D1556793

THE RELUCTANT VILLAIN

JAMES L WILLIAMS

The Book Guild Ltd

First published in Great Britain in 2021 by
The Book Guild Ltd
9 Priory Business Park
Wistow Road, Kibworth
Leicestershire, LE8 0RX
Freephone: 0800 999 2982
www.bookguild.co.uk
Email: info@bookguild.co.uk
Twitter: @bookguild

Copyright © 2021 James L Williams

The right of James L Williams to be identified as the author of this
work has been asserted by him in accordance with the
Copyright, Design and Patents Act 1988.

All rights reserved. No part of this publication may be
reproduced, transmitted, or stored in a retrieval system, in any form or by any means,
without permission in writing from the publisher, nor be otherwise circulated in
any form of binding or cover other than that in which it is published and without
a similar condition being imposed on the subsequent purchaser.

This work is entirely fictitious and bears no resemblance to any persons living or dead.

Typeset in Minion Pro

Printed and bound in Great Britain by CPI Group (UK) Ltd, Croydon, CR0 4YY

ISBN 978 1913551 506

British Library Cataloguing in Publication Data.
A catalogue record for this book is available from the British Library.

My brother, Geoff Williams, for his ongoing support and advice.

Helen Sage MBE and June Totterdell for their continued editing help and support.

1

"Mr Bishop, I have told you on more than one occasion, I am not going to pay you any protection or insurance money, as you call it. And if you ask me again I will inform the police. Now if there is nothing else, I have a business to run. Goodbye!"

Graham Bishop stood his ground. He tried another angle. "How many break-ins have happened around here in the past month? Four or maybe five? Can you afford to turn up one morning and find your shop has been burnt to the ground?"

David Evans was about to comment but neither man had heard the shop door open. Both gave a little gasp when Sergeant Peter Proudfoot spoke.

"Up to your old tricks again are you, Bishop? We don't take too kindly to people moving in from other parts of the country thinking they can antagonise our shopkeepers," said Proudfoot stepping past Bishop as he addressed the shopkeeper.

"Are you okay, Mr Evans?"

Not knowing how much the officer had heard of their conversation Evans gave a weak smile and said quietly, "Just a minor misunderstanding, Sergeant. Mr Bishop and I have concluded our business."

"In that case, Bishop, I want a word with you outside. Afternoon, Mr Evans," he said, as he faced Bishop and defied him to remain.

As the two men approached the door an elderly lady was about to enter the shop, but Bishop barred her way and didn't step back until Proudfoot tapped him on the shoulder. "Forgetting our manners aren't we, Graham?"

But all he got back was a sullen stare and the sergeant had to pull him back by his arm to allow the woman room to pass.

She mouthed a silent 'thank you' to the officer but stared straight at Bishop for a couple of seconds. The man couldn't match her gaze and looked away. The two men then left the shop as the woman walked towards the shopkeeper with a warm smile on her features.

"Good afternoon, David, is it too much to hope that horrible man has finally been arrested?"

Even though the woman had lived in the area for more than fifty years, traces of her upbringing in Bavaria, Germany, could still be detected in her accent.

"I'm afraid we have no such luck, Mrs Stockwell, but the sergeant is talking to him outside. Have you come to collect the present for your husband?"

She raised both hands to her cheeks and spoke in a hushed tone.

"Is it here? Oh, please let me see it!"

The shopkeeper smiled and reached down into a drawer behind the counter and took out an ornate box which he handed to the woman. Before opening the box, she spoke in the same hushed tone.

"Have you had time to engrave it as I asked?"

Evans said nothing but indicated to her to open the box, which she did with trembling hands. On doing so, she gasped, and a couple of tears trickled down her cheeks as she held up the item.

"Oh David, it is so beautiful! Please tell me, when did it arrive and who did the engraving?"

Evans smiled and called over his shoulder.

"Gerald, can you spare a minute please? Someone wants to speak to you."

"Coming, Mr Evans, I just need to clean this grease off my hands," replied a young voice from the rear of the premises.

"He is finishing cutting a set of keys for the supermarket and needs to deliver them to the manager who cannot get into his storeroom. Someone tried to break in last night but all they did was damage the lock. The present arrived by courier this morning and Gerald spent the rest of the time putting on the details you requested. Does it come up to your expectations?"

"Yes, yes. In fact I have not seen such beautiful work since I came here from Germany." A few more tears ran down her cheeks.

Moments later a youth, of medium height and build, appeared next to the shopkeeper, wiping his hands with an old rag. Turning to the youth Evans said proudly, "Gerald, Mrs Stockwell wants to thank you for your work this morning."

Gerald nodded, slightly embarrassed, and the customer stepped forward and gave him a big hug and a kiss on both cheeks. Taken aback by this friendly assault Gerald's face went crimson and he stammered, "Glad you like it, Mrs Stockwell."

She took both his hands in her own, looked intently into the youth's eyes, and spoke quietly.

"Gerald, I was just telling Mr Evans that I have not seen such beautiful handiwork since I watched my father at work before the war."

It was common local knowledge that she had arrived in Britain in the mid-thirties, a refugee before the outbreak of war, and had married Robin Stockwell just after her twenty-first birthday. She continued, still looking intently into his eyes,

3

"Gerald, you are my hero!" and she kissed him on both cheeks once again, causing him even more embarrassment.

She continued speaking, "If you continue using these hands with their natural skills you will become very successful. Take care of them, my dear. But a word of caution. Do not let others distract you from this path you have chosen, or the success you deserve will elude you," and she gave him another kiss on both cheeks before releasing his hands.

The youth nodded and returned to the workshop at the rear of the premises.

"Yes, you are right, Mrs Stockwell, he has a bright future ahead if he continues. I wish I was nineteen again. Now, let me wrap this up for you so you can take it home to your husband."

She looked thoughtful for a few moments before speaking. "No, David. Please wrap it up in nice paper but keep it here and bring it along to the gathering with your wife. I don't want Robin to find the present before the party."

Once again Proudfoot had entered the shop while the two were engrossed in conversation. "Buying secret presents are we, Mrs Stockwell; a special occasion perhaps?"

"Oh, Sergeant, you move too quietly for a big man," she admonished him sweetly, before continuing, "Yes, it is our golden wedding anniversary this weekend."

"Congratulations, Mrs Stockwell. Actually, Marjorie and I are celebrating our silver wedding the following weekend and I too am making use of Mr Evans' selection of gifts for all occasions."

The last remark brought a laugh from the others as this was the slogan in the shop window. "Then you and your wife must join us at our gathering on Sunday," the woman insisted.

"I'm sorry, Mrs Stockwell, we have both changed our work pattern to ensure we are both free for the following weekend."

She smiled and then sighed and took one of his large hands in both her own.

"Never mind, perhaps another time. How is Mr Newsham enjoying his new work? We haven't seen him for a couple of weeks. I hope he has not forgotten his invite for Sunday."

Proudfoot gently extracted his hand from the warm embrace of Mrs Stockwell. His hand continued to tingle for several seconds after the release of the grip.

"Ernie is settling in at the sports centre complex, Mrs Stockwell. He is looking for a couple of assistants to help with the maintenance side of work so if either of you hear of someone who can help then pass on the word."

"I will leave you gentlemen to talk in peace. Please do not forget my package on Sunday, David." She gave each man a smile and short nod before leaving the shop.

"A wonderful woman," the shopkeeper announced.

"Yes indeed," agreed Proudfoot, "and now, I am here to look at your selection of gifts that will hopefully impress my wife."

"Very well, if you give me a price range in mind, I can show you a selection of items to consider."

***

In fact, Ernie was now only looking for one more assistant as an ideal candidate had wandered into the sports centre cafe a couple of days earlier. He was back in again that morning and Ernie kept a watchful eye on him as his police training told him this lad could be trouble. He had been sitting at the table nearest the door with the same glass of coke for at least twenty minutes.

Ernie made mental notes of the youth as he observed him toying with his drink and looking around the cafe, watching other people, checking to see if anyone left unattended bags or items of clothing within grabbing distance. Keeping a close watch on the youth Ernie moved to stand near the top of the stairs of the balcony that ran around three quarters of the cafe.

From this vantage point he corrected his assumption of the age of the youth. More a young man in his early twenties, no more than twenty-two at most but with a childlike, almost baby face. Tall, just over six feet, a lean frame but with broad shoulders and strong arms. He could be dangerous in a fight, but Ernie had tackled bigger, stronger men in the past and had been victorious. He spotted what was about to happen a split second before the man could react.

A young woman who had come into the cafe for a drink after a session in the swimming pool next door left her bag unattended while she went to buy a coffee from the cafe bar. She had taken some change from her purse and left the remaining money on top of her holdall. Ernie had the advantage of moving quickly and silently down the stairs behind the would-be thief while he had to wait until the woman had moved far enough away to give him the opportunity to pounce.

She had to manoeuvre around a couple of tables to reach the counter and even though the man was not looking in her general direction his concentration was solely on her movements. This allowed Ernie the opportunity to stand less than two paces behind him without being noticed. Deciding that the woman was far enough away, the man stood up and moved towards his target.

His right hand was inches away from the purse when he felt a vice-like grip on his elbow and a voice whispered in his ear, "Play this right and you won't get arrested!"

The man turned his head slowly and looked back at his captor.

"What's the bloody game, mister, I saw the money first," he said, in a strong Yorkshire accent.

The woman must have heard the exchange and looked back in their direction. She took a couple of paces towards them and called, "Excuse me, that's my bag. What do you think you're doing?"

Ernie released his grip on the man's arm and pointed at several signs on the walls surrounding the cafe.

"It's all in order, miss, I'm the manager and you obviously haven't read the signs."

The signs read in quite prominent letters: *Do not leave any items of value unattended. They are your responsibility and our insurance does not extend to cover the loss of such items.*

Ernie spoke again, "This gentleman indicated to me what you had done and as manager I came down to make sure there was no misunderstanding. Isn't that right, sir?" and he looked directly at the man as he made his final remark.

"Yeah, as he said, you never know who's watching you these days," and returned Ernie's look.

The woman muttered her thanks, still a little suspicious as to both men's intentions. She picked up her belongings and walked back towards the cafe counter. Ernie waited until the woman had moved out of hearing distance and indicated to his companion to lead the way up the stairs. Having little option, he followed Ernie's instructions and sat down at a table in the corner of the balcony.

Ernie sat opposite, thus blocking off any means of escape to his guest.

"Okay, what's your name and where are you from?"

After a few moments the man replied, "Mark."

"Mark who?" Ernie responded.

To which came back the defiant reply, "Mark is all you're getting for now. So who are you then?"

Ernie had come across hundreds of people in his time like Mark and he knew from experience there was no point in pushing too hard at first. "Okay, my name is Ernie Newsham and as well as being manager of this place, I'm an ex-copper. Where are you from, Mark? Somewhere up north I'll guess."

Mark swore under his breath, sighed and looked up at the ceiling for several seconds. Sensing he would get no more

7

response, Ernie continued, "Mark. You came in here yesterday afternoon and went through the same routine and after nearly an hour of watching for an opportunity you gave up and left. I've lost track of how many times blokes like you have wandered in with the same plan. So again! Where are you from and how did you end up here?"

He had decided to put some pressure on Mark but if it didn't work he would let him go and report his description to his ex-colleagues. But he hoped it would not come to that as he had a gut feeling he could make some use of this man in the plans he was developing.

Mark sighed once more and looked back at Ernie.

"Halifax in Yorkshire. I thumbed a lift from a long-distance lorry driver with the intention of heading down towards Bristol. But the bastard was bent and made a pass at me but I showed him!"

Sensing there might be a chance to have a hold on the man Ernie silently switched on the mini recorder in his pocket. "Go on, what happened?"

Mark hesitated for a few seconds before speaking. "This bloke said he was carrying some important gear. He didn't say what. He said he shouldn't be giving anyone lifts in his lorry but he felt sorry for me, so he picked me up. Anyway, it was late at night so nobody could see me in the dark cab. He started making remarks about my features, called me 'baby face' a couple of times and when I said I hated that bloody name his manner changed.

"He said he was going to stop and pick up some more fags and two cups of coffee for us then we would pull into a lay-by and we could get to know each other a lot better. I knew what he had in mind, so I made my own plans."

"What were those plans then?" asked Ernie.

Mark gave a sneer. "That fat bastard will think twice about picking up kids just for his own satisfaction, the pervert! While he was getting his fags and coffee in a cafe we stopped outside, I got out a small bottle of olive oil I had in my bag. See, I keep getting this ear infection and that stuff is supposed to be good for that kind of thing. Anyway, I soaked a little wad of cotton wool with the oil and pushed it into the cigarette lighter he had in his dashboard. I didn't push the lighter right in, he would have to do that when we stopped for what he thought was going to be his bit of fun."

"What if he didn't want to have a fag? You were taking a chance, weren't you?" Ernie asked.

Mark smiled.

"No chance, that bloke was a chain-smoker. We stopped four times on the way and each time he lit up as soon as he stopped. The floor of the cab was covered in fag ends and paper, right pigsty it were. He brought his stuff back to the lorry and announced that there was a spot about a mile down the road he knew about and was going to stop there. It was sheltered from the road and had a small wooded area on the left side.

"He pulled the lorry off the road and said to me 'Right, my little stud, time for action'. I had to think quickly so I told him I needed to have a crap in the woods. He said something like 'No tricks or else!'.

"He took out a fag and rammed in the cigarette lighter and I grabbed my bag and only got half out the door when all hell broke loose. Smoke poured out of the dashboard and the lighter unit shot out of its socket and landed amongst the rubbish on the floor."

Mark continued, "He shouted something and dived out of his door. I thought he was going to chase and grab me but instead he grabbed a fire extinguisher that was attached to the outside of the cab but I don't think it was working. By now I'd legged it into the woods and when I looked back the whole cab was in flames and he was on his mobile phone."

Ernie interrupted.

"I heard about a lorry fire about six miles from here. So that was your handiwork, was it? You like starting fires then?"

"Yeah, it gives me a buzz at times. After that I stayed in the woods until it was daylight and walked into this town. I've been sleeping rough for the last two nights."

Ernie reached into his pocket to switch off the recorder before asking, "What kind of jobs did you do back home? Have you got any qualifications of any kind?"

Mark gave a sarcastic laugh before answering with not a little venom in his voice. "Oh sure! The only thing I'm qualified in is looking out for me, and they don't teach that at no college. Jobs? I've worked in a garage from time to time, helping to strip down and reassemble motors and other bits of machinery. Nothing permanent, just drifting from one job to another."

Ernie's ears pricked up at the mention of his guest's experiences with machinery; it could be a way of enticing Mark to stick around for a while and get him involved in the ex-policeman's other plans.

"If I offered you a job here at the centre and found you some digs would you be willing to help me in another venture I've just started?"

Mark was immediately suspicious of Ernie's motives. Why should this stranger, especially an ex-copper, make him an offer like this on their first meeting? He was always told by his older brother, 'You don't get ought for nowt'.

"What's the catch?" he said, staring at Ernie.

The manager smiled having already guessed this would be the man's reaction. "You work here at the centre assembling and servicing equipment in the gymnasium next door; that will be your main role during opening hours. On odd occasions I might need you to, let's say, help me enforce my new security business. Your main role will be strictly legitimate, paid by the council who own the centre, the second role will be cash in hand."

Mark snorted in disgust. "Employed by the council? That means bloody paperwork and National Insurance numbers which I have never had. The second role could sound interesting though."

Ernie shook his head. "You can't have one without the other. If it's your NI number that bothers you I can easily get around that little hurdle. No, Mark, it's all or nothing and I need your answer before you leave here, or I make a phone call to my ex-colleagues in the local force about your little confession just now."

"You bastard," Mark snarled. "It's only your word against mine. I can deny ever meeting you."

Ernie smiled and took the recorder from his pocket and played back a small portion of what had been said earlier.

"There are also CCTV cameras in this place and I'm sure I could find that woman you tried to rob earlier and get her to make a statement. Come on, Mark, you'll never get a better offer than this if you live until you're sixty, which I doubt you will ever see if you carry on in your own fashion."

Mark looked down at his hands and his thoughts against Ernie couldn't have been darker. But he kept them to himself and said quietly, "Okay, but no trying to trace my family. Apart from my older brother, Kevin, the rest can go to hell, and that includes my mum and that sprat of a boyfriend she's living with now."

"What happened to your father? Is he dead or just not on the scene any more?"

Mark sneered.

"That scum? He ran out on us when I was only eight years old. If Kev hadn't been around to watch over me I'd have gone under years ago. He knows I've left the area cos he gave me some money to scarper."

Ernie listened carefully but said nothing. He was sure Mark wanted to get more off his chest and he did.

"Kev is a member of one of the gangs in Leeds and they were trying to get me involved with them but Kev doesn't trust some of them so he gave me money to disappear. He taught me how to look after myself and a few other tricks besides. He even taught me how to handle guns."

Ernie suddenly became wary.

"You're not carrying, are you?"

Mark had noticed Ernie's sudden change in attitude and toyed with the idea of playing him along but decided he couldn't afford to do so right now. But later, things might be different.

"No, Kev keeps them with him but if I need anything, he would let me have it."

"Good, I can cover for most circumstances, but guns would be difficult to explain. Right, a couple of things before I send you to those digs I mentioned. I'll need you to help move stuff from place to place. Can you drive, and do you have a licence?"

"Yes and no, work it out for yourself," Mark replied.

Ernie ignored the taunt.

"Okay, what surname do you want on the licence? And one final point, this is important! From time to time I have some ex-colleagues from the local force come in to do some rehab work for getting their fitness levels up to return to duty. I'll identify them to you so under no circumstances allow yourself to become a focus of their attention."

Mark nodded and answered, "I'll use my mum's surname; it's Yarrow."

Ernie wrote an address on a sheet of paper and passed it to his companion. "This is where you can stay for the next few days until I find somewhere more permanent for you. By the way, have you eaten today?"

Mark looked at the address and shook his head. "No, where is this place? I don't know my way around this town yet."

Ernie stood up and took two £20 notes from his pocket and passed them to Mark along with a map of the town.

"That should keep you from starving for the next few days. Study that map and spend the rest of today and tomorrow familiarising yourself with details of side streets and back alleys. Report back here on Saturday morning at nine o'clock."

"I never get up that early, especially on a weekend," moaned Mark.

"You do now! And don't get into any kind of bother. Or else!" Ernie responded and tapped the recorder in his pocket.

Mark glared back at him but said nothing and walked towards the stairs and the exit of the building.

Once he was sure his guest had gone, Ernie walked into the cafe and found the young woman Mark had tried to steal from earlier. He sat down at the table she occupied and smiled at her.

"Well done, Sally, it worked like a dream. He's just the type I was looking for. Here's your bonus." He passed Sally fifty pounds.

She took the money and stuffed it into the pocket of her jeans.

"If you say so, Mr N, but I wouldn't fancy being around that bloke by myself for a minute longer than necessary. He's got shifty eyes and gives me the creeps."

"Well, he's going to be around here for a while, but I don't think he will bother you. I'll keep him on a short leash," Ernie reassured her.

Sally stood up and made her farewell. "Any time you want a similar favour you only have to ask but let's be clear, that's as far as it goes. I'll be at the library if you do."

2

Robin Stockwell picked up the phone just before the answer machine cut in. He spoke quietly into the handset. His wife, Stella, was resting in the next room before she finished the final preparations for their anniversary party that evening.

"This is Robin Stockwell, who is calling please?" He recognised the voice on the other end of the line immediately.

"Robin, it's Ernie Newsham. Listen, I'm sorry but I can't come to your party tonight. I had a delivery of equipment for the gymnasium late yesterday and I'm showing my new worker how to assemble and test the machines. Please accept my best wishes to you and Stella for a happy golden wedding anniversary and I'll drop in my present to you tomorrow."

"Oh, I'm sorry you can't make it tonight, Ernie, we were both looking forward to your company. Who is your new helper?"

Ernie didn't want to give too many details about Mark, so he simply said, "New lad from outside the area – good with his hands, but some of this stuff is new to him so he needs plenty of supervision. I'd like to chat a bit more, Robin, but if we don't crack on, we'll be here till gone midnight. Regards to Stella. Bye!" and the line went dead.

Robin returned the handset to its cradle but decided not to disturb Stella to pass on the news until she had rested for a little longer. She had been preparing food for the gathering since early that morning and had only stopped to rest when Robin pointed out to her that she looked tired and wouldn't enjoy herself later is she didn't have a nap.

About ten minutes after the phone rang Stella walked into the living room and asked who had called.

"Ernie Newsham. I'm afraid he won't be coming tonight, something about assembling new equipment for tomorrow. He sends his best wishes," Robin replied, as he finished polishing the wine glasses.

Stella gave a slight frown and tapped her husband on his shoulder.

"Robin, how many times has Ernie pulled out of meetings and other gatherings at the last moment? I can think of at least half a dozen in the past couple of months. Have we upset him in any way?"

Her husband paused and thought for a moment. "Yes, you're right, dear, it does always seem to happen at very short notice. Still, I suppose he is trying to establish himself at the leisure centre and make a success of his endeavours. However, this is a very special occasion for us and I would have thought he would have wanted to be here to show his appreciation of how we helped him in the past."

Stella smiled and chided her husband. "Robin! He was someone who needed our help at the time and it's not our decision to pick and choose who we help."

He returned her smile, "I'm sorry, you're right of course, Stella. But he's not the same person he was nine months ago. I suppose he is still a little resentful that he didn't get his job back despite all the things you did to help him. Now enough of Ernie. Remind me who is coming tonight; I keep forgetting who we've invited."

"You don't forget, Robin, you just have a nice way of changing the subject. Let me think... there is Jenny, Mr and Mrs Evans, Gemma Watson and the Byewaters. I believe that is everyone."

A sad smile briefly crossed her features. "It would have been nice if Natalie and her stepfather could have come but I fully understand she couldn't make it because of her studies."

Robin noted the omission of their daughter's name, Patricia, from the list. She had died seven years earlier from a kidney complication and had passed away very suddenly. Her second husband, Frank, had always adored Natalie and had taken care of his adopted daughter just as if she was one of his own. Robin put his arm on his wife's shoulders.

"We could make a surprise visit when Natalie graduates in a year's time."

Stella turned away from her husband to hide the single tear running down her cheek.

"Yes, that would be nice," she said and busied herself re-arranging some napkins.

Their guests started arriving just before eight o'clock. As expected, Jenny Potter arrived first followed shortly after by Gemma Watson. Both ladies came with the express intention of assisting in any last-minute tasks being required, but the Stockwells had everything prepared for their social evening.

Jenny started with an advance apology. "I am so sorry, Stella, I don't want to be too late in going home as my new kitten has not settled in properly and Fish is still wary of him."

Robin managed to hide a smile behind a hand as she spoke. Apart from a sister and niece she had no other family beside her cats.

"As you only live a few houses away from here, you can easily pop over to check them out from time to time but I'm sure they will be fine. Cats know how to work things out – better than humans in some cases."

This last remark caused smiles amongst the gathering apart from Jenny who pressed her point forward.

"Oh, I'm sure they do but the kitten is very shy and apt to leave a little package on the carpet if it gets too nervous."

This brought more little laughs but before anyone could advance the conversation, the doorbell rang and Robin excused himself to answer the summons.

"Is it male or female and have you given the kitten a name yet, Jenny?" Gemma asked.

"He's a ginger tom and I'm going to call him Biscuit," the proud owner announced.

Robin came into the room followed by Ralph and Hazel Byewater. Greetings were exchanged and drinks passed around but once again the doorbell was rung. This time Stella went to the door to greet the caller. As she had hoped, it was David Evans and his wife, Sandra.

As they entered, David passed Stella a package which she gratefully took and placed it in a drawer of the cabinet in the hallway. Stella showed her guests into the lounge and once again, greetings were exchanged. Jenny Potter enquired, "Is Mr Newsham coming tonight?"

Robin replied quietly, "No, Jenny, he phoned earlier to say he was too busy to come as he had work to complete at the Leisure Centre."

While he was speaking, Stella took the opportunity to slip out of the room to retrieve the package that David had passed to her upon arriving. She cleared her throat to speak.

"It is a pity Ernie could not come tonight but we are so pleased that you all could attend to celebrate our golden wedding anniversary with us, aren't we, Robin?"

Robin nodded and was about to make a small speech of his own, but Stella continued speaking. "Forgive me for being so hasty, Robin, but I cannot wait a moment longer to give you this gift as a token of my love for you and our fifty happy years together."

With that, she planted a kiss on both cheeks of her husband and thrust the package into his hands. He stood there, a little taken aback and then said quietly, "Stella, what is this package? We exchanged our personal presents to each other this morning."

She smiled. "Open it and see, Robin. It is just a little extra surprise."

Robin carried out his wife's wish with not a little puzzlement as they had never, in all their married life, tried to catch each other out with surprise presents. He undid the wrapping and opened the small presentation box and gave a little gasp as he viewed its contents. Unable to keep her own inquisitiveness to herself Jenny asked what the mystery present was. Robin held it up for all to see. It was a gold cigarette lighter, engraved on one side with the letters, RS, inside a heart with the numbers 41-91 underneath. He passed it around the gathering for all to inspect and as they did so he went to his wife and gave her a long embrace and a full kiss on her mouth and simply said, "Why?"

Stella gave a little laugh and replied, "Now I will not have to spend the rest of my life going around picking up spent matches when you light up your cigars."

Robin laughed and stood back, then gave his wife another hug. The guests joined in the laughter and Ralph Byewater retrieved the bottle of champagne he had brought in earlier and announced, "I think it's time we all drank a toast to the happy couple."

Glasses were filled and the toast formally announced. Gemma asked Stella, "When do you plan to visit your granddaughter next, or will she be coming over here to visit you?"

Stella hesitated before speaking. "Natalie is in the middle of her studies at present so it is more likely that we will have to travel to Canada to see her. Please excuse me, Gemma, I must pay a visit to the bathroom," and she left the room with her head bowed.

Moments later Jenny said she wanted to go and check on her cats. Robin told her not to be more than five minutes or he would come looking for her. She promised that she would be back in that time so he gave her a spare key to let herself back in to the flat. As Jenny passed the bathroom door on her way out a strange sound could be heard coming from within, but it was not repeated so she hurried out to her cats.

True to her word, Jenny arrived back within the time stipulated by Robin and as she passed the bathroom door it opened, and Stella stepped out dabbing her eyes with a lace handkerchief. Both women stopped and stared at each other. Stella was the first to speak.

"Oh, Jenny, you startled me. Please don't mention to anyone you saw me wiping my eyes. It is merely the emotion of the occasion and I am not used to drinking alcohol. Promise me?"

Jenny could only nod in acceptance of what she had been asked not to reveal and Stella squeezed one of her hands in thanks.

As they both re-entered the lounge David was speaking.

"Yes, Robin, I'm afraid it's true. I have decided to sell the business as Sandra wants to retire to the south coast to be nearer our elder daughter and grandchildren while Catherine goes to Cambridge University next year."

"But what about young Gerald, David? What will he do?" Stella asked upon rejoining the conversation.

Robin looked a little bemused. "Who is this Gerald?"

Stella replied, "He is the young man who so expertly engraved your lighter for me. As I told him, he has a special gift when it comes to that skill and he must develop it to advance in life."

"Oh, in that case, I must go and thank him myself."

David Evans gave a little chuckle. "There's no big rush, Robin, I haven't even formally put the business on the market yet. Anyway, whoever takes it on would be foolish to dispense with someone of Gerald's talents."

***

Ernie was indeed busy later that evening. He had explained in detail to Mark how his security enforcement plans would work and the purpose of the night's exercise. Their van, with the logo of Acme Security on its front doors, stopped and parked in a side street next to the building site owned by Byewater Construction. It was foggy, just after midnight and there was nobody around to observe their actions. An eight-foot-high wire fence topped with razor wire had been built around the site.

There was a double gate in one section of the fence secured by a single padlock. Checking to make sure the coast was clear, Ernie and Mark got out of the van, both wearing padded jackets and gloves. Mark was carrying a large pair of bolt cutters and made short work of removing the padlock.

Once the gates were open Ernie reversed their van into the yard. Mark had already moved to one of the Portakabins in one corner of the site and treated the padlock on that door with the same swift efficiency as before.

Ernie joined him and they quickly removed various items of equipment and put them into the back of the van. When Ernie gave the signal, Mark moved to the next Portakabin and broke inside but instead of removing items he quickly started a fire amongst some work overalls and closed the door before joining his partner in the van.

The whole operation had taken less than five minutes from start to finish.

As Ernie drove carefully away so as not to attract attention, Mark asked, "I don't get it, what do we need with bloody sledgehammers, fire extinguishers and the other rubbish? We'll get next to nothing if we try and flog them."

Ernie sighed, "Like I told you earlier, Mark, that was just to give an example and warning to a couple of businesses nearby that having a security patrol keeping an eye on their premises is a worthwhile investment. I know Byewater and he wouldn't fall for our little security scam. I'll bet that within twenty-four hours there will be a real security firm on the case. But that won't help the people I'm targeting."

By the time they arrived back at the centre two fire engines with sirens blaring had passed them heading in the direction of the construction yard. Ernie pulled into the car park at the rear of the centre and parked by the double doors.

Both men got out of the van and removed the plastic signs from the front doors of the van and took them along with their haul of items into the building and up the stairs into the room overlooking Ernie's office.

It was the first time Mark had been in this room and he was surprised at the number of items that were stacked in the corner.

3

Over the next few weeks Ernie managed to convince four more businesses to accept his security patrol offer following the fire at the construction yard. Three paid a monthly retainer, while the fourth paid in kind, using surplus stock in lieu of payment.

A month after announcing his intention to sell his business David Evans called Gerald into his back office to give him the latest news. "Gerald, I just want to let you know I've had a firm offer for the business and the prospective buyer is coming here next week to go over final details. He has assured me that you will have a place in his plans for expanding the customer base and that there is no need for you to look elsewhere for work. Two things I want to share with you. I will introduce you to Mr Matthews on Thursday. The second point is, because you have worked so hard on your skills as an engraver I will pay your college fees for a further two years so you can complete your course and take your exams. Also, I will make sure Mr Matthews is aware of your college commitments."

Gerald only managed to stammer out an acknowledgement to the first point and then added, "You're very kind, Mr Evans, but it won't be the same here without you and Catherine. Can I ask, what is she going to do when you leave?"

"As you know she is going to university in Cambridge next year. She will continue to work here until the end of the year and then she starts a temporary job in Newmarket in the National Stud College for six months. I don't know when Mr Matthews plans on taking over but I expect it won't be until at least the end of January. Oh, by the way, how is your grandmother keeping these days? Are you still managing to maintain the flat in good order?"

David Evans also owned the building where Gerald and his ageing relative resided. He had lived with her for the past seven years, ever since his parents were killed in a car crash and his grandmother took him under her wing.

"What about the rent and any work to be carried out on the flat?" Gerald asked.

"Before I leave, I will give you my bank details so you can continue the payments as at present. Any work needed doing on the flat, call our usual builder in and send me the bill so that I can sort out payments."

"I'm sorry you and Catherine are leaving, Mr Evans. I've enjoyed working with you both and thank you for your friendship towards my grandmother and me."

"Well, I hope we will all keep in touch and you can update me on how Mr Matthews is dealing with, shall I say, some of our more eccentric customers."

Gerald smiled – he knew who his boss was referring to – and went back into the shop to be confronted by Graham Bishop.

"Where the hell is your boss, kid?"

Gerald knew better than to antagonise this man who lived a short distance from his grandmother's flat.

"Can I help, Mr Bishop? Mr Evans is busy in his office right now."

"I want to speak to the organ grinder not his pipsqueak monkey. Get out of my way!"

Without thinking of what he was doing Gerald stepped forward to block the older man's attempt to pass through into the back of the shop. "Sorry, Mr Bishop, no customers allowed beyond this point unless Mr Evans says so," Gerald said in an apologetic voice.

Bishop drew back his right arm with the intention of punching the youngster, but a voice from the rear of the store stopped him in mid motion. "Don't you dare hit any of my staff!"

"Then tell this bloody kid to get out of my way!" snarled Bishop.

"Gerald, please go and finish the order for Mr Perkins while Mr Bishop and I have a talk."

Gerald nodded and walked past Evans. He understood the coded message his boss had given him. There was no customer called Perkins; instead he was to stand just out of Bishop's sight and listen in case there was any trouble.

Waiting until he thought they were alone, Bishop spoke to Evans in a hoarse whisper. "What's this I hear you're doing a runner! If you are skipping town I want three months' money right now and the name of the geezer who's taking over this dump."

The shopkeeper stared up at his aggressor and spoke in an even tone. "Mr Bishop, I am not doing a runner, I'm retiring and selling my business to a man who owns a chain of stores in other towns. I have told you a dozen times I have no intention of paying you any protection money. So if there is nothing else I can help you with, please leave my shop now."

Bishop stood motionless with his mouth wide open, then he stepped forward and shouted, "You snivelling apology for a man, you'll pay up or I'll burn this place to the ground with you in it and Matthews will have inherited a pile of ashes."

"I heard that threat," Gerald said stepping back into full view.

"So did I!" said a young woman standing in the doorway. Sally had come in to purchase some refills for her pens. Bishop glared at both of the younger people, then at Evans before storming out of the shop.

"He's not on your Christmas card list is he, Mr Evans?" Sally said with a grin.

"Most definitely not, Sally. Thank you for distracting him. His type don't like witnesses to see what nastiness they are up to."

Sally walked up to the counter and spoke to his assistant. "Hi Gerry, I've not seen you in the library lately. Gone off my coffee, have you?"

Gerald blushed. Sally was the only one to use that name, but he didn't mind her doing so.

"No, we are getting ready for a stock audit for the new owner…" then he realised he might have spoken out of turn.

His boss noted his hesitation. "It's all right, Gerald, if Bishop knows, then half the town must be in on my secret."

Sally sprang to Gerald's defence. "I'm afraid it is. It's all people are talking about. Whoever is taking over will have a lot to live up to to meet your standards, Mr Evans."

It was the shopkeeper's turn to colour slightly. "Thank you for your comment, Sally, but with Gerald still here I'm sure people will be happy with the service they receive."

The woman raised her eyebrows in Gerald's direction causing more discomfort to him, made her purchase and left the two men to their thoughts.

"So what's it to be, Gerald or Gerry?" Evans asked his assistant. "We've always known you as Gerald, yet Sally seems to have special privileges."

Gerry coloured once more and said quietly, "Sally thinks the name Gerald makes me sound too old, so she prefers Gerry. I don't mind either."

He slipped back into the rear of the shop before his boss could comment further. However, a memory of the previous New Year's celebrations was rekindled and he was so deep in those memories he didn't notice Catherine coming into the room to pack an order for a customer. She greeted Gerry but got no response, so she playfully gave him a dig in the ribs.

"What's her name then, Mister Starry-eyed?"

"Sorry? Did you say something, Catherine?" Gerry asked.

"Never mind! Listen, Gerry, can I ask you something?" she said quietly.

He nodded.

"I need to tell someone about this. It's driving me barmy and I've got to get it off my chest."

Unsure of what she was talking about he looked quizzically at her. She continued in hushed tones, "You know I'm leaving after Christmas to go to work in Newmarket before going to university next autumn. Don't tell my dad but I don't know if I want to go to uni after all. I'd much rather stay in Newmarket to look after horses."

"When did you have a change of heart? You've done nothing but talk about how excited you are regarding your move to Cambridge."

She was silent for a few moments. "Dad has always been keen on someone from the family going to uni and we all thought Colin would go one day but he opted for the Royal Navy instead. If I pull out now, well, I don't want to think how dad will feel."

Gerry was about to speak when Evans called out from the shop. "Gerald, can I have a hand here, please? We have customers waiting to be served."

He went back to the shop and served two customers before returning to join Catherine. "Right, where were we?"

Catherine shook her head. "It will take too long to explain now, I've got to catch the last post with this parcel. Meet me in the library at seven o'clock. It's open late tonight," she said, picking up the package while leaving him to his own thoughts.

After Catherine had left, the shop was quiet again and her father said innocently, "You and Catherine were in deep conversation earlier, anything I should know?"

Taken aback by the direct question, Gerry could only blurt out "She was talking about university and Newmarket and how—" but his boss interrupted him.

"I hope she is looking forward to university, but if she has any reservations, I would prefer her to be honest and tell me. The last thing I want is for Catherine to feel she has no choice in the matter."

Another customer came into the shop so he went to serve him. Gerald heaved a huge sigh of relief. Now he had some good news for Catherine.

***

Catherine was approaching the post office, but her path was suddenly blocked by Graham Bishop. "Well, if it isn't the shopkeeper's would-be university graduate! And what's in the parcel? I reckon that might pay a small part of what Daddy owes me. Hand it over!" and he tried to snatch the package from her grasp.

But Catherine had read his intentions and stepped back out of his reach.

"Get your hands off! This is already paid for and I'm going to make sure it goes to the right person," she shouted back at him.

Bishop made another attempt to grab the package from her and this time he managed to get a handful of her jacket collar. Despite her struggles he held on and dragged the girl towards him. He had hold of the package with his free hand and was about to run off before a loud voice caused him to hesitate.

"Bishop! Let go of her right now!" Ernie Newsham's voice held enough of a threat for the assailant to release his grip.

"Are you okay, Catherine? Not bothering you is he?" he said while still keeping both eyes firmly on Bishop.

"I was on my way to post this package to a customer when he grabbed me," she replied.

Ernie took the package from Bishop's hand and gazed at the address.

"Sorry Graham, it's not got your name on it. What makes you think it was for you?"

Bishop remained silent and Ernie nodded to the girl and passed the package to her.

"Well, off you go, love, before the post office closes."

She gave him a quick smile, nodded her thanks and glared at Bishop before turning on her heels and headed towards her destination. Ernie waited and watched her until she disappeared inside the post office. He then turned to Bishop.

"Let's you and me go and have a little talk somewhere quiet, Mr Bishop." The sarcasm and threat in his voice was not lost on the other man but he stood his ground defiantly.

"You and me don't have anything to talk about; you're not a copper any more in case you'd forgotten."

Ernie took a step closer to the man and spoke quietly but forcibly. "Oh yes we do! I now run a security patrol around here and a couple of my new customers have told me that you are their biggest concern."

When Bishop said nothing, Ernie continued, "Threats to my customers could suddenly become very unhealthy for you. Stick to your normal game of burglary, but not from my clients. Savvy?"

"You're saying I can do burglary outside your area and you'll do nothing about it? What's your game, Newsham?"

Ernie spoke even more quietly. "My game is this: if you come across any stuff that's too hot to handle, maybe we can do business. That's all I will say and, of course, I will deny this conversation ever took place if you think of speaking out of turn. Who do you think anyone would believe, you, a known villain or me, an ex-copper."

Bishop glared and said, "I'll think about it," and went to walk away but Ernie grabbed his arm.

"Not so fast, friend Graham. You're staying here until Catherine comes back so that I can escort her home. Just in case you had other ideas!"

The two men stood in silence until Catherine reappeared and Ernie walked with her back to her father's shop. When they entered the premises together Evans looked a little concerned.

"Are you all right, Catherine? I was expecting you back about ten minutes ago. I'm about to close up and Gerald has gone home."

"Yes, I'm fine, Dad. Mr Newsham and I bumped into each other and he said he would walk back with me, just like a gentleman would," and she gave Ernie a little smile before walking past her father into the rear of the shop.

Evans waited until he and Ernie were alone.

"Is that right, Ernie, you just bumped into each other?" the scepticism written all over his face.

"Well, there were a couple of dodgy characters hanging around so I thought it would be wiser to make sure she got back safely. Anyway, what's this I hear about taking early retirement? And who is taking over?"

Evans smiled. "Matthews' Hardware is buying me out in January. I don't have the energy or inclination to carry on and besides, I couldn't compete with his prices."

"Price isn't everything, David, quality plays a big part also, which I've heard Matthews doesn't get anywhere near matching you."

"Nice of you to say so, Ernie. How are things at the leisure centre? Going well, I hope."

Ernie smiled. "Couldn't be better."

***

Catherine, the only customer, was by the book section on horses when Gerry came into the library. Sally greeted him as he entered. "My, we are honoured, come to return that book? Excuse me, what was it called now? Ah, I remember! *In Praise of Older Women*. Or have you got something else on your mind?"

Gerry smiled and spotted Catherine and Sally nodded in realisation. "No funny business, you two, or I'll have to ask you to leave!" she said in mock seriousness, then added, "Can I interest you in a cup of coffee?"

Catherine called out, "Yes please, and can I have one of those chocolate muffins as well? I haven't had my dinner yet."

"Getting into the student habit already, Catherine? Don't skip too many real meals or you'll end up like the rest of the crowd, relying on the booze for your energy."

When Sally saw Catherine's reaction, she bit her lip and left to organise the beverages.

Gerry reached his co-worker's side and said quietly, "Hit a raw nerve, did she?"

Catherine merely nodded and took the book she had been reading to a table in the far corner and Gerry followed. They sat in silence until Sally had returned with the coffee and a cake for each of them. She wanted to apologise for her earlier comment but decided to wait for a more appropriate moment.

Gerry finally spoke after taking a bite from his cake. "So what's giving you doubts about Cambridge then?"

She took a couple of bites from her cake and looked around to make sure nobody else had entered the library before answering. "It's all this talk about boozing, and the thought of Freshers' Day just gives me the idea that it will just be one long hangover. I like a drink, but to get absolutely paralytic and throwing up all over the place is just not me. I know it's supposed to be about bonding and the like but I don't want to go through that just to be one of the in-crowd!"

"What about the subjects you chose? I thought you liked art. I've seen some of your sketches and think they are brilliant," Gerry said softly.

"Thanks, Gerry, but I honestly believe my A level art will be enough to get me through what I want in life. Why is it so vital that we must all have degrees to be looked on as being a successful person?" The last part of Catherine's comment was said loud enough for Sally to hear and she looked at the couple briefly.

Gerry finished his coffee and cake before replying. "Sounds like you've convinced yourself that Cambridge is not for you. Seems to me you should speak to your mum and dad. Somehow, I don't think it will be that difficult to bring them round to your way of thinking. Have you thought about other universities? What about your school friends; where are they going to study?"

She looked down at her half-eaten cake and pushed it in front of Gerry.

"Most are going to Bristol but there are no places left there, but the culture will still be the same. Maybe you're right about talking to my parents. Here, have this, I've lost my appetite."

"Thanks. What about Newmarket? Is that still in your plans?"

"Too right it is! That could be my dream move."

They both stood up, picked up their cups and plates and walked back to the counter where Sally was waiting. Catherine said, "Might as well get it over and done with right now."

Sally hesitated before speaking. "I couldn't help hear you two talking but Catherine, take this from one who's been through the same quandary. University can be a great place if that's what your heart is set on but on the other side of things it can be a gut-buster, if you get my meaning."

Catherine nodded her thanks. Sally continued, "You should listen to Gerry sometimes, not always mind. He's not just a pretty face and freckles."

"I don't have freckles!" Gerry protested.

Sally laughed. "Oh yes you have, Gerald! And I know exactly where but he doesn't have them in the usual places, Catherine."

"Tell me," the younger female said.

"Sorry, love, you will have to find out for yourself, but behave yourselves, you two!" Sally replied and turned away.

Outside the library Catherine looked at Gerry with a look of expectancy on her face. "Well?"

"Well what? I've got no idea what she's on about," Gerry said in a defensive voice.

Catherine grabbed his arm.

"Gerry! You and Sally were the talk of the sixth form last New Year's Eve. She was practically carrying you back to her place."

He was silent for a few moments as he walked her back to her parents' house.

"I'd twisted my ankle. She had offered to treat it, that's all."

"I bet you enjoyed the treatment!" she said and ran ahead, as Gerry tried to grab her arm. When he caught up with her he said, "You're too young to know about such things."

She laughed. "Too young, Gerry? I will be eighteen next March. We will have to compare notes sometime," and gave him a peck on the cheek.

He took her hand and said quietly, "Perhaps, before you leave for Newmarket anyway."

They walked the rest of the way in silence, still holding hands.

He then walked to the flat he shared with his elderly grandmother. He had lived there since he was twelve years old when both his parents were killed in what he was told had been a motorway pile-up. Now they were the only surviving relatives left from what once was a large family.

The ground-floor, two-bedroom apartment entrance was on the side of the four-storey building and had a small ramp up to the doorway. Gerry unlocked the door and called out as he went inside. "Hi Gran, it's me, sorry I'm late."

A stout woman in her mid-seventies came out of the lounge and gave him a warm smile. "That's all right, dear, I only put your dinner back in the oven to keep warm about ten minutes ago. Been out with your friends?"

Gerry took his coat off and hung it on the coat stand in the hallway.

"Sort of. Mr Evans' daughter, Catherine, wanted to ask me something and we went to the library for a coffee."

"Tell me about it after you've eaten your dinner, dear. It's your favourite; cottage pie. Don't forget to wash your hands first."

Gerry smiled. Her last comment was made every time he came home. The old lady also had a faint smile on her face. She had noticed the thin smear of lipstick on Gerry's cheek which he now spotted as he washed his hands and hastily cleaned his face.

He took his dinner out of the oven and sat at the small table in the kitchen. His gran made a wonderful cottage pie and when he finished he washed the plate and utensils and left them to dry in the rack. He then made them both a cup of tea and took them into the lounge and placed both cups on a coffee table next to where the old lady was sitting.

"So what have you been up to today, Gran? Today was card club day, wasn't it?"

She took a sip of her tea before answering, "Yes, but I didn't go, Gerald. I went to see the doctor about this niggle in my side."

"Is that still bothering you? I thought it had cleared up after the doctor gave you some tablets last week."

She shifted uncomfortably in her seat. "They did for a while, but I saw a different doctor today, a locum called Dr Chown. He's much younger and taller than Dr Bowden, and he is sending me for an X-ray on Friday."

Gerry looked concerned. "You haven't had a fall, have you?"

"No, not since I slipped on that wet floor last year. Now, that's enough about me, tell me what you have been up to."

Gerry knew not to try and push his gran any further about her ailment; her last comment was her signal to say she wouldn't talk about herself and there would be no point in further questions. Instead, he told her about Mr Evans' decision to sell his business but that his own future seemed to be secure.

She gave a little smile. "I know about Mr Evans, dear, the doctor's receptionist told me the whole story. What that woman doesn't know about other people's lives just isn't worth knowing. I don't want to worry you, dear, but that man Matthews, who is taking over from Mr Evans, doesn't have a very good reputation from what I have heard."

"What do you mean, Gran?"

"Well, he has a habit of working his staff very hard and is always looking to cut corners and costs. Is your college course going to carry on? I hear Mrs Stockwell is very pleased with the engraving you did on her husband's lighter. You must keep practising those skills."

"Mr Evans said he will pay my college tuition fees right up to my final exams. As for Mrs Stockwell she did thank me but she also scared me a little."

"Scared you? How did she do that, Gerald?" she asked, with more than a little concern in her voice.

Gerry thought for a moment while he chose his words carefully. "She thanked me for engraving the lighter and said something about not seeing similar work since she was in Germany. She also gave me a kiss on both cheeks before…"

The old lady smiled with a twinkle in her eyes. "It seems like lots of women are kissing you on the cheek. Is there anything I should know, Gerald?"

He looked in confusion at her before remembering the mark on his face earlier.

"Oh that! It was Catherine who was messing around. Anyway, as I was saying, after Mrs Stockwell thanked me she took hold of both my hands in hers and stared at me as she spoke. Gran, it was almost like she was trying to hypnotise me or read my thoughts. It was quite an unnerving feeling. And her hands felt so hot, I was glad when she let go of them."

Mrs Reynolds looked down at her own hands for several moments and Gerry thought she was about to cry but she recovered her composure and spoke. "Mrs, and to a lesser degree, Mr Stockwell have some unique talents and you would be wise to take heed of what she told you."

Nothing more was spoken about the subject and half an hour later the old lady made herself a cup of cocoa and retired to her bed.

Gerry sat alone for some time thinking about what his gran had said and recalled some of Mrs Stockwell's words.

'Don't let others distract you from your chosen path.'

He couldn't think of anything that would persuade him to give up his engraving work so what did she know about his future?

After mulling things over and over in his mind for a further twenty minutes he also went to his bed. The two women in his dreams were not the elderly ladies but Catherine and Sally. Both were trying to pull him in a different direction.

4

Percival Matthews walked into the hardware store as if he already owned the premises, picking up items, having a cursory look at prices and then discarding them, not always in their proper position.

Gerry, not having ever met this person who had just entered the shop, watched his actions and asked politely, "Can I help you, sir?"

Matthews looked at the young man with disdain written all over his face.

"Just tell the manager I'm here, he's expecting me!"

Unruffled Gerry kept his cool although this man's manner didn't go down too well with him. He was about to ask his name, but David Evans came through from his office at the rear of the shop.

"Thank you, Gerald, I will take over now. Good morning, Mr Matthews, I wasn't expecting you for another half an hour."

Matthews ignored the last remark and deliberately made a point of looking around the shop.

"Not very busy today, are you? I've been standing outside for the past twenty minutes and only seen one person come in."

"It's probably due to the Thursday-morning market. It's usually quieter for a couple of hours. I'm sure things will pick up later. Come on through to the office and I'll make you a drink. Coffee?"

Looking at Gerry he said, "The boy can make the drinks. I will have tea – not weak, milk and two sugars!"

Evans turned to face Gerry, gave a quick wink and led Matthews into his office. Waiting until the office door was closed Gerry was about to make an obscene gesture in that direction but he heard the shop door open. Turning around he faced a male customer with a very youthful face that he hadn't previously seen in the area.

"Can I help?" Gerry asked the stranger.

"You sell lighter fluid in this place, mate?" was the reply in a distinctive northern accent.

Gerry went behind the counter and produced three items.

"These are the three we stock; any particular brand?"

"The cheapest one will do. I've been trying to get hold of some all bloody morning. You've got some nice stuff in here, must be a bit pricey."

Gerry took no notice of the last comment, told him the price of the lighter fluid, took a five-pound note from the man and went to the other counter to get change from the till. His back was not turned for more than a second but he was suddenly aware that the man had moved quickly and silently towards one of the other displays and was about to put something into his pocket.

"Those cufflinks cost upwards of £50 if you're interested in buying them!" he said in a loud voice and moved forward towards the door to cut off the stranger's escape route.

Realising he had been spotted Mark gave a half laugh and put the item back in its place. He took his change from Gerry and left the shop.

Gerry watched the man disappear and suddenly remembered he hadn't made Matthews his tea and the same for his boss who had a drink at this time of morning. Luckily, the kettle had not long boiled and he took the drinks in, after first knocking on the office door and waiting for the summons to enter.

Matthews gave Gerry another of his disdainful looks.

"Took your time, didn't you?" then turned to the shop owner, "Is he always this slow? When I give my staff an instruction, I expect immediate response."

Before his boss could defend him, Gerry spoke. "A customer arrived just after you came in here and Mr Evans has trained me to attend to them as a priority." He turned and closed the door as he left the office.

Evans only just managed to restrain himself from smiling at his assistant's remark.

"Gerry is a very efficient lad and handles all the engraving work and key-cutting duties as well as his normal tasks."

Matthews didn't take kindly to being spoken to in such a manner by staff members and made a mental note of Gerry's attitude. He simply commented, "I don't know if there will be much hand engraving work being done when I take over. It's mostly done by staff in my other shops. I'm looking for staff who can service computers and the like."

"I didn't realise you were intending to change the stock portfolio to such an extent. What plans do you have for my current stock, if you don't mind me asking?" Evans enquired, thinking of how long it had taken him to build up his business to the high prominence it now held in the area.

Matthews sensed the feeling of disappointment in the owner's voice and he decided to push the knife in deeper.

"If you agree to my improved terms we have discussed, I'll take over straight after the Christmas break and hold a closing-down sale. What I can't dispose of in the following month I'll get rid of in my bric-a-brac shop."

David Evans suddenly had grave doubts about the wisdom of selling his business to this man. However, having rejected two other offers, he knew he had to go through with the sale to Matthews. There was only one concern left to resolve.

"What about young Gerry? He's a good sales person as well as carrying out the tasks I mentioned just now. He lives with his grandmother and his wages and her pension are the only income they have coming in. He also has another two years left to go on his college course before he takes his exam which I have paid for on his behalf. Incidentally, Mr Matthews, Gerry will be learning to use a computer as well as engraving work but he wants to maintain his manual skills as well. His course also includes training to be a locksmith."

Matthews' mind was ticking over at a fast pace, but he gave nothing away in his next question. "I've seen a girl working here on my previous visits. Having a pretty thing like her around sometimes brings in the customers?"

Evans stared back at Matthews for several seconds before speaking quite deliberately. "That girl is my daughter and she is leaving to take up a temporary job in Newmarket before going to Cambridge University, so you will have to find another 'pretty thing' to attract your kind of customer."

Matthews suddenly realised he could put the purchase of the shop in jeopardy if he pushed Evans any further, but he wasn't the type of person to apologise.

"Hmm, so that means you're only leaving me with one member of your staff. Can I rely on that boy not to swindle me? I've taken over too many shops where the previous boss has left me with staff who have tried to, let's say, help themselves."

Evans held up his hand and spoke again in a voice that was fast running out of patience. "I think what is more to the point, Mr Matthews, is Gerald going to have a future in your business or are you going to find a way of pushing him out once you've established yourself here?"

Again, Matthews avoided giving a straight answer. "If you say he's reliable and willing to learn new methods and style of working I'll give him a chance to prove himself. But I don't have much use for a hand engraver; one of my sons does that."

Evans smiled. "But to what standard, I wonder. Gerald completed a task last week that had a customer comparing it to work her father, a man with nearly thirty years' experience, used to carry out. That is why I am paying for Gerald to continue his studies in the technical college, who also find his work exemplary and to the highest possible standard."

"Do you pay him when he attends college?"

"Why, yes of course! I wish I could pay him a higher wage but instead, I've paid for his course and exam fees."

Matthews didn't reply but made a mental note to either cancel Gerry's course or pay him less than this mug was doing. Instead he said, "Well, if you accept my new terms, namely, I take over straight after Christmas when you hand over the keys, I don't think there is anything further to discuss."

David Evans thought for a moment and then asked, "You mentioned little or no engraving; what about the key-cutting business? We do find that quite lucrative at times, especially when Gerry goes to their premises to solve such problems."

Matthews shook his head. "No chance, I've got a more modern machine at one of my other shops. I'll get rid of yours for scrap if it's still here when I take over."

Nodding his head Evans rose to his feet and offered his hand to Matthews. "I think that concludes our meeting, Mr Matthews. I will amend and draw up the paperwork and have it sent to your solicitors by the beginning of next week."

The other man gave a limp shake of the hand and turned to leave. He walked through the shop, totally ignoring Gerry as if he didn't exist. Evans walked up to Gerry and putting a hand on one of his assistant's shoulders he said, "I'm afraid you might have an uncomfortable time with Mr Matthews if you don't keep your head down and work very hard."

"What about my engraving and key-cutting jobs, Mr Evans? Those cover more than fifty per cent of the work I do here."

The shopkeeper looked forlornly around his pride and joy he had built up over the past thirty-five years, not sure how to share his concerns with the lad. But he had always been honest so he faced him and spoke softly. "Mr Matthews believes his son is capable of taking on those duties, despite what I explained to him about your skills. I also get the feeling that he is not in favour of you completing your college course, but I could be wrong on that score."

Gerry stood speechless for several seconds, then he blurted out, "What does he expect me to do then, Mr Evans? Just serve customers and sweep the floor or serve him tea? You know how much I enjoy the engraving work and helping people who have locked themselves out of their homes or shops. I'd go crazy doing nothing but serving all day long!"

Evans indicated for them both to go into his office, leaving the door open to listen out for customers. He told Gerry to sit down while he made them both a cup of tea, allowing the youngster time to try and gather his thoughts. When he returned with the drinks, he was relieved to see Gerry had regained his composure. Facing his assistant across the office desk he started to speak.

"First, Gerry, I must apologise to you; the sale of my business has not turned out in the manner I had hoped for. Mr Matthews laid out his plans this morning and frankly, it depresses me to think about what he intends to do."

Gerry looked blankly back at his boss who held up one hand for silence.

"Let me finish first, Gerry, then you can ask as many questions as you like."

He then proceeded to explain what Matthews' plans were for the business and he felt it only fair to give details of what would be expected of his assistant. Gerry listened intently and did not speak for a couple of minutes, trying to digest the news. Finally he said, "If it's as you think, Mr Evans, I can kiss the engraving goodbye and the college course. I know a bit about computers and similar gadgets but I wouldn't say I was a fountain of knowledge concerning their repairs. Would he send me on a course to gain that EXPERTISE instead or have you paid the course fees for nothing?"

It was Evans' turn to sit in silence for a time before responding, "I will be perfectly honest with you, Gerry, I believe it's his intention to bring in his own staff to do the majority of the work and push you to one side. Then he will try to find grounds on which to dismiss you. But on no account must you just walk out and leave. You wouldn't get any benefit money if you did that.

"I have a plan in mind to help you but I must speak to my solicitor to check my facts first. However, do not worry about the rent of the flat you and your grandmother live in. If you do have the misfortune to lose your job I will waive the rent payments until you find other employment. I would prefer it if you told no one about this conversation until I have checked with the solicitor and am clear on what I can do to help you."

"I don't know if I should tell Gran about this situation, she's not been herself lately and I don't want to worry her unnecessarily."

"Then don't say anything until we know more. And I don't want you thinking all is lost. You are like a second son to me and…"

A man's voice from the doorway made both Gerry and Evans look up in startled surprise.

"A bit old for adopting, aren't you, Dad?"

"Colin! What are you doing here?" the shopkeeper said smiling broadly as he stood up and went and exchanged a hug with the man.

"I've been standing here for the past couple of minutes and didn't want to interrupt. But it sounds a bit grim. How are you, Gerry?"

Gerry stood up, also smiling, and warmly shook the man by his offered hand. "I'm okay. Do you want a hot drink or something?"

Colin nodded. Gerry checked with his boss for approval, which was given, and was about to leave the two men to talk family business when he noticed something about Colin's appearance.

"Colin, that's a different uniform compared to the one you wore the last time I saw you."

"Doesn't miss much, does he, Dad? Yes, I'm now a petty officer but you don't have to call me sir, not just yet anyway."

Gerry offered his congratulations and left the two men to talk in private. Father and son moved into the office and Colin sat in the chair vacated by Gerry. His father was about to speak, but Colin held up a hand.

"Sorry, Dad, I'll explain why I'm here after you tell me the news about the sale of the business. Doesn't sound too friendly from what I heard just now."

Evans had almost finished explaining the problems when Gerry knocked on the door and waited for the summons before entering with the drinks. Colin gave a quick signal to his father to end the conversation on the matter of the sale, indicating it could be continued later. Gerry was about to leave the room when Colin spoke. "Yes, one of the reasons for my flying visit is to take advantage of Gerry's talents."

The other occupants of the room looked equally puzzled so he explained, "This might come as a bit of a shock to you, Dad, but I'm about to get engaged and I want young Gerry here to do some engraving for me."

Again, both men were stunned into silence before they both offered their congratulations to Colin.

Gerry spoke first. "Who's the lucky or should I say unlucky girl?" and he managed to dodge the half-hearted attempt by Colin to grab him.

"Watch it, sunshine, I can still arrange to have you press-ganged. Look, I haven't got much time right now but I would like you to engrave a jewellery box with this message." He passed Gerry a piece of folded paper along with a large package.

Reading the message Gerry laughed. "Wow, it must be love! Two interlocking hearts with your initials and a date. If you don't mind me asking, Colin, what do the initials 'ZP' stand for?"

"Zoe Parker. And yes, Dad, it is Zoe, your solicitor's daughter."

"Well, well, what a small world. How soon do you want this done? I will make it a priority task for Gerry if need be," Evans said, and gave his son another hug and shook his hand vigorously once more.

"Gerry, I know it's very short notice, but I have to be back on board my ship in Avonmouth near Bristol by nine this evening."

Gerry took another look at the drawing and asked to see the jewellery box. Colin opened the package and passed the contents to Gerry.

Evans senior and Gerry inspected the box with critical eyes and asked Colin where he purchased the item.

"I saw it in Hong Kong last year when we were on a tour in the area. I admit it's not the greatest work of art but it was all I could afford at the time."

"Mm," was all his father would say before summoning Gerry into a storeroom at the rear. Colin stayed in the shop in case someone came in to buy something. Moments later the shop door opened and Ernie Newsham walked in. Looking at Colin it took a moment for him to identify the man in uniform.

"Hello, Colin, I didn't recognise you at first. How are you?" and extended his hand in friendship.

"Hi, Mr Newsham, how are tricks with you these days?"

"Doing pretty well as a matter of fact. Is Gerry around by any chance? I need him to cut some keys for me."

Before Colin could answer the two men reappeared from the back of the shop carrying a similar box to the one shown to them earlier.

Ernie stepped forward and spoke to Evans. "I'm sorry for butting in but could Gerry cut me another set of van keys for the new bloke who is working for me as I want to hang on to the spare set in case he loses them."

Evans looked at Gerry and gave him a nod of approval so the assistant took the keys and went to his workbench behind the counter. He finished the task and was paid by Ernie who left the shop without saying a word which drew a quizzical glance from Evans senior but he resumed his conversation with his son. Gerry joined Colin and his father just as Evans senior was saying, "Colin, you can and will accept this box! Yes, it is probably worth more than the one you bought in Hong Kong but I only want you to have the best. Consider it as an engagement present from your mother and me."

Colin shook his head but he knew better than to argue with his father when he was in this mood. Once again hugs were exchanged between the two.

"Right, Gerry, Colin is going to visit his mother and sister for the next few hours. If you can start on the job in hand as soon as you've had your lunch and we'll see how much progress you make by closing time."

Gerry nodded and Colin gave him a slap on the shoulder as a sign of appreciation.

"Thanks, Gerry, I'll catch you later."

Once Colin had left them alone Evans asked Gerry if Ernie had made any comment.

"Only that he had to get back to the centre as he was expecting an urgent delivery. Why, is something wrong?"

"No, don't worry. He just seemed very anxious not to get into conversation with Colin. I wonder why?"

***

Ernie had very good reason not to hang around talking to anyone because he had to return the van keys to their rightful owner. The driver of the van was sitting on a wall next to his vehicle. He was a thickset man with a drinker's paunch and when he saw Ernie approaching him, he stood up and commented, "Took your bloody time, didn't you? If he finds out, I'm dead!"

"Stop moaning, I'm back now. Here's your keys back and the fifty quid I promised. Remember, give me a ring when it's ready."

Harry nodded and climbed into his van without another word.

5

Returning from lunch, Gerry briefly called on his grandmother to tell her he might be late coming home because of the extra work. By the time Colin arrived back at the shop three quarters of the engraving had been carried out but the more delicate work would take almost as long to complete.

Colin looked carefully over Gerry's shoulder to observe progress, stood back, and said to his father, "God, this lad has got some talent!"

His father nodded in agreement and asked, "Everything okay at home? I'm sure they had a bit of a shock when you made your announcement."

"Yes, they were pleased as punch but I got the usual sarcastic remarks from Catherine. Dad, I think you need to have a talk with her about Cambridge. She seems to have lost her initial enthusiasm about going. Mum didn't hear us speaking so I'm not sure if she knows anything."

Evans senior shook his head in frustration.

"I have to admit whenever the subject has arisen she has quickly tried to talk about something else and I've been meaning to press her but I'll try and find time tonight."

"Fine but go easy on her, Dad. She's torn between staying quiet and disappointing you and Mum."

His father sighed; Catherine always confided in her big brother first.

"Don't worry, I will. While you are here with Gerry, I want to call on Albert Parker with these papers to sign. I need to talk with him on another business matter, and of course, discuss the wedding plans?"

"There's no rush on that last part. When you leave, I'll lock up."

The shop owner gathered some papers together and left the premises after which, Colin locked the door and turned the lights off in the main shop area. He sat down on an office chair watching Gerry continue with his task. After nearly ten minutes he put down his tools and announced, "I'll have to leave it for about fifteen minutes for the metal to settle down. Any chance of a coffee, Colin?"

Colin went and made them both a hot drink and after sitting in silence for a couple of minutes he spoke. "Gerry, I hope you don't mind me asking, do you make it a habit of cutting vehicle keys?"

The lad looked back at him for several seconds before answering. "I've only done it once before for Mr Newsham after your dad said it was okay. Why?"

"That kind of work is normally confined to vehicle main agents or dealers. Both of you could get into trouble if the word spread. Ernie Newsham would know that, being an ex-copper. Yes, those dealers charge about ten times what you do, but I believe it's against the law. Tell me straight if I'm sticking my nose in, but I wouldn't carry on that practice when Matthews takes over. I've heard things in the past that make him sound a dodgy character to deal with. He's got no qualms about dropping others in the brown stuff to save his own skin."

"Thanks, I'll bear your comments in mind and crack on with the engraving. I should finish in about an hour. You don't have to stay here if you've got better things to do. Nobody is likely to bother me."

Colin thought for a moment and stood up. "Well, I was thinking…"

Before he could finish speaking a loud banging came from the shop doorway. He moved forward quickly and was two paces from the door when a strident voice called out, "Open up, Evans, I know you're in there, I can see your light. We've got things to sort out", and the banging on the door began again.

Colin turned towards Gerry and asked quietly, "Do you recognise that character?"

Gerry put down his tools and nodded. "It's Graham Bishop, one of the local petty criminals who keeps making threats against your dad."

The sailor's eyes lit up.

"Oh, does he now! Well, Mr Bishop, you're in for a rather nasty shock. Nobody threatens a member of my family and gets away with it."

He reached the door and had it unlocked and open in seconds.

Bishop started to speak. "About bloody time…" and stopped when he saw that he was confronted by a younger man in uniform, of equal height to himself but broader and looking more formidable than the elderly shopkeeper he was expecting to confront.

"Isn't life full of nasty surprises, Mr Bishop?"

The startled man was grabbed by one shoulder and dragged into the shop and the door pushed closed behind him.

Colin wasted no time in further pleasantries.

"So you're the gutter rat who has been threatening my father. Fancy your chances against me do you, big boy? I've bounced much larger scum across the ship's gymnasium and not raised a single bead of sweat in the process."

49

To emphasise his last remark the sailor transferred his grip to the front of Bishop's coat and raised him so that the villain had to stand on tiptoe in order to continue breathing. After a few seconds Colin allowed the man to stand normally on his feet. Bishop started to blurt out, "I don't know what you're talking about, mate, there must be some mistake. I…"

Without turning Colin called out, "Gerry, are you sure?"

"All true," was all Gerry said. Bishop managed to look at Gerry and for a fleeting moment menace emitted from his gaze. However, Colin didn't miss the look.

"The mistake is all yours, friend Bishop! But if I hear you've threatened any member of my family I will bounce you around this town like those space hoppers we had as kids. And that warning covers my friend Gerry and his family."

He released his grip on Bishop, spun him round to face the door and gave him a hard shove to his back. As he unlocked the door he spun the man around once more to face him and said, quietly at first, "This was your first and final warning. So GET OUT and STAY away from my father's shop."

And the unfortunate man was propelled through the doorway and landed in a heap outside. He scrambled to his feet and ran off like a scared rabbit.

Colin locked the door and called to Gerry. "I enjoyed that! If he comes near here again or makes any kind of nuisance of himself I want to know."

Gerry half laughed and returned to his work.

"I'll have a word with Dad before I leave to get the full picture, but that puts paid to me leaving you here on your own."

It was another ninety minutes before Gerry was satisfied that his task was completed to his satisfaction and he presented the finished article to Colin who inspected the box with pure admiration at Gerry's handiwork. He announced, "When Zoe sees this she will want to come and thank you personally and I'm sure you will be on the guest list for the wedding."

"Glad you like it, Colin, and congratulations on your engagement."

They shook hands. Colin offered Gerry a lift home but he refused saying he needed to clean his tools before leaving the premises.

The next morning David Evans told Gerry that the whole family wanted to thank him for completing such a fine piece of work. When she came in later Catherine gave him a kiss on the cheek while nobody was looking.

Later that morning her father called Gerry into his office. He invited him to sit down.

"As you know I went to see my solicitor yesterday evening and we discussed the potential problem with Mr Matthews honouring my pledge to you, concerning your college course. He came up with the following plan. He's written a letter for you to give to the college stating that only you or I can cancel the course and if any time remains unused, or exams not taken by you and you alone, upon termination of the course, you and you alone will be entitled to those fees not spent."

"But why should I terminate the course, Mr Evans? You know how hard I've studied and worked for those qualifications."

The shopkeeper smiled. "Yes, I do know, but this is to safeguard any move Matthews might make to pocket the money himself. I cannot be absolutely certain he would do that, but better to be forearmed to cover that eventuality. And if he does do such a thing and, God forbid, dismisses you, then you will at least have some money to fall back on until you find something different."

Gerry sighed but otherwise remained silent, looking down at his hands.

Evans continued, "I'm sorry things have turned out this way but as contracts have been agreed I cannot pull out of the sale. Here is the letter Mr Parker has drawn up for you. Keep it safe, in case, or should I say, until you need it."

"What if Matthews ignores the letter or just rips it up? What do I do then?"

Evans couldn't help but smile. "Then you go to see Mr Parker and he will come with you to confront Matthews with another copy of this letter. Matthews will think twice about taking on a solicitor. The man is arrogant but he's no fool."

Gerry looked up and took the letter offered to him. Evans had one more thing to tell him. "There is one additional measure I have taken but I cannot mention any more for the moment. If I don't inform you what that measure is, then Mr Parker knows the details."

"Is that all, Mr Evans? I would like to get back to work so that I can take my mind off Mr Matthews and his plans."

"There is one other matter, Gerry. I will be finishing on Christmas Eve and he takes over after Boxing Day. It seems the lease runs out on one of his other shops on 31 December and he wants to move the stock from that shop to here."

"But we don't have the room, Mr Evans. You remember we had an extra delivery of Christmas stock on Monday and the storeroom is nearly full."

"That will be Mr Matthews' problem to sort out. He has a couple of vans he can use for temporary storage. I'm more concerned about making our customers aware of the change in the type of stock he will be selling. Let's leave the future to him to worry about. We have the next five weeks to get ourselves through."

Gerry stood up and went back to his work. He didn't see the look of concern that took over the features of his boss.

Word soon spread around the town that David Evans was selling his business and to whom. His regular customers called in to see if there were any bargains to be had and some were rewarded for their support over the many years. Gerry's skills were also in high demand and he was almost too busy to have time to worry about his own future.

Catherine worked extra hours but she didn't mention anything more about university to Gerry until the Saturday before her father was due to hand over the business. Then, on a rare moment of solitude they had together, they talked in his work area to the rear of the shop.

"Gerry, I've made up my mind about university, and Colin backed me up in front of Mum and Dad. I've decided that I can't start uni if I don't feel I can stick it through to the end. I'm grateful to you for trying to point out the alternatives but I know in my heart that it's not for me."

Gerry didn't reply for several seconds, he had his own problems to sort out, but didn't want to upset his friend.

"Well, if you've made up your mind then go for it one hundred per cent. I wish I had something definite to focus on right now."

She put a hand on his arm. "Gerry, I'm sorry you've been left in such a mess. Dad is racking his brains trying to think up ways of helping you. You don't feel that he's leaving you in the lurch, do you?"

He had to bite his tongue before replying. He felt bad for thinking the way he did but he really didn't care about other people's problems at this moment. He merely said quietly, "I'm glad you've sorted yourself out and no, it's not your dad I'm blaming, it's that slimy toad Matthews. I just wish your dad hadn't taken up his offer."

Catherine turned away to hide the tears that were beginning to well up in her eyes. Then she turned round suddenly and grabbed Gerry so quickly in her embrace that they both nearly fell over. He steadied himself and returned her embrace, also aware that he too was feeling quite emotional. Just as quickly, Catherine released herself and ran to the toilet leaving him with confused feelings.

He wiped his eyes that had also moistened and was about to continue his work, when he heard his boss call "Gerry, customer waiting."

Making sure his eyes did not betray his emotions he went back into the shop and was dismayed to see the customer waiting for him was Stella Stockwell.

"Gerald, I wanted to come and see you to wish you a happy Christmas and to see Mr Evans before he retires. Tell me, is your grandmother well?"

Taken slightly aback at the mention of his grandmother he hesitated before replying. "Grandma? Oh yes, Mrs Stockwell, she's fine. Busy baking far too much for the two of us. You would think she was expecting half the town to drop in for something to eat."

"Yes, yes. She is a fine cook. Do not be surprised if you have many visitors to sample her food. Before I forget, I want to give you this little gift as a small thank you for the work you did for me a couple of months ago." She gave him a small box with a little bow holding its cover.

Colouring slightly, he stammered, "Thank you very much, Mrs Stockwell, you didn't have to buy me anything, it was my pleasure."

"Yes, I did! This might sound a little strange to you right now but do this for me. If you cannot wear the gift, I want you to give it to your first love. Do you understand me?"

Looking confused he said, "My first love? I don't have anyone but Grandma; is that who you mean?"

She laughed merrily. "No! Your grandmother is not who I mean! You do not have a special girl or woman in your life? Well, Gerald, you will know who I mean in the near future."

Before he could answer or react, she leaned forward and gave him a kiss on both cheeks. As she pulled away from him Gerry could have sworn there were tears in her eyes. She turned around and waved at David Evans who was serving another customer and left the shop. Once they were alone in the shop, Gerry approached his boss and asked, "Is Mrs Stockwell okay? She seemed very emotional when I finished serving her."

Evans thought for a moment and sighed. "It might be that she doesn't feel as if she wants to come back here when Mr Matthews takes over. I've had quite a few of our regular customers expressing those views. It will be entirely up to him to rebuild customer loyalty for himself, although if he does change the stock and scope of the shop I fancy many of our faithful customers won't be coming back in a hurry."

"They are not the only ones. I think Catherine is also pretty upset about finishing here. I hope you don't mind me saying, Mr Evans, she hasn't been happy about university for some time and I think she's made the right decision."

His boss looked at him wistfully. "Time will tell, Gerry, time will tell. Only three more days to go. Let's try and get through them without too much heartache."

Before closing his shop for the last time David Evans gave Gerry a new set of engraving tools and a large bunch of master keys as well as one other surprise. "I've marked your initials on both those sets so there can be no doubt as to their ownership. Also, Mr Matthews said he intends scrapping the key-cutting machine so I will do that for him."

For a moment Gerry looked crestfallen but his boss held up one hand and continued, "Well, not exactly scrap the machine, Gerry, I will have it dismantled and set up again for you in the basement of your grandmother's flat. It's not the most modern piece of equipment but it will be something for you to use if and when necessary. It can be sorted out when we come in to do the final stocktaking during the holiday period."

These duties were duly carried out and David Evans' final words to his assistant were, "It's been a pleasure having you work for me, Gerry, and I have written a reference for you to give to any new employer if you should ever need one. But please remember, don't be late on your first day working for your new boss!"

Firm handshakes were exchanged when they had finished and as soon as they parted Gerry made a rare visit to one of the local pubs where Sally also happened to be visiting. Inevitably they ended up in her flat where she consoled him for a few hours, taking his mind off the worries that had plagued his thoughts.

6

Before leaving home to start his first day of working for his new boss, Gerry asked his grandmother if she had received the results of tests carried out at her hospital appointment.

"Nothing to worry about, dear, just old age catching up with me. I just need to take things a bit slower and rest more than I have been lately."

"Is there anything in the way of shopping you want me to collect on the way home tonight, Gran? The shops should still be open when I finish work."

She thought for a moment and then a smile crossed her features. "One thing we haven't had in ages is a nice piece of liver. If you can get about a pound of liver I can make a casserole with some bacon that should stretch for a couple of meals. Get it from the butchers on the high street; Mr Thomas knows just what kind of liver I like. Yes, I'm looking forward to that already."

Gerry nodded and promised to do as she asked.

***

"What time do you call this then? Didn't your old boss tell you I wanted you to start at seven thirty today?"

Gerry looked at his watch. He clearly remembered Mr Evans telling him that Matthews didn't want him at work before eight o'clock. But he wasn't going to argue with the man.

"Sorry, Mr Matthews, he must have forgotten in the rush of sorting things out for you."

Matthews gave a sneer. "I bet you forgot, not him. First and last warning, I don't tolerate lateness. Now go to the storeroom and help Harry pack this crap you used to sell. I need space to bring in quality stock."

Harry, a large man who shambled across the room rather than walked, turned to look at Gerry as he entered the storeroom. His breath smelt of stale beer as he spoke. "About bloody time too, kid, I was told I'd have help right from the start. Bring in the stuff off the counter by the door and I'll start packing it into boxes. When all the boxes are full you can take them out to the van in the yard."

Gerry bit his tongue. If everybody was going to pick on him and treat him like their gopher, he would start looking for other work right away. By the time he had cleared the stock from the counter and the display cabinet behind, Gerry had made more than a dozen journeys back and forth to the storeroom.

It was warm work and Gerry was looking forward to a cup of tea. He asked Harry if he wanted a drink at the same time. His reply stunned the lad.

"Only if you're paying!"

"Paying? What do you mean? Mr Evans has left enough tea and coffee to last nearly a week."

Harry gave a sarcastic laugh. "Huh! Fifty pence a cup is what you pay when you work for Matthews, kiddo. No freebies here!"

"Any charge for a glass of water, is there?" Gerry asked with a hint of his own sarcasm.

Harry looked at him and said with the hint of a smile, "No, but don't drink too much or he'll charge you for going to have a pee."

Gerry turned around and went into the bathroom at the rear and looked for the glass that was normally by the sink but it was nowhere to be seen. He came out and went into the kitchen to pick up a cup. He turned around and found his path blocked by his boss. "It's fifty pence a cup for you."

Gerry stared at him for a moment. *No*, he thought, *I'm not taking the bait.* So he replied as pleasantly as he could. "Yes, Harry told me. Is there any charge for a cup of water, Mr Matthews?"

Matthews looked back at him, shook his head and went back into the shop.

After having his drink Gerry continued to remove stock from the counters and took it to Harry for packing. This routine continued until well past Gerry's normal dinner break so he decided it was time he found out how much, if any, he was allowed.

Matthews was busy talking in hushed tones to a man in his office so Gerry had to wait for a further ten minutes before he could speak to his boss. The curt response was typical of the man.

"Thirty minutes and don't be late this time. Remember you've had your final warning!"

Gerry nodded his thanks and as soon as he left the shop he sprinted to the butcher's shop to buy some liver for his gran. But he was to be disappointed. Mr Thomas said regretfully, "I'm sorry, Gerald, I've sold out but I'm expecting a fresh delivery this afternoon. Pop in on your way home from work to check if it's come in."

Gerry nodded. He had wasted nearly ten minutes on this errand, so he barely had time to pick up a packet of crisps and a chocolate bar before returning to his work.

Upon returning he was told to start unloading the new van that was now parked at the rear of the shop. These boxes were heavier and bulkier than those that he had removed earlier. These were marked simply, 'Electrical Equipment' and were placed in the corner of the storeroom. There were two other men Gerry had not seen before dismantling the display units behind the counters. The only items for sale left in the shop were office accessories and sundries.

By the time he had finished unloading the van Gerry was beginning to feel the exertion and was ready for a drink of some kind. He went over to Matthews and asked if he could have a cup of coffee and offered him some money to pay for the beverage. To his surprise his boss refused to take the money. Instead he said curtly, "You don't pay me now, I'll take it out of your wages. Don't worry, I keep a tally on what you drink each day."

Gerry went into the kitchen area and found Harry drinking a cup of coffee. He tried to strike up a conversation with the man.

"Those boxes you've been packing, are those going to Mr Matthews' bric-a-brac shop?"

Harry looked at him as if he was a little simple and then a realisation dawned on him. "Ah! That's what he told your ex-boss, was it? Another mug he's caught out!" and laughed.

"Sorry, I don't understand."

Harry turned to wash out his empty cup before answering, "Kid, that's what he tells people like your old boss. The stuff that remains in the shop, or what's left of it, goes to the slop shops as he calls them. The stuff I've packed up goes into storage until he has enough to make a trip to London worthwhile. His brother has got a shop there where he can sell that stuff for double the price he paid your boss."

Seeing the look of surprise on Gerry's face he laughed and walked out of the kitchen.

After washing up his own cup Gerry went back into the shop to find out what his next task entailed. It was to help Harry remove those packed boxes and stack them into the now empty van. By the time they had finished it was past the usual time for the shop to close and Gerry suddenly remembered the promise he had made to his grandmother.

"Is it okay if I finish now, Mr Matthews? I have to collect something my grandmother is waiting for."

Matthews looked at his watch and frowned.

"Didn't Evans tell you that I run flexi time here? That means you finish when all the work is done for the day."

Gerry looked around the shop. From what he could see there was nothing left to do.

Matthews did the same and then said, "Okay, you can skip off this time but don't forget your time is my time and if there's work to be completed you will stay behind to finish no matter what time it is. Go on, get out before I change my mind!"

Gerry muttered his thanks, grabbed his coat and left the shop, hoping he was not too late to catch Mr Thomas at the butcher's shop. To his dismay, as he arrived the man was locking up his premises. "Sorry, Mr Thomas, am I too late to collect Gran's liver order?"

The butcher smiled and passed a plastic bag to him.

"No, Gerald. I was about to deliver it to your flat. I know Mr Matthews' reputation for making his staff work late. You can pay me another time for the meat."

Heaving a sigh of relief Gerry thanked the butcher and returned to his flat, quite exhausted after a day of heavy lifting and carrying.

After their meal was finished and the table cleared Mrs Reynolds couldn't help but notice how deflated and lost Gerry appeared.

"Is there anything wrong, love? You're not your usual self tonight. Didn't your first day go too well with Mr Matthews?"

Not wishing to worry his grandmother Gerry replied quietly, "I suppose I'll have to find a way of adapting to his methods, but he's not the easiest person to get along with. And the bloke I'm working alongside isn't exactly a bundle of laughs either."

"Never mind, Gerry, it all takes time to settle into new ways of working. Are you meeting any of your friends tonight?"

"No, Gran, I think I'll have an early night." With that, he rose and gave his gran a kiss on the cheek and went to his room after saying goodnight.

She brooded for several moments and then decided that now was not the time to tell the lad what the doctor had really said to her when they talked about the results of her tests. *What will he do when I'm gone? He will have no family to turn to for help or advice.* She dabbed her eyes and tried to concentrate on something else, but to no avail.

The next two days followed a similar routine to his first under Matthews but at least Gerry did manage to serve some customers although they each indicated that it would be their last visit if the stock didn't revert to its former choice.

He tried to tell his new boss about the comments, but Matthews sneered and said, "They're not the type of clientele I want in this shop anyway."

New lockable counters and display cabinets had been fitted and were full of items such as mobile phones, computer accessories and peripherals.

After his experience of being told he would have to pay for his beverages Gerry took the liberty of taking a flask of coffee into work. He couldn't afford to pay, as over the week the cost would mount up. When he entered the kitchen on the third morning he found Harry helping himself to a drink from his flask. Harry turned round to see the look of annoyance on Gerry's face.

"We share things here, kid. You can have a fag if you want."

"I don't smoke," was Gerry's terse reply.

Harry shrugged and said, "Well, you can't say I didn't offer," and proceeded to top up his cup, defying the younger man to challenge him further. Knowing he was no match for the older man Gerry made sure he drank the remains of the coffee from the flask and went back to work. Matthews had a message for him.

"No college for you tomorrow. They phoned me up and said your tutor is off sick this week so you can come in here and my son, Quentin, will give you a crash course in the stock we hold."

Now that his lunch break was only half an hour instead of an hour as with Mr Evans, he was limited to eating cold snacks instead of going into one of the nearby cafes for something hot. Fortunately those three days working for Matthews had been dry, even if a little cold, so he purchased his food and sat on one of the benches in the town square. On this particular lunchtime he was joined by Ernie Newsham who asked if he could join him. Gerry nodded and finished his snack and washed it down with a can of ice cold tea.

"I notice your new boss doesn't hang about in clearing out Mr Evans' old stock. Any idea what's happening to it?"

Gerry was glad to vent his anger at Matthews' apparent deception of his old boss.

"He told Mr Evans he was going to sell off the old stock in his bric-a-brac shops, but Harry told me he's taking the quality merchandise to London to sell in his brother's shop for twice the price he paid for it. I reckon Mr Evans has lost out on at least a couple of thousand pounds."

Ernie shook his head. "Poor David, he didn't deserve that kind of treatment, he was an honest bloke who served this community."

Gerry nodded. "Yes, and the last thing on his mind would be to cheat anyone else."

Ernie was quiet for a moment before he said casually, "So when was this stuff taken to London, or is it still nearby?"

Gerry walked right into Ernie's trap. "No, it's still there. We've loaded it all into one of Matthews' vans that's parked in the yard at the back. It hasn't gone yet because there's supposed to be some stuff arriving from another shop he's clearing out."

"How blokes like Matthews get away with tricks like that is almost criminal," Ernie said in a resigned voice.

Gerry looked at his watch and stood up. "Oh heck! I've got to go now, Mr Newsham, or he'll dock my wages for being late."

Ernie smiled. "That's okay, Gerry, see you around."

He ran back to the shop and found his boss waiting for him.

"Evans said you were a good timekeeper. Frankly, I'm not impressed. Go and give Harry a hand transferring goods from my other van to the one you've put stuff in from here. If you can't get it all in the van then bring the surplus into the shop. And make sure those items don't get marked in any way. If they do it's coming out of your wages."

He joined Gerry and they both walked into the backyard where Harry was rearranging items in the first van. Matthews went and spoke to the older man before returning indoors.

"Okay, as he's already told you, no marks or scratches on these new items or we'll both lose wages and if we do, I'll take it out on your hide, so watch it!"

Right at that moment, Gerry couldn't decide who he detested most out of the two men. True to form, they worked well past their normal finishing time and when he arrived home Gerry was full of anger towards both of them.

He went to bed earlier than normal for the second night in succession in a mixed state of exhaustion and depression. But others would be toiling a lot later and would be pleased with their night's work.

7

Ernie and Mark waited in the shadows at the rear of the shop until all other sensible people had retired for the night. When all was clear they moved to the entrance of the shop yard. Ernie took out a folded, thin strip of metal from inside his coat and opened it to its full length.

He pushed the metal through the gap between the edge of the large door and the gatepost and manoeuvred it up and down until he located the latch that kept the door closed. He had visited the yard on a number of occasions whilst on the pretence of advising the previous owner on security matters. David Evans had asked if it would have been advisable to fit a strong lock onto the gate frame, but Ernie had said it would not be necessary as there was nothing of value in the yard. The expense of adjustments to the gate to incorporate a lock would not be justified as the rear of the building had sufficient security methods to deter any would-be burglars. Evans never left his van in the yard overnight as he used it for his own transport needs, and he trusted Ernie's advice as a friend of long standing.

Ernie found the latch and lifted the end out of its position and the gate swung open silently on its well-oiled hinges. There was a light on in the rear of the building and the door opened and Harry stepped out to meet the two burglars.

"Took your time, didn't you? I thought this would be finished by now, and who is this kid?"

"Keep your voice down! When you told me Matthews wanted you to stay as night watchman I had to change my plans. Never mind who this is; the less you know the better."

Mark had stayed in the shadows as Ernie had instructed him.

"What happens now?" Harry asked.

"This!"

And Ernie's punch to his head caught Harry completely by surprise. To add to his discomfort, when he fell the big man banged the other side of his face on the edge of the shop door. He started moaning as Ernie knelt over him to speak.

"Remember what I told you to say; get it right and there will be an extra bonus for you. Get it wrong and you know what will happen. Wait at least an hour before calling the police."

Then he gave him a not-too-gentle kick in his ribs. After removing the van keys from the prone man's jacket pocket, Ernie unlocked the rear door of the van to make sure Harry hadn't been lying about the contents.

Satisfied, he closed and locked the rear door, Ernie climbed into the driver's seat and started the engine and signalled to Mark to close the gates once the van was clear of the yard and get into the passenger seat.

The van was driven to the rear entrance of the leisure centre and Mark got out and opened the large doors to allow Ernie to reverse inside, after which he closed them to avoid prying eyes.

"Okay, I reckon we have no more than twenty-five minutes to unload this lot and get back on the road."

The unloading and storing of the stolen goods was accomplished within Ernie's time limit. Mark picked up his equipment for the final part of the operation and he climbed into the driver's seat of the van and once Ernie had opened the centre doors, he watched Mark disappear out of the car park.

After locking up the building Ernie followed the van to its final destination in his own car.

Ernie caught up with Mark on a large piece of waste ground behind some derelict buildings and left his car parked a safe distance from the van. Mark was busy pouring the contents of a can of petrol inside the passenger compartment and then threw the can inside the rear of the van. Ernie approached him and asked, "What have you done with the spare keys?"

Mark answered without turning around. "On the floor, as you said. This is the bit I enjoy the most. Stand back if you don't want to fry."

He took an aerosol can and a lighter from his pocket, judged the direction of any wind and went round to the passenger door to open it. He called to Ernie, "As soon as I fire my little flame-thrower into the van and I'm out of the way, slam the door quickly. I don't want to be caught in any backdraft from the flames. Ready?"

Ernie nodded. Mark operated the aerosol and lit the lighter, taking great care not to spray himself or his clothes with the contents. He leapt backwards and Ernie slammed the door shut. For a brief moment very little happened, then the flames ignited the petrol. There followed a dull thumping sound and the whole interior of the passenger compartment filled with a mass of flames.

The two men ran for the car and left the area at high speed, but once they were clear Ernie slowed down to observe the local speed limit. He glanced at Mark.

"One day you're going to get it wrong with that lighter trick," he said.

Mark gave a clenched fist salute to himself and laughed. "Not me! I'm too good at my job."

Ernie drove to his own house and told Mark to change out of the clothes he was wearing and put fresh things on before occupying the settee on which he was to sleep.

***

Gerry rose from his bed extra early the next morning. Instead of the usual bowl of cereal and cup of tea, he cooked himself a full breakfast. His energy levels had suffered because of his rushed lunches over the previous few days. Mrs Reynolds came into the kitchen just as he was finishing eating.

"What's this, Gerry? You don't normally eat a full breakfast. You're not skipping lunch, are you?"

"Morning, Gran. No, Mr Matthews has shortened my lunch break, so I don't have time to eat even a decent snack. Sorry, I can't stop to chat now, if I'm late he'll dock some of my wages."

She shook her head as Gerry grabbed his coat and went outside.

As he approached the shop it was evident that something was not all as it should be. For a start, he hadn't seen so many police officers in the area at one time before. He tried to enter the shop, but his way was barred by a WPC.

"Sorry, sir, nobody is allowed in. You will have to come back later."

"But I work here," he said, slightly bemused. "What's going on?"

She nodded and told him to stay where he was and on no account to leave the area. So Gerry did as he was told and waited. It took the WPC a good couple of minutes to return and then she told him to follow her. She led him through the store and out into the backyard where the vans had been parked the previous night. Matthews was talking to a police officer while a man in civilian clothes was paying close attention to the back gate. On seeing Gerry, Matthews turned round abruptly, and said with some venom, "You're late again! Remember what I said before about docking your wages, and this morning of all days!"

The three other occupants in the yard turned to judge Gerry's reaction to this outburst but he looked baffled at the activity going on around him. He answered Matthews' remark. "I wasn't late, Mr Matthews, I was outside the shop before eight o'clock but was prevented from coming in."

The WPC nodded to her colleagues to confirm the fact and she told Matthews, "That's true, sir, he arrived just after seven fifty-five."

Relieved that his story had been confirmed Gerry asked, "Where's Harry? He's always here before me."

"In hospital!" Matthews barked out without turning round.

Even more confusion showed on Gerry's face and the other uniformed officer indicated that he should follow him into the shop while the WPC engaged Matthews in conversation. The officer told Gerry to take a seat in the kitchen and then he asked the lad to go over his movements from when he left work the previous evening. Gerry began with a question, "Before I do, can you tell me what's up with Harry? Why is he in hospital?"

"Mate of yours, is he?"

"No way! A work colleague maybe, but a mate? No chance."

The officer thought for a moment before replying. "Okay, all I can tell you is that Harry was beaten up last night and the van full of goods was stolen. Now, tell me what your movements were last night after finishing work."

Gerry explained that he had left work just before six thirty at the same time as Harry. He had gone home to his gran's flat, had a cooked supper, watched television with her and had gone to bed just after nine o'clock because he was tired after all the lifting and carrying he had done that afternoon. The officer interrupted him. "You said Harry left at the same time as you. Did you leave in the same direction?"

"No, I live the other side of Market Street and turned left after leaving here. I looked back and saw Harry go into the Butler's Arms just across the road."

The lapel radio on the officer's uniform buzzed before he could ask another question and he stood up and walked to the front of the shop to speak in private. Even so, Gerry managed to hear some of his responses.

"Where?"; "Anything left?" and "That's odd, why do that, I wonder?" and then the conversation ended. He walked out to the yard and passed on part of his conversation with Matthews and his colleagues. Matthews swore and kicked something over that clattered around the yard. Then the officer returned to continue talking to Gerry.

"Okay, where were we? Right, did you know that Harry sometimes doubled up as security for your boss when required?"

"I've only worked for Mr Matthews since Monday so how would I know Harry's routine? I don't have a routine of my own. I was supposed to be at college today, but the boss told me it had been cancelled this week because the tutor was off sick. I was looking forward to going to get away from here for a while."

"What course is that?" asked the officer.

"Hand engraving and computer training at Muller Road College," Gerry said sullenly.

The officer seemed puzzled. "Who is your course tutor, Gerry, if you don't mind me asking?"

"Lee Bradley, and he's the best!"

"Describe him to me," which Gerry did.

The officer spoke on his radio and seconds later the WPC came into the room.

"Okay, Gerry, give the name of your tutor and describe him to my colleague."

Gerry did so and the WPC smiled.

"Now tell her what your boss said yesterday afternoon."

"That my course was cancelled because Lee was off sick all week."

The woman shook her head. "My name is WPC Bradley and I'm married to Lee and he's as right as rain."

"Think very carefully before answering, Gerry. Did you have anything to do with this robbery last night? Don't say anything until I come back from talking to your boss," and left the room while the WPC stayed with Gerry.

In the yard the officer asked Matthews, "How well do you know young Gerry, Mr Matthews?"

"I inherited him from the previous owner and he's not a very good timekeeper. I would get rid of him if I could find someone to take his place but I suppose I'm stuck with him for now."

"Mr Matthews, did you receive a phone call yesterday to say Gerry's course at college was not running today?"

"I can't remember such trivial things. What has that got to do with this robbery anyway?"

The officer pressed him further. "It's to do with the simple matter of whether we can trust that Gerry is speaking the truth. Now, Mr Matthews, did you or did you not receive a phone call yesterday concerning the course that Gerry was supposed to attend at college today. Yes or no?"

"Are you taking his word over mine? He's slow, sullen and I think he resents me for taking over the cosy workplace his ex-boss kept for him."

The officer took in a deep breath and exhaled slowly. "Mr Matthews, I realise this is a stressful time for you. However, I have reason to believe that either he is lying, or I am being sidetracked in my investigation. If I have to, I can have a record of your incoming calls made to you yesterday. In order to do that I would have to ask my superiors to sanction such an enquiry. In that case you would both have to accompany me and my colleague to the police station. So, for the last time, Mr Matthews, is the answer yes or no?"

Matthews sighed. "No, damn him, but why do you take his word over mine? I'm a well-respected..."

The officer held up a hand. "Enough! The tutor who you claimed was off sick happens to be married to my colleague and she confirms that her husband is at work today! Whatever your motive could be for trying to get the lad in trouble, frankly, is none of my business. We've wasted the best part of an hour trying to sort this pointless exercise of yours out. Now, have you anything further to add to your statement?"

Matthews shook his head. The officer called to ask his detective colleague if he was finished investigating. He nodded and came over to speak.

"Plenty of old prints but nothing new or unsmudged but I'll take the prints of Mr Matthews and the lad and the bloke in hospital just to eliminate them."

Matthews became more indignant and asked, "What do you need my fingerprints for? Are you seriously thinking I set this up myself? What about the boy? Have you checked if he told any of his mates about what was in the van?"

The uniformed officer spoke quietly and deliberately, "As my colleague said, we need to eliminate your prints and those of your employees from our enquiries. Speaking off the record, I think you have tried your best to get young Gerry into as much trouble as you can and I don't believe he has anything to do with this robbery."

He re-entered the shop to tell his colleague and Gerry what had taken place. Turning to Gerry he said, "It's none of my business but if I were you, I would look for a better employer to work for sooner rather than later. One other matter, the detective will want to take your fingerprints, just like your boss, so that they can distinguish them from any others he's found."

"Am I still a suspect concerning the robbery?"

"Not unless you have anything to say to make me think differently."

Gerry shook his head.

"I'll tell Lee, my husband, the reason you didn't go to college today. So don't worry," the WPC added as they prepared to leave. Matthews called to them before they left.

"One minute, you said the van was burnt out with nothing left inside; can't you get any clues from there?"

"It's too early to say but I wouldn't hold out too much hope. Good morning, Mr Matthews," was the final comment from the male officer.

Matthews swore and stormed into his office. Five minutes later he came out and shouted at Gerry, "I don't pay you to sit around doing nothing. Do something useful like making me a cup of coffee."

Gerry stood up and went into the kitchen. He pondered whether to ask his boss what his reason was for telling lies about college. He had the right to know and was going to have an answer!

By the time he took the drink to the office, another man, in his late twenties, was waiting in the office with Matthews. Both ignored him but as he was about to go back out his boss said curtly, "Gerry, this is my son, Quentin. He's going to show you how to distinguish a mobile phone from a cordless phone. First, make him a drink as well."

"Tea, not too strong, milk and no sugar, please, Gerry. Meet me in the workshop in a few minutes." Quentin spoke with more friendliness than the lad had heard from his father since they first met.

Gerry had not bothered to bring a flask in that morning, unaware of what had happened the night before, so he expected Harry to be at work and wasn't going to provide him with free drinks. He took the opportunity to make himself a cup using the same teabag as he had for Quentin.

Gerry was joined by Quentin in the workshop and they sat opposite each other while they finished their drinks but as Gerry finished his cup Matthews senior stuck his head round the door and said smugly, "I'll add that cup you made for yourself to your list of drinks for the week."

Gerry protested, "I used the same teabag after making Quentin's tea!"

Matthews was about to respond but his son beat him by saying, "Come off it, Dad, you can charge it to me if you have to," which received a low growl from his father but no other comment.

Once they were alone Quentin said quietly, "You're learning fast, Gerry. He'll try and get away with charging you for anything he thinks he can. He was even like that with me and my brother at first, but we stood our ground."

"What's your brother's name?" was the only thing that came to mind. Quentin seemed to be on the level, but Gerry wasn't taking any more chances with any of the Matthews family until he got to know each one a lot better.

"He's called Oswald, poor bloke! He's in his early thirties and left home about ten years ago. Probably had enough of Dad's tight ways with money. Once I get my degree in computer science, he won't see me for dust either."

"Your father said that you are supposed to teach me about the new stock we're going to be selling here. I know how to do the basics with computers but don't ask me to take one apart or repair one that's broken."

Quentin laughed. "No chance! All I will be showing you is how to sell accessories such as cables and the various bags for tablets and laptops. There will be somebody from one of Dad's other shops to deal with selling all the gadgets, etc. That person will also know about the repair side of things. Keep this to yourself for now, but I think he's planning on selling non-electrical items as well. I don't know but you may be more suited to selling that kind of stuff."

Gerry wanted to say he would much rather be doing the work he did before the shop was taken over by this family.

However, even though Quentin seemed a lot friendlier he wasn't ready to trust him just yet. Instead he simply said, "I can only give it a go."

His companion nodded and rose from his seat.

"Okay, let's give it a start. We'll go through the items stored in the new counter and display cabinets that you need to know about," and he led the way back into the shop. His father was waiting for him.

"I'm going out to check on Harry. The hospital said he's been discharged so I want to hear his version of events of last night. And he better have a good story or he's out on his ear!"

"Steady, Dad. You need him for all the odd jobs you can't get anyone else to do."

Matthews fumed and muttered, "If he doesn't satisfy me then he's out! And this mug will have to do his work or he'll be walking as well."

Gerry was about to speak out but Quentin stepped in between the two and moved Gerry towards the display units and away from his father's comments.

"See you later, Dad."

Matthews glared briefly at his son's back and turned around and stormed out of the shop. Once he had gone Quentin spoke to Gerry in a calming manner.

"You nearly walked into his trap. You were about to answer back, and if you had, you would have been out the door post-haste."

"Sorry, Quentin, but if he continues to talk about me in that way without getting any reaction he's mistaken."

"Then kiss this job goodbye because he will push and push until you do react, then boom! Come on, let's go through the stock and see how you get on."

They had been working for about half an hour when a customer entered the shop. It was the same man Gerry had stopped stealing on his previous visit before Christmas. As if nothing had happened, he cheekily asked, "Hi, mate, got any more of that lighter fluid?"

Then he stopped and saw the changes that had been made since his last visit and paid particular attention to the electrical items Quentin had placed on the counter.

"Wow, that's a nice bit of gear, much better than the crap you used to stock."

Before he moved to the counter where the last few items of old stock were housed Gerry managed to signal to Quentin to keep a watch on the stranger.

"Only one left I'm afraid and it's a bit more expensive than the last one you bought. Do you still want it?"

"Ain't got much soddin' choice, have I, mate!" he moaned, paying Gerry and made a point of counting his change before walking out without saying another word.

Once they were alone Quentin asked, "I got your signal. Know him, do you?"

"Last time he came in for the same item he tried to pinch an expensive set of cufflinks but I stopped him."

"Yeah, he didn't seem to have two pennies to rub together yet he paid a lot of attention to the stuff on the counter. That's one thing Dad won't know about, the dubious characters in the area."

Gerry agreed and they returned to the task of identifying stock and their uses. Quentin complimented Gerry on his ability to understand the uses and techniques of the equipment and they completed the task early in the afternoon a few minutes before Matthews senior arrived, still in an apparently foul mood.

"How is Harry?" Quentin enquired. It took a few minutes for his father to reply.

"Fewer bruises than the stupid fool deserves. He heard someone throwing stones over the gate and some were hitting the van windscreen so he went out to chase what he thought were kids just mucking about. Before he knew it, two blokes jumped him and knocked him out. They pinched the van keys and scarpered. The police told me this morning the van was found but it had been burnt out after being unloaded. And the insurance company is being funny about paying up."

He went into his office and slammed the door.

Quentin turned to Gerry, "Give me five minutes with him and then bring us both in a cup of tea and make one for yourself; you deserve it after your work this afternoon."

Gerry did as he was instructed and found his boss in a slightly calmer mood. Quentin was explaining how well Gerry had picked up his new tasks.

"He picks things up quite quickly. He's got the potential to do well if you give him a chance."

Matthews looked at his assistant. "I'll be the judge of that. I take a bit more convincing than you."

Quentin persevered with his defence of Gerry. "He identified a potential shoplifter this morning. I wouldn't have had a clue, but Gerry gave me a signal to keep an eye on him."

All Matthews could say in a sullen voice was, "That's what I pay him for. It's his job to spot characters like that."

Quentin shook his head. His father never valued his staff, unless they wore a short skirt.

Two other customers came in later and Gerry served them with the correct new stock even though Quentin was nearby if required. Again, this didn't impress his father.

8

Harry returned to work after the weekend with a plaster covering a cut below his right ear. He seemed intent on getting back in favour with his boss and tried to cause trouble for Gerry. By now, however, the lad was wise to most of his tricks and able to avoid the traps.

On the Wednesday of that week two locals came in, at different times, to purchase the same product from the old stock. The first to come in was Graham Bishop and he made his purchase, looked around briefly at the new items before leaving. Matthews asked Gerry if he knew the person who had just purchased a tube of super glue.

"That's Graham Bishop; he made a couple of threats against Mr Evans. I think he runs a small kind of protection racket around the area. I don't know if Mr Evans ever paid him anything."

"If any of his kind come around here offering threats, they'll wish they had never been born."

About forty-five minutes before the shop was due to close Ernie Newsham entered the premises. He, too, looked around at the displays. "Quite a change from before, Gerry. How are you adjusting to your role? I don't think David had the knowledge or inclination to diversify to such an extent. Let's see, any bargains in the clearance sale of old stock?" he asked the young assistant.

Then he spotted the two remaining tubes of super glue, picked them up and asked Gerry the price. After he was told, Ernie thought for a moment and then nodded his head. "Not sure if I'll find a use for them but at least it's one less item on your stock check list," and he left the shop.

Once again Matthews asked Gerry for details of the latest customer.

"Totally the opposite to Bishop. That was Ernie Newsham, a former policeman who now runs the leisure centre. I believe he's also started a private security patrol of sorts."

Matthews was clearly interested in the latter part of Gerry's information and made a note to find out more details. For once Gerry thought he had been seen in some sort of positive light by his boss. However, his feeling of success was short-lived.

"I've got a new worker starting here tomorrow. She will be in charge of sales and when I'm not around you take orders from her. Understand?"

"Yes, Mr Matthews," was his assistant's reply but he felt like saying a lot more. It seemed that everyone could give him orders around here.

Matthews' voice broke into his thought. "Make yourself useful and check if Harry needs a hand unpacking the latest delivery. If he's finished go and sweep out the yard."

Gerry was finding it increasingly difficult not to lose his self-control. His boss was always finding the most menial tasks for him to do and giving more responsible jobs to others.

Later that afternoon Ernie returned to the shop. Moments later Matthews and his visitor went out into the backyard and stayed there for several minutes. Gerry heard the last few words of a conversation.

Ernie was saying, "… but remember, Mr Matthews, there won't be much point putting a decent lock on that flimsy gate. You need to replace that as well."

The shop-owner made a non-committal sound and showed his visitor out of the door. He turned to Gerry, who was rearranging stock after his boss had left it in the wrong places, as was his want after serving customers.

"I'm going to buy a mortise lock for the back gate. Then you can demonstrate your locksmith's skills to me and prove that you are at least learning something at that college."

"Excuse me for saying so, Mr Matthews, but didn't Mr Newsham mention something about replacing the back gate before fitting a new lock?" Gerry said quietly.

"That gate is strong enough, he's just looking for extra work for his mates. And I'll thank you not to eavesdrop on my conversations in future!"

Matthews didn't return for more than an hour and he was in a foul mood.

"That damned ironmonger wouldn't sell me this blasted lock at wholesale price, the tight-fisted bastard! Since you have college tomorrow you will have to fix it now. Get your tools and put this on the gate before you finish."

The shop was due to close in less than twenty minutes and Gerry knew he wouldn't finish in that time but it was the first proper job he had been given in more than a fortnight, so he was glad to take on the task.

However, he hadn't banked on Matthews standing over him and watching while he finished the job which was completed in just over half an hour. It had started raining so the owner went back into the shop to find an umbrella and he stood behind Gerry, making sure he was not getting wet while leaving his assistant exposed to the elements.

His boss checked the finished article and gave the gate and its frame a good shake.

"Is that the best you can do? It doesn't feel very secure to me."

Gerry replaced his equipment in the toolbox before replying, "It's the best I can do considering the condition of the gate and frame, Mr Matthews. As Mr Newsham recommended, fitting a stronger gate would be the best solution."

Matthews glared back at him. "I will be the judge of that! And in future, as I've already told you once, don't listen in on my private conversations if you know what's good for you."

He turned around on his heels and kicked his assistant's toolbox, spilling some of the contents onto the floor.

Before he could stop himself, Gerry blurted out, "Careful! It took me a long time and a lot of money to put together that kit."

Matthews turned around slowly, looked down at the tools strewn across the pavement, and quite deliberately kicked a couple of them into the roadway. He stared back at Gerry, daring him to make another comment.

His assistant stared back for a moment, then bent down and retrieved his tools and put them away in the box. He remembered what his old boss had told him about not walking into such traps and went back into the shop, put on his coat and headed for the door, still carrying his tools. Matthews called to him as he opened the door to leave.

"And don't be late in the morning."

Gerry stopped and looked over his shoulder at his boss.

"As you reminded me earlier, tomorrow is my college day, Mr Matthews. I will be in on time on Friday," and left before his boss had time to respond.

He arrived home, soaked to the skin after being drenched by a passing motorist who seemed to drive through the large puddle next to the pavement Gerry just happened to be walking on at that moment. He didn't think it was his boss driving the car but it wouldn't have surprised him if that had been the case.

***

He entered the flat and called to tell his grandmother that he was going to get changed out of his wet clothes before sitting down to dinner. His mind was so occupied by the train of events that he had been put through, he didn't notice his grandmother had not responded to his call. It was only after he returned to the bedroom to finish changing into dry clothes that his mind was alerted to the situation. Quickly, he finished getting dressed. He checked the kitchen and dining area first to see if she was there but the light was not on and a quick check told him the oven had not been used. He found out why when he walked into the darkened living room and put on the light. She was slumped in her favourite chair, still wearing her outdoor clothes. It was quite clear that she had been crying earlier. Feeling more than a little alarmed he went to her side and gently touched an arm and asked quietly, "Gran? Is there something wrong, are you not well?"

It took a couple more gentle prods to her arm before he got any response. She opened her eyes, looked around with some confusion on her features, before recognising her surroundings. She then tried to stand up, but Gerry put a hand on her shoulder and gently prevented her from rising.

"Stay where you are for now, Gran, let me get you a drink before you try moving."

She nodded and settled back in the chair while Gerry went to fetch her a drink of water. He came back with the drink and passed it to her, allowing her time to become familiar with her surroundings before asking, "What happened, Gran? What have you been up to today?"

She took a couple more sips of water before speaking. "I went to the meeting as usual this afternoon and was about to leave when Mrs Stockwell invited me to go for a cup of coffee with her. It was quite strange; she was telling me how much she would miss being around with her husband and friends and I asked her why I was being told these details."

"Did she tell you why?"

"Not at first, but when I pressed her, she changed the subject and told me not to worry about her but to prepare myself for things to come in the near future."

Gerry stayed silent for a moment before asking, "Prepare yourself for what, Gran? Is she trying to give a message of some sort but can't explain things clearly to you? You used to go to her meetings with Mr Stockwell but stopped because, well, some of their discussions upset you when they talked about family members who were no longer alive, like Mum and Dad."

Mrs Reynolds took out her hankie and started dabbing her eyes and she spoke in a shaky voice. "I'm all right now, Gerry. Can we stop talking about it? What do you want for your tea? I'm afraid I haven't prepared anything. If I give you some money you can go to the chip shop and get yourself something to eat."

"What about you? You probably haven't eaten since dinnertime."

"Don't worry about me, Gerry, I will have some soup later."

He was not convinced by her answer but now was not the time to argue so he put on his coat and went out into the rainy evening once more. The Willow Gardens chip shop was less than ten minutes away and the evening rush for their cuisine had not started. The Chinese lady owner knew him and as usual, wanted to have a long chat about the goings-on around the town.

Gerry only managed to extract himself from the conversation when another customer arrived. By the time he returned home his trip had taken the best part of half an hour. Going into the kitchen, he smiled on spotting what his grandmother had done for him. On the table were two slices of buttered bread for his chip butty he always had as a treat. If she could think of such things then she must have got over her upset from the afternoon. Gerry finished his meal and finding his grandmother was not in the living room he gently knocked on her bedroom door. Calling out for him to enter, she was sitting on her bed with a large case open in front of her while examining its contents.

He had often wondered what she kept in the old, battered case and had longed to find out but never dared to ask.

There were more than two dozen items either on the bed or still to be removed from the case. Each item was wrapped in soft tissue paper and kept inside a cloth bag. A small handwritten piece of paper was pinned to each bag to identify their contents.

"It's time I told you about our family history, Gerry. If you've finished your tea I will explain some background details. Sit down next to me, dear."

Gerry did as she requested, and suddenly a mixture of excitement coupled with a little dread of what he was about to hear overcame him. She began speaking. "What you see in front of you goes back at least four generations of our family history. First, I will tell you briefly about your mother's possessions, such as her rings and necklaces. She also collected many trinkets picked up in sales. Most of them only have sentimental value but one or two items do have an interesting history. But I want to put them aside for a moment and tell you about some items that your great-great-grandfather brought home from South Africa."

"What was he doing in South Africa, Gran?" Gerry asked, his mind suddenly filling with fantasies of a great hero from the family's past.

She smiled ruefully, "It's not what you are thinking, Gerry. Andrew Silas Patterson was a convicted thief who escaped arrest and probable transportation to Australia by escaping as a stowaway on a boat to South Africa. Once over there, he found work, mainly in the gold mines, but occasionally returned to his criminal ways; sometimes stealing from the mines but quite often from the local native workers. But he, and other thieves, were very devious in the way they stole from the workers. Cheap trinkets and baubles that traders had brought to the area would

84

be exchanged for more valuable native artefacts which would then be sent back home to be sold for great profit. But Silas made a very bad mistake because one of the natives he tricked was the son of the tribal chief. The chief knew he would get nowhere if he approached the white authorities because they would believe Silas rather than the natives at every opportunity."

She continued, "Instead he consulted a local witch-doctor who came up with a cunning remedy. A curse was put on all of the items stolen so if anyone sold them for profit, that person would meet a sticky end. This message was conveyed to Silas who laughed off the curse."

Before she could continue with her story, the phone rang and Gerry went to answer the call. He returned a couple of minutes later with a slight smile on his face.

"Who was that, dear?" enquired his grandmother.

"My course tutor at the college checking if I am going to be in class tomorrow. I told him I would definitely be attending. He just wanted to make sure after Mr Matthews' attempt to stop me a couple of weeks ago."

"Good, that man is very devious, you must be wary of him at all times. Now where was I? Yes, I remember. Silas eventually returned to this country after making his fortune in the gold fields and through his trickery."

Gerry held up his hand to ask a question. "But, Gran, you said at the beginning that he fled to Africa because he was about to be transported. Surely the authorities would have arrested him even after his long stay?"

"Quite right, Gerry, normally they would have done so but Silas came home as some sort of hero. He had been in Africa for more than twenty years but he left the gold fields at the start of the Boer War to become a scout for the British Army. He was even decorated for his service and gallantry."

As she finished her remark, she opened another pouch and withdrew a box containing a medal.

The ribbon on the medal was badly faded but the inscription was as clear as if it had been done just yesterday. It was the Queen's South Africa medal. Gerry put his hand out to remove the medal from its box, but his grandmother pushed his hand away and said firmly, "No, Gerald! On no account must you take the medal out of its box. There is something unpleasant about the medal and the other items that Silas brought home with him from South Africa."

Gerry was about to laugh but managed to stop himself when he saw the earnest expression on her pallid face. He simply asked, "What do you mean, Gran? It's not going to bite me, is it?"

He was not prepared for her reaction as she closed the box and placed it back in the cloth bag and returned it to the suitcase which she closed firmly.

"Gerald! You are clearly not ready to be told the whole story and its implications. Now I am tired and want to get ready for bed so please leave my room. Goodnight, dear." She turned away from him but not quickly enough to hide the tears that were welling up in her eyes.

He mumbled his own 'goodnight' and left the room, with feelings of surprise and not a little confusion. She had never spoken to him with so much hurt and anger in her voice since he had moved into the flat to live. He sat in the lounge for more than an hour trying to digest the events of the evening but couldn't come to any rational conclusion as to its meaning.

It would not be too long before he found out through several interlinked events that would change his life over the next six months to something he could not envisage at this moment in time.

9

If he had expected his day at college to be a relief from his job worries, then Gerry had to think again. Lee, his tutor, had to tell him on several occasions to concentrate on what he was doing. Two practice pieces of work had to be thrown away as Gerry had made very basic errors in their design. When the class broke up for its mid-morning break Lee took Gerry to one side.

"Gerry, I don't know what's bothering you but the work you're producing is, well, total rubbish. My wife didn't go into any details but she told me you're having a hard time at work with your new boss. There's nothing I can do about that but you need to buck up your ideas. It might be better if you go home for the rest of the day and come back next week when I hope you will be back to your normal self. Go and have your coffee break and if you don't come back for the next lesson I'll say you went home sick. Okay?"

Gerry stood, thinking for a moment before replying. "I'm sorry, Lee, it's not just work that's winding me up. I promise I'll do better after the break. I don't want to go home. I need something to occupy my mind."

His tutor tapped him on the shoulder. "Off you go then and it doesn't matter if you're a few minutes late coming back."

He joined a couple of his classmates in the refectory and one of them, Jack, asked, "What's her name then, Gerry? Must be pretty special for you to balls up your work like that."

Gerry forced a smile. "Not female problems, Jack, more to do with work. If you hear of any jobs going, give me a shout."

"Miserly Matthews up to his usual tricks again, is he?"

Gerry nodded and told his friends about some of the things that had happened but didn't mention the robbery until one of the others at the table spoke.

"I heard about Matthews being turned over and that fat slob Harry having a bit of a kicking. Couldn't have happened to two more qualified cretins."

Gerry didn't volunteer any further information in case it got back to the police or his boss. The others left him to return to the class while he finished his coffee. He decided also it would be best to try and talk to his grandmother when he got back home as he was still feeling guilty about making her angry and upset.

Having decided on the proposed actions he would take when he finished his day at college the rest of his time in class was more productive and earnt praise from Lee for his change in attitude.

However, when he arrived back home, Mrs Reynolds was not waiting for him in either the lounge or kitchen and Gerry felt a moment of panic until he knocked on her bedroom door and he was relieved to hear her voice.

"Hello, dear, your dinner is in the oven keeping warm. I'm rather busy at this moment doing some writing. I will let you know when I've finished."

Even though her voice sounded normal there was a finality about it that told him not to disturb her for any reason. After eating and clearing the dishes he spent the rest of the evening brooding and waiting anxiously to make peace with his grandmother.

She came briefly out of her room more than an hour later, simply to announce she was tired and would be going straight to her bed and not bother to have her usual late evening hot drink. A repeat performance occurred the following evening and it wasn't until the Sunday afternoon that Gerry was able to confront her.

"Gran, I'm sorry I upset you the other night when you were trying to tell me something about the medal and its significance. I promise not to make fun of anything you tell me about that and the other pieces."

She stared at him for several seconds trying to assess his mood. Finally, a smile spread across her features and she nodded once and spoke. "Very well, Gerald, we will have some tea then I will explain everything to you. But remember, on no account must you tell anyone else about these items."

He heaved a sigh of relief and smiled back at her. "I promise, Gran, it's our secret and nobody else will know."

After eating and clearing the dishes from the table, she asked Gerry to bring the suitcase into the living room so that the contents could be looked at in more detail. He was a little surprised at its weight and how his gran had managed to move it. He placed it on the settee, but before opening the case she continued the story of how Patterson had accumulated his ill-gotten gains.

"The other night I told you how a witch-doctor was supposed to have put a curse on the items Silas had stolen from his tribe. It seems that the curse also extended to any items Silas had accrued in his time in South Africa, including the medal he was awarded and any other items he came by illegally. According to Silas's son, my father, the curse would only be invoked if those items were sold for profit or stolen by anyone else. Furthermore, if the items were ever stolen then the curse would not only affect the thief but also extend to any male member of the thief's family. It seems there is no end to this curse."

Gerry held up his hand to ask, "Is there any proof of this happening?"

Mrs Reynolds spoke in a very quiet voice, "My father took the curse seriously and told me the story and became very nervous when his father was killed less than a year after his return to this country. On the day before his death, Silas had removed a gold nugget from the case and taken it to be valued. No money had been agreed for the price of the gold but that seemed to be enough to invoke the curse. On his way home from a meeting the next day Silas was knocked over and killed by a horse-drawn tram."

Gerry was silent for a few moments but felt he had to ask another question. "But, Gran, why didn't the curse affect your father, or did it?"

She gave a faint smile. "No, it didn't affect him or me for that matter because neither of us tried to sell any of the items. We looked after them carefully. However, I'm afraid your father took no notice of the curse."

A feeling of apprehension came over Gerry as he asked in a shaky voice, "What did he do, Gran?"

She took hold of one of his hands before replying. "About two weeks before their accident he and your mother took some of her trinkets to be valued as they wanted money to take you on holiday as a special birthday treat. The trinkets were almost worthless but somehow, either by accident or deliberately, a ring that was part of the items from Africa had been mixed in amongst your mother's trinkets."

Even before he asked the question Gerry was sure he knew the answer. "The person they went to meet recognised the ring as being valuable and persuaded them to sell it?"

She nodded and brushed away a tear. "He was an authority on African artefacts and had worked out the origin of the ring. He tried to persuade your parents to take the rest of the items Silas had stolen to show him but they refused. So he agreed to pay them a fraction of the value of the ring and they collected the money from the buyer on the night of their accident."

It was Gerry's turn to wipe away tears from his eyes and both were silent for several minutes until he asked the question that nobody had ever provided him with the full answer to. "What actually happened in their accident? I always remember Dad as being such a careful driver."

Mrs Reynolds took hold of his hand again. "Before they left the meeting with the buyer your mother phoned me and told me they had received £500 for the ring and were going to have a celebration meal before coming back home. You were staying with friends that night and I received a phone call from the police just after midnight to tell me there had been a bad accident. All they would tell me was it appeared that your father went through a yellow light at a crossroads and he was hit by another vehicle on an emergency call and both your mum and dad were killed instantly."

She broke off and they hugged each other for several minutes, both crying quietly. Gerry seemed to change at that moment; a cold, fanatical desire to find out who was really to blame for the death of his parents overwhelmed him.

"Who was driving the emergency vehicle that hit them, Gran?"

She hesitated for a long moment. "Gerald, it's not important now. They're gone and knowing won't bring them back. Please, let things rest in the knowledge that they were only thinking of you."

Gerry's outburst shocked and frightened her. He removed his hand from her grasp and thumped the settee with such force that the items in the suitcase bounced with the power of the blow. Without realising what effect it might have on his elderly relative, he shouted, "Well, it's bloody important to me! I need to know!"

Mrs Reynolds almost fell off the edge of her seat in shocked response to Gerry's outburst. Floods of tears ran down her cheeks and the sight of this brought him to his senses. He tried to mumble an apology and take her hand again but it was brushed aside and she pointed to the door for him to leave. He hesitated momentarily but knew he had overstepped the mark and he left the room to go into his bedroom. He could hear the sounds of grief coming from his gran's room but knew she wouldn't respond to any apology from him at this moment.

Neither could he fully understand or explain his own outburst. It was completely out of character. Perhaps after a night's sleep they would be in a better frame of mind to talk. However, that conciliatory talk would not take place for several weeks.

Gerry also had a night lacking in sleep, waking the next morning with insufficient time to even have breakfast, let alone make peace with his grandmother.

***

Matthews was waiting in the shop doorway as Gerry arrived, slightly out of breath, after running the last half mile to make sure he wasn't late thus giving his boss the opportunity to dismiss him.

"And about time too. Get into the storeroom and take over from Harry. I need him to do some meaningful work that you can't be trusted with."

Gerry knew from that remark that it would be the most mundane task Matthews could find for him to carry out. But before he could get to the sanctuary of the storeroom he came face to face with a woman in her mid-twenties. She was almost as tall as Gerry and the clothes she wore did little to cover her rather interesting figure, from the low-cut blouse to one of the shortest skirts Gerry had seen in ages. Any thoughts he had about asking the woman if he could help her were cut short by Matthews' sardonic tone.

"You can stop gawping at her, boy. When I'm not here Miss Spires will be in charge so you take orders from her. Now go and relieve Harry like I told you."

Gerry gave a little nod in Abigail's direction, but she seemed to look straight through him as if he wasn't even in the room. He understood right away that she wouldn't dream of accepting him as a fellow employee. She was the boss's favourite and everyone better realise that fact from the very beginning.

Gerry walked into the storeroom and was greeted by Harry's gruff tone. "Where the hell were you yesterday?"

By now, Gerry wished he had not bothered getting up and coming to work so he responded in kind to Harry's comment. "Yesterday was my college day and the boss knew that so it's not my problem if he didn't bother to tell you."

This was the first time he had stood up to the big man's constant sniping and surprisingly Harry laughed and said, "Wow! Talking tough because there's a bit of skirt working here now. Take my advice, sunshine, steer well clear of that Abigail, she's poison."

Gerry laughed back. "I've already got the message loud and clear."

Matthews' voice bellowed from the shop. "Harry! Tell the kid what to do and let's get moving. I want to pick up that new van today, not next Christmas."

Harry mouthed an obscenity in the direction of their boss and quickly told Gerry his task. "Make a list of all this crap that you used to sell, number of items and each individual price. There's a pen and pad on the table. Best of luck, mate!"

Gerry looked at the items to be listed which were scattered around the floor. There was no semblance of order as Harry had left them. His first task was to put the items in neat piles to establish their category and number of each item. He had almost completed that first task when Abigail called his name. "Gerry, make me a cup of coffee, will you? Milk with two sugars."

He noted the lack of courtesy in her request so he wanted to establish who was paying for the beverage. When he enquired as to this fact Abigail gave him a haughty look and said scornfully, "I've never paid for any drink in my life, so just pull your finger out and make it!"

As he returned to the kitchen area the thought crossed his mind, *I can believe that your ladyship*, so he decided he was entitled to a drink as well. After making the drinks he returned to his task in the storeroom. Boss's pet or not he wasn't going to put up with much more of this place. Apart from fixing the lock on the gate he hadn't done what he could call worthwhile work in nearly six weeks of being employed by Matthews. He decided the time had now come to look elsewhere for gainful employment.

An hour later he was summoned again to serve Abigail, receiving the same lack of thanks or courtesy.

Shortly after midday, she announced it was time for her lunch and would be back in due course. This lunch break lasted more than ninety minutes. On her return, Gerry announced he was leaving to have his own break. Abigail promptly stated, "Mr Matthews told me you're only allowed half an hour for your lunch so don't be late."

On his return, Gerry made a point of looking at his watch and noted he had only taken twenty-eight minutes and nodded in the woman's direction. She ignored his action until it was time for yet another coffee break. Two more followed that afternoon. As Gerry was taking the final drink to Abigail, Matthews arrived back from his day out with Harry tagging behind. He smiled at the woman and had a short conversation with her before turning to Gerry.

"How many cups is that you've had today then? Remember to let me know so I can take it from your wages."

He turned back to Abigail and asked her to confirm.

"He's had five cups to my knowledge, although I don't know if he had any while I was on my dinner break."

Gerry spoke up for himself, "Actually, Abigail, I only had four cups. I made myself a cup each time you requested a cup of coffee. And I didn't have a drink while you were out on your ninety-minute lunch break."

She looked daggers at Gerry, but Matthews interjected, "Well, that's at least four cups to pay for by you and if Abigail was out that long for lunch, it's none of your business."

Gerry was about to make a comment when a tap on his shoulder distracted him. It was Harry.

"If you've finished making that list we need to load the stuff into the new van. Is that right, Mr Matthews?"

Gerry nodded and seeing the look in Harry's eyes understood the message, and followed the big man into the yard where the new van had been parked.

Once out of earshot of the shop Harry turned to his fellow workmate.

"I told you before that bitch is poison. They set you up concerning her lunch break. Like it or not, you and me will have to work together to keep our jobs or Lady Muck will conjure up some way of getting rid of one or both of us."

Gerry didn't trust Harry but decided to take his advice for the moment.

It took them nearly half an hour to load the van, by which time the shop was due to close. As they finished Matthews came into the yard and announced, "Right Harry, take it to my discount shop in Hereford Street. He can go with you to help unload."

He left before Gerry could ask how long this extra work would take so he turned to Harry. "Hereford Street is over the other side of town. By the time we get there in the rush-hour traffic and unload the van, I won't get home much before seven."

"You want to argue the point with the boss? Remember what I just told you. We need to stick together. If there's time I can drop you off near your home but there's no guarantee."

Gerry was tired and thoroughly fed up but he knew it would be silly to talk himself out of a job at this precise moment. So he reluctantly got into the van and sat in total silence as they crawled through the heavy traffic to their destination in Hereford Street. Inevitably, it was busier than normal partially because of the heavy rain now falling.

Gerry was carrying the last box of stock into the shop's storeroom when the manager called Harry to take a phone call from Matthews. The younger worker had a premonition of what was about to happen. And he was correct!

Harry followed Gerry into the storeroom trying to hide the smile on his features, but it didn't fool Gerry. "Sorry, mate, the boss wants me to take the van to one of the other shops to be ready for loading more stock to be moved tomorrow morning. It's further away from your place so I suggest you get a bus or start walking." With that final comment, he turned on his heels and as he went back into the shop, Gerry could clearly hear the two men laughing.

Dropping the final box onto the floor Gerry marched into the shop and confronted the manager. "I don't suppose you can lend me the money for my bus fare home?"

Both men laughed again. "Not a cat in hell's chance, kid. This is a proper business, not a charity shop. Now move yourself, I want to close up and go home as well."

It was nearly eight o'clock by the time Gerry got home, soaked to the skin. His grandmother had left him a note to say his dinner was in the oven and she was having an early night.

Just as well, Gerry thought. The mood he was in it wouldn't take much for another argument to start over the suitcase and its contents.

10

For the second morning in succession Matthews was waiting inside the shop for Gerry to arrive. "Don't take your coat off, you're needed over in Hereford Street. One of the workers has phoned in sick and you will have to cover for him."

Gerry sneezed and after wiping his nose he said, "I'll need some money for the bus fare, Mr Matthews, or it will take me the best part of an hour to get there."

His boss did not look too pleased.

"Use your own money and keep the ticket and I'll reimburse you in your next pay packet."

Now wise to his boss's penny-pinching attitude Gerry looked him straight in the face and lied. "Sorry, Mr Matthews, I didn't bring any money with me this morning."

For one moment the shop owner looked as if he was about to explode, then he took in a deep breath and walked over to Abigail who was standing next to the cash till and asked in clipped tones, "Give me £5 out of the till, please, and pass me the receipt book."

"Here's the money; date and sign the book and bring back any change along with any tickets, or you will have to pay back the full amount to me in person."

He handed Gerry the money after the receipt book was signed. However, Gerry hesitated on being handed the money.

"Do you mind if I have the money in loose change, Mr Matthews? Some bus drivers insist on having the correct money or give you a credit note in exchange."

Percival Matthews stared back at his assistant and after a few moments, he called to the woman without taking his gaze from Gerry, "Abigail! £5 in change, please!"

He then snatched the £5 note from Gerry's hand and left the change on the counter for him to retrieve. Gerry made a point of counting the money before putting it in his pocket.

"Tony, the manager, will be watching your timekeeping and the same rules apply regarding any drinks you may have. So don't hang about here, get a move on. If you're not at the Hereford Road shop by nine fifteen I'll be taking it out of your wages," and he dismissed Gerry by turning his back on him.

Because it was a Saturday there was slightly less commuter traffic and he reached his destination in good time.

Tony didn't seem to be such a stickler for detail as their boss, but Gerry was taking no chances, so he stuck to the rules about drink breaks and simply didn't take any.

By lunchtime the manager had noticed Gerry's unwillingness to have beverages and he commented, "Old Percy's rules don't apply here to drink breaks. I put up the cash for that so help yourself, but don't take any liberties with the length of time you take."

Gerry nodded his thanks. He was more familiar with the items on sale at this shop and the more relaxed atmosphere and was not too upset when Tony announced, "Gerry, I've just had a call from the boss to say you're to come back here on Monday and possibly stay until the end of the week to cover for my usual staff member. Is that okay with you?"

"That's fine by me but will I get my bus fares paid? This isn't my normal place of work."

Tony couldn't answer but told him to keep his bus tickets anyway.

The next day was a Sunday and Gerry saw very little of his grandmother, so he didn't have the opportunity to bring up the subject of how his parents died. This stalemate lasted through the whole of the following week and he was glad of the opportunity to call in the library and have a conversation with Sally on the following Friday evening.

After exchanging pleasantries Sally asked him how his job was going and after the health of his grandmother. Gerry told her about how he was treated in work by everyone and how he wished he could find another job. Sally was silent for a couple of minutes before speaking quietly, "It's not the kind of work you might have done before, but Ernie Newsham is looking for a second assistant at the leisure centre. But Gerry, if you do go there to work, watch out for the other new bloke. He's called Mark. He's sly, devious and has a cruel streak in him. Ernie's got his measure, but you be careful of him."

Gerry asked, "What's he look like, Sal?"

"Quite tall, muscular but slim if you know what I mean and he's got what you might call a kid's face; some would call it a baby face. Oh, and he's got a Yorkshire accent."

Gerry gave a half laugh. "Sounds like the bloke who came into the shop a couple of times. I caught him trying to pinch something the first time. I'm certain I'd know the bloke again if I saw him."

Sally touched his arm. "Okay, but be careful of him, Gerry. I'm sure Ernie's aware of his tricks but I wouldn't turn my back on him too many times."

He took hold of her hand that was pressing on his arm and smiled. "Are you applying to be my guardian angel, Sal? I'm sure there's a vacancy."

She blushed slightly and quickly changed the subject. "How's your gran? I haven't seen her in the library for ages. She used to be one of my regulars."

Gerry frowned and took a few moments to reply. "We haven't been hitting it off too well lately. I think she may have a health problem but I can never find a way to bring the subject up with her. And there's other issues that have cropped up between us over the past week or so."

"Like what?"

Not wishing to break his promise to his grandmother he only made a passing comment about the suitcase, its contents, and how it seemed to worry the old lady. He wanted to ask Sally if she knew anything about his parents' accident. But Sally's interest had been aroused by his mention of the mystery suitcase and she gave his arm a squeeze.

"Come on, Gerry, tell me about your family's hidden treasures. Is it pirate gold or something?"

Realising he had divulged too much he simply said, "Nothing like that, just medals and stuff one of her ancestors brought back from South Africa at the beginning of this century. I can't say any more, I promised Gran. Can we talk about my parents, please, Sal? You were around when they died."

She looked at her watch. "I'll be closing up in about twenty minutes. We could go for a drink or back to my place where there aren't any nosey parkers to listen in on our chat."

But other ears had already picked up their conversation and Graham Bishop standing in the next aisle of books had been listening intently for several minutes. Neither of them saw him leave with the gleam of greed in his eyes.

"Sorry, Sal, I'm working in another shop this week and have to catch a bus and daren't be late. How about tomorrow night and then it doesn't matter if I get up late?"

Sally raised her eyebrows but there was a hint of mischief in them. "Being a bit presumptuous, aren't we, young Gerald? It sounds like you have other things on your mind!"

Realising what he had just said he blushed and tried to stammer an apology, but Sally stopped him and laughed. "Tell your gran you're eating out tomorrow night and she might not see you until Sunday. That is if you survive my cooking and other talents!"

He looked into her eyes. "You know me, I could never resist a challenge," and on that comment they both stood up, squeezed hands and parted company, both with a keen anticipation of what the following evening might bring.

His final day at the Hereford Street branch progressed smoothly and a phone call from his boss confirmed that he was to report back to his normal place of work on the following Monday.

As he had not had contact with his grandmother the previous evening Gerry had left a note to say he wouldn't want any food making for him and that he would be spending the evening, and possibly the night, with friends.

True to her word, Sally cooked a wonderful meal for two and afterwards Gerry insisted on doing the washing-up before they settled down with a bottle of wine and an intimate chat. She teased him mercilessly about being too domesticated and one day some woman would take advantage of that fact. He countered her teasing by saying he was open to offers and that she better hurry before someone else beat her. Sally just laughed but he could tell by the look on her face she might consider the challenge.

Whether it was the relaxed atmosphere brought on by the wine, neither of them mentioned the previous evening's subjects and quite soon after the second bottle of wine was consumed they retired to Sally's warm and comfortable bed.

They had previously spent several similar nights together but this one surpassed all of them in their intimacy and passion and it lasted until the early hours of the morning before both fell asleep exhausted but satisfied.

A howling wind and heavy rain splattering the window of the bedroom awoke them just before midday. After a late breakfast and once the bad weather had subsided, Gerry was sent on his way with Sally's final words giving him food for thought.

"I was saving up to buy a dishwasher but I might have to reconsider whether that money could be put to better use."

Over the next couple of months such thoughts would be far from the forefront of their minds and forthcoming events would change their lives forever.

**

On his return on the Monday, Gerry discovered the true reason for him being sent to the other store in Hereford Street. His workspace at the back of the shop had been completely transformed and it was now taken up by equipment, presumably for the new repair workshop that Quentin had mentioned. His remaining tools had been dumped in a bin in the corner. He retrieved them and took everything he owned back home to his flat. However, one item was missing. His original set of master keys was nowhere to be found. He made enquiries with both Harry and Abigail but got no positive response from either.

Fortunately, he had kept the new set of keys David Evans had given him back at home.

He had only been back at his usual place of work for a couple of days when events began to unfold in ominous ways.

Matthews and Harry were on one of their stock-moving missions on that Wednesday afternoon when Abigail's strident call had Gerry dashing into the main shop area from his most hated duties of brushing the backyard.

"Gerry! Come here quick and tell this old biddy to get lost."

On entering the shop, the first thing he noticed was Stella Stockwell leaning against one of the counters, apparently fighting for breath and almost on the point of collapse. He shouted at Abigail to fetch a chair and then a drink of water. She hesitated for a moment but on seeing the look of deep concern on his face she did his bidding as Gerry went to support Mrs Stockwell.

Abigail brought in the chair and then fetched the drink, returning to find Gerry talking quietly to the old lady.

"Mrs Stockwell, are you sure you don't want me to call an ambulance for you?"

She put a shaky hand on his forearm and spoke hoarsely, "No, Gerald, thank you. Please allow me to rest here for a few minutes and then I shall be on my way. Bless you, my dear."

He was not taken in by her assurances and spoke firmly but gently to her, "Mrs Stockwell, if you won't let me call for an ambulance then I will order a taxi and take you home to your husband. I can't let you walk out of here on your own, you look as if you might collapse at any moment. My gran would box my ears if she found out I let you leave in this state."

She smiled weakly. "Gerald, you are a good boy. I will do a deal with you. You can order a taxi if you promise to take me to a friend's house near to where I live and she will walk home with me after. You see, my husband has a lot of worries at the moment and I don't want to start him having concerns about me as well."

Abigail had been listening to their conversation and spoke to Gerry in a hushed voice, "Look, I want this sorted right now before the boss comes back. I'll order the taxi. Has she got money for the fare and what's the address?"

Stella looked directly at Abigail and spoke in a clear yet stern voice. "I do not want charity from anyone. I do have the fare and I would like to go to Somerset Street. Thank you."

Both Abigail and Gerry were taken aback by the coldness in her response and the woman left to make the phone call.

While Abigail was out of earshot Stella took hold of Gerry's arm in a surprisingly strong grip and spoke in a hushed tone once more. "Gerald. You will not tell anybody about this, not even your grandmother. It is very important to me, you understand?" She did not release her grip on his arm until he nodded in agreement.

Abigail returned and confirmed the imminent arrival of the taxi and said to Gerry, "Don't be long, or you'll have some explaining to do to Mr Matthews."

Having heard the comment Stella gave Abigail a withering look but said nothing. For her part, Abigail suddenly went bright pink and stood open-mouthed for several seconds before regaining her composure. The taxi arrived within the next couple of minutes and Gerry helped Stella climb into the back of the cab where he joined her.

Once the vehicle started moving Stella seemed to make a full recovery and said to the taxi driver, "Driver, please take me to the corner of Somerset Street where we will get out."

Gerry looked a bit confused at her change in demeanour and was about to speak when Stella tapped his leg and held up one finger for silence.

"I am feeling much better now and I've just remembered that my friend is not home today so there is no point in calling on her. We will get out of this taxi and you can walk me the short distance to my home."

Another tap on his leg made it clear there was no point in arguing.

Having reached their destination they got out of the vehicle and Stella paid the driver. He drove away. Before they started walking to Stella's home she turned to face Gerry.

"Gerald, please remember what I said, not a word to your grandmother or anyone else, please. Now tell me, how is she in herself? The last time we spoke she was very nervous concerning something that she was reluctant to talk to me about."

Not sure if he should talk to her regarding the suitcase and its contents he remained silent for a few moments before he finally blurted, "We haven't been getting on too well lately, ever since Gran showed me the contents of an old suitcase that's been passed down through the family."

Stella let out a short gasp and then spoke earnestly. "I told her she should not open that case again; it has a bad feeling surrounding it. Please, Gerald, do not touch anything from inside that case; it will bring you only bad luck."

He couldn't help let out a small laugh at her words and was shocked at her reaction. She grabbed both his wrists in a vice-like grip, and stared at him intently. When she finally spoke the venom in her voice was apparent.

"Do not make fun of such things, Gerald. That suitcase harbours only evil and to even think that way may be a threat to you."

Just as quickly she released his arms and looked down at the ground for several seconds and when she looked up at him again, it was with the face of the sweet old lady he knew. When she spoke a second time it was with her usual soft nature.

"Please do not worry about that case any more, Gerald. It has been arranged that it will not be your concern for much longer. Now, dear, no more talk. Walk me to my door, please, and remember my words when I spoke to you about my Robin's present."

He hadn't forgotten those words and they continued walking to the door of her flat. Then she turned to face him and gave him a kiss on both cheeks and silently mouthed the word 'Goodbye'.

He didn't know how long he stood alone on the pavement until a voice behind him said, "Excuse me, can I get past please?"

He turned around to face a woman with a toddler in a pushchair. He mumbled an apology and turned around to walk back to his workplace, not really sure if Mrs Stockwell had really been ill or she had engineered the whole episode just to talk to him. But why?

11

By the time he returned to the shop Matthews and Harry were back and his boss was in one of his predictably foul moods.

"What the hell do you think you're playing at, Reynolds? I don't employ you to skive off to take some old crone home when she pulls the wool over your stupid eyes by pretending to be about to kick the bucket!"

For the umpteenth time, Gerry bit his tongue to hold back from telling Matthews what to do with his job. Instead, he spoke in a subdued tone, "Mrs Stockwell has helped a lot of people in this town for many years. It wouldn't pay to ignore her call for help when she needed it. Your local trade would disappear overnight if news got out that your staff didn't at least try and help her."

Matthews was still out for blood but changed his direction of attack.

"I'm not running a charity here, my lad, so if you've taken time off without permission you can lose a day's pay for your 'kindness' so maybe you'll think twice if this ever happens again. Now go and make drinks for me, Abigail and Harry. At least we've been doing proper work while you've been playing nursemaid."

This last remark brought a smirk from Abigail as she spoke. "Mr Matthews, he also ordered me to phone for a taxi on the shop phone."

"That will also come off your wages along with the cost of those drinks you're about to make so get a move on before I fine you even more!"

With a last glance at Abigail Gerry went into the kitchen.

He had finally decided that he would follow Sally's suggestion and visit Ernie Newsham to see if there was a vacancy for him. He couldn't imagine Ernie being as hard a taskmaster as his current boss.

Matthews and Abigail were in his office and when Gerry took in their drinks they stopped talking and waited until he had left before resuming their conversation. Harry was removing boxes from the van parked in the yard. He mumbled a form of thanks for the drink and said, "Told you that bitch was poison, didn't I? The boss said you can help me unload these boxes and store them in the unit in the yard."

"What's he flogging this time or is that a trade secret?"

Harry laughed. "If it's going cheap, he'll find a market for anything. Sports stuff, mostly trainers and tops, just bankrupt stock from a place in the Midlands."

Gerry tried to change the subject as he wanted to know something about the refurbishment of the workshop.

"Who cleared out the workshop before the new stock was put in?" Harry pointed to himself as he took another mouthful of tea.

Gerry continued, "I found most of my kit in the bin but there was something missing that I wanted to keep. Did you come across a bunch of skeleton keys by any chance?"

Harry shook his head and looked quickly away from Gerry before he put his empty cup down and motioned to his companion to move towards the van.

He spoke quietly. "I wasn't there the whole time. Miss

Droopy Drawers went in before me and she put your stuff in the bin so it might be worth asking her about those keys."

"That will have to wait until Friday. She's busy with the boss now and tomorrow is my college day, thank God."

Harry smiled. "He's not going to let you carry on going to college. He wants you here so that he can extract every ounce of sweat from you, remember this is for future reference, kid."

"Well, if he does manage to stop me attending college then he will have broken an agreement with my old boss, and it will cost him."

Harry gave another sardonic laugh. "Breaking agreements with people is what he lives for. He will say or sign anything to get his way in a deal, then break it at the first opportunity. Mark my words, it won't cost him a bean!"

Gerry didn't want to take the conversation any further so he kept quiet, but he made a mental note of checking on his ex-boss's solicitor in case he needed advice.

It was another late finish for Gerry. Nevertheless, he had decided to call at the leisure centre to check if Ernie Newsham still had a vacancy. However, he was out of luck. As he approached the car park at the rear of the centre he saw Ernie drive away in a van marked Acme Security. In the passenger seat he could clearly see the other occupant was the man Sally had called Mark. This was the same person who had tried to steal from the shop when it was still owned by David Evans. Did Ernie know this man was capable of such crimes? Did he want to work alongside such a character? He remembered Sally's description of Mark, and then compared him with his current work colleagues and decided he couldn't do any worse by at least enquiring.

On arriving home he tried to talk to his grandmother about the incident involving Stella Stockwell, but as soon as he mentioned Mrs Stockwell's comments about the suitcase his gran stood up abruptly and spoke only to say, "I thought I told you not to mention that case to anyone, especially not her!"

As she left the room, she called back to tell him she was going to bed and did not wish to be disturbed.

His hopes for a friendlier atmosphere at college were sadly misplaced and he could not understand why his tutor was very cool, almost hostile, towards him. By the time the morning coffee break arrived Gerry could take it no longer and confronted Lee, his tutor, after the rest of the group had left the room.

"Lee, can I have a word with you, please? I can't seem to do anything right by you today. Have I offended anyone?"

Lee continued to clear books away from his desk before looking directly at Gerry. He crossed his arms in front of his chest and said, "In view of what your boss told me I was a bit surprised you had the nerve to come in at all today."

Gerry didn't give him a chance to continue speaking. He held up his hand and almost shouted back at his tutor, "What's that conniving sod up to now? I want to know what he said about me!"

Lee hesitated for a moment and invited Gerry to take a seat before he spoke. "Well, I shouldn't be repeating this but as we've known each other for a few terms I'll be straight with you. In his exact words, 'Gerry says he is fed up coming here, learning nothing and being treated like a thirteen-year-old and he doesn't want to continue on such a crap course'.

"I've never treated any of my students like thirteen-year-old kids and apart from a couple of minor bloomers, you've been my star pupil. In that time you've been keen to learn and never given any indication you were unhappy attending. He also went on to say that in view of your so called 'feelings' towards the course he will be contacting the principal to have the rest of your course and exam fees refunded. He did that late yesterday evening and I had to face the principal this morning to explain why a student had such poor views of my course."

Gerry sank back in his chair, suddenly feeling as if his whole world was crumbling around him. Lee watched his student closely for a minute before asking, "Gerry, tell me, is any of what your boss said true?"

Shaking his head, Gerry replied in a husky voice, "Lee, I couldn't have asked for a better teacher and a more interesting course and I've never felt like you were treating me like a young kid. All Matthews wants to do is claim the course and exam fees for himself. Mr Evans paid for them and warned me to be careful of him doing just that."

It was Lee's turn to sit back in his chair but instead of looking defeated he banged his fist on the table and swore loudly before apologising. Then he stood up and beckoned Gerry to follow him.

"Come on, Gerry, we're off to the bursar's office. I just hope they haven't sent that payment through to Matthews. If they have, then there's not much I can do."

On their way, Gerry told Lee about the letter David Evans had given him and the instructions relayed to his solicitor.

"Hmmm, that could prove interesting. We might have to talk to the principal in that case as well."

It was not good news from the bursar. On instructions from the principal himself the payment had been sent to Matthews' own account that morning. By now, the morning break would have finished and the tutor returned to tell his assistant to take charge while he talked to the principal on an urgent matter.

It took several minutes to convince the principal's secretary that the matter required his immediate attention, and another ten minutes while her boss finished his current appointment.

"Mr Bradley, I hope this is as important as you make out. I am very busy this morning and I believe you should be taking your class at this moment. Who is this with you?" He finished with a nod in Gerry's direction.

"This is Gerry Reynolds, the person we were discussing this morning. He has given me some very important information that you should be aware of, Mr Spires."

At the mention of the principal's surname, a sudden thought came into Gerry's head, but he kept quiet for the time being.

Lee then proceeded to tell his boss about his conversation earlier that morning with Gerry, including the mention of the possible involvement of Albert Parker, the solicitor. He finished by saying, "If you check Gerry's class record and achievements it should indicate to you that he is a hard-working student and has been a model pupil who has given no indication of being unhappy in his time at the college."

The principal sighed and opened a folder on his desk.

Gerry could clearly see his name on the front cover. The first couple of pages were read before he spoke. "Why should a solicitor be involved in this matter? I fail to see the connection."

Gerry took this as a signal to speak out. "Mr Spires, I used to work for David Evans until Mr Matthews took over the business. It was Mr Evans who paid for my course and exam fees and he was concerned that Mr Matthews would try something like this. So he drew up a letter with the aid of his solicitor to state that if the course was cancelled for any reason the money would be paid to me. Mr Parker is supposed to have written to you on this matter."

Spires held up his hand for silence and pressed his intercom button on his phone.

"Miss Partridge, can you check if I had a letter sent to me by an Albert Parker, a solicitor, in the past couple of months, please?" He turned back to Gerry. "Are you saying those comments that Mr Matthews attributed to you are false?"

"Completely. I've always looked forward to, and enjoyed learning new skills with Mr Bradley and you can ask the other students if I've been disruptive in class at any time."

Spires tapped his fingers on his desk several times before speaking. "This leaves you with a problem then, young man. Unless you can get Mr Matthews to return the fees, or alternatively you can find other funds yourself, I cannot see any way of reinstating you on the course. Correct me if I'm wrong, Mr Bradley, but I believe there is a list of several capable students waiting to join your class."

Bradley looked at Gerry and then asked his boss, "How long has Gerry got to find any alternative funds?"

Spires looked at Gerry. "You have until the bursar's office closes at four thirty tomorrow afternoon. Oh, you must also have an employer who will give you a reference stating you will complete the course and attend on a regular basis."

Gerry slumped back in his chair and his tutor looked away. There was a knock on the door and the principal's secretary entered the room with a letter and handed it to Spires. He read the letter carefully and then repeated the process before announcing, "It seems that your former employer, Mr Evans, did try to protect your interests. However, Mr Matthews assured me he had a legal right to those fees and was prepared to go to court to get hold of them. I think you should go to speak to Mr Parker to seek advice and find out if Mr Evans is willing to fight Matthews in court.

"In the meantime, I have to consider the college's position and if you can find other funding by tomorrow afternoon and stay in employment you will be reinstated on Mr Bradley's course. I have other matters to attend to so this meeting is at an end."

He rose from his chair and opened the door for his two guests and watched them leave. Once they had left he closed the door and went to his phone and dialled a number. When the call was answered he spoke quickly. "Abigail, tell Percy the money has been transferred to his account, but the lad Reynolds has a solicitor on the case so be prepared for trouble."

Lee took Gerry into a small office next to his classroom and invited him to sit down.

"I'm really sorry, Gerry, I wish there was something else I could do to help but since the principal is involved I have to step back as he has the final say in this matter. But as he said, go to your old boss's solicitor and find out if he can come up with anything."

"Thanks, Lee. Even if I get some money back Matthews will find a way to sack me and that means I couldn't attend the course anyway. One thing, the principal, does he have a daughter called Abigail?"

Lee shook his head. "He's got two sons but he does have a niece, and I'm sure her name is Abigail. Why do you ask?"

Gerry explained the connection and Lee let out a low whistle.

"You're really up against it. Chances are Spires has already warned her of our meeting. Look, I have to go back to the class now but if there's anything I can help with, a reference or something, let me know. Do you want to say cheerio to your classmates?"

Gerry shook his head, said nothing and left the college, feeling the weight of the whole world on his young shoulders.

He walked to the local park and sat on a bench for the next half an hour trying to find something positive to concentrate on, oblivious to the steady drizzle and increasing wind. It was only when the rain became heavier that he decided to find an indoor venue. He headed for the library, hoping Sally would be there to give good counsel to him.

No such luck! The woman on duty told him Sally had a pre-arranged appointment with her doctor and would not be back on duty until later that afternoon. Where now? He was so preoccupied with trying to think of any solution he bumped into another person walking past the library as he came out. This person was of solid build and Gerry bounced back a couple of steps. The man gave a slight laugh and said, "Take it easy, lad, you could do yourself, or somebody else, a mischief charging around like that."

Ernie looked carefully at Gerry. "What's up, Gerry? You look as if you've lost a tenner and found a penny. Why the glum features?"

It took a few moments for Gerry to register what had happened. "Oh, sorry, Mr Newsham, are you okay?"

"In a lot better state than you, it seems. Anything you want to talk about or is it too personal?"

Before Gerry could reply, an ambulance, sirens blaring and blue lights flashing, roared past. Both men watched the vehicle speed away towards the centre of town. Only when it was out of sight did Gerry speak, first checking nobody else was within hearing range. "Thanks to my boss, Matthews, I've been kicked off my college course and will probably lose my job."

Ernie suppressed the smile he was aching to expose. This was just the situation he had bargained for, so he spoke quietly. "I can't talk now, Gerry, but if you come to the centre at about three o'clock you can tell me what's happened. Is that okay?"

Remembering what Sally had repeated to him just a few days ago, he sighed and nodded his head. "Thanks, Mr Newsham, I'll be there."

Ernie let out a smile, tapped Gerry on the shoulder and walked briskly away. Gerry decided he would go home, making the excuse that his tutor was ill if his gran started asking awkward questions. He was beginning to think his troubles were being resolved but events nearby would unfold to shatter that illusion.

***

Jenny Potter looked out of her living room window and was shocked to see an ambulance, rear doors open, parked outside the Stockwell residence. She had been baking in the kitchen at the rear of her house and had heard approaching sirens but decided not to investigate as her cake was due to come out of the oven at any moment.

Having surveyed the scene she grabbed hold of her coat and was about to cross the street when the two medics came out of the Stockwells', followed closely by Robin. The stretcher had a prone figure laying on it, which could only be Stella, Jenny surmised.

She was about to call out to Robin when he followed the stretcher into the rear of the ambulance, doors were closed and they drove away at speed, once again sirens blaring and lights flashing.

Jenny was left standing on the pavement, unsure what to do or think. She stayed in the same position for at least five minutes not comprehending quite what she had witnessed. Ernie found her standing on the pavement next to her gate, staring into the distance. He called her name but got no response so he gently tapped her on the shoulder. She let out a stifled scream and looked round at him, visibly relaxing as she looked into a familiar face. Ernie repeated his unanswered query.

"Jenny, is everything okay? You look as if you've, well, seen a ghost."

"Oh, Mr Newsham, something terrible has happened. Stella has been taken away in an ambulance. What could be the matter with her?"

"Was Robin with her or is he still at home?" he asked.

"No, no. Mr Stockwell got into the ambulance with her. I don't know what to do, Mr Newsham!"

It was obvious to Ernie that Jenny was in a state of shock so he gently, but firmly, took her arm and led her back to the open door of the house. She hesitated at the entrance and then spoke, "Would you like to come in for a cup of tea, Mr Newsham?"

It was Ernie's turn to show hesitation. He didn't want to get drawn into a long conversation with Jenny. He knew that once she started talking it could prove a little difficult in withdrawing. He said, "I will come in for ten minutes but I do have an appointment to attend, so I can't afford to stay any longer."

Jenny appeared happy with that compromise and invited her guest into the living room while she went to the kitchen to make the tea. Her two cats were waiting but as soon as Ernie stepped into the room both felines dashed past him into the hallway. Jenny was aware of the situation and looked a bit puzzled until Ernie announced, "I'm not really a cat person so your two probably sensed that fact."

They made general conversation for the first few minutes while drinking their tea. When the silence became a little strained Ernie got up and left with a promise to enquire about Stella's welfare and notify Jenny when he knew something. She did the same but once Ernie had gone she realised she had no way of contacting him.

***

On his arrival home Gerry suddenly remembered his gran usually went out on a Thursday afternoon so he had the house to himself. He found the letter his old boss had given him about contacting Albert Parker and he noted the phone number and dialled the solicitor's office. A female answered the phone and when he asked to speak to her boss she replied, "I'm sorry, sir, Mr Parker is out of the office for the rest of this week. Can one of the other partners assist you?"

Gerry was about to hang up but on the spur of the moment he decided to explain his problem and as he spoke, he could hear the woman typing notes on her computer. When he had finished speaking, she read back her notes to Gerry to confirm they were correct. He agreed.

"By coincidence, Mr Parker is visiting Mr Evans this evening and I can leave him a message if you wish."

Gerry knew he didn't have any other choice, so he accepted her offer and gave his home number as contact details. He put the phone down and made himself a quick snack before going to meet Ernie.

***

He found Ernie talking to the man who he had seen in the passenger seat of the van the previous evening. Gerry stood well back from the two men, not wishing to have any contact with the younger person but Ernie noticed him waiting and called him over. Reluctantly Gerry approached the couple and Ernie made the introductions.

"Gerry, this is Mark. Mark, Gerry here might be joining us soon."

Neither of the two attempted to shake hands as Ernie carefully observed, but he didn't say anything further to Mark who walked away.

"Okay, Gerry, go upstairs and grab one of the tables in the corner. I need to check something in the office. I'll be along in a couple of shakes."

Gerry followed Ernie's instructions and found a suitable table, far enough away from the three other people on the balcony. Meanwhile Ernie retrieved the small recorder and put in a new tape then slipped the recorder into one of his pockets.

He rejoined Gerry and asked him if he wanted a drink. Gerry nodded and asked for an orange juice which Ernie went to collect. While he waited for Ernie, Gerry looked around the facilities. The cafeteria below was quiet with only about half a dozen people either seated or waiting to be served. He could see Mark removing items from a stack of boxes in the far corner and carry the items into a room which had a sign saying 'Gymnasium'.

"You two have met before then."

Gerry had been so deep in his thoughts he hadn't noticed Ernie return with the drinks.

"Yes, he came into the shop a couple of times."

Gerry hesitated before continuing, "I think you should know, Mr Newsham, he tried to steal something from the shop when Mr Evans was the owner."

"First of all, Gerry, call me Ernie, we're all on first name responses here. Thanks for telling me that; I'll have a word with Mark later."

He slipped his hand into his pocket to switch on the recorder before continuing, "When we met this morning you looked like you didn't know which way to turn. Want to let me know what your problem is?"

Gerry spent the next ten minutes going over the details of his woes since Matthews took over from David Evans. He finished by talking about the plans Evans had drawn up with his solicitor apparently to foil Matthews from stealing his course and exam fees.

At the mention of Parker's name, Ernie became a little wary. He didn't want anyone like that taking an interest in his current operation, so he made a suggestion to Gerry. "Tell Mr Parker what you said about Matthews lying to the college; he's probably broken several employment laws in the process. Have you got any plans or ideas of what work you would do if things went pear-shaped with Matthews?"

Not wishing to give the name of his source Gerry asked, "I've heard you might be looking for another assistant to help around the centre. Is that true?"

Ernie was about to reply but he felt the recorder switch off as the tape reached the end of its spool. He had to turn the tape over but couldn't do so in front of Gerry, so he stood up, apologised and made an excuse to go to the bathroom. He came back a few minutes later, having turned the tape over and also decided on his strategy.

Having switched the recorder back on he sat down facing Gerry.

"There is a vacancy here but there are some things you have to accept along with the everyday run-of-the-mill tasks. You might be aware that as well as running this centre I also run a small security service for local businesses. You would be expected to help in that area, from time to time, no questions asked!"

Gerry looked a little pensive at Ernie's last remark.

"You don't mean the kind of service that bloke Bishop offers? Sorry, Mr Newsham, I'm not going to threaten anyone!"

Ernie gave a short laugh. "I wouldn't dream of asking you to threaten anybody, Gerry. If people don't want my security I'm obliged to point out the risks they could be taking. In the end it's their decision and if they don't listen to my advice, then so be it. Anyway, what experience do you have of our friend Bishop?"

Gerry told him about the time he threatened to burn down the Evans shop.

Again, Ernie laughed. "That's Bishop for you, all threats and no action. If he bothers any of my clients he will be sorry he ever came to this town."

Gerry then remembered what happened when Colin Evans confronted Bishop and the subsequent action that followed. This time both men laughed. Ernie then moved the subject on to another area.

"If I remember correctly you used to do some locksmith duties for David. Do you still have a set of skeleton keys and the key-cutting machine in the shop?"

The discussion was now moving into an area that Gerry yearned to be doing more often and he walked into Ernie's trap.

"Before he left Mr Evans gave me the key-cutting equipment and it's now in the basement of Gran's flat. He also gave me a brand new set of master keys which are better than the old set I used. That was quite lucky really; while I was away working at his other shop Matthews cleared out my old work area to accommodate his computer repair business and my old set of keys disappeared. I was fortunate that I managed to retrieve my box of engraving tools."

Ernie suddenly felt it was his birthday and he was celebrating Christmas at the same time. He put as much concern as he could into his reply. "That's not good; a set of skeleton keys in the wrong hands could prove problematic for a security firm like mine. Don't worry, Gerry, there's no blame attached to you. If anybody is at fault it's Matthews."

The relief was clear on Gerry's features and he wanted to move the conversation on to other areas.

"What kind of work would I be doing in the centre?"

Ernie was also happy to progress to speaking about other areas. It was too early in their relationship to push his young companion into a corner just yet.

"Tell me if I'm barking up the wrong tree, Gerry, but you must be pretty handy when it comes to fixing machinery. I'm talking about assembling and dismantling bits of equipment. For example, like the kit in the gymnasium."

Gerry looked a little pensive at first so he broached the question, "If you have the manuals for the equipment, I could give it a go? But I can't be sure until I try."

Ernie nodded. "At least you're honest about it, which I like. It's things like pumps, the type we have in the swimming pool. Oh, and can you swim? Mark stays well away from the pool in case he falls in. None of his family learned or so he says."

Gerry had mixed feelings. "Yes, I can swim. In fact, I was thinking of taking up swimming to get fitter. I also have a first aid certificate in lifesaving techniques. As for the pump, isn't that covered under a maintenance contract with the council?"

"That's correct, but I sometimes have to drain the pool to clean it out on health grounds. I just meant switching the pump on and off and maybe operating a steam cleaner. Mark is not too hot on those kinds of things. Look, Gerry, I have other things to attend to right now so if you've got no further questions, I have a couple of pieces of advice for you."

Gerry shook his head, so Ernie made his final point.

"Right now, you still have a job, and until Matthews makes his move, which he will do, don't do anything to give him cause to sack you. With what you've told me, the solicitor should have enough grounds to at least get you some holiday pay. If he forces your hand and you have no choice but to walk away from the job, then again Parker could claim constructive dismissal on your behalf. Don't tell anyone that you have another job lined up. I still have to notify the council I've found my second assistant and the paperwork could take a couple of weeks to sort out."

With that final comment he stood up and offered his hand to Gerry who accepted it with a smile. At least Gerry knew things weren't such a disaster after all. But all his worries were not over as he would find out once he returned to his flat.

12

On returning to the flat he once again found his gran in a distressed state, sitting in her favourite armchair, still wearing her outdoor coat. He knelt by her side.

"What's the matter, Gran? Is something wrong?"

At first all she could do was nod her head, so Gerry gave her time to compose herself. It took nearly five minutes of several sobs and sniffles before she finally spoke.

"I heard some dreadful news this afternoon, Gerald. Mrs Stockwell was rushed into hospital and somebody said she wouldn't last the night."

He took her hand in his own and said quietly, "That's just speculation, Gran. Just wait and see. Mrs Stockwell is very resilient, and she could make a full recovery. I'll make you a cup of tea. That will make you feel better."

After a few moments she released his hand and nodded. Gerry went into the kitchen and thought about what he would say if his gran started asking questions concerning his early arrival home. He found a packet of her favourite biscuits and took them out with the two cups of tea. Sure enough, she enquired as to his early return.

"Mr Bradley had an appointment and the class finished early, Gran," he said after finishing his second biscuit. There was an uneasy silence for several minutes which was interrupted by the phone suddenly ringing. With surprising speed the old lady moved quickly to the phone before Gerry had time to answer it.

Mrs Reynolds spoke into the receiver. "Hello? Yes, that's correct. You want to speak to my Gerald? Who is this calling? Mr Parker did you say?"

Gerry had not expected the call from the solicitor to be made this early and it put him in an awkward position. How could he talk about events at the college in front of his grandmother without arousing her suspicions? To his relief, she handed the receiver to him and walked out of the room.

"Hello, Mr Parker, I thought you wouldn't be calling until this evening."

Parker's reply was terse and rather abrupt. "Well, I'm here now so give me the details as quickly as possible; I have a train to catch that leaves in less than ten minutes."

Gerry went over the events of the day, including the meeting with the principal. The solicitor asked a couple of questions and after hearing the replies he spoke in a much friendlier manner.

"Right, Gerald, I will be back in my office tomorrow morning. Do you intend going into work tomorrow or will you wait until I arrive? I would suggest you go to work as normal but don't bring up the subject of your course and exam fees if you can possibly help. If you feel uncomfortable just say I will be calling in to speak to Mr Matthews before lunchtime."

Gerry said he would go into work and wait there for the solicitor and the line went dead. He nearly jumped out of his skin when his gran asked him from the doorway, "Are you in some kind of trouble, Gerald? Why were you speaking to that solicitor?"

There was no point in trying to hide the facts from her any more, so he told his gran the minimum of details but hopefully enough to satisfy her curiosity. Not so.

"Gerald, people usually contact solicitors when they are in trouble. If you are not in trouble why do you need a solicitor? I know Mr Matthews is a difficult man to deal with at times but if you explain the situation calmly to him, I'm sure he will see your point of view."

Gerry took in a deep breath. "Gran, ever since Mr Evans handed over the shop to Matthews my life has been a misery working for him. He gives me the most menial tasks to do and if I want a hot drink he charges me for it. He is now trying to cheat me out of money I was told by Mr Evans would be mine if my college course and exams were cancelled. Matthews cancelled both yesterday evening and lied to the college principal saying I was a troublemaker. If I don't get this money, I will have nothing to give towards the rent and food until I get a new job. I didn't want to worry you about money but now you know everything. Does that satisfy you?"

The shocked look on her face immediately told him he had gone too far. She sat back in her chair, tears welling up and he tried to console her but it had no effect. Her sobs cut into him like a knife and he hung his head in shame. After a few minutes he heard her speak. "In all the time we have been living together, Gerald, you have never spoken to me in that way. I can only put it down to the fact that those items I showed you in the case have caused this bad feeling between us."

Gerry stood up. "I'm sorry for talking to you like that, Gran, I promise I'll make it up to you," and he walked out of the room. Moments later she heard the front door close and she burst into more floods of tears.

He must have walked around the town for more than an hour in the cold drizzle and finally went back to the library. At least Sally would understand. The woman who was on duty when he had called earlier was about to close up, so he asked if Sally was around.

"No, dear, she phoned in sick and will be away for a couple of days. I told her you called and she gave me a message for you.

She is feeling under the weather and doesn't want any visitors in case anything is passed on to you and will be back in touch when she has recovered."

Grudgingly he made his way back to the flat.

As he approached his home a figure was standing in the shadows who appeared to be watching the flat where he lived. Gerry turned in his direction but as soon as he did so the watcher moved away very quickly and disappeared down a side street. He toyed with the idea of trying to find that person but by now he was tired and hungry so he turned for home.

His grandmother had retired to her room but had left a note for him saying she would be out for most of tomorrow. However, she had made him a sandwich and left him a piece of his favourite cake. Gerry saw this as a sign that he was forgiven for now.

***

Taking Mr Parker's advice Gerry turned up for work on time and was a little bemused at the almost, but not quite, friendly atmosphere in the shop. Abigail even said, "Good morning, Gerry" and Harry even offered to make him a cup of tea. No sign of the boss so he asked Abigail what his duties were for the time being.

"Someone brought in a camcorder that needs repairing but I don't have the time or inclination to waste energy on it at the moment. Put it in the outside storeroom for now, then you can go and ask Harry if he needs any help."

He found the box with the damaged item, marked 'Property of Councillor Fred Barnes' and after asking Harry for the keys, deposited it as instructed in the outside storeroom.

Harry was unpacking fresh stock for the display cabinets, so he helped by marking all the accessories with the same serial number on the packaging.

He had been working at this task for more than thirty minutes when the boss arrived. Gerry caught him winking at Abigail before he spoke. "Good day at college yesterday, Gerry?"

In response Gerry made a non-committal grunt. *Let's see who is laughing once the solicitor has been to speak with you, Mr 'Clever Dick'.*

The boss was in his office completing the weekly pay cheques when Parker arrived, and once he had introduced himself and his reason for calling, Abigail dashed into the manager's office. She came back out looking flustered and invited the solicitor to go in and meet Mr Matthews.

The meeting went on for about forty minutes and on a couple of occasions Matthews was heard raising his voice. When the meeting finally ended both men came out, Matthews glaring daggers in Gerry's direction but Mr Parker looking calmness personified. He spoke just loud enough for everyone to hear.

"Gerald, I've concluded our business with Mr Matthews, and he has given permission for you to accompany me to my car where I need you to sign some papers. It shouldn't take more than thirty minutes."

He turned, nodded at both Matthews and Abigail and said, "Good morning to you both," and indicated for Gerry to collect his coat and follow him out of the door.

No words were spoken until the two men had walked past two blocks of shops where they stopped and the solicitor asked, "Which bank do you pay your wages into, Gerald?"

Gerry gave the name of the bank and street where it was located. Parker nodded and led Gerry to his car which was parked two doors away from the bank. They got into the car and Parker opened his briefcase.

"Sign these papers, please. They will indicate to Mr Evans that I have discharged my duties as per his instructions."

After he took back the papers from Gerry, he handed him an envelope and asked him to open it. Inside were two cheques.

One was his weekly wages and the other a cheque for a little over £1,000.

Letting out a small whistle Gerry said, "Thank you, Mr Parker, I didn't realise Mr Evans paid that much for the college course and exams."

"That's not the full amount, I'm afraid. I had to concede that you attended college on six occasions while employed by Mr Matthews and so he was entitled for those days' payment."

"It doesn't matter now, but I only attended five college days because Mr Matthews told me college had been cancelled on one day which was a lie."

The solicitor smiled and shook his head, "Well if you say that doesn't matter, we will leave things as they are. At least it will give him a small moral victory. Now we will go to your bank and pay them into your account. I just want to make sure Matthews doesn't try and stop those cheques."

"I don't normally get paid until Saturday, so why have I been paid a day early?"

Parker smiled. "He was sorting the payroll out so I hinted it would be a sign of no bad feelings towards you if he let me take your pay cheque along with the one for the college fees. He blustered and swore a little, but I made him see sense in the end."

Gerry suddenly thought, "I need to contact Mr Evans to thank him for sorting this matter out. Do you have his phone number by any chance?"

Parker shook his head. "I do, but it won't help you. Mr and Mrs Evans are leaving on a month-long cruise at midday today so it will have to wait until they come back."

They got out of the car and went to the bank and deposited the cheques without further bother.

Mr Parker turned to his companion. "I've done all I can for you at this moment and if you require further advice don't hesitate to contact me. However, if Mr Matthews digs his heels in and wants to go to court in future, I will have to speak to Mr Evans to see how far he wants to support you."

Gerry nodded and, as they left the bank, they shook hands and the young man returned to work, wondering what kind of reception awaited him. The answer was a little surprising because the shop was closed, and no lights could be seen inside. He stood outside for a couple of minutes until he spotted Harry coming back from an early lunch break.

"What's going on, Harry? Are they inside or have they gone to lunch as well?"

"No idea, kid. You and I have to collect more stuff from another of his businesses and bring it back here. Just as well, he's in a right bad mood. Even Abigail had a mouthful of abuse from him before he calmed down and left with her."

"What kind of stuff are we collecting this time; more bankrupt junk?" Gerry asked, relieved to be putting off facing his boss.

"Bit better quality junk this time; portable radios, cameras and the like. It's the shop next to the travel agents on the main high street. We're also supposed to dismantle the shelving and stands as well. We could make it a two-day job if we work to my system?" And he gave a wink.

Before leaving they collected together several boxes to carry back the stock and loaded them into the back of the van.

It only took twenty minutes to find the shop. Harry pulled up outside and they both got out of the van and approached the main shop doorway. Harry took out a key ring with two keys on it but it was obvious to Gerry neither key would fit the shop's lock. After a few minutes of banging and cursing by Harry he gave up his attempts and stood back to appraise the situation.

"Excuse me, sir, you can't leave that van parked there or I will have to give you a ticket."

Both men turned to find a traffic warden about to produce a parking ticket.

Harry was not in the best of moods by now and he turned aggressively to face the warden.

"Look, mate, we're here to remove the stock from this shop. If I can't park outside, where the hell do I leave the bloody van?"

The warden, taller and fitter than the driver, looked scornfully at Harry. He met his type almost every day on his beat and wasn't impressed by the man's attitude. He pointed past the travel agency next door. "You do just like the other traders around here. You can get that van down the lane that runs behind the shop. I'll be back in five minutes and if you haven't moved, you'll get a ticket," and he walked away before Harry could comment.

Gerry spoke. "Let me have those keys, Harry, and I'll go and check if they fit the back door. If they don't, there's no point in moving the van round there."

Harry gave the door of the shop another kick before sullenly handing the keys to Gerry who ran past the shop next door and followed the lane until he was behind the middle building in the rank of three shops. He chose one of the keys and it fitted the door and within seconds Gerry was inside the main shop area. He was about to tap on the window to indicate to Harry to move the van to the rear of the shop when a loud wailing sound began. The premises were fitted with an alarm.

He looked around for the security box that housed the alarm electronics and found it after a frantic thirty-second search and switched it off with the second key on the key ring.

Harry was standing outside laughing at Gerry's effort to find the alarm switch but stopped laughing when he was joined by another man who came from the shop next door.

"What's going on here?" demanded Andrew Phillips, the proprietor of the travel agency.

Harry looked him up and down before speaking with the hint of violence in his voice. "What's it got to do with you, smart arse?"

Phillips took a step backwards but still managed to say, "I know the owner of this shop and you're not one of his workers. I've a mind to call the police if you threaten me!"

Slowly Harry drew out some papers from his jacket pocket and waved them in front of the man's face.

"For your information, Mr Nosey Parker, I work for the new owner of the shop and I've got orders to remove the flaming stuff inside. You got any objections then, buddy!?"

Phillips took another step back and abruptly returned to his shop. However, Harry's problems were not over. While he was having his altercation with the travel agent the traffic warden had returned and quietly placed a ticket on the windscreen of the van and walked away.

Gerry had seen each event through the shop window and ran back out to the front just as Harry discovered the parking ticket. To say he was not best pleased was a big understatement. Gerry took his life in his own hands when he stood in front of his workmate to stop him going into the shop to beat up the travel agent.

"Get out of my way, kid!" Harry growled but Gerry stood his ground and spoke as calmly as he could under the circumstances.

"Harry, listen! It's not the travel agent who got us into this mess, it's Matthews. He didn't give you the right keys, or tell you about the parking, or the alarm system."

The big man was about to push Gerry to one side but then started laughing. "Oh no, it wasn't the boss who gave me the details, it was Miss Droopy Drawers, Abigail. Let's see the little madam talk her way out of this mess."

First checking to make sure the van would have sufficient room to manoeuvre down the alley, Harry instructed Gerry to guide him past the large refuse bins which were situated at various points along the route. This process took another fifteen minutes and did nothing to improve Harry's mood changes. They removed the boxes from the van and went into the shop to start packing the containers. It soon became evident they did not have enough boxes to remove all the stock.

Harry signalled to Gerry to stop removing items from cabinets.

"I'm going to load this stuff into the van. Have a look around to see if you can find any tools to dismantle the shelves. I wasn't told anything about display cabinets being removed so we'll have to go back for instructions."

Gerry searched for any kind of tools but found none so started checking the shelf fittings to see what was required. He helped Harry put the remaining boxes into the van and they drove slowly away from the area.

It was just starting to get dark when they returned to their home base. The shop was still closed up so the van was driven into the yard after the gate had been opened. Harry had a key for the side door and Gerry was about to speak as they went in, but the driver put a finger to his lips for silence. They could hear a man laughing and giggles from a female voice. The two men looked at each other and smiled knowingly. Harry said in a loud voice, "Check the front door is secure, Gerry, and I'll have a look in the offices to see if anyone's still around."

There was a male curse and a female stifled scream followed by a desperate plea from the female, "For Christ's sake, Percy, don't let them come in! I can't find my bra or knickers!"

"Shut up, you silly bitch!" came the hissed reply from her boss.

Moments later the office door was opened with just enough room for Matthews to squeeze out sideways, his shirt hurriedly tucked into his trousers. He smiled nervously at his employees.

"Harry, Gerry, I wasn't expecting you two to come back so soon. Abigail and I were having discussions about..." when he realised the zip on his trousers was undone and he turned around to make himself more presentable. On turning to face the two men again, he had regained his composure and started shouting.

"Why the hell have you come back here? You were supposed to take the shelving to Tony's shop in Hereford Street along with what stock he could handle and bring the rest here. You can't have finished that work already."

Harry cleared his throat. "Mr Matthews, no mention was made of Hereford Street, we didn't have the key to the front door, and I got a parking ticket for hanging around outside the shop while we tried to get in through the back entrance."

Gerry added, "Nobody said anything about an alarm system and there were no tools to dismantle the shelving units. Oh, and what do we do about the display cabinets?"

Matthews rounded on his young assistant. "Who asked you to speak? You've already cost me a fair bit of money today so keep your mouth shut until I say you can talk!"

Gerry slowly turned his head in the direction of the office door that Abigail was standing in, now fully dressed. Matthews understood the silent message and calmed down and cleared his throat.

"Hum. Gerry, go and put the kettle on and make us all a hot drink while I talk to Harry. Please?"

Gerry was amused at the inclusion of the word 'please'. He nearly fainted when Abigail repeated the word in her request for two sugars in her coffee, although he noticed it was said through gritted teeth.

After making the drinks and delivering them to his colleagues Gerry decided to throw an observation of his into the conversation.

"If my skeleton keys hadn't gone missing last week there wouldn't have been any problem getting into the shop through the front door."

Harry concentrated on sipping his tea, Abigail flushed a bright pink while Matthews remarked, "You were given all the keys by Abigail, Harry, so what was the problem?"

Harry seized the opportunity with both hands. "I was only given two keys, one for the back door and the other Gerry used to switch off the alarm which I wasn't told about. The busybody from next door came to find out what was going on and while I was dealing with him the bloody traffic warden crept up and stuck the ticket on the van which I don't expect to have to pay, Mr Matthews."

Matthews looked directly at Abigail and said quite smugly, "I will sort out the cost of the ticket later but as for the missing key, Abigail, I gave them to you on that fancy key ring."

She flushed even more and stuttered, "That is a very nice key ring and you said I could keep it. I was removing the keys from the ring when a customer came in and I found the main key after Harry had gone for lunch. I'm sorry, Percy, sorry, I mean, Mr Matthews."

She received another stare from her boss who, after a moment's thought, decided, "As you've got stock in the van, unload that here and then go back to finish collecting the rest of the gear. I'll look for some tools and you can collect them in the morning."

Harry made a show of looking at his watch and said quietly, "If it's all the same to you, Mr Matthews, we can unload the van in the morning and then go back to finish off."

Matthews was beginning to get the message that the price he would have to pay for their silence would drag on for some time unless he could find a way of halting this mini mutiny. He nodded but said nothing.

The two men left via the side door leaving their boss and Abigail to resume their 'discussions'.

***

His grandmother had a cooked meal waiting for him upon his return. After he had finished and washed up Gerry asked her if there was any news concerning Mrs Stockwell. She shook her head and, shortly after, retired to her room for the night.

He considered trying to contact Sally but thought it best to respect her wishes for privacy for now.

The next morning as promised, the tools, along with the key to the front door of the shop, were waiting for them, but only the boss was in attendance. Abigail was nowhere to be seen. Matthews sent Gerry out to start unloading the van while he spoke to Harry in private, who was very subdued upon coming back to continue the unloading. When that task was completed they collected more boxes and left to carry on with their previous day's work.

13

On arriving at the shop Gerry was about to get out of the vehicle but Harry told him to wait.

"A piece of advice, kid, don't try and use yesterday afternoon's discovery of Matthews and Droopy Drawers' little adventure as a means of having an easier life. He's already got me by the short and curlies. Just keep your mouth shut or he'll do the same to you."

Gerry gave a short laugh. "What Matthews has got over you is your business, Harry, but he's going to get rid of me as soon as he can anyway, it's only a matter of time."

Harry shrugged his shoulders and indicated to his companion to guide him down the alley to the back of the shop. Two other men were standing outside, surveying the rear of the travel agents. One was the manager of the premises, the other was Ernie Newsham. As the van reversed towards them Phillips and Newsham went back inside.

Gerry and Harry recommenced their work of loading the remaining stock into boxes and placing them in the van. That part of their task was almost complete when Ernie approached them. He gave Gerry a brief smile and spoke to his companion. "Hello, Harry, Mr Matthews expanding his empire even more is he? What happened to the previous owner?"

Harry was glad of the chance of a short break; he was blowing rather hard.

"Hi, Mr Newsham. Usual method; owner dies, wife doesn't have much business knowledge, so the boss comes along with an offer she can't refuse."

Without waiting to be invited Ernie looked in one of the boxes and commented, "Good quality merchandise here. I'm sure Mr Matthews has an outlet for this kind of thing – as long as he doesn't overstretch himself that is."

He turned to Gerry. "I didn't expect to bump into you here, Gerry. Anything exciting happening at base?"

Before Gerry had a chance to reply Ernie turned to the older man.

"Watch out for this lad, Harry, he's got a bright future ahead of him if he plays his cards right. Anyway, I've concluded my business here but I'm sure our paths will cross again fairly soon."

As he walked away Harry pointed to the rear door of the shop and indicated to Gerry to follow him.

"Pal of yours, is he? All I'll say to you is, don't put all your trust in him just because he's an ex-copper. Believe me, that guy is no saint. Now, I'll finish packing the rest of this stuff. You get the tools and start dismantling those shelves. Somebody else is coming to sort out the display cabinets."

It took them nearly three hours to dismantle and remove what they could of the shelves and have lunch in a nearby cafe. Before leaving the premises, they made it secure and reactivated the alarm system.

Tony, manager of the Hereford Street store, greeted them with a sour look and a barbed comment. "Matthews told me you would be here and finished dumping the stuff by three o'clock. You'd better get your skates on because I'm not staying a minute later than my closing time. And don't block my normal stock in with that junk. Put it to one side against the rear wall."

He chucked the outside storeroom keys at Harry and returned to deal with his customers. With the extra task of making space for the new items in the van the two men completed their work with only ten minutes to spare before the shop closed. Tony's final comment was to Gerry. "You might be working here again next week, Gerry. My usual helper has phoned in long-term sick."

This news didn't disappoint Gerry. The more time he spent away from his boss's company the more it suited him down to the ground.

Heavier than usual traffic, mainly due to bargain hunters in the new shopping mall, had blighted their progress back to their home base and Matthews was his usual belligerent self. He demanded to know why they took so long in emptying the shop of its stock and then arriving back well after closing time.

Gerry left it to his companion to try and give a plausible explanation. Their boss was not to be appeased. He ranted on for a full twenty minutes, which were full of threats varying from docking a full day's pay to possible dismissal. In the end Gerry had heard enough and his outburst caught Matthews off guard.

"Mr Matthews. We did everything you told us to do yesterday and today. You never told us how much stock there was to move. We weren't told about the parking restrictions and you didn't supply us with the correct tools for the job which meant it took a lot longer to dismantle the shelving. We also had to shift a lot of stuff around before we could find space in the Hereford storeroom. We've worked our bloody socks off today. And as it's well past closing time and you don't pay overtime, I'm going home. Goodnight!" and he left the shop with both men staring open-mouthed.

***

Mrs Reynolds was on the phone when Gerry arrived home that evening. His grandmother was speaking on the phone when he entered the room. She put the receiver down once she saw him and walked quietly out. Whatever the phone call had been about, it had visibly upset the old lady.

There was no meal waiting for him, so he waited for a few minutes before knocking on her bedroom door. After he knocked a second time he was invited to enter. It was evident she had been crying for some time.

His grandmother indicated for him to sit on the bed next to her and the old lady took hold of both his hands. She gathered herself and spoke in a shaky voice. "Gerald, I've some very sad news. Mrs Stockwell died in hospital this morning. It seems she had lung cancer and nobody, not even her husband, knew about it."

He immediately put an arm around her shoulders, and she leaned into him, sobbing heavily. They remained in this position for more than ten minutes and only moved when the phone rang once more. Gerry asked her if she wanted him to answer the call but she shook her head and went to take the message herself.

She was only out of her room briefly and returned, wiping her eyes with her handkerchief. She sat back down next to her grandson.

"That was another call asking if I had heard the news about Mrs Stockwell. Would you take any more calls, please, Gerald? I'm finding the whole situation too upsetting."

He nodded and then told her about the incident in the shop when Mrs Stockwell was in a near state of collapse. His grandmother wanted more details of this incident which he divulged to her, then finished by saying, "You knew her better than me, Gran, but when I offered to get the taxi to drop us outside her house she insisted on getting out around the corner and walking part of the way with me. There was no way she would accept any advice."

She thought for a moment and then nodded in agreement.

"Yes, I understand. When she used that stare of hers, everyone knew she would have the final word, including her husband. Now I will go and prepare something for you to eat but I just don't have an appetite at the moment."

Gerry offered to cook himself a meal, but she insisted, claiming it would take her mind off events.

After eating his meal the rest of the evening was spent with idle chat and reflections his grandmother had of the Stockwells, and how they had been an important part of the fabric of the community.

The following day being a Sunday meant Gerry would be home to watch over his elderly relative, to make sure she didn't get too depressed and anxious. On the Monday morning he checked she was in a fit state to take care of herself and he had the phone number of his workplace.

Matthews greeted him in his usual manner. "What the hell are you doing here? Didn't Tony tell you his assistant was off sick? Get over there right now and don't come back here until I tell you to!"

Gerry knew that if he had taken the initiative and gone straight to Hereford Street it would have been wrong anyway. *Damned if I do and damned if I don't* was the thought that went through his mind as he left.

The contrast in the working atmosphere between the two shops couldn't have been more marked. Tony was pleased to see Gerry and insisted on making him a hot drink before his assistant started work.

During a quiet period just after lunch Tony asked him, "You're a good worker, Gerry, would you consider being transferred here on a permanent basis? My usual assistant has health problems and I can't be certain from day to day if he will be coming in or not, but you don't have to make a decision right now. Think about it for a few days and maybe give me the answer at the end of the week."

After a more productive and friendlier day at work Gerry was feeling more relaxed but his grandmother put an end to that feeling when she told him about her day.

"Gerald, where have you been today? I rang your work number and a rather rude woman told me you weren't there and that you were not allowed personal calls at work, then she hung up after swearing at me."

Gerry nearly swore himself but managed to hold back. It could only have been Abigail who answered the phone.

"Sorry, Gran, I've been sent to another branch and will be there all week. Why were you trying to get hold of me?"

"First of all, I have been told that Mrs Stockwell's funeral is on this coming Friday at midday. Then Sally called in to say she is moving to live somewhere in Derbyshire to be near her sister who is, I think, expecting a baby. She gave me some contact details but said not to try and get in touch until the weekend."

At this moment in time he didn't particularly want to pursue the matter further anyway.

Gerry arrived at work on time the next morning and who should be waiting for him but Percival Matthews. He tried to hide the look of disappointment when he saw Gerry approaching but his mood was quite clear.

"I knew you wouldn't defy me, I am the boss and you know it! Now go and tell Tony to come here. He's in the storeroom. And don't forget, I will be checking on you at every opportunity until you can't put up with me any longer."

Gerry walked away without rising to his boss's bait. He could bide his time but not for much longer.

His thoughts turned to Sally and he was puzzled by the fact that she had never even mentioned having a sister or relatives in Derbyshire. So he concentrated on the other part of the phone call his gran had made to the shop and the reaction of that bitch, Abigail. All employees knew that Matthews had set up a phone link between all his shops, purely for him to keep on the backs of the managers when he felt the need. Gerry decided to use that link to speak to Abigail to find out what the reasons were for not transferring the call.

That morning was busier than usual, added to which Harry delivered nearly two boxes of trainers another one of their shops couldn't sell. These trainers, mostly white, had silver buckles on the heels, although some were missing either one or both buckles. Tony commented, "Another duff line we have to flog. If the other shops couldn't sell them, what hope have we got? My storeroom is full of junk like that."

During mid-afternoon Gerry took advantage of a quiet period to try and phone Abigail after getting Tony's permission to use the phone, but inevitably, it was Matthews who took the call. "What the hell do you want, Gerry? If you've got time to use the phone it must be quiet over there so you can come back here to do some work."

Gerry had to pick his words carefully, so he changed tack slightly before coming to the main point of his call.

"Oh, I'm glad it's you, Mr Matthews, I need to make a request to have this coming Friday off to attend a funeral. A close friend of my grandmother's has died suddenly, and I need to accompany her to the service."

Matthews barked back down the phone, "Definitely not! Only attending funerals for close relatives is the rule."

Gerry tried to protest. "Mr Matthews, this news has badly shaken my grandmother and she hasn't been well herself lately. Apart from that there is nobody else to accompany her."

"Again, no! That's twice I've told you, and if you ask again you can find another job and good riddance!" The line went dead.

Gerry was sorely tempted to ring back but decided not to give his boss the excuse to carry out his repeated threats. If Gran didn't have any reliable person to look after her at the funeral, then Matthews could stick his job.

Five minutes later, while he was serving a customer, the phone rang and Tony took the call. He came back out of the office shortly after and took over Gerry's serving duties.

"Mr Matthews is on the phone for you, Gerry."

He picked up the receiver and it was obvious from his boss's tone his mood had not improved.

"Answer me this. Was it your grandmother who phoned here yesterday and this funeral you're talking about, is it that woman who came into the shop last week you took home in the taxi?"

"Correct on both counts, Mr Matthews, and can I say there was no call for Abigail to swear at my grandmother. She was already upset at the news of the death of her friend without having to put up with that."

Matthews lowered his voice slightly. "Abigail had every right to reply as she did. We were busy and I'm not running a personal answering service. Don't forget, report for work on Friday or else. Now put Tony back on the phone."

Gerry quite deliberately dropped the receiver on the desk but not before he clearly heard Abigail's laughter. Tony was kept on the phone for what seemed like an age to Gerry. When he came back into the shop his face was like thunder.

There was no communication between them until it was time to close the shop. When this was completed Tony said, "The boss told me that if you don't show up for work while you're working here I have to let him know immediately, or if you phone in sick. Then he will come round here and fire you on the spot. Why has he got it in for you, Gerry?"

As Tony had been straight with him, Gerry decided to tell him about the events since Matthews had taken control of his place of work, including the discovery he and Harry had made on the previous Friday. Tony let out a long chortle when this was mentioned.

"He just won't learn. Abigail is at least the third woman he's been carrying on with, to my knowledge. The first one got pregnant, and the second one tried to blackmail him by threatening to tell his wife. His two sons found out and called her bluff but I'm damn sure it cost them a pretty penny."

Gerry shook his head. "Well, I'm not going down the blackmail route to keep my job. Anyway, I would need Harry to back me up and I don't trust him any more than Matthews. But if my grandmother needs me to go with her to the funeral, I'm going, and that's that!"

"I'd like to help you, Gerry, but my hands are tied. I've got a wife and three kids to consider so I can't put my own job at risk."

Gerry nodded. He wouldn't want anyone else to suffer from Matthews' vengeful actions. When he returned home, he decided to tell his grandmother about his situation and the threats of reprisals if he didn't attend work on Friday.

However, he need not have worried. Mrs Reynolds knew that the vast majority of those attending the funeral would be from her generation or slightly younger. She felt sure Gerald would feel out of place so she had made discreet enquiries as to who would be attending. Those enquiries had been prompted by an incident earlier that very afternoon.

They had finished eating their meal and the dishes washed and cleared away before Gerry tried to bring up the subject, but his gran interrupted him as he was about to speak.

"Let me speak first, please, there is something I must tell you. Now, Gerald, I know you said you would go with me to the funeral on Friday but I'm not sure you will feel comfortable with so many strangers and elderly people around. Therefore I have spoken to Mrs Byewater, who is a former nurse, and she and her husband will collect me and bring me home. So there is no need for you to take time off work on my behalf. Now, what is it you wanted to say, dear?"

Gerry scratched his head, feeling a little perplexed, and he said jokingly, "You spent too much time in Mrs Stockwell's company, Gran. I was about to tell you that my boss told me if I took time off for the funeral he would fire me."

Rather than be amused at her grandson's comment, Mrs Reynolds went quite pale and sat open-mouthed for nearly a minute and she failed to hear Gerry's question. So he repeated what he had said, but with more concern in his voice. "Gran, are you okay? You've gone very pale. Can I get you a drink or something?"

His raised voice stirred her into responding. "Gerald, what you said was uncalled for, but also very true."

He was even more puzzled. "I'm sorry, Gran, I wasn't mocking Mrs Stockwell's memory, but I don't understand your other comment."

It was her turn to smile. "You know I often have a little nap in the afternoon. Well, today was no different but this time I had a very vivid dream, or at least I think it was a dream. I was visited by Mrs Stockwell and she told me that you were very busy and couldn't come to her funeral and she was very pleased at that thought. Why, I don't know. Anyway, she said it had been arranged that Mr and Mrs Byewater would collect me and bring me back home after the funeral."

He was beginning to think his gran was getting confused and said gently, "Gran, you told me you had already arranged with Mrs Byewater to be collected."

She shook her head, looking more serious now.

"No, Gerald. I had this 'dream' before I rang her. When I spoke to Hazel Byewater she told me that she was on the point of calling me because the same thing had happened to her. She was in her bedroom and she suddenly felt tired, so she lay down on the bed and apparently fell asleep. And the same message came to her from Mrs Stockwell, but with one addition."

Gerry felt less comfortable at what she said next.

"Mrs Stockwell also mentioned that we would both have trouble caused by another person in your work. And it would be something you had dreaded happening."

"I bet it will be Abigail but nothing she could do bothers me."

Shaking her head, Mrs Reynolds spoke again. "Not a female, Gerald, another man has already done something that will come to light very soon but you won't have confirmation until sometime later."

He sat staring into the distance wondering what this would mean and was unaware of his grandmother leaving the room to make a cup of tea for them both. She also brought in a plate adorned with his favourite ginger biscuits. This was her coded message for 'let's accept things as they are'.

At least now he could go into work on Friday and not fall foul of Matthews' endeavours to fire him but he would still have to be on his guard.

Wednesday and Thursday passed by without any more threats or calls from his boss and after making sure his gran's plans were still going ahead he left for work on the Friday morning. He arrived a few minutes before the shop was due to open so he had to ring the bell for attention.

The door was opened by Percival Matthews and Gerry wasn't sure if the man was about to cry out in frustration. Instead his boss said, "Don't think you'll fool me. I'll be checking at regular intervals to make sure you're still here. What time is the funeral due to begin and where is it being held?"

"At the Arnos Vale Crematorium in Bristol, starting at midday," Gerry replied, knowing full well Matthews would have already checked. His boss gave a scowl and turned around to speak to Tony. He talked in a loud enough voice so that both would hear.

"Tony, I will be phoning in to check that Reynolds is still at work in this shop. He knows that if he tries to skive off to attend the funeral of this Stockwell person he will be fired. If you connive with him in any way to trick me I will also be looking for a new manager for this shop. Is that clear to both of you?"

Tony nodded and said, "Clear and fully understood, Mr Matthews."

"Good, I might call in later if I'm in the area."

Giving a contemptuous look in Gerry's direction Matthews walked out of the door with an air of victory he felt he had gained over his staff.

"Well, I think we both know what's at stake, Gerry. And you can bet your last fiver he will make sure he's in the area later!"

Gerry gave a little laugh and Tony looked at him with a hint of irritation. "I fail to see the funny side. He means exactly what he said!"

Gerry cleared his throat and coughed, "Sorry Tony, I wasn't laughing at what he said to us but it's all a waste of time on his part. My gran has made other arrangements to go with some friends to the funeral. She didn't feel I would fit in with the crowd that will be there, and I think she is right. So chase around as much as you like, Mr Matthews, you're only wasting your own time and petrol."

Tony let out a laugh and said, "And it couldn't happen to a better person. Come on, I'll put the kettle on to celebrate."

True to his word, Matthews returned to the shop twice that morning and on each occasion, he went into the manager's office to speak to Tony. While they were talking in their second meeting just after midday the phone rang and Gerry answered. It was the manager of one of the other shops who asked if the boss was there and said he needed to speak to him urgently. Gerry knocked on the office door and told Matthews there was a message on the phone that required his immediate attention. Cursing under his breath he picked up the receiver. "What the hell is wrong now?"

He listened to the message, cursed, and slammed the receiver down and called to Tony. "Tony! I've got to go to the Broadmead shop. They've had a power cut, the only shop in the block it seems. I'm going to check it out. If Abigail rings to speak to me let her know what's happening."

He stormed out of the shop and moments later the lights went out there as well. Tony found a torch and went to inspect the fuse box but a cursory look told him there was nothing wrong in that area. He came back into the shop and was about to report his findings when the phone rang. Gerry picked up the receiver.

"Hello, Hereford Street shop, can I help?"

"For God's sake, Gerry, is Percy there? I need to speak to him now!"

It was Abigail and she sounded almost hysterical.

"No, he left a few minutes ago to go to the Broadmead shop. They've had a power cut, but he said…"

He didn't have time to finish before Abigail's strident voice interrupted him. "The bloody lights have gone out here as well. Did you hear the laughter?"

Gerry wasn't sure he had heard her correctly. "Laughter? What are you talking about, Abigail? Nobody's laughing here."

"I don't mean you were laughing, you stupid little sod. When the lights went out I definitely heard the sound of a woman's laughter, an old woman, just like that old crone who you said had died. I want Percy back."

And then Gerry heard a crashing sound followed closely by Abigail's screams just before she dropped the phone.

Gerry shouted her name into the receiver and Tony came to find out what had happened. Gerry explained while periodically calling Abigail's name.

Finally, the receiver was picked up and Harry's voice called back, "What's all this racket about, kid? I was in the storeroom putting up those shelves when one section collapsed. Her ladyship screamed, I came in to see what had got her knickers in a twist and she grabs her coat and disappears out the front door as if she had a crowd of zombies on her tail. Oh, and there's no bloody lights on here."

That was the longest passage of speaking Gerry had heard Harry utter since they had met, and he sounded out of breath at the sheer effort.

Tony took over the call. "Harry, it's Tony, seems like the shops in the Matthews' empire have all experienced power failures, all at the same time. The boss should be on his way back to you by now, but I can't see how we can operate with no lights or power. If the power is not restored within one hour I would say there's no point in trying to stay open. The weird thing is every other business around us has power; what about you?"

There was silence while Harry went to check Tony's statement and he came back to confirm the exact same situation.

"Well, I for one am not sitting around here while there's a nice warm pub across the road. I'll give it thirty minutes and then I'm off!" was Harry's closing remarks and the line went dead.

"We can't afford such liberties like Harry so I'm afraid we're stuck here unless the boss gets back to us."

Within five seconds of Tony putting the receiver down the phone rang again. Matthews' irritation was evident.

"Tony, what the hell is going on? I've been trying to get hold of you and Abigail for the past ten minutes but both lines were engaged. I've had to call in an engineer to sort this problem out. God knows that will cost me. How busy are you? I might have to use your shop as base. Oh, is that layabout kid still there, or has he done a runner?"

Tony shook his head and smiled. He was almost going to enjoy passing on his bit of news.

"Gerry is still here, Mr Matthews. But I'm afraid this shop will be no good as your base as we are without power, along with Abigail, who according to Harry, ran out of the shop screaming after their lights also went out."

At this news Matthews started to panic. "Abigail? What's happened to her!? If that drunken slob has laid a finger on her I'll kill him…"

Tony had to shout his boss's name several times to get his attention, finally resorting to using his first name before it had any effect.

"PERCY! Abigail is fine, just a little upset and Harry has done nothing. Now what are we supposed to do here? If you have to get an engineer to the other shop, will we have to do the same? With respect, I think we may as well close up and call it a day. No lights, power or heating; nobody will want to come in here today. So do I have your permission to close the shop?"

There was silence for several seconds then a defeated Matthews spoke. "I suppose you will have to. But everyone has to be back at their posts tomorrow morning unless you hear different from me, and that includes that Gerry!"

After hanging up Tony relayed the good news to Gerry and said he would give him a lift home once they had closed up for the day.

It wasn't yet two thirty in the afternoon and Gerry had worked out he would be home before his grandmother, and he could have a cup of tea waiting for her. Things could get back to normal very soon, he hoped.

But not so!

14

Tony dropped him off just around the corner from the flat after promising to ring him in the morning with any developments regarding the power failure.

As soon as Gerry opened the front door he had a sense of foreboding. There was a very faint aroma in the air which he didn't recognise. He stood in the small hallway that led directly to the two bedrooms for a few seconds, before heading in that direction. He ignored the living room, which was normally his first port of call.

The first door was his bedroom but all seemed in order so he next opened the door of his gran's room and as he did so, he heard a faint groan and sobbing coming from within. Pushing the door gently open he found his grandmother on her knees next to the bed. On top of the bed was the old suitcase, but this time, it was empty of any of its previous contents. Beside the case was one of the cloth bags that had held some of the items. It was now empty, apart from the label pinned to the opening.

He picked up the bag to read the label. The writing sent a chill down his spine: 'Patricia's favourite jewellery'.

His mother's most treasured possessions, the only items that remained of her memory. Now those had been stolen from him.

But under where the bag had lain was something even more significant; the bunch of skeleton keys that had gone missing from his work.

He knelt down by his grandmother and gently put an arm around her shoulders. She leaned against him, still sobbing gently. After what seemed like an age, she suddenly stood up and made space so she could sit on the bed. She dabbed her eyes with a lace handkerchief and cleared her throat to speak. But first Gerry had to know something important.

"Gran, did this happen before you came home from the funeral or was there someone here when you got back?"

She shook her head and began speaking, "No, dear, Mr and Mrs Byewater brought me home early because I didn't want to go to the meal that had been set up for those attending. I knew they wanted to go back because there were so many old friends they hadn't seen for years, although Mr and Mrs Evans, your old boss and his wife, weren't present, which surprised some, especially Mr Stockwell."

"I was told by Mr Parker that they were leaving to go on a month's cruise last Saturday, so I'm sure they would have left before the news broke about Mrs Stockwell's death."

"Ah, that explains things. I must telephone them tonight," she replied.

"But Gran, we have to phone the police to tell them about the burglary."

Gerry was not prepared for what happened next. Mrs Reynolds stood up and spoke with determination. "NO, Gerald, they will not be told. In fact, nobody else is to know about this incident. Those cursed items are now out of our lives forever and perhaps we can now have some peace."

Gerry stood open-mouthed unable to comprehend what she had said, before he countered with more than a little anger, "Don't tell anyone? Some of those things were Mum and Dad's personal belongings and by rights they should be coming to me once you've gone. No, Gran, I've got every right to get those items back and I WILL phone the police!" and he turned around to leave the room.

His grandmother tried to block his progress to the door, but he managed to brush past. She shouted after him, "Gerald, please, I forbid it!"

His last words to her were, "Like hell I'll let them go!"

As he opened the front door, he heard the loud thump of a body falling. He hesitated before dashing back to her room. Mrs Reynolds lay unconscious on the floor next to her bed.

He was immediately filled with remorse and tried to revive her, the person who had cared for him for most of the last seven years. But she did not respond to his coaxing or cries.

He went to the phone on her bedside cabinet and dialled 999. When the operator answered, he asked for an ambulance, gave the details requested and followed the instructions he was given to check pulse and breathing and look for any signs that his gran might have struck her head when falling.

Her pulse was weak and breathing very shallow but there were no signs of having struck her head on any item of furniture or other injuries. As he knelt beside his only remaining relative the telephone operator reassured him that an ambulance was on the way and kept asking him to check the pulse and breathing of his gran. Finally, after what seemed like an age, he could hear the siren of the approaching emergency vehicle. He dashed to open the front door just as it pulled up outside.

Within five minutes of the vehicle arriving Mrs Reynolds was placed in the back of the ambulance. Gerry quickly made the flat safe and secure and joined her inside the vehicle. They reached the local hospital in less than six minutes.

Gerry was told to wait outside the emergency cubicle while staff checked his grandmother to ascertain her condition. It was a further agonising wait of just under an hour before a doctor came out to speak with him. He asked Gerry to describe what had happened prior to her collapse. He did so but played down the reason for the argument and his sudden feeling of hostility he had felt towards his elderly relative.

After hearing what Gerry had to say, the doctor replied, "She seems to be in some kind of coma, brought on by sudden shock and her heartbeat is slightly irregular. Is she under any medical observation by her GP?"

Gerry remembered the appointments she had been having over the past couple of months but couldn't give the doctor any idea of the reason for these visits. After giving details of the surgery she attended Gerry was advised to go for a cup of tea and come back in about an hour.

He managed to find a table in a corner that wasn't close to other patrons of the cafeteria and tried to make some sense of the chaotic events of the past few hours. A feeling of shame and regret came over him once more as he remembered his own outburst of anger towards his grandmother. After a while he forced these feelings to the back of his mind and focused on another issue that he couldn't understand.

How did the old set of skeleton keys suddenly reappear? Obviously, the burglar had got them from somewhere or somebody.

That somebody was the next question to answer. Only three people knew they had gone missing and could have committed the crime themselves, or more likely passed them onto the burglar. It was either Matthews, Abigail or Harry. It had to be one of them who was involved.

Any one of the three could have taken the keys but could any of them have committed the burglary? Abigail and Harry were together in the shop and could give each other an alibi, added to which, Abigail was hysterical at the time of the power cuts and like Harry, didn't know the times when their flat would be unoccupied.

Matthews knew the time of the funeral but would have been too preoccupied with sorting out the power problems at his shops. So, as he had surmised earlier, none of them would have had time to break into the flat. Back to the issue of the keys.

Any one of them could have taken the keys and passed them on to the burglar. But nobody else knew about the suitcase and its contents, yet nothing else was stolen as far as he could tell.

Gerry's thoughts went back to his gran. Why didn't she want the police notified about the burglary? She had said something about the curse being gone. So what! He thought, *Curse or no bloody curse those things would have been mine and now they're gone.*

Another thought came to him. He had tried on a number of occasions to get his gran to give him more details of his parents' accident. If something happened to her how would he ever find out? That thought caused a few tears to run down his cheeks and he quickly wiped them away before anyone else noticed. Moments later he felt a tap on his shoulder and looked up to find Ernie standing behind him.

"Are you okay, Gerry?"

Gerry cleared his throat before answering. "Oh, hi, Mr Newsham. What are you doing here?"

Ernie pulled up another chair and sat opposite him.

"I bumped into a neighbour of yours in town and they told me about your grandmother being put into an ambulance followed by you getting in as well. I made a few enquiries to find out where the ambulance had taken you so I came along to see if you needed any support. Look, your tea has gone cold, I'll get us both a cup. Hang on there while I organise it. Do you want anything to eat?"

Gerry shook his head. Even though he hadn't eaten since breakfast time food was the last thought on his mind at present.

Ernie returned with the tea and a couple of mini packets of biscuits, which he placed on the table between them. He stirred his tea and opened one of the packets before speaking in a soft friendly voice. "Want to tell me what happened, Gerry?"

Gerry took a sip of the near-scalding liquid but didn't seem to notice its heat.

"We had a series of power cuts in all the shops and they couldn't be fixed right away so Matthews had no choice but to give us the rest of the day off. I was working in the Hereford Street branch so Tony, the manager, gave me a lift home and dropped me round the corner. This was just before three o'clock when I arrived back home."

He then related the events as they unfolded ending with the heated argument between himself and his grandmother. The reason for her not wanting the police involved still rankled with him and he told Ernie so. Ernie asked him the question, "Would you be able to give the police a list and description of those items that were stolen?"

Gerry visibly slumped in his chair. "Not really, the only thing she showed me was the box holding a medal her ancestor won during the Boer War. She never got round to showing me specific items in detail. But mentioned things like raw diamonds and small gold nuggets this ancestor had stolen. Along with some tribal items he conned people out of in exchange for trinkets."

Ernie sat back, drank some tea and looked around the cafeteria. He leaned forward and spoke quietly, "This isn't the time or place to discuss such things. Can I suggest we go and see the doctor in A&E to check on your grandmother's condition? Depending on what you are told we could go back to the flat and have a look around. Agreed?"

Gerry hesitated, drank his tea and ate a couple of biscuits before replying, "I suppose you're right; I've been putting off going back to see him in case it's bad news."

He wiped his eyes before standing up to leave.

Ernie stood up beside him and put a hand on his shoulder.

"I'll come along with you and ask any difficult questions if you'd prefer; it's up to you."

Gerry nodded and they went back to find the A&E doctor he had spoken to earlier. They had to wait a further twenty minutes before the doctor had finished with another patient and he led them into a side room and closed the door.

The doctor began by asking, "Is this a relative or friend with you, Mr Reynolds, and do I have your permission to speak frankly in his presence?"

Gerry nodded, so the doctor continued, "Your grandmother is still unconscious and in some form of coma. Her GP confirmed she is indeed on medication for an irregular heartbeat although she has no papers to indicate this, or what the medication entails. She should carry that information with her at all times to assist any medical person in circumstances such as this. She is quite weak. There are indications she has eaten very little in maybe the past ten days. Did you have meals together, Mr Reynolds?"

Gerry thought before answering. "Only on Sundays. I work full-time and I always left for work before she got up and on most evenings she told me she had already eaten before I arrived home. Could a sudden shock have caused this coma?" Gerry asked, but unseen by the doctor Ernie gave him a quick tap on his ankle and spoke up.

"What Gerry is referring to is that a close friend of his grandmother died recently, and she attended the funeral today. I was there and she seemed anxious not to hang around for the spread afterwards. In fact, she arranged for some of the mourners to take her straight home after the service."

He glanced at Gerry, almost defying him to divulge any more information. Gerry took the hint.

The doctor digested that news for a few moments before continuing with his report.

"That could have a bearing on things I suppose, but there might be other underlying issues that further tests might divulge. In the meantime, she has been moved to a medical ward and you are free to go and see her if you wish, but I have to tell you my thoughts first on what could happen. She is on a drip to give her some form of nourishment and this may stabilise her and in time improve matters. However, Mr Reynolds, I have to be honest with you, if your grandmother has lost the will to live or to fight, all the medical interventions in the world won't help. I'm sorry but she has to want to recover or have a reason to do so. Now, do you have any questions?"

Gerry shook his head and looked down at the floor. Ernie asked, "You say she is on a drip; is she on a ventilator or heart machine, Doctor?"

"No, if she was on either then the decision of what to do next might have to be made sooner rather than later. Right now, let's say the ball is in her court. If there's nothing else I'll get a nurse to take you to the ward. I'm sorry, Mr Reynolds, I wish I could give you more positive news," the doctor said as he rose to show them out.

A nurse took them to the high dependency ward and without saying anything to either Ernie or Gerry she spoke to the staff nurse in charge. "Staff, the son and grandson of Mrs Reynolds have come to see her. Is it okay to show them into her room?"

Ernie was first to react, almost with a look of horror on his face, "I'm sorry, Nurse, this is the grandson of Mrs Reynolds, and I'm just a close friend. Her son died in a car crash several years ago."

"Oh, I apologise. I just assumed you were both related," the nurse replied.

Ernie's comment alerted something in Gerry's mind. Perhaps he knew some details of his parents' death, and he would quiz him later. He had also noticed how pale Ernie's face was at the nurse's initial comment. But it was only a fleeting moment and Ernie recovered his composure and tapped Gerry on the shoulder and whispered in his ear, "It's only fitting that you go in on your own, Gerry. I'll wait out here for you."

He followed the nurse into the room and stood by the side of the bed, just about managing to control the trembling in his body. This was his fault she was lying in the hospital bed. The nurse brought a chair for him to sit next to his gran and he nodded his thanks.

"You can hold her hand if you want to. It may help her to recognise a familiar touch. Have you eaten lately, Mr Reynolds?" she asked in a sympathetic tone.

"Not lately, but I'll be okay, thanks."

She left the room and Ernie came in moments later. He motioned to Gerry to come outside for a moment which he did reluctantly.

"Gerry, it may be wiser if you stayed here for a while. I've got a late evening appointment, but I can check if you're still here and pick you up if you need a lift home."

Before he could reply the nurse returned with a cup of tea and a sandwich and gave it to Gerry. "I think you might be feeling hungry and you can stay as long as you like."

He took the offering and said to Ernie, "Thanks, Mr Newsham, I should be okay for getting home. Besides, the walk in the fresh air might do me some good."

Ernie nodded and walked away. Gerry followed the nurse into the room. He sat back down again and after glancing at the plate of sandwiches a couple of times he suddenly realised how hungry he was, so they were eagerly devoured and the tea was also consumed.

After washing his hands in the small washbasin in the corner of the room Gerry sat down by the bed and gently took hold of one of his grandmother's hands. They felt so limp and lifeless, for a moment he thought she was already gone. But he held on and began to take some comfort from the contact.

He wasn't sure how much later it was when the nurse came back into the room. She went to the other side of the bed and checked the old lady's pulse and took her temperature. When she finished writing the results on the chart at the bottom of the bed she said quietly, "I'm going off duty in about fifteen minutes but I'll tell the night staff you're here. Can I suggest you go home eventually and try to have a good night's rest? The next few days could be long and tiring for you. Goodnight."

He nodded his thanks and stayed where he was. Sometime later, someone tapped him on the shoulder and he woke up and found himself looking at a middle-aged nurse. She spoke in a hushed tone, "Mr Reynolds, I've looked in on you twice since coming on duty and each time you've been fast asleep. Why don't you go home and have a proper rest? I don't think anything will happen tonight."

Gerry looked at his watch and was surprised to see it was fast approaching midnight. He released his gran's hand, stood up and had a little stretch before acknowledging the nurse and leaving the hospital.

While he had been resting others had been busy in making use of the enforced darkness that had befallen certain premises within the town.

Ernie and Mark in their official-looking jackets and caps parked their van near the rear entrance to Matthews' shop they had visited a few months earlier. They walked around the front of the building and made a show of checking the front door was secure. There was nobody else around so they walked back to the van and Mark retrieved a crowbar and pillow from inside the van and went to work on forcing the lock on the gate to the yard.

He pushed the end of the crowbar into the gap between the edge of the gate and frame and pressed the pillow over the area to muffle the sound of breaking timber. Having one final check to make sure nobody was around, he rammed the bar further into the gap and gave a sudden twist of his wrist. The weakened timber of the gate gave way. Mark had plenty of practice doing this kind of work and he pushed the gate to its full opening, allowing Ernie to reverse into the yard. The gate was pushed closed and kept in that position with the help of a large stone.

Ernie ran to the door leading into the main building but found it was locked. Mark gave a soft whistle to alert his partner and Ernie joined him by the door to the outside storeroom. The key was still in the lock!

Using their torches they identified the boxes with the electrical items that Gerry and Harry removed from the shop the previous weekend. The items were placed in the rear of the van in a silent and efficient manner. Ernie shone his torch to pick out any items that might be of value and the light fell on the box containing the damaged camcorder placed there by Gerry. He quickly checked the label and knowing the name of the owner he picked it up and put the final item in the rear of the van. The storeroom door was closed, then locked. He put the key in his pocket.

Ernie signalled to Mark who went to open the gate and check the coast was clear. He got into the driver's seat and started the engine. Mark opened the gate once more and the van moved out of the yard. The gate was pulled closed so as not to attract attention and Mark climbed into the passenger seat. They moved quietly away. From start to finish the operation had taken less than ten minutes.

As they drove down a street near their destination Ernie spotted a hunched figure walking slowly and he pulled over to the kerbside.

He told Mark to open his door and take up the middle seat and called out to the person, "Hi, Gerry, just going home. Climb in and I'll give you a lift."

Gerry hesitated for a moment until he recognised Ernie's voice. "Oh, hi, Mr Newsham, I am a bit knackered, sure you've got room?"

Ernie nodded and Gerry started to climb into the vehicle until he recognised Mark. Noticing his wariness Ernie gave

Mark a light dig in his ribs. Mark responded by saying in a pleasant voice that even Ernie was surprised to hear, "Hi, Gerry, sorry to hear about your gran. How are things at the hospital?"

Taken slightly aback by his comment Gerry said nothing at first but once he was in the van he answered, "Oh, about the same, thanks for asking."

The journey to Gerry's flat was finished in complete silence until they arrived in the street next to the front door. Ernie spoke as Gerry got out, "If you need a hand with anything tomorrow, give me a shout and have a good night's sleep if you can."

As he drove away Ernie complimented Mark on his surprising comment to Gerry. "That was good, I need you two to get on together if he joins our team. Right, let's get back to the centre and unload. I'm intrigued to find out what the councillor has brought in for repair."

15

Percival Matthews picked up the phone in his lounge and answered irritably, "Hello, who is it?"

Sergeant Proudfoot cleared his throat before replying, "Clapfield South Police Station, Mr Matthews. Sergeant Proudfoot speaking."

Matthews quickly changed his manner. "Oh, good morning, Sergeant, what can I do for you?"

"Mr Matthews, one of our patrols was called to an incident at the rear of one of your shops last night because the gate was swinging backwards and forwards and making quite a racket. We took several calls about this and when officers attended they discovered that the gate had been forced open and the lock broken."

"Oh, for God's sake, how many more problems do I have to sort out?" Matthews shouted down the phone.

Proudfoot continued calmly, "If you let me finish, please. The officers made a quick check around the rear of your premises but found nothing else out of order, apart from one observation they made at the front door. There was a sign on the door stating, 'Shop closed due to complete power failure.'"

"That's correct. We did have a power failure yesterday afternoon. In fact, the same thing happened in three of my shops."

"Well, Mr Matthews, it's a possibility that someone read that sign and had visions of it affecting the alarm system you have on the premises. But as I said, there doesn't seem to have been any attempt at forced entry. However, you have a few upset neighbours who had a disturbed night's sleep because of the gate banging. Anyway, I'm sure you have other things to deal with, as have I. Good morning."

Matthews put the phone down. On the one hand he felt annoyed at the prospect of having the cost of fixing a stronger gate and frame, but on the other, nothing seemed to have been stolen.

Once again, his phone rang. This time it was Tony.

"Mr Matthews? The electrician reckons we will need a new mains fuse box as the old one is partly burnt out. It's at least a four-hour job and that's if he can get hold of a new box. It was lucky it didn't start a fire. What do I tell Gerry? Come in or stay at home?"

Matthews nearly blew a fuse of his own at the news that Gerry was not in work yet.

"What! It's gone nine o'clock. He should be there by now. As soon as he gets in send him round to help Harry measure up for a new gate and frame. I've just had the police on telling me some little bastards broke the old lock and damaged the frame. Reynolds fixed the lock so he can pay for a replacement. And tell me what time he gets in. He'll lose money there as well."

He put the phone down before Tony could give him any more bad news.

Tony found Gerry's number and rang him to pass on Matthews' instructions. He let the phone ring for nearly a minute and was about to put the phone down when he heard a slurred voice on the other end.

The constant ringing had finally penetrated Gerry's deep sleep but even then, it didn't register with him where he was lying. He was not in his own bed. The sound was nearby and too loud to allow him to ignore.

He struggled up from the settee and shambled over to the phone on the coffee table. He had fallen asleep in his day clothes and had even forgotten to close the curtains when he had come in after midnight. Even the living room light was still on.

Gerry hesitated for a moment before picking up the phone. What if it was the hospital with bad news? He shivered and his hand trembled as he picked up the receiver. "Hello?"

"Gerry? It's Tony. Look, Matthews has just phoned. You have to go and give Harry a hand to measure the gate and frame in the backyard of the shop."

Gerry was confused. "What are you talking about, Tony? I'm not going anywhere until I've had breakfast and phoned the hospital."

It was his manager's turn to feel confused. "Hospital? Gerry, have you been on the razzle all night? Get a move on, sunshine, Matthews is on the warpath and he's looking for scapegoats!"

"No, Tony, I'm not going anywhere right now."

He proceeded to give the barest of details of what happened after he had been dropped off the previous afternoon.

Tony let out a low whistle before speaking. "Well, Gerry, I know what my priorities would be in those circumstances. Ring the hospital to find out any news of your gran and get over there even if they say she's improving. I'll explain the situation to Matthews and tell him that is your number one priority until things improve. He phoned me just now and said something about a broken lock on the back gate that you fixed but that's his worry. Give me a ring at the shop if you need anything. Still no power, but I can get on with a few things anyway."

Gerry muttered his thanks and hung up. He rang the hospital and was told his gran was comfortable but the doctors had not made their rounds so it would be best to ring later to get more news. He put down the receiver and a sudden thought crossed his mind. His gran had said about only ringing Sally after the weekend, but where had she left the note with the number? He searched all the obvious places it could be, but found nothing. He pondered what to do next.

He finally decided to call into a nearby cafe for breakfast and then visit the library with the hope that one of Sally's colleagues would have a contact number for her.

***

Ernie had the feeling that it was suddenly Christmas or his birthday and he had won the lottery all at the same time.

This stroke of good fortune came about when he opened the box containing the malfunctioning video camcorder they had found in the storeroom of the shop. He knew Councillor Barnes to be a little lacking in the operating, or knowledge of repairing most mechanical items.

It took Ernie less than thirty seconds to release the jammed video compartment and discover that no damage had been done to the film itself. He took the film into the living room and placed it into the VCR player and pressed the play button. For the first minute the quality of the film was quite poor and Ernie stopped it playing and pressed the fast-forward function. He nearly fell off his chair when he recognised three of the four people on the film:

The two men, Councillor Barnes and Andrew Phillips the travel agent, and Sally from the library. It took him a further minute to put a name to the other woman and then he remembered her. It was Abigail, who worked for Percy Matthews.

For the first few minutes it all seemed perfectly innocent with drinks and general banter. Then the mood suddenly changed when Phillips made an attempt to grope Sally. She reacted by shouting and slapped him across the face and stormed out of the room. The camera was temporarily turned off but when it was switched back on again the remaining guests, minus Sally, were all in various stages of undress. They had also been joined by another woman, who Ernie guessed was about Sally's age but had a fuller figure and was slightly taller than her. He would have to contact the library assistant to get the name of the stranger. Sally would have no choice in withholding that information from him. He knew too much about her past and she would have to cooperate.

Ernie was a man of the world and guessed what was going to happen next and he was not disappointed. The film ran on for more than two hours and the final scenes had Ernie laughing and clapping his hands. It clearly showed the two men paying money to Abigail before she left the room.

This was the kind of evidence he needed to persuade the two men at least, that it would be unwise not to fully agree with his demands. He would not approach the woman for the time being. As for Sally, she must have had some idea of why the party had been arranged but had left before anything incriminating had begun so she could be ruled out of any blackmail pressures.

He needed to make copies of parts of the video but didn't have any blank tapes to hand, but knew where he could purchase some.

***

Gerry entered the library after eating his meal and was disappointed to find the person in charge was not someone known to him, so he enquired when he could speak to Sally's friend. The man was reluctant to give details and simply stated they were now one staff member short and the rota for the following week hadn't been drawn up, therefore Gerry would have to call in at another time to speak to someone else.

At this point he decided he would go straight to the hospital without even checking if there was any further news of his grandmother. On arrival at the ward he was invited to go into an office and speak to a Staff Nurse Lamb who was in charge.

"There is no real change in your grandmother's condition, Mr Reynolds. The doctor examined her this morning and he can give no clue as to when and if she will regain consciousness. I'm sorry but there's nothing else I can tell you. You are welcome to visit her at any time you feel the need if that is what you want to do."

He sat staring into the distance, trying to comprehend how much his life had been turned upside down since the beginning of the year. Was it all down to Matthews after he took over the shop from David Evans, or did that stuff in the suitcase really have a curse on it?

No! he decided. That was just nonsense put into his gran's head by the Stockwell woman and now she was gone and that should be the end of that rubbish. But why had Sally suddenly disappeared from his life just when he thought their relationship was beginning to be more meaningful to him? He had to find the telephone number his gran had written down and discover the truth from her as to why she had left.

Matthews was also to blame, not only for his hostile attitude but for allowing his skeleton keys to go missing. If the thief hadn't stolen those bloody things his gran wouldn't be in this hospital now. *I'm going to sort things out with that bastard once and for all*, he decided. As he stood up to leave, he heard the staff nurse say something to him.

"I'm sorry, I didn't catch what you said," he mumbled.

"I said, your tea is getting cold. I put it in front of you nearly ten minutes ago but you've been staring into space. Drink up and I'll take you to see your grandmother," she said in a gentle voice.

But Gerry suddenly felt very claustrophobic and needed to be away from the hospital smells and orderly chaos he felt was trying to envelop him. He took a step towards the door and said in a slightly strangled voice, "Sorry about the tea but I have things to do. I'll be back in later to see my gran. Bye."

Seeing the distressed look on his face she tried to persuade him to sit down but he left and almost ran out of the building in his haste to be clear of its surroundings. Gerry forced himself to walk at a more normal pace to give time to form a plan of action once he arrived at his place of work.

However, the shop was already in enough turmoil before he arrived. Abigail and Harry were in the middle of a heated exchange and Matthews was having difficulty in stopping them coming to blows.

"I've already told you, Miss High-and-Mighty, I locked up the outside storeroom to come in and find out why you were screaming your bloody head off, but you had already disappeared out of here. Then I put the key on the counter…"

Abigail shouted, red in the face and fists clenched tightly,

"Then why isn't the damn key here now, Mister Beer-Belly?"

Matthews had heard enough from his staff and banged his fist on the top of a nearby counter.

"That's enough from you two! I have more than my fair share of problems without both of you acting like kids arguing in a playground over some stupid nonsense. What happened to the container I left in the drawer of the old desk in the workshop? Which one of you sorted it out before you dumped it, Harry?"

Harry remained silent, wondering if he had walked into a trap set by the others. Then he remembered, "I didn't sort out any of those desks or cupboards, Mr Matthews. You told her to do it while I emptied the van so that we could dump the junk somewhere," and he gave a defiant stare in Abigail's direction. *Talk yourself out of that, bitch*, he mused to himself.

It was now the woman's turn to be on the defensive. She remembered the situation clearly and Harry, damn him, was correct. So, she tried deflecting the blame in another direction. "I searched all the drawers and cupboards and didn't find any containers holding any keys. You know me, Mr Matthews, I'm very meticulous in my work. It could only have been the kid, Gerry, who took those keys or got rid of them."

They were all too busy hurling accusations around, trying to lay the blame on each other, to notice that a fourth person had entered the shop from the yard. On arriving, Gerry found the front door still locked with the closed sign and reason for the closure still on the door, so he gambled that the gate at the rear might be open and was proved correct. His anger had only subsided slightly since leaving the hospital but when he spoke in quiet, measured tones the other three turned with guilt showing on their faces.

"If you remember, Abigail, I was not here the week you three refurbished the work area around the back and wasn't even told it was going to happen. In fact, Mr Matthews, you made sure I was out of the way by sending me to Tony's shop for the whole week." He paused to let his words sink in and then continued, "As a matter of fact, the container with the spare keys was in the bottom drawer of the desk, along with my toolbox and a set of skeleton keys that Mr Evans allowed me to keep. When I returned here after the work was completed I found my toolbox had been dumped in the bins outside, but there was no sign of the container with the spare keys or my skeleton keys. So whoever dumped part of my personal belongings in the bin couldn't have failed to find the other items."

The shop owner tried to change the subject back to Gerry.

"So your tools were dumped in the bin; you got them back, didn't you? What I want to know is where you've been all morning. I generously gave you the rest of yesterday afternoon off as part of your holiday entitlement and now you wander in here two hours later than everyone else and start accusing one of us of stealing some keys of yours."

Gerry felt the anger start to build up once more and there was no mistaking the menace in his voice.

"Yes, Mr Matthews! I did get my tools back but whoever took those skeleton keys did one of two things. First they were thrown away or, whichever one of you took them, passed them on to someone else. And that 'someone else' used them to break into my grandmother's flat and stole all her precious and personal belongings. I got home from Tony's shop and found my gran in a distressed state and shortly afterwards she collapsed and I had to call an ambulance to get her to hospital. You want to know where I've been, Mr Matthews? Well, I was with my grandmother from three o'clock until after midnight and again this morning. She's lying in a coma and the doctors don't know if she will recover!"

He practically screamed out the last few words and kicked the door of one of the display units with such force it came off its hinges. They all stared at him in stunned silence but again it was Matthews who was the first to recover his composure.

"How does that have anything to do with any of us? You can't come in here, throw accusations around and damage my property. I've a good mind to sack you right now!"

Gerry turned to face his boss. Only his need to fully explain prevented him from punching Matthews right there and then. Instead he took a deep breath before speaking, "This is what it's got to do with at least one of you three. When I got back home I told you I found my grandmother in a distressed state kneeling on her bedroom floor with an empty suitcase which had contained her personal treasures open on the bed. Next to the case, on the bed, were my missing keys. Only you three knew my gran would be at the funeral and that I was in Tony's shop yesterday. The only lucky thing about this incident is that she never came home while the burglar was still there. So if I find out which one of you is involved you'd better find a safe hole to crawl into."

Matthews was silent for several seconds before asking, "So we can expect a visit from the police regarding these allegations, can we?"

This was the one question that Gerry had not anticipated and his apparent reluctance to answer was seized on by his boss.

"Assuming, of course, the police have been contacted. And I am guessing they have not! So, you think you can come in here and accuse one or all of us of stealing those keys, do you?"

Gerry tried to deflect the attack, but he realised he was on dodgy ground. "It's my grandmother's flat that was burgled, also it was her possessions that were stolen so it would be her decision to call the police. Right now she's not in a fit state to decide."

Matthews shook his head and knew he had found a flaw in Gerry's defence. "No, no. You could still report a crime has been committed. The police would investigate and see if it was worth pursuing. No, Gerry, you're trying to cover your own tracks and want to deflect from the truth by using those missing keys to drag innocent people into your affairs. I've had enough of your lies, poor timekeeping and below average commitment to working for me. I knew you were not worth employing from the moment I first saw you. You're fired. Harry, throw him out!"

Before he could react Gerry was grabbed from behind by the larger man and forced towards the front door which Abigail had gleefully unlocked. He tried to resist but he was no match for Harry and he was propelled into the street where he landed on his side. He tried to roll over and rise but Harry put a large boot on his chest.

"Nobody accuses me of anything and gets away with it. Go on, try and get up and I'll kick six bells out of you, kid!"

"You'll do nothing of the kind, Harry! Let him go or I'll dish out some of your own medicine to you!"

Harry turned around to see who had challenged him and came face to face with Ernie Newsham who was accompanied by Mark. Harry only hesitated for a split second before retreating into the shop, locking the door behind him.

Mark offered Gerry his hand and it was accepted but Gerry was visibly shaken by the ordeal and Ernie took note of his demeanour before speaking in a friendly voice, "Let's find somewhere quieter to talk and you can give me your version of what happened."

They found a cafe further down the street with only a couple of other clients inside. Ernie ordered two teas and cakes and sent Mark on an errand to enable Gerry to talk more openly to him. They sat in a corner, well out of earshot of others and after a couple of minutes Ernie said, "Whatever that incident with Harry was about I'm guessing it was done on orders from Matthews. Am I right?"

Gerry merely nodded but said nothing so Ernie continued, "Look, Gerry, we can get through this a lot quicker if you tell me the details, rather than me asking you questions and you nodding or shaking your head in response."

Gerry remained silent for a full minute, then he sighed deeply and told Ernie the events of the morning. When he had finished Ernie asked him a couple of questions.

"Do you have any idea how many items were in the case and could you describe any of them?"

"Judging by the number of cloth bags I saw on another occasion there must have been at least two dozen items, but I was only shown two or three at most."

Ernie was thoughtful for a moment, digesting the facts so he asked another question, "Did your gran tell you what was in some of the other bags but didn't show you?"

Before replying Gerry looked over both shoulders to make sure nobody else could hear when he gave his answer, "It's too long a story as to how they came into the family's possession but she said there were uncut diamonds, maybe a few gold nuggets, most of my mum's jewellery and some tribal relics her relative had picked up in South Africa."

It was Ernie's turn to sit in stunned silence and when he was about to comment Mark came back into the cafe. Ernie excused himself for a moment and spoke to his assistant and gave him some money before returning to the table.

"Sorry about that, Mark is getting himself a drink and cake but he won't join us as I told him you were talking personal issues and didn't want anyone else to hear. As for the things you've just told me, there are no precise details of the items to give the police and your gran's reluctance to report a crime wouldn't help matters. In the circumstances I don't think they would have much to get their teeth into, but tell me, why doesn't your grandmother want the police involved? After all, some of those items would have been passed down to you."

Gerry looked around before answering in a hushed voice, "She believes there was a curse put on the tribal items and that curse has contaminated the rest of the things that were alongside them in the case."

A faint smile crossed Ernie's face and he only just managed to hold back the laughter and Gerry had noted the reaction and wouldn't say any more.

"Come on, Gerry, surely you don't believe that kind of nonsense."

A thought suddenly crossed Gerry's mind and he spoke without pausing to think what reaction it might have on his future. "You knew Mrs Stockwell because gran said you were in the group or circle she and her husband ran. So you might have the answer to a question that has been bothering me for years. Gran said my dad and mum took one of those tribal items to have it valued by some bloke who collected those kind of things. He kept the item for a while and then called my parents with an offer. They accepted his price and went to collect the money." He continued, "On the way back they were involved in a car accident and both my parents were killed. I've never been told the full story but Gran believed they were killed because they sold that item and it was the curse that killed them. I understand you were still in the police at that time; do you know what really happened?"

Gerry couldn't understand why Ernie had turned a deathly white and seemed to be having trouble with his breathing.

"Are you okay, Ernie? Have I said something wrong?"

Ernie shook a hand in denial and slowly the colour came back to his features and his breathing became more regular. However, it was at least another minute before he was ready to speak.

"Sorry about that, Gerry, I wasn't expecting such a question like that from you. Listen, I probably can help you with some limited information on that matter but this is neither the time nor place to talk about it. So if it's okay with you I can come round, say Sunday evening, to your flat and tell you all I know about the accident. I could also have a brief look around to see if there are any clues regarding the burglary."

Immediately after finishing talking, Ernie stood up so Gerry had little choice but to accept the offer and they walked over to Mark who was examining the contents of a bag he had brought into the cafe.

Ernie turned his attention to Mark and asked, "Did he have enough of those items I ordered?"

Mark nodded and stood up ready to leave but Ernie held up a hand.

"Hold on, Mark, slight change of plans. I'm going to be busy tomorrow night so you will have to do the security patrol yourself, but I'll explain more later. I guess you will be visiting the hospital later, Gerry. In the meantime, let me know if there's anything you need help with."

They parted company outside the cafe and Gerry returned to the flat before his visit to see his gran. When he was out of hearing range Ernie turned to Mark.

"I should be in a position to make Gerry an offer he can't refuse after my meeting with him on Sunday and we'll have our new recruit. Meanwhile, it doesn't look as if Matthews has discovered his loss, thanks to Harry leaving the key in the storeroom door," and both men chuckled as they walked back to the leisure centre.

Gerry made himself a snack and had another look to try and find the note with Sally's phone number but without success. By the time he arrived at the hospital it was after three o'clock and he was relieved to note there was a different staff nurse on duty. She told him there had been no change in his gran's condition and the next doctor's visit would take place the following morning.

He sat with his gran for more than an hour, holding her hand throughout but getting no response from his periodic squeezes of her hand. A feeling of depression started to come over him and feeling a little guilty he left and went back home.

He made a second search of the flat in an attempt to find Sally's number but instead of that he found the box with the brooch that Stella Stockwell had given him and recalled the words that accompanied the gift. 'If you cannot wear the gift I want you to give it to your first love'. He immediately thought of Sally. Why had he taken so long to accept the obvious?

But why had she left so suddenly without even a hint of her plans? Did she truly have the same feelings towards him as he was experiencing now? What would he do if she just laughed off his advances?

The phone rang at least three times before it registered in his mind and he dashed into the living room to pick up the receiver. Then he hesitated; what if it was the hospital with bad news? He stood motionless for several seconds until a female voice on the phone penetrated his thoughts. "Hello? Hello? Is anyone there?"

Gerry heaved a sigh of relief. "Hi, Sally, I'm glad it's you, I couldn't find your new number anywhere."

"Oh? Isn't your gran there? I gave her all the details when I phoned last time. I know she wrote them down because I asked her to repeat what I had said. Is anything wrong there? You sound a bit, well, strange!"

He cleared his throat and told her all the news, from Mrs Stockwell's death, his gran's collapse and him being fired by Matthews. The only thing he left out was the theft of the contents from the suitcase. It was Sally's turn to be stunned into silence for the moment. When she spoke once more, there was a husky tone to her voice, "God, Gerry, I feel terrible! When you needed me most I wasn't there for you. I'm so sorry."

At these words he felt a great flood of emotion come over him. *She really does care!* He cleared his throat once more and asked, "Are you okay, Sal? Gran said something about your sister being pregnant and you had to leave to help her. I didn't realise you even had a sister."

The silence on the other end of the line bothered Gerry. Was there something Sally wasn't telling him? He asked if she was still on the phone and moments later a nervous laugh answered him. "Yes, everything's okay here. Listen, it's better I tell you face to face about what's going on but I'm a bit under the weather right now and I can't come down to see you for a couple of weeks and I'm still settling in up here. Maybe when I'm sorted out you could come up for a visit?"

"I would like to do that but right now I have to be near the hospital in case things change with Gran. Also, I'm seeing Ernie tomorrow evening on a different matter although I've got a feeling he might offer me a job at the leisure centre."

"Remember what I said about Ernie, he can be very persuasive, and he can talk you into doing things you could regret later.

"Have a think about this, Gerry. If you moved up here, you could find something to your liking and I'm not just talking about work." The last phrase was said with a distinct air of suggestiveness surrounding the words.

Gerry took the hint. "Getting the best of both worlds, I like the sound of that."

Then her tone became a little more serious. "Okay, Gerry, I have things to do now so I'll give you my address and phone number if you have a pen and paper handy."

He asked her to wait a moment and when he was ready she gave him the details. They spoke for a couple of minutes longer before she hung up. Gerry left the pad with the details on the table by the phone.

Sally sat back on the settee, putting both hands in a cupped motion over the bump that was starting to become more prominent. She knew Gerry was the father but would he accept that as the truth.

Her morning sickness was starting to ease but she didn't feel confident in travelling far at present and besides, there was the first scan due soon and she was feeling slightly nervous about what it would show. Was the doctor right in his diagnosis? Could it really be twins?

16

There was no change in his grandmother's condition, nevertheless Gerry sat by her bed for more than an hour, but his thoughts were focused on his conversation with Sally the night before.

It wasn't so much what she had said, more about what had not been mentioned that exercised Gerry's thoughts. Sally's colleague at the library had spoken about a visit to the doctor's and almost immediately after, Sally moves to another town miles away without telling anyone the reason. Also, he could not recall her ever mentioning a sister, or for that matter, any other family member.

Before leaving the ward, he asked the nurse in charge, more in hope than anything else, if there were any signs of improvement in his gran's condition. She checked the notes and shook her head but did say the doctor would be doing his rounds later that day and if there was any sign of change, he would be informed.

Ernie arrived a lot earlier than he had expected, and Gerry had only just finished eating when the doorbell rang.

Showing his guest into the living room, it had been his intention to formulate a clear set of questions to ask Ernie about the accident but his mind was not fully on that subject, even though he had wanted answers for many years and this seemed to be the perfect opportunity. Right now, he wouldn't have minded a small postponement for a short while.

However, Ernie had gone through all the possible questions, and a few others besides, that Gerry was likely to ask, and he was determined to control their meeting.

Ernie began by asking about his grandmother and repeated his offer to assist and advise Gerry in any way required. He was confident that the lad hadn't given sufficient thought to all eventualities. Then when that time dawned, he would close the trap very smoothly on Gerry without him realising what he had stepped into until it was too late.

"Okay, Gerry, you asked me about the accident that killed your parents. That was a nasty business all round and the reason it caught me out yesterday in the cafe is very simple really. I was the second officer in that patrol car that was involved in the accident."

He had anticipated Gerry's reaction and he was correct down to the last detail. He sat in stunned silence and was unable to form a coherent response so Ernie continued with the biased view that made him look like the prime victim of the crash.

"We were on an emergency call and my oppo was driving and he went through a set of red and amber lights and hit the other car that must have also gone through a red light. Both cars overturned and I was flung out into someone's front garden. The medics thought I had broken my back, although with the injuries I suffered it wouldn't have been much worse if I had done. Anyway, as a result I was not considered to be fit enough to carry on in the force, despite me going through hell to get fit again. I have to say a lot of credit has to go to Mrs Stockwell who proved the doubters wrong by using her special skills to heal me. I ended up with a small police pension and had to take on the job of running the centre to make ends meet. And I lost a good mate in Joe. He got away with a few cracked ribs and other cuts and bruises but after the crash his wife left him and emigrated to the States. What we didn't know about Joe was that he had taken to drinking and that possibly slowed up his reactions and maybe he could have avoided hitting the other car. Sad thing, after his wife left him he got flung out of the force because of his drinking and within six months he committed suicide. I lost a good mate through that accident."

"And I lost my parents." Gerry spoke with a hint of bitterness.

Ernie gave some acknowledgement to his comment but continued, "Yes, that was bad luck, but I believe your grandmother was paid a compensation package, presumably to look after you."

Gerry tried again to switch the tone of the conversation back to his parents. "But if your mate had been drinking, he should have been prosecuted for dangerous driving or drink driving. Didn't that happen?"

Ernie sat slightly forward and looked down at his hands before replying. "I spent several months in hospital and apart from a statement I made over a month later I wasn't involved in the enquiry. Somebody even suggested that I was driving the patrol car but Joe admitted it was him. You see, Gerry, I also suffered some memory lapses for a while, and they looked on me as an unreliable witness. I did hear from one source that they found some traces of alcohol in your father's blood but he wasn't over the limit but that could have impaired his reactions. I'm not…"

Before he could continue there was a loud crash in another room and the sound of breaking glass. Both jumped up and went to check each room. Gerry found the cause in his grandmother's bedroom. There was an old fireplace with a mantelpiece surround in the bedroom and a long oblong mirror hanging above the fireplace had fallen and broken into several slivers of glass. One of those jagged pieces was sticking into the pillows on the bed. Another piece of glass had knocked the phone off the bedside cabinet. Gerry picked up the phone and placed it back in its proper place and noticed the time flashing on the handset. It was just after 7.42 p.m.

Ernie joined him and told him to find any old newspapers to wrap the glass in and then place the remains of the mirror frame along with the glass in the rubbish bin outside.

Ernie wanted to have a brief look around to see if there were any clues left behind by the burglar. Gerry explained where he had found the empty suitcase, along with the cloth bag and his keys which Ernie wanted to see. He noticed the label on the cloth bag and asked if all the items were in separate bags and marked in a similar fashion. Gerry confirmed these facts.

"I remember you telling me before that there were quite a few tribal relics and uncut diamonds and gold nuggets amongst the stolen items. They won't be easy to get rid of in a hurry unless the thief has a ready-made source to dispose of them.

"I'm guessing it's a local thief who wouldn't have the know-how what to do with them so they could still be around. I'll make some discreet enquiries. Remind me, Gerry, why didn't your grandmother want the police involved?"

"According to family sources there was supposed to be a curse on the relics and anyone who handled them or sold them on would come to a sticky end. Gran said that Mum and Dad were on their way back from selling one of the smaller relics to a specialist dealer somewhere out of town. They were on their way home after stopping for a meal to celebrate."

Ernie gave a little smile. "Sheer coincidence and a small bit of bad luck more likely. Let's go back into the living room and we can talk a bit about you working with me and Mark."

They had only been sitting down for a couple of minutes when the phone rang. Gerry said he would take the call in his gran's bedroom. After all, if it was Sally calling again he certainly didn't want Ernie eavesdropping in on his conversation. But the call was from the hospital to tell him the doctor would like to speak to him in the morning at about ten o'clock. Gerry agreed to attend and returned to the living room. However, in the time he was absent from the room Ernie had noticed Sally's name on the notepad along with her address so he hastily copied them onto another page he had torn from the notepad before Gerry returned.

"Why don't you come to the centre tomorrow morning and we can discuss in more detail what the job offers and go over any paperwork to make it official with the council. I've got some work to do at home in the afternoon so you and Mark can have a chat and get to know each other a bit better."

Gerry held up a hand. "Sorry, Ernie, that depends entirely on what happens at the hospital. Something has changed in my gran's condition and I will be seeing the doctor in the morning."

Ernie held back the irritation he was feeling at this potential spoiler to his plans so he came up with the following offer. "How about I drop you off at the hospital for your appointment, wait for you outside and then take you back to the centre? You can have what you want to eat off the menu at my expense. Deal?"

Gerry felt trapped. He didn't fancy the idea of spending the whole afternoon in Mark's company but he felt he had no option but to agree to Ernie's offer. He grudgingly nodded his acceptance.

They both stood up, shook hands and Ernie left after agreeing a time for him to collect Gerry in the morning.

***

The doctor was waiting for Gerry in the ward office and it was apparent from the serious look on his face that he was the bearer of bad news. He invited Gerry to sit down before he explained the situation.

"Mr Reynolds, yesterday evening we believe your grandmother suffered a stroke and her prospects of recovery are not promising. It happened not long after she was checked at just after 7.30 p.m. and I was called to attend at 7.50 p.m."

Gerry's features must have betrayed his thought at the mention of the timing and all he could visualise was the time on the phone in the bedroom flashing at 7.42 p.m.

"Mr Reynolds, did you hear what I said?" the doctor asked again.

Gerry came out of his trance-like state. "Sorry, no, Doctor, would you tell me again please?"

"I said, your grandmother is on an intravenous drip and a breathing ventilator and she is comfortable at present."

Gerry swallowed and asked, surprisingly to himself, in a calm voice, "You said her prospects are not good. In that case, how long has she got left?"

The doctor had wanted to avoid going down that road but as the young man seemed ready to receive the bad news he continued, "It used to be that if a stroke victim could last the first ten days there was a reasonable chance of a limited recovery. However, as your grandmother was already in a coma, I cannot see that rule applying. Putting it bluntly, she could go tomorrow or, she could last longer than that. There is no way of telling. We will make things as comfortable as possible for her but that's all I can promise. If you have no further questions, I must continue my ward rounds."

Gerry stood up to leave but the nurse attending the meeting put a hand on his arm. "You can still go and see your gran. Would you like a cup of tea? You look in need of one."

He gave her a weak smile and said in a husky voice, "I'll go and see her briefly but I have someone outside waiting to give me a lift. Maybe next time I'll have the tea," and he followed her to his gran's bed.

Five minutes later, after a brief visit to the toilet to compose himself, he was sitting in Ernie's car being driven to the centre. Ernie asked how the meeting went but he gave only the briefest details. He didn't want to chance breaking down in front of anybody. He was a man. Men didn't cry in public; well, at least he wasn't going to!

But Ernie read the signs. However, it didn't suit him to make alternative arrangements that afternoon. He needed the answer to one question and Gerry had unwittingly provided the only source to give him that answer.

As the two men had already met there was no need for formal introductions so he reminded Mark on what to show Gerry and to take him to the cafe when he decided he wanted to eat. Gerry said he wasn't hungry and wanted to get on with the reason for his visit. Once he was sure Mark and Gerry were getting on with things, Ernie left them to carry on. He headed to his agreed collection point to meet another person.

The round trip would take at least six hours so speed was of importance to them.

Mark took Gerry into the fringes of the gymnasium and gave a brief description of what would be required. They were about to leave when a female voice called out, "Gerry, isn't it? Can I have a word?"

A tall, very fit woman dressed in her workout kit walked over to them. Gerry recognised her as WPC Bradley, his ex-tutor's wife.

"Are you joining up here or just looking around, Gerry. Lee told me what happened at the college. That sounds typically like the kind of stroke Matthews would pull."

Gerry nodded. "Yeah, and he gave me the sack on Saturday, so I'm starting work here. Mark is showing me round. But what are you doing here? You look plenty fit enough to me."

She smiled. "Steady on, young man, I'm happily married as you know. Actually, I've got my annual medical and fitness test coming up so I'm putting in extra work just to make sure I pass. Sorry I can't stop to chat, I'm on duty in an hour. Bye." And she walked back to the weights bench.

After she had gone and the two had walked to the other side of the room, Mark said, "You jammy sod! I've been trying to chat that one up since she started coming here last week and now, I find out she's married."

"And she's a copper as well!" Gerry told him.

And the look of horror on Mark's face told him everything. He was no friend of the police.

"Bloody hell! Ernie told me some coppers come in here, but I didn't put her as one of them. Thanks, mate, you've saved my bacon."

They bypassed the cafe and went into the pool area after walking through a door that had a sign reading: 'Pool closed. No lifeguard in attendance'.

"I don't feel happy in this place, it gives me the creeps," Mark said as they entered. Gerry immediately noticed that his colleague kept a safe distance from the edge of the pool.

"Let me guess, you can't swim," he said. "Didn't you learn at school or your parents take you swimming when you were a kid?"

Mark turned to face him. "My parents take me swimming? Do me a favour, mate! They took me nowhere and taught me nowt! In fact, my dad buggered off before I was ten years old and then my mum shacked up with some other louse. No! None of them bastards did anything for me or my brother, Kev. If it wasn't for him, I'd have more than likely ended up in some kids' home. You were lucky having parents that did anything for you. Me? Absolutely sod all."

The bitterness was quite evident in his voice as he spoke.

In his angry state Mark hadn't noticed he had strayed in his direction and was walking at an angle towards the pool. He also hadn't seen the hosepipe lying across his path.

Too late he realised the danger and before he could stop his forward momentum his foot caught on the pipe and he toppled towards the edge. Gerry tried to grab his arm but missed and Mark fell headlong into the pool with a frantic yell.

Frantically Gerry looked around for something he could pass to his colleague to grab hold of but Mark's wild thrashing was taking him further away from the side of the pool.

There was only one other course of action to take. Removing his shoes and jacket he jumped into the pool to try and aid Mark. He was waving his arms in all directions thus making it difficult for Gerry to get near him and he ignored his shouts to calm down. Mark briefly went under the surface of the water and when he came back up again his shouts and thrashing gained even more urgency.

Gerry managed to get behind Mark and put his hands under his armpits and slowly pull him backwards while kicking his feet to propel them to the side of the pool. But Mark was heavier and stronger, Gerry had not swum for many months and he soon began to tire.

There was the sound of two people jumping into the pool and seconds later the lifeguard took hold of Mark and guided him to the ladder at the end of the pool. The other person took up the same position that Gerry had adopted and started swimming backwards in the same direction with him relaxing against the chest of his rescuer.

By the time they reached the ladder the lifeguard had Mark standing on one of the lower rungs but supporting himself by gripping tightly to the rest of the frame.

Gerry took hold of the ladder frame and turned around to thank his rescuer who was pulling herself out of the pool. It was Karen Bradley and her top and shorts clung to her body, showing off all her contours in a very provocative manner.

She offered Gerry her hand which he accepted and with very little effort, pulled him out of the water. He stood staring at the woman standing in her wet clothes for several seconds and she gave a small laugh.

"Well, at least you've made a quick recovery. Come over here and sit down for a few minutes." She gently, but firmly, led him to a bench by the wall of the pool. Seconds later they were joined by Mark and the lifeguard who was less than pleased.

"Can you give a good reason why you two came in here when the sign on the door said the pool was closed and I wasn't around?"

Mark was still catching his breath, so Gerry spoke, "This is my first day at work here and Ernie told Mark to show me round the centre. I can swim but haven't been near a pool in a couple of years and I'm way out of practice. Mark was telling me he never learnt to swim but he tripped over the hosepipe on the other side and fell in."

The lifeguard softened his tone only slightly. "Well, if you're going to work around here I'm going to recommend to Ernie that you get some practice in pretty sharpish and Mark has some lessons. Wait here and I'll get you all some gowns and towels from the reception desk."

He left the three others by the pool.

By now Mark had recovered sufficiently to take an interest in the woman sitting next to Gerry. She, in turn, didn't appreciate his ogling of her and told him in no uncertain terms.

"Put your eyeballs back in their sockets, sunshine, didn't your parents tell you it's rude to stare?"

Mark's eyes flashed and he retorted, "My parents abandoned me when I were ten. They never taught me bugger all."

WPC Bradley had encountered numerous young people who told a similar story and she knew from experience it would be counterproductive to pursue the matter further, so she spoke in a softer voice, "Okay, forget my last comment. Once the lifeguard returns with robes and towels go and get changed out of those wet clothes. Then get a hot, sweet drink inside yourselves. This little incident might have shaken you up more than you realise. It's Mark, isn't it? If you want to talk to anyone about your situation I can put you in touch with someone who might be able to help."

Mark looked back at her and sneered, "No thanks, I've had my fill of do-gooders and bloody therapists. Just a waste of time and space if you ask me."

He deliberately turned to look in the opposite direction. She looked at Gerry, shrugged her shoulders and shook her head before getting to her feet, then walked to meet the lifeguard who had just entered the pool area carrying towels and robes.

The two talked briefly before she took her items and headed for the changing room.

Craig, the lifeguard, gave the remaining items to Mark and Gerry.

"Go and get out of those wet clothes and bring them back to me and I'll get them put into the drying room. When Ernie comes back I'm going to talk to him about your swimming limitations, especially you, Mark."

The two did as instructed and returned with their wet clothes and gave them to Craig who told them to come back in about an hour to collect them. They had hardly spoken to each other since the incident and Gerry was about to speak but Mark beat him to it.

"I suppose I should say thanks for trying to rescue me back there. But if that Craig thinks he'll get me back in that pool again he can go and take a running jump. And if I ever meet up with my old man, I'll push him under and hold him there until he croaks."

Gerry laughed, "You could only do that if you learn to swim properly and hope he hasn't learnt in the meantime. Assuming of course, he's still alive and your paths cross."

"Well, I'm not holding my breath and if he don't come near here, all well and good. Otherwise…"

***

Ernie's companion didn't make the appointed meeting place so he made the journey by himself. It would mean a change of plans because as well as the visit he would have to check the immediate area to make sure future visits would prove beneficial.

Sally had been surprised when he turned up at her door and she refused to let him in until he disclosed how he discovered her whereabouts. However, he made it quite clear that Gerry should not find out about his visit and she reluctantly agreed. He then explained the reason for his visit.

"I have come across a homemade video in which you played a minor role along with four other people. Now I know you made an early exit after slapping one of the other participants across his face. I recognise three of those people but the woman who took your place I've not seen before. Who is she?"

Sally gave a little smile; she now knew the reason for his visit.

"You're too late, Ernie, she died about three years ago from a drugs overdose, so you will have to cross her off your list of blackmail targets."

Ernie coloured slightly at the answer she had given but he was not fully convinced yet. He repeated his question with a hint of menace. "The name, Sally. I need her name."

"Barbara Hutchinson. Check it out with your colleagues. They found her body in the fishermen's shack next to the jetty. She used the money she got from that little show to buy the drugs. I can't prove it but I'm convinced that bitch Abigail was her supplier."

"Are you still in touch with her?" Ernie asked.

"No way! She offered me some stuff once but I told her where she could shove it. I've seen what that does to kids and don't want any part of it. That's the reason I quit university."

Ernie's thoughts raced ahead; so now he had another hook into Abigail. As Sally turned to reach for a tissue from a box to blow her nose he noticed something and his question caught her completely off guard.

"When's the baby due, Sally?"

The look on her face confirmed his suspicions and no answer was necessary but she said quietly, "I'll tell the father the answer to that when I see him."

Ernie stood up and as he turned to leave something caught his attention for a brief moment. The flames in the gas fire were not the usual colour he would have expected. All he said as he left was enough to earn silence about his visit.

"I don't think either of us has cause to mention my visit here today. Agreed?"

Sally nodded and closed the door behind him. She had known Ernie for many years and things were never straightforward, especially if you had to agree with the man. Gerry would have to be very careful if and when he dealt with Ernie.

She suddenly felt very tired and wiped her nose once more, hoping she wasn't catching a cold. Even though it was not yet eight o'clock she decided to have an early night and went to bed.

17

Mark and Gerry had no alternative but to sit around waiting for their clothes to dry. During that time as they spoke it became apparent to each of them they had more in common than either had realised.

Due to differing circumstances neither had received proper parental guidance in their informative years.

Gerry's parents had a more stable relationship and he wanted for nothing, except perhaps more love and affection. They were both ambitious business people and that was their number one focus in life. Even from his earliest years he could remember being left with his grandmother while Mum and Dad were away on business trips or holidaying with other couples.

He could only ever remember going on holiday abroad with them on one occasion. They went to Spain for ten days and he was ill most of the time because the local food didn't agree with him. His parents' social life was hampered to such an extent his father wanted to come back after only four days but they couldn't arrange a flight. When they did arrive back home he recalled his mother saying to her mum, they wouldn't take Gerald on holiday abroad again. Holidays after that were confined to day trips to the seaside.

Gerry was a bright lad at school and he was keen to learn. However, it was only due to his grandmother's persistence that he continued his studies after his parents' accident. Gaining enough qualifications to be considered for a place at university, he insisted instead on finding a job in order to support his grandmother as payback for all the sacrifices she had made in raising him.

Mark's parents rarely seemed to have had enough spare money to visit any of the seaside resorts or local attractions. Yet his mother would spend most evenings playing bingo while his father frequented the local pubs on a regular basis. His father could never hold down a proper job so supplemented his income by breaking into local shops and houses.

The local police began to take an interest in his activities and he decided to move out of the area, thus leaving his family to fend for themselves. Not that his wife and two sons missed having him around; he would often return home from his escapades in a drunken state and the boys learnt at an early age to stay well out of his way on those occasions.

While both parents were away the childminding duties for Mark were left in the hands of his older brother, Kevin, who sometimes abandoned his younger brother at home while he followed his own criminal pursuits with the gang he had joined.

Mark was also a quick learner and in his early years wanted to become a policeman. This ambition was thwarted by his minor criminal involvement with some of Kevin's friends. He was caught shoplifting on a number of occasions and appeared in the juvenile court. Due to his brother's influence he began to see the police as his enemy, preventing him from obtaining things his school friends had received by legitimate means. After his court appearance he resorted to starting small fires in his school which eventually led to his expulsion.

He would have been in more serious trouble until some of Kevin's gang friends persuaded a witness not to give evidence against him in an assault charge. Finally, Kevin decided it would be better if Mark was sent far away from the influence of his friends to try and start afresh.

"Gerry. Look, I'm not very good at expressing my thoughts but nobody else I know would have jumped in to save my skin so thanks, mate, I owe you one."

Slightly embarrassed, Gerry smiled and shrugged his shoulders. "Next time there may not be anyone around to save you so why don't you take up Craig's advice and learn to swim? Places like this usually run classes for beginners of all ages."

Mark shook his head. "That's not for me. I'd be too embarrassed learning with a bunch of kids or old fogeys."

This made Gerry laugh for the first time in ages. "If you did fall in again and there was nobody there to rescue you, embarrassment would be the least of your worries; you'd be dead!"

Once they had retrieved their dry clothes Mark resumed his guided tour of the centre. He finished by taking Gerry to the locked room above Ernie's office. Before he unlocked the door, he said, "Don't tell Ernie I showed you what's in here; he'd have my guts for garters if he knew."

He unlocked the door and switched on the light which shone feebly and didn't do much to lessen the gloom. More than half the floor area was covered in boxes of varying sizes, some partially open.

Gerry gasped. He couldn't be certain, but he was sure he recognised some of the items in the open boxes. He looked around and then asked, "Where does this lot come from? This looks more like a shop's storeroom than one for a centre like this. Come on, Mark, cough up, where's it from?"

Mark gave a triumphant laugh. "This is what me and Ernie pick up some nights when we go on our security patrol, either from punters who won't pay up or from those idiots who think they're too clever."

It didn't take long for Gerry to realise the bigger picture.

"You mean the two of you nicked it? That's it. I don't want anything to do with this kind of work. I'm leaving right now, and Ernie can keep his flaming job."

He turned to leave the room, but the doorway was blocked by a familiar figure. Ernie stood still, saying nothing, but the expression on his face spoke volumes. Gerry tried to push past but he was no match for the ex-policeman.

"Not so fast, young Gerry. I was hoping to hold this conversation at a later date but it looks like there's no time like the present. Follow me downstairs to my office and don't be stupid enough to try and run. Mark, lock up for now and we'll speak later."

There was hidden menace in his last remark.

He unlocked the door to his office and told Gerry to go in first and he then closed the door behind them, inviting Gerry to sit down in front of the desk.

Ernie took the seat behind the desk and appraised the young man sitting opposite. He leant back in his chair, saying nothing, knowing from past interview techniques he had used in the police that his guest would be feeling uncomfortable and would eventually break the silence. It didn't take more than a couple of minutes before Gerry spoke. "Ernie, I don't want anything to do with what I've just seen upstairs, and I can forget what Mark told me. That's your business and I want nothing at all to do with it. I'm not the person you need here and won't get involved in anything illegal."

He started to rise from his chair, but Ernie barked out an order. "Sit down! You're not going anywhere until I say so. And for your information, Gerry, you are already well and truly involved in my business, so keep your mouth shut and listen! Remember when I came into your shop before Christmas and you were talking with Colin Evans? I bought in a set of van keys for you to copy and those keys weren't mine. They belonged to a van full of stock that was stolen from Matthews' backyard and later found burnt out. You performed a similar service for me a few months earlier. Yes, David Evans gave the go-ahead then and those were my own keys. I was just testing the water to see if your boss would cooperate. He never thought to challenge me and neither did you. Don't forget, Gerry, ignorance is no defence in the eyes of the law."

Gerry stared back at him, not able to quite comprehend what he had just heard. Then he remembered the words of caution Sally had mentioned, and Colin's reaction after he had sorted out the van keys for Ernie. Added to those remarks was the double-edged advice about his future given to him by Stella Stockwell.

He asked nervously, "What plans do you have for me then? Mark may be the type to pinch anything that's not nailed down, but I've never stolen anything in my life. Please, Ernie, you know I've got enough problems of my own right now without getting involved in this kind of work."

Ernie's voice lost a little of its menace, but it was nowhere near as friendly as the tone Gerry was used to. "I know you've got troubles, Gerry, and I can help you sort most of them out. But everything has its price. Look, you don't have a job and the type of things you're good at Matthews has got covered in this town and sly bastard that he is, he has a fair bit of influence within the business community. Do you have any savings? What about your rent, and God forbid, if something happens to your gran, do you have enough money to cover the funeral expenses? I can help you with some of those things but if you don't join me and Mark you'll be in debt up to your ears in no time."

He let his comments sink in before continuing, "I'm not asking you to go round beating up people or breaking into their houses. I leave that kind of thing to people like Graham Bishop. What we do is go to business people and offer them a security service for a regular fee. Some see the sense in what we offer, others need, let's say, a little persuasion to understand the situation. I choose my clients carefully and only select those who can afford my services. The small traders and those who are struggling we leave alone. They're not worth the hassle anyway."

Gerry thought carefully before speaking, "You mean people like Matthews, I suppose. But his shop in Hereford Street is run by a decent bloke who's got a young family. If you targeted his shop he would suffer at least as much as Matthews, if not more."

Ernie smiled. "I don't intend to hit his shops for a while. From what you say it doesn't look as if he's discovered our last little venture on Friday night. When we picked you up walking home from the hospital, the van was full of gear from the storeroom in your home base. Once we had got into the yard someone had conveniently left the key in the storeroom door. I've still got it here with me," and he took a key from the drawer of his desk. Gerry looked at it and confirmed it was the one that had gone missing. He even had a little smile.

"I bet that was Harry who left it in the door. Both him and Abigail were in a right panic when the power failed."

The mention of the woman's name reminded Ernie that he had other business to attend to before the following morning. He looked at his watch and stood up. "Okay, Gerry, you know the deal. It would be unfortunate if you tried to back out. I couldn't afford to let you discuss my business with anyone else so let's have your answer now; in or out?"

Gerry knew he was trapped. His head was spinning at the dramatic change in Ernie's manner and the events of the day. He bowed his head and said quietly, "I've got no choice. In, damn it!"

Ernie stood over him and spoke in his more friendly tone, "Good, all I need from you now is your assurance that this conversation goes no further. I won't drop you in at the deep end. I'll choose the first target you will be involved with very carefully. In the meantime, concentrate on your grandmother for the next couple of days, then call in to have another chat."

The mention of his gran seemed to clear his head. He was supposed to ring or call in at the hospital this evening. It was past nine o'clock so a phone call would be better.

He stood up and tried to leave but Ernie held his arm and forced him to shake hands.

"There, the deal is done and agreed now." He released his hand and allowed him to leave.

Beryl, the receptionist, unlocked the front door of the centre and let him out with a cheery 'Goodnight'.

The chilly night air helped him to clear his head and concentrate on what was his current priority, namely phoning the hospital. Much to his relief, the nurse on duty reported no change in his gran's condition and that the doctor would be doing his rounds in the morning and there would be an update later.

He tried to think if he had any way of escaping Ernie's clutches but could find no other person he knew who could give him the protection required. He wasn't going to worry Sally with his problems though he did toy with the idea of possibly looking for a job in her area. But how long would it take Ernie to discover his new whereabouts? And that could put Sally in danger.

No, he had been naive in trusting the honesty of others. Well, if he had been drawn into the shady world of Ernie Newsham, he would have to be very careful and make sure his back was covered at all times.

The next day he went through the motions of going to the Job Centre in the vain hope of finding work that matched his skills, but his hopes were soon dashed when all that was on offer was stacking shelves at various supermarkets. He had always worked hard and never tried to cheat anyone and with a good boss like David Evans he had felt that the future only held positive benefits for him.

Then along came Percy Matthews. The total opposite of Mr Evans. Even his own sons couldn't abide his working practices. He treated his staff like dirt, except for Abigail. He could only think of Tony who had similar morals to himself.

So he tried to look on the positive side of working for Ernie at the leisure centre. He had to admit that it was in Ernie's own self-interest to make sure he didn't get caught, or arouse the suspicions of others. But also knew that once he had taken part in one of Ernie's illegal ventures he would be snared in his web of crime with no way out.

***

Ernie was also busy, making copies of the video he had obtained. He made four complete copies along with as many duplicates of each participant's involvement. If they tried to deny it or to delay in cooperating, he could always make additional copies and threaten to send them to their families or the authorities. Then, of course, the price would go up.

He decided to approach the two men first. After his meeting with Sally he now had an extra lever against Abigail.

Sally, also, could prove to be a problem but his visit had also given him a clue on how to gain her silence and prevent her from assisting or influencing Gerry. He didn't finish his copying and editing tasks until well after midnight and coupled with his long round trip earlier he decided not to do his nightly security patrol. Unwittingly, this proved to be a minor godsend as two properties in a new area he had planned on offering his services were broken into that night.

One of these businesses was a popular local restaurant and the perpetrators had only managed to steal a laptop computer from an office but had also started a small fire in one of the toilets. When Ernie heard about this, he questioned Mark about his movements that night.

"Okay, it was me, I started the fire and took their bloody laptop. I tried to go in for a meal the other day with Beryl and they turned us away just cos I was wearing jeans. Bloody snobs!"

Ernie grabbed Mark by his collar and put his face within inches of his employee.

"You stupid idiot! What have I told you about not drawing attention to yourself? If the police investigate and ask if the manager or his staff know of anyone with a grudge against them and your description is given? Your baby-face features make you stand out a mile. Keep a low profile for the next week or so and don't do anything on the break-in front without my clear say-so. Understood?"

Mark was seething inwardly at Ernie's repeated jibe at his youthful looks but he bit his tongue and mumbled an apology.

Ernie calmed down a little but decided on a unique way of teaching Mark a lesson.

"Okay, apology accepted but seeing as you have to keep low for a while, I'm going to get Craig to give you private swimming lessons. And if you fail to attend those lessons then I'll get one of the female instructors to sort you out."

Mark stood open-mouthed for a second and tried to protest but Ernie had walked away, partly to hide the smirk on his face. He knew how Mark tried to look like the macho man in front of the female staff and wouldn't want to lose face in front of any of them.

***

Each subsequent visit to the hospital put Gerry in a more depressed mood and he slowly realised that even if his grandmother recovered most of her faculties it would be very doubtful that the hospital would release her into his care.

He spoke with the nursing staff and told them he wouldn't be able to visit every day as he was starting a new job. Even though this was true he still felt guilty, but he knew if he didn't have something positive to concentrate on it would drag him deeper into a depressive state. Not that the prospects of being involved in Ernie's shady work prospects filled him with much comfort.

He contacted Ernie and said he was ready to start work on the understanding he could visit the hospital at a moment's notice, which his new boss agreed would be acceptable.

The first few days were rather boring and repetitive, consisting mostly of reading manuals on assembling and dismantling the various fitness machines. Mark would be with him most of the time and they started to build up a working relationship.

However, Mark would be summoned by Craig, the lifeguard, to carry out some duty and upon his return Gerry noticed his companion's damp hair. On the third occasion of this routine occurring he waited about ten minutes before going to investigate the reason for Mark's absence. He had a good idea of what he would find and was correct. Mark was having his enforced swimming lessons. Not wishing to embarrass his colleague Gerry did not mention any knowledge of the discovery.

On the Tuesday of the following week the inevitable happened. Ernie came running from his office and told Gerry to grab his coat and follow him. He had visions of this being his first security patrol but was mystified as it was late afternoon and nowhere near getting dark. Gerry had been so absorbed in his work of assembling a new cross-trainer machine he had forgotten all about his other concerns. Ernie's first comment as they got into the car refocused his mind very quickly.

"Brace yourself, lad, you're wanted over at the hospital asap. It doesn't look good."

Gerry was surprised at how calm he felt. Visions of being in a blind panic had haunted him in the past when he first thought of what he would feel like at this moment.

They were shown into the side ward where a nurse was sitting by the side of his gran's bed. At a first glance he couldn't see any difference in his grandmother's condition but on closer inspection he noted her breathing was much shallower and less frequent.

The nurse stood up and left the room. Ernie tapped Gerry on the shoulder and spoke quietly, "I'll be back in a few minutes. I'll go and see if the doctor is around," and he closed the door behind him, leaving Gerry sitting down and holding his grandmother's hand.

He had never been very religious, not attending any church since his parents' funeral but without realising what he was doing, he silently said the Lord's Prayer. It was only on finishing he knew it was his farewell to the old lady who had cared and guided him for almost seven years.

A gentle hand on his shoulder made him turn around and Staff Nurse Lamb whispered quietly, "Would you like to go outside for a few minutes, Gerry, while we make her more comfortable?"

He nodded, stood up and went outside to stand against a wall next to Ernie, neither man saying anything. Gerry could feel his companion watching him from time to time but he chose to ignore it and look away.

It was nearly fifteen minutes before the staff nurse came out of the room and she gently took hold of Gerry's arm and led him back into the room and Ernie followed behind.

"I'm very sorry, Gerry, she's gone," was all she said but continued to hold onto his arm until he moved to sit down next to the bed.

She looked at peace. He was aware of Ernie and the nurse talking quietly but couldn't make out what they were saying, not that he really cared.

He wasn't sure how long he had been sitting by the bed but eventually Ernie came over to him and spoke. "We can't do any more here, Gerry. I'll take you back to the flat where we can have a chat."

He stood up, kissed his grandmother on the forehead, the numbness inside blocking all emotions he felt and he turned and walked past Ernie without saying a word.

Neither spoke on the journey back to the flat until Ernie parked the car and switched off the engine. Gerry was about to get out when Ernie spoke, "Don't bottle up your emotions, Gerry. Even men are allowed to cry sometimes."

Gerry looked back at him and said coldly, "That's not for me! Look, I'd rather be on my own for now so I'll see you in the morning. Thanks for the lift."

He got out of the car before Ernie could reply, walked to the door of his flat, let himself in and slammed the door behind him. Ernie contemplated following him but decided to let him do things his way. There were lessons he would have to learn for himself.

The flat was cold and felt unfriendly. It was never this way when his gran was alive. He went into her bedroom and looked in each and every drawer and cupboard, something he never dared do in the past. But now he had control of anything and everything in his life, all decisions would be made by him; no more asking for permission to bring a friend into the flat.

In fact, he had only sought the consent of his gran on one occasion. He had asked if he could bring Catherine, his ex-boss's daughter, to come and listen to some of his records. He had assured the old lady they would not play the music too loud, and he was convinced they kept to that promise.

Yet every fifteen minutes there was a soft knock on the door followed by his gran's voice, "I think you should turn that down, please, Gerald."

On the third time this occurred, Catherine whispered to him, "It's not the music, Gerry. She thinks we're up to something. She doesn't trust us to behave."

After the fourth interruption Catherine grabbed her coat and left. Gerry went to talk to his gran and ask the real reason for her repeated visits to his room and she calmly answered, "I just wanted to be sure you were both safe, dear."

It took several seconds for the penny to drop but he was too dumbfounded to respond. And he didn't tell Catherine either. Needless to say, that was the first and last time he invited anyone around to the flat.

From now on, things would be different. He would invite whoever he liked when he liked. And the first one he would invite to join him would be Sally, once she had finished helping her sister. It still nagged him to try and remember her ever mentioning another relative. Was there another reason for her sudden absence? But what? On thinking of Sally he decided to phone her and tell her the news about his gran. Perhaps that would influence her early return to him.

Nobody picked up the phone and it cut into the answer machine. He didn't want to leave a message, so he hung up.

***

Sally was not at home as she was making her third visit to her new GP within a fortnight. At first, she had put down the feeling of nausea and headaches to extended morning sickness. However, the symptoms soon disappeared after leaving her flat. Her doctor carried out some tests but couldn't come up with a definitive answer, so she went back home and went straight to bed, even though it was still early evening.

Gerry had started to remove his grandmother's clothes, not really sure how to get rid of them. He was surprised at the amount of clothing she had acquired over the years. As he emptied the last drawer, the truth hit him.

She wasn't coming back. He would never hear her soft, calming voice again or be able to go to her for advice.

There would be no more hot, nutritious meals waiting for him when he got home from work. There was nobody else he could call family. He was on his own.

All these reminders hit him like a hammer blow to his chest and he fell back sobbing into the mound of clothes on her bed. He must have cried himself to sleep because when he finally woke the room was cold with the first light of dawn beginning to show in the clear, frosty sky of another day.

Moving into his own room and removing his jacket and shoes he slid under the warm covers of his bed. He instantly fell back to sleep once more, only to be awoken by the constant ringing of the phone in the living room. He hoped it would be Sally, but instead Ernie's voice greeted him.

"How are you feeling now, lad?"

Gerry cleared his throat and replied, "Much better after some sleep. Oh and thanks, Ernie, I took your advice and feel a lot better for it."

His new boss didn't push him on that subject but continued, "Good, now comes the difficult bit. Getting the death registered and organising the funeral. I don't suppose you've had time to look for any life insurance policies or similar documents?"

Gerry had to clear his throat again before speaking. "No, I started going through her clothes and wondered what to do with them. There's a heck of a lot of them."

Ernie cut in. "Forget the clothes. It's paperwork you should concentrate on for now. Look, I've got a few calls to make this afternoon so if you're up to it, I need you here with Mark. Then tonight I'll come round to help you go through any documents we can find. Deal?"

Gerry accepted the offer, made himself a quick breakfast before going back to work. Mark was aware of what had happened and after a very brief commiseration he stayed clear of his workmate, which suited Gerry perfectly. All he wanted to do was clear his mind of any thoughts of what had happened to his gran. She was gone now and he had grieved for her and that was that. Or so he thought!

***

Ernie's first call was to Andrew Phillips Travel Agency and the unsuspecting manager showed him into his back office. He was expecting his visitor to have come to talk about security arrangements and its cost. The latter would be the biggest surprise.

Ernie began, "I don't have much time, Andrew, and I won't beat about the bush. Something came into my possession last week and I think you might like to see what that is. Can we use your video recorder and TV monitor over in the corner?"

Andrew Phillips suddenly became suspicious and asked the reason why that was necessary. Ernie said nothing and went over to the equipment that the travel agent used to show prospective holiday advertising videos to his clients. Ernie switched it on and inserted a video he had taken out of his briefcase. After switching the equipment on he walked back to the office door to make sure they wouldn't be disturbed and watched for Phillips' reaction.

It took less than five seconds for the significance of Ernie's visit to dawn on the travel agent. He had turned very pale and without turning his gaze from the screen he asked, "How did you get hold of this tape?"

Ernie let the video run for another minute before returning to switch the equipment off. He turned to face his host.

"That doesn't matter right now, just confirm to me who the other participants are and how much you paid the women."

Phillips confirmed the names that Sally had given him and he said his fee was £1,000, but he didn't know how much Fred Barnes paid as he paid for the venue which he named as a motel on one of the junctions on the motorway.

Ernie whistled. "£1,000? That's some fee for just a few hours of hanky-panky! Why so high?"

Phillips spoke with a hint of anger in his voice. "There was supposed to be a second meeting taking place but neither of the women turned up. Not that we were in a position to report them. Now I need to know, how did you get hold of the video?"

"Let's just say, the owner of the recorder was a little careless in his choice of repairer when he couldn't open the camera."

"And what does Mr Barnes have to say about your involvement?"

Ernie knew Fred Barnes would want to keep this episode firmly under wraps, so he used this as a lever against Phillips.

"He will cooperate and doesn't want any scandal. He can't afford to let his church group know anything, or the police authority for that matter."

Andrew Phillips gave a little sigh of relief. He didn't belong to any such groups. "How much do I have to pay for this tape and your silence?"

Ernie smiled. "The tape is yours; I have the master and several copies. The fee? Right now, nothing, but in future I may need air tickets and certain information only you can provide."

The travel agent suddenly asked, "What's to stop me going to the police? Fred Barnes can look after himself."

Ernie played his second trump card. "Oh, the reason the women didn't turn up was because one of them died from a drugs overdose. Drugs she purchased with the money you two paid her. So life would get very complicated for you both."

Phillips visibly slumped in his seat. He knew he was beaten.

He muttered, "All right, Mr Newsham, what happens next?"

Ernie stood up before replying. "Nothing right now, I'll be in touch at the appropriate time. Now if you will show me out, please. Let's make it look like a good meeting for your assistant's benefit."

Reluctantly Phillips obliged, and after showing his visitor out, he told his assistant that he was not to be disturbed under any circumstances for at least an hour. He went back to his office and locked the door to ensure his privacy would not be disturbed, then switched on the television and video recorder.

Councillor Fred Barnes was in a council meeting, so Ernie left him a message to arrange a meeting as a matter of urgency. He went back to the centre to collect Gerry in order to help him sort out his grandmother's affairs.

Back at the flat Ernie suggested that Gerry should search for and check any relevant official-looking paperwork, while he did the same in the living room and kitchen.

After more than two hours of searching Gerry had found a life insurance policy on his gran and the rental agreement on the flat, but no will or power of attorney documents. There were also bank statements dating back more than eight years.

Ernie had found an interesting list of items hidden in the pages of the old lady's bible but he decided not to show it to Gerry. He put the note into an inside pocket of his coat and went back to find his assistant in the bedroom.

Having looked at the paperwork Gerry had found, Ernie commented, "First of all, you will have to register the death and once you have the certificate you can claim on the policy and close her bank account. Didn't you find your own or her birth certificates?"

Gerry shook his head, puzzled as to why he would need those details, so Ernie explained the barest reasons but kept back some of the more important ones, thus keeping Gerry reliant on his counsel until the matters had been resolved.

Ernie had one more thought. "Have you got an up-to-date passport for identification purposes?"

Again, Gerry shook his head. "No, my old passport ran out three years ago and the photo in it was taken when I was still at junior school."

Ernie appeared to look serious for a moment but underneath he was even more pleased as Gerry's reliance on him had now increased.

"Okay, Gerry. That might delay things a little but let me sort out those details for you. Tomorrow morning, we need to collect the death certificate from the hospital and get you a new passport photo. In the meantime, find some bags to put all your gran's clothes in and we can take them to a charity shop; also things like handbags or ornaments you don't want to keep. Try and keep your mind occupied for the next few days and it will help you come to terms with what's happened. You can always give me a ring at the centre if you have any questions or problems you're not sure how to tackle. I have to leave now. I need to go out on my security patrol with Mark tonight."

With that final comment Ernie left the flat, satisfied he now had enough control over Gerry to manipulate him even deeper into his plans.

***

On arriving back at the centre, he went into his office to have a second look at the list he had found inside the bible. As he had first surmised it was a comprehensive list of the items that had been stolen from the flat. He had to read the list several times to grasp the possible

value of the items. Judging from their detail he was convinced that whoever stole them, that person would have great difficulty in disposing of them locally. It would mean having to make discreet enquiries amongst the villains he knew to discover if any knowledge concerning these items was known. And he knew exactly who he would approach first.

18

Graham Bishop had gone to ground. Despite his many contacts Ernie couldn't discover his whereabouts and had to temporarily call a halt to his search, but not before he broke into Bishop's flat where he made a surprising discovery.

He had Gerry's second set of skeleton keys and after making sure Bishop was not around, he gained entry to his abode. Personal belongings were strewn around and Ernie surmised his target had only left for a short while and would be back at some time later.

He failed to find any signs of the items on the list he had found in the bible, but another discovery caught him by surprise. An old school photo of two young boys gave Ernie food for thought. On the back of the photo was a rough note which simply said: 'My lads.'

The younger boy in the picture, looked nothing like Graham Bishop but the older one could have been Bishop's younger brother.

Something was nagging Ernie. What was the connection, aside from the photo, that he knew needed to be uncovered.

Bishop was from Yorkshire, judging by his accent, and so was Mark but there was no resemblance between the two. It was time he delved deeper into Mark's past, if only to dismiss any connection. He made one other important discovery, Bishop's real name.

He replaced the photo in exactly the same position where he had found it and checked to make sure he had not left anything out of place.

Later that evening as they were driving around, supposedly checking on the security of their clients' properties, but also looking for potential new targets, Ernie pulled into a side street and casually asked Mark, "I've got to sort out a passport for Gerry as he's got no other form of photographic identification. What about you, Mark? I don't suppose you have a passport either?"

Mark was watching a young woman walk past and replied without taking his eyes off her. "Never needed one."

Ernie waited until the woman had disappeared around a corner before continuing, "You might not have needed one in the past but there may come a time in the future when you have to go abroad for whatever reason. As I mentioned, I'm sorting one out for Gerry; getting one for you would be just as simple. I don't suppose you have a recent photo of yourself?"

Mark hesitated before taking out an old battered wallet. "The only photo I've got is of me with my brother, Kev; that's no good, is it?"

Ernie frowned. "Not really, but let's have a look, you've mentioned big brother a lot. I'd like to see if there's any family resemblance."

Mark gave a sarcastic laugh as he passed the photo to Ernie.

"You've got to be bloody joking. I don't look anything like Kevin. He's the spitting image of our dad, poor sod. I take after our mum."

Ernie switched on the interior light of the van. He took the photo from Mark, glanced quickly at it and then turned to observe something imaginary across the road.

Eureka. It was Kevin he had seen in the picture back at Bishop's flat. But was Mark aware his father now lived in the same town? His next question clarified the situation more clearly.

"It doesn't sound as if you have much time for your father. What if you suddenly met up somewhere?"

Mark's reaction was instant and venomous. "I'd kill the bastard. If he had looked after me like a proper father should, I could have made a decent fist of my life. You won't believe this but when I were a kid I wanted to be a copper but he put paid to all that."

"What about Kevin? Does he feel the same way about him?"

"Yeah, but for different reasons which I ain't talking about," was Mark's response as he turned to face the pavement, signalling to Ernie not to pursue the matter any further.

He passed the photo back to Mark and started the van's engine and continued their surveillance tour of the area.

***

The next afternoon Ernie carried out his promises to assist Gerry in sorting out the affairs of his grandmother. In a further search of the flat, things were made slightly easier because Gerry had found birth certificates and other official documents, including another insurance policy to be paid on his gran's death.

The visit to a local undertaker's was the most difficult task to accomplish. Gerry had no idea of what was expected of him and it fell to Ernie to finalise the arrangements. The most awkward moment came when the undertaker's fee was announced.

Gerry was speechless and stood with his mouth wide open until Ernie tapped him on the ankle. Outside the funeral parlour Gerry managed to find his voice.

"Ernie, why did you agree to his price? I don't have anything like that amount of money, not even if the insurance policies pay up the full amount."

"Don't worry about money for now, I'll cover any extra you haven't got, and we can sort it out at another time. Anyway, how do you feel about coming out with me tonight on one of my patrols; something to take your mind off things?"

Ernie had deliberately engineered the situation, knowing Gerry would feel obliged to agree, and it worked.

"Okay, but I don't know what I will be able to do. Will Mark be coming along?"

"No, I'm giving him the night off for once. You can do his job instead. Get some rest and grab something to eat. Then meet me back at the rear of the centre at ten o'clock."

Gerry was so relieved to have other things to occupy his mind he was unaware of the trap Ernie had set for him. The second part would be to implicate the lad into assisting in a robbery.

Gerry was wondering when to inform David Evans about his gran's death and that he was now working for Ernie. True, his ex-boss had said there would be no problem about a delay in paying rent on the flat if he lost his job. However, he wasn't sure of the reaction if he suggested that there would be a new tenant to replace his gran. And he already knew who he would ask.

Ernie was waiting in the van for Gerry when he arrived and handed him a padded jacket and told him to try it on for size. It was close to a perfect fit so he got into the passenger seat and they pulled out of the car park and headed towards the southern side of town.

They chatted idly for a while until Ernie asked, "I forgot to check, Gerry, do you have a full driving licence?"

Gerry nodded. "Yes, but I've never had enough money to buy my own car. It's not been a priority of mine."

Ernie shrugged his shoulders. "In that case, it might give me the opportunity to have a night off from time to time and you and Mark can show your worth."

Five minutes later he pulled up in a side street next to a warehouse. "I'm going to take a walk round this block to check things out. Then you can do the same and report any suspicious activities, okay?"

Gerry flinched. "What if you miss seeing someone and they jump me instead? I wouldn't stand a chance."

Ernie smiled. "This place is always quiet. I just want you to see if you can pick out any potential weaknesses in their security. Don't worry, Gerry, I'll be following about fifty yards behind you in the van."

Ernie got out of the van after picking up a torch and a two-foot-long nightstick. He then walked slowly down the road before turning a corner and disappearing.

Expecting Ernie to reappear from behind, Gerry kept watch in the wing mirror but it was fully ten minutes before his new boss came back around the corner in front of the van. Ernie got in and sat in the driver's seat before speaking. "Slight change of plan; they've locked the gate at the end of the road so I couldn't walk all the way round. You do the same and I'll follow you in the van and I can turn around at the end."

He handed Gerry the torch but kept the nightstick in the van.

"Off you go then, lad, just relax and walk as if you belong here."

Gerry didn't feel relaxed or if he belonged anywhere except at home but he tried to put on an air of confidence as he walked down the road. After turning the corner he moved a further twenty yards and noted a narrow alley on his left. He stopped, switched on the torch and shone it into the darkness. To his astonishment a man stood by several large boxes and started beckoning towards him.

He looked back and saw Ernie drive the van past him at speed and turn the vehicle around and come back in his direction. A voice called out quietly, "Gerry. Get your arse down here and give me a bloody hand."

He recognised Mark's voice immediately and ran towards him. "What the hell's going on, Mark?"

By now, Ernie had stopped the van by the alley entrance and had the back of the van open and he also called out, "Come on you two, move yourselves before someone sees us."

Mark thrust one box into Gerry's arms and picked up another and ran towards the van. Without thinking about what he had been drawn into, Gerry followed him with his box.

Throwing his box into the van Mark sprinted down the alley to collect another box and Gerry followed suit. When all four boxes had been deposited into the vehicle the three men got into their seats and Ernie drove away. From the moment Gerry had first spotted Mark, to their leaving the scene had taken less than ninety seconds.

"Gerry, you did okay, but speed is of the essence in this game. Right, we're off to meet the Market Man to deliver his request."

It was only at that moment that Gerry realised the whole situation had been set up as some sort of initiation into the group. There were also mixed feelings about the lack of trust Ernie had shown in him by not divulging beforehand what was about to happen.

Contrasting that feeling, a buzz of excitement had taken hold of him during the episode and he could still savour its effect.

Mark had noticed his colleague's look of excitement.

"That were a good crack, Gerry, you did okay, mate."

Ernie nodded in agreement and commented, "Yes, welcome to the group. As I said we will meet up with our contact and you, Gerry, will get your first bonus payment."

Ernie drove onto the motorway and headed north to keep their rendezvous with the person called the Market Man. After driving for under an hour they pulled into a motorway service station and headed for an area of the car park that was almost deserted apart from a van larger than their own. But Ernie wasn't intending to stop. Instead he flashed his headlights twice as he drew up behind the other vehicle. Almost immediately, the larger van's engine started up and it pulled out in front of them and it proceeded to lead the way out of the service station.

To Gerry's surprise, the lead van drove back onto the motorway and headed back in the direction they had come from, but came off the motorway at the next junction. The two vans joined a dual carriageway and carried on for a further two miles before the lead van indicated that he was pulling into a large lay-by hidden from the main road by a clump of trees. Both vehicles stopped and Ernie switched off his engine. He and Mark got out. Gerry started to follow them but Ernie held up his hand.

"No, Gerry, you wait here until I signal you it's safe to get out. I need to speak with the Market Man first."

Gerry did as he was told and watched his colleagues meet up with their contact. When the man alighted from his van Gerry could only stare open-mouthed at the man's stature. He was only a few inches short of seven feet tall but of only medium build which gave him a rather odd appearance.

The three men greeted each other and talked for a couple of minutes, during which time, Ernie pointed back at his van on a number of occasions. All three turned around to face Ernie's van but it was the tall stranger who approached the van on his own. He climbed into the driver's seat and said nothing, appraising Gerry silently. Then he spoke with a well-educated voice that, for some reason, caught Gerry by surprise.

"Well, young Gerry. You've joined Mr Newsham's band of brigands to make your fortune, I suppose. If, however, you decide at any time in the future to inform the authorities of our arrangement, it will take your relatives a long time to find your remains. Do you understand my meaning, Gerry?" and as he finished speaking he briefly undid the long coat he was wearing to reveal an eighteen-inch-long machete in its sheath strapped to his belt. Once he was sure the weapon had been seen he closed the coat again.

His last words were spoken with such implied menace that Gerry could only nod several times.

The man got out of the van and said in a more pleasant tone, "Time to unload the goodies you have brought me; we all need to get back to our respective homes."

He walked back to the rear of his van and opened it up to receive the items. Gerry joined Ernie and Mark at the rear of their own van to collect the boxes they had brought along.

However, as well as the four boxes Gerry and Mark had dumped in the van there were at least a dozen other smaller but heavier containers to be transferred.

When the task was completed, Ernie sent the other two back to sit in the van while he received the payment for the items. The two men shook hands and moved back to their respective vehicles. Before Ernie had got back in the driver's seat the other van had pulled away and disappeared down the dual carriageway. Ernie only started the van's engine after he passed some money to Gerry.

"Here's the bonus I promised you. Market Man was very pleased with his merchandise and added £20 to your bonus. He's not normally that generous so you must have made a good impression."

Gerry gave a nervous laugh. "He certainly made an impression on me with that damn knife of his. Does he always carry that thing around with him?"

Mark was the first to reply. "Only when he's collecting or delivering stuff. He's a good bloke once you get to know him but I'd never cross him."

Ernie turned right onto the dual carriageway and headed for home, his next operation already decided. Stealing to order was getting more lucrative by the day. He still had to confront Fred Barnes regarding the video clips and the lever to be used to gain the councillor's full cooperation.

***

The day of Mrs Reynolds' funeral finally arrived. Ernie had kept Gerry busy with maintenance tasks in the centre but he was unsure of what reaction there might be from him on the day.

With help from catering staff at the centre Ernie had arranged a small meal for those attending the funeral. But it was a pointless gesture. Apart from Gerry and Ernie, only four other people came to the crematorium and they returned to their homes after the service was over. Gerry had kept his composure until he and Ernie returned to the centre, then he vented his feelings.

"Where were all those people she helped in the past? All those she visited when they had troubles or were sick? Those people she cooked meals for when they weren't capable of doing so for themselves? She would spend hours slaving away in her kitchen to prepare food for those bastards. And not one could bother coming to her funeral. Well, if that's the thanks you get around here for helping folk, this town can go to hell for all I fucking care."

He stood up suddenly and stormed out of the centre before Ernie or Mark could react.

Gerry spent the next two hours wandering aimlessly around the town, unaware of the constant drizzle that fell. Finding himself across the road from his old workplace, he was not sure how long he stood there but in all that time not a soul entered the shop.

Eventually the door opened and a figure came out and shouted something in his direction. It was Harry and when Gerry ignored him he waited for a break in the traffic and started to cross the road. This registered something in Gerry's mind and he turned and quickly walked away.

He carried on walking past a rank of shops and he suddenly went into one purely on impulse. It was an off-licence store with a queue of four people waiting to be served, but there were no staff members to be seen.

He looked around to see if anyone had noticed him but all the customers were only interested in their purchases. He quietly picked up a bottle off the nearest shelf, turned around and left the store.

He walked quickly away, glancing over his shoulder a couple of times to check if anyone was following but nobody seemed interested in him. As he faced forward again he almost collided with a large figure walking in his direction and nearly dropped the bottle.

"Steady on, lad. You'll do yourself or someone else a mischief dashing around like that," Sergeant Proudfoot said, putting a hand on Gerry's shoulder to steady him.

Gerry stammered an apology and tried to get past the officer but he put out a restraining hand, and said, "You're Gerry who used to work at Mr Evans' shop, aren't you? I was sorry to hear about your grandmother. She was a well-respected lady around here. Please accept my condolences for your loss."

Gerry was lost for words and he felt as if he might burst into tears at any moment. This man was the first person to show any genuine remorse. Not even Ernie had aired such a comment. However, he managed to hold himself together and said quietly, "Thanks for that, Sergeant. I'm in a bit of a rush. I need to get out of these wet clothes. Can I go now?"

Proudfoot eyed the bottle and commented, "I didn't put you down as a port drinker. You're not going to drink all that on your own, are you?"

Gerry noticed the label on the bottle for the first time.

"Oh no, I've got a friend coming around later who likes this stuff."

The sergeant was not fully convinced by the answer but stepped to one side to let Gerry pass.

Walking away he could feel the sergeant's eyes watching him and Gerry broke into a sweat as he hurried for home clinging tightly to the bottle.

He changed out of his wet clothes, thinking back to how easy it had been to steal the bottle of port. He felt that excitement buzz once more.

He poured himself a large glass of the liquid and took a mouthful, almost gagging on the heavy, sweet taste as its warmth ran down his throat. Events of the last couple of weeks had changed his views on life and how it appeared you had to put number one first and let the rest fend for themselves. In the past he had followed his gran's advice and put other people's needs before his own but now he was free to run with the wild herd and it gave him an inner glow.

What to do next, he thought. Get totally drunk? Or make plans for his future?

He remembered his plan for sharing the flat with someone and he knew what to do about that. Before carrying out his intentions he poured himself another large glass of port and felt a little light-headed.

He found the notepad by the phone, still on the page with Sally's details, so without hesitation he dialled her number. It rang more than a dozen times before the answer machine cut in. He tried to speak clearly but the drink had started to take effect and his message was not as coherent as he had wished.

"Hi Sal, I need to speak to you. Things have happened here and I want you to come and join me at the flat. Give me a call back, okay?"

He put the phone down and wondered where she was, while suddenly feeling nervous about what he had offered her. Would she call him back? Would she accept his offer? Anyway, why had she gone away and not told him she was leaving?

That last thought bothered him, and he poured himself another drink, noticing with slightly blurred vision that there was less than a third of the contents left in the bottle.

Not finding any answers to his own questions, he finished

the remaining port in the next half hour and fell into a deep, drunken stupor on his gran's bed.

The persistent ringing finally penetrated his heavy, drunken sleep but on trying to stand up to retrieve the phone he almost fell backwards onto the bed, so he carefully sidled along the edge to pick up the receiver. He spoke blearily into the handset, "Hello, who is it?"

There was a brief pause before he heard Sally's voice.

"Gerry? Are you okay? You sound as if you've had a skinful. Your message didn't make much sense, is there a problem?"

Ignoring her questions, he asked one of his own in a pleading tone, "Sally, where have you been and why didn't you tell me you were leaving me? I need you here, Sal. I've had a lousy week. Will you come back here to live with me? Please, Sal, I need to know."

This was not the Gerry she knew. Something was wrong and the concern showed in her voice.

"Gerry, take a deep breath and try to calm down. There's something wrong. Tell me, what's the matter, love?"

Hearing her soft, calming voice Gerry broke down into floods of tears, the recent events proving too much for him. She called his name several times before he finally managed to compose himself.

"I'm sorry, Sally, it's just that Gran died last week and Ernie was the only one who helped me. So can you come and stay with me, Sal?"

Sally let out a small gasp at his news. She had to choose her words carefully so that they wouldn't cause him more upset.

"Gerry, I'm so sorry about your gran, I didn't realise she was so ill. Listen, it's not possible for me to travel down to you right now but why don't you come up and stay with me for a while. I can look after you a lot better up here. Does that sound good?"

He hesitated before answering, "I suppose I could come there but why can't you come to me?"

"It's too complicated to explain over the phone but I've got some news to share with you. Tell me you'll come to me, please, Gerry."

Hearing her pleading, he made his decision. "Okay, Sal, I'll tell Ernie I need some time to get my head together."

She spoke firmly, "Don't tell Ernie you're coming here, Gerry. He will try to stop you. Pack some warm clothes, it's been a bit nippy here lately, and book the first coach you can get on. I promise you won't regret it."

Accepting her reason he promised he wouldn't say anything to Ernie and said he would let her know the time of his coach's arrival.

After putting the phone down Sally felt a slight movement in her tummy and before she could stop herself, she said quietly, "Behave yourselves in there, you two, daddy's coming to see you," and she giggled to herself.

Then she felt a moment of trepidation. What if Gerry didn't accept her word that he was the father? She knew with a hundred per cent certainty that he was, but would he believe her?

If he didn't, then so be it. She had made her mind up and wouldn't change it for anyone. Gerry would have to decide for himself what he was going to do.

Having made enquiries about the availability of a seat on the next coach to Matlock Gerry packed a sports holdall with warm clothes for a short trip to the Peak District, convinced he could talk Sally into returning home with him. After some thought he also packed the gift Stella Stockwell had given him, hoping it would be a lucky charm.

Ernie only appeared to put up token resistance to him taking time off work, but in reality he knew exactly where Gerry was going despite his evasiveness. If he didn't return over the weekend, Ernie decided he would go to confront the two of them and put paid to any plans Sally had made for taking Gerry away.

The coach journey had taken far longer than planned and Gerry was not only tired but hungry as well. He was looking forward to enjoying some of Sally's home cooking and most of all her special brand of tender loving care.

**

The taxi driver who had driven him from Matlock Coach Station turned in his seat and told Gerry, "This is the street you want, mate, but it's been blocked off for some reason by a police car so you'll have to walk the last fifty yards to your final destination. That will be six quid for the journey."

After retrieving his holdall from the boot of the taxi and paying the driver Gerry started to walk down the street. He had only walked about twenty metres before a police officer blocked any chance of further progress.

"That's far enough, young man, where do you think you're going? This street is closed to everyone apart from residents. What's your address?"

Gerry gave him Sally's address and added, "I'm visiting my girlfriend. She invited me up for a few days."

The officer looked at a list containing names and addresses and told Gerry to wait while he went to talk on his car radio. Minutes later another officer, this time an inspector, walked quickly towards the police car. After a brief conversation between the two policemen the senior officer approached Gerry and asked him to confirm the name and address he was visiting.

Gerry obliged and the first feelings of concern started to nag at him.

Several people were standing around, curiously waiting for events to unfold, keen to witness the first drama that had taken place in their midst.

He tried to ask the officer what the problem was but was

totally ignored as they approached a building that had blue police tape across the gate leading to the flat. On viewing the tape Gerry's apprehension quickly rose. He spoke again, unable to keep the concern out of his voice. "Look, Officer, what's going on here? Is this Sally's flat or not?"

The inspector turned to look at him and said quietly, "Are you saying, Mr Reynolds, that this is your first visit to this flat?"

Gerry nodded, and for the first time, noticed the curtains were drawn even though it was still daylight. His attention was then drawn to an ambulance parked a few metres away with both its doors open and the crew standing by awaiting instructions.

A man dressed in civilian clothes carrying a medical bag ducked under the blue tape and came out of the flat and Gerry heard his brief comment to the inspector.

"I've finished in there; you can remove the body now."

Those words felt like a hammer blow and Gerry had to grab hold of the gatepost to prevent himself from falling. The doctor noticed this and saw the look of distress on the young man's face. A brief comment from the policeman told the medic what he wanted to know.

He gently, but firmly, took hold of Gerry's arm and led him to the rear of the ambulance and a female medic helped the doctor to get Gerry to sit on the rear step of the vehicle.

It took Gerry two attempts to ask, "What's happened to Sally? Please, someone tell me."

The doctor replied softly, "Was she a friend of yours?"

That first word told Gerry everything and he tried to stand up and run to the flat but the two medics were too quick for him and prevented his escape.

He started to sob uncontrollably.

The medical staff, with the aid of a policeman, managed to manoeuvre Gerry into the rear of the ambulance and close the doors with Gerry and the doctor inside.

Allowing his patient time to regain some composure the doctor eventually asked Gerry what his relationship was to the woman who had died and the last time they had met. Between more sobs he explained the reason for his visit.

Doing a quick mental calculation, the doctor decided not to mention that Sally had miscarried twins, especially as the young man had made no comment about the woman's pregnancy. This was news that would be too much for Gerry to bear at this moment in time and he kept his comments to himself.

Twenty minutes later a soft knock on the door of the ambulance found the police inspector waiting with a message that they would like to complete the operation of removing the body so they could complete their investigation of the scene of the suspicious death.

Gerry had regained some of his composure and was led to a police car to be taken to the nearest police station so that he could write a statement and make plans to either stay in the area or arrange travel back to Clapfield. He chose the latter and called Ernie who promised to leave at once.

With nowhere else to go he stayed at the police station, accepting the offer of a hot drink and a sandwich. But he had no real appetite and only ate part of the food before discarding it. Gerry was given some form of privacy by being taken to an interview room not currently in use, so he could gather his thoughts. After a short time he fell into an exhausted, fitful sleep.

A hand shaking his shoulder woke him and it took moments for him to recognise his surroundings and see Ernie standing over him. "You've had a hard day, Gerry, let's go home, lad."

Gerry picked up his holdall and stopped in the open doorway and suddenly said, "I don't know what happened to Sally, nobody has told me anything."

Ernie took his arm and led him out of the room before speaking. "I asked for some details and I'll tell you on the way home if you're ready."

Gerry allowed himself to be led out of the police station to Ernie's car. To his relief, Mark was not waiting for them. The fewer people he had to speak to, the better.

Not that much conversation took place with Ernie anyway. As soon as he got into the car Gerry reclined his seat and tried to go to sleep once more. But it was a forlorn hope. Visions of Sally came flooding back and he was constantly wiping tears from his eyes.

Ernie observed these actions and decided to stop at a motorway service station. Gerry needed to talk. It was starting to get dark and there were a few areas deserted of any other commuters. He chose a place in the corner that was furthest from the service building. He gave Gerry a gentle shake of his shoulder to get his attention.

"It might seem a little premature but you need to get things off your chest. What were you told about the circumstances back in the police station?"

Gerry sniffled and tried to ignore the question, but Ernie gave him another nudge.

"Come on, Gerry, you won't get any peace until you talk things over."

Reluctantly he opened his eyes and spoke gruffly. "What's there to say? She's dead; that's all that matters, isn't it?"

Ernie sighed. "She died from carbon-monoxide poisoning. She wouldn't have realised what was happening to her. It doesn't happen the minute you're exposed to the gas, it's a gradual thing that creeps up on you, just like dozing off to sleep but you don't wake up. Even if you were there, unless you knew what to look for, you would have been just as vulnerable as Sally, and probably just as dead."

Gerry stared out of the car door's window. "Better off if I was dead as well. She was the only real friend I had. We were made for each other. Now she's gone."

And the tears began to well up once more.

Ernie wanted to say more but now was not the time. Instead he asked his companion if he wanted a hot drink or something to eat. A single shake of the head was all he received in response, so he started the engine and drove back onto the motorway and headed for home.

19

For the following three months after his wife's funeral, Robin Stockwell took little interest in his pharmacy work and limited his opening hours to requests from regular customers he knew personally. Most came to purchase special lotions he made up for them, but this custom began to dwindle and he had to make a decision whether to continue working.

After much thought, he decided to plan a trip to Scotland in early spring. The couple had spent several holidays in those parts, walking and sampling the various amenities in the area.

He had often expressed an interest in producing a perfume, using the prime ingredient heather from the slopes of the Scottish Munros, mountains that stood above three thousand feet. The idea was hatched in his mind after a rare visit they had made to North Wales, where a local chemist had produced a similar item, called Snowdon Heather™.

Being a qualified chemist himself Robin knew the process of producing such an item. The blending, testing and discovering the ideal aroma would be the time-consuming part, but now he had the freedom to pursue his dream and it was with Stella's blessing as she had foreseen the demise of the small independent chemist.

Long before anyone knew about her terminal illness, Jenny Potter had been made to promise her friend that, if ever the need arose, she would make Robin a Sunday roast dinner on a weekly basis. Always keen to return past favours it never dawned on Jenny to question why such a situation might ever become necessary.

On one of those Sundays when she had delivered his meal Robin confided in her.

"I think my days as a dispensing pharmacist are numbered, Jenny. Another pharmacy chain has opened a shop a few streets away and I've already lost some of my regular customers. If it wasn't for the odd herbal remedy that Stella showed me how to prepare and my lotions, I wouldn't have anyone coming through my doors. I think I will have to diversify or close the shop for good."

Jenny was horrified at such a thought. "Oh Robin! After all you and Stella have done for the people around here, surely not!"

Robin gave a faint smile. "That's the harsh reality of business I'm afraid, Jenny. If people can buy the same things I sell for a lower price from another source, it's only natural they will go for the cheaper deal. You can't blame them really."

"But what will you do? Does that mean you will have to sell the shop and move away?" she asked, very near to tears.

"Don't worry about me, Jenny. I still have some savings to fall back on if required. However, I do have an idea I want to pursue. Stella told me to follow my dreams and I still have one in mind. I've often thought about making a brand of perfume from natural ingredients and I'm going up to Scotland in a few weeks' time to collect some samples of them. It won't be the same without Stella to guide and encourage me but she would still want me to try at least. I will let you know the dates of my trip nearer the time."

Over the next few months he made several such trips to Scotland to identify and collect local flora he thought might make a unique blend. Numerous attempts were made and he came close to admitting defeat but his promise to Stella fuelled his determination to succeed.

Ernie was also showing great determination in his endeavours to entice Gerry back into his security business. The lad hung around his flat for nearly four weeks after returning home. Nobody had contacted him personally about Sally's funeral so that event passed by without his attendance. Little did he know, Ernie had given his own details to the police and when he was informed of the post-mortem verdict and date of the funeral, he had not notified Gerry.

Mark made frequent visits to his colleague and Gerry slowly accepted him as a confidant. Sometimes he would give vent to his anger, on other occasions he would despair at the cruel misfortune that had befallen him.

In one of those latter moments he pleaded with Mark to ask Ernie if he had heard any news from the police in Matlock.

Mark already knew the answer but passed on the message to Ernie who had been waiting patiently for this moment to arrive. The next day Ernie invited Gerry to meet him at his house where he could play his trump card.

"I'm a little ashamed to tell you this, Gerry, but the Matlock police lost your contact details. The post-mortem and funeral took place last week."

As Ernie anticipated Gerry flew into a rage and cursed the police for their incompetence and denying him the opportunity to say farewell to Sally. When he had calmed down Ernie dropped his bombshell.

"I'm truly sorry to have to tell you this, Gerry, but there's still more bad news you need to know about Sally. I don't know if you were aware, but she was nearly fifteen weeks pregnant, but that's not all, I'm afraid. I came across a video that doesn't put her in a very good light."

"Sally? Pregnant? You've been given wrong information,

Ernie. She was in Derbyshire to look after her sister who was expecting, not Sally."

Ernie shook his head. "Sorry, Gerry, she misled you. I've known Sally since she was a teenager. She was an only child, no brothers or sisters, possibly the odd cousin somewhere. There are several things you didn't know about her in those younger years."

He then selected a video and placed it in the recorder. Gerry sat stunned for several moments before asking about the significance of the video to this conversation.

"I found it in a camcorder we picked up from your old boss's storeroom. Take my word for it. You don't need to see it."

Ernie knew Gerry would fall into his trap.

"I'll decide that. Show me, damn it."

He gave Gerry a second chance to change his mind but the offer was declined. Ernie sighed and switched on the equipment.

He played the video past the point where Sally slapped the face of the travel agent and stopped it when it became evident what the whole evening was all about. Gerry jumped up and ran to the bathroom to be violently sick. He didn't come back into the living room for a further ten minutes where Ernie pushed a glass into his hand and advised him to drink it in one swallow.

Gerry duly obliged and coughed a couple of times at the sharp taste of the alcohol, then sat quietly, staring into the void before asking, "Is there any more news of Sally you want to drag through the dirt?"

Ernie shook his head. "No, it seems she left at that point and another woman took her place. At least she had the sense to do that. I'm sorry, Gerry, that wasn't easy for me either. I liked Sally, she had a decent heart but was led astray on some occasions, and you needed to know the truth."

"Did I? But what about the others in that video? Is anything going to be done about them? I recognise that bitch Abigail and the bloke Sally slapped; that's the travel agent you were talking to when Harry and I were clearing out that shop. I don't know the other man. Who was he?"

Ernie could sense that Gerry wanted someone else to be hurt just like he was hurting now, so he gave him his wish.

"This is what I plan on doing. The wife of Percy Matthews is the power behind his business. It's her money that helped set him up in the first place. There are a few clips you haven't seen on that video revealing Abigail in all her glory.

"Along with those clips and some information I gleaned from another source, it seems that Abigail obtained drugs for the woman who took Sally's place. That same woman died from a drugs overdose a couple of weeks later.

"Mrs Matthews will be receiving those details along with the clips I mentioned, and I bet Miss Abigail won't be seen in her shops again."

Gerry visibly relaxed but wanted more assurance from Ernie.

"Did you try and blackmail Sally in the same way?"

Ernie smiled. "I wouldn't have bothered trying, Gerry, Sally would have called my bluff. And besides, what could I blackmail her with; slapping Phillips for trying to grope her?"

Gerry tensed up again. "I'll do more than slap him if our paths cross."

Ernie shook his head. "I've got a more fitting punishment for both those men. Leave it to me, my method is more long term. Now, I have a big favour to ask you but it will also benefit us all."

Sensing some kind of trap Gerry asked warily, "What does it involve?"

"I would like Mark to move in and share the flat with you. You get on a lot better these days and I would feel happier if you didn't spend a lot of your time alone. It will also supplement your rent and I can help you draft a letter to David Evans to explain your reasons."

Sitting motionless for a while Gerry gave great thought to the request and finally agreed, but with a couple of conditions.

"I need a few days to move my stuff into Gran's room first. But I will also have the final say if it doesn't work out to my satisfaction."

Ernie stood up. "That's only right you have the final say, but Mark will still have to pay an equal share of costs. Take your time sorting the rooms out. Then we can get back to work as a team once again."

Gerry understood the meaning behind those words but now he wasn't daunted by the path he would be following.

Being honest and hard-working has only brought me grief so let's try the other way, he decided. *What do I have to lose now?*

The two men shook hands and as Gerry left his house, Ernie put into motion his plans to keep his promise to make other people pay. As a result, Percy Matthews would lose control of his business in spectacular fashion.

***

Mrs Matthews found a package addressed to her on the doormat when she came downstairs one morning. Thinking it was something her beloved Percy had ordered as a surprise present for her she ripped open the package. Most of her days at home alone were spent watching television or going through her mountain of film videos she had accumulated over the years.

Assuming it was the latest film her husband had ordered for her she went into the kitchen to make a cup of coffee, toasted and buttered four crumpets before going into the spacious lounge to watch her new present. The daily cleaning lady wouldn't be coming for at least two hours so she anticipated there would be enough time to watch the film and get dressed before she would be disturbed. Percy had left for work as usual at 7 a.m. and would not be home until early evening.

Ernie had edited the clips on the video so that Abigail was on screen most of the time and the film lasted less than fifteen minutes. Mr and Mrs Matthews had not had sex together for at least two years so on the first showing of the film Mrs M thought her husband had sent the film to help rekindle their relationship and was more than a little flushed at the end of the first showing. She had not paid much attention to the features of the cast, such were the distractions on view.

She ate three of the crumpets and drank half of the coffee before replaying the video. There was something familiar about one of the women but she couldn't remember where she had seen the face before.

Retrieving the packaging she searched for any clues to the identity of the cast. There was nothing apart from a short note which read: 'All play and no work at the boss's demands. We recommend you investigate.'

Mrs Matthews was in the middle of finishing the remains of her now cold cup of coffee as she read the note and almost choked on the drink. She spat out the coffee over the expensive thick-pile carpet and dropped the cup on the floor as recognition of one of the females dawned on her. It was that tart who worked for Percy.

She was about to pick up the phone to order her husband to return home immediately, then a better idea came to her.

Confronting the two of them at work would be far more satisfying and she could demand that Percy fire the bitch on the spot. The shop had recently taken delivery of some tele-recorders so she could show him the evidence without giving him the chance to use his usual delaying tactics.

Before going upstairs to get dressed she phoned for a taxi to collect her in half an hour by which time the cleaner would have arrived.

As she got into the taxi the driver was instructed to put the bill on Mr Matthews' account and to wait for her to finish her business and return home. That would be the smallest amount he would pay if he didn't do her bidding.

Abigail was serving a customer when Cynthia Matthews walked into the shop, swept past the counter and headed straight for the manager's office. Harry didn't recognise this rather large lady marching through and asked if he could assist her. The tone of her voice should have told him that trouble was brewing.

"Is my husband in his office?"

Harry nodded and tried to at least delay her advance but Cynthia was not going to be held up by some pot-bellied individual and entered her husband's office without knocking and waiting for a response.

Percy sat in his chair, feet up on the desk while he idly rubbed his crotch, anticipating the liaison he and Abigail had planned when the shop closed for lunch and Harry had been sent out on some minor mission.

"So this is how you run this business I fund. Lounging around and dreaming of that tart you call a sales executive."

Percy almost toppled backwards out of his chair. Was this some kind of nightmare? His wife never came into any of his shops, let alone charge in like an enraged elephant without first being announced.

He managed to get to his feet, smiled feebly at his wife and closed the door behind her to try and lessen any further damage to his reputation. However, it was too late.

Abigail had turned a bright crimson on hearing the taunt directed at her and the customer who had been more interested in her cleavage than the item she was demonstrating suddenly decided he wasn't in the market for the product, apologised and left the shop.

Harry looked on slightly bemused, first at Abigail and then in the direction of the manager's office. He noted the glare directed at him as the door was closed by his boss and instinctively knew the blame would be entirely his and nobody else.

Meanwhile, Percy Matthews was trying to placate his wife by offering her a seat, still not sure if his dearly beloved had lost her mind.

"Cynthia, please have a seat. Can I get you a cup of something, dearest?"

Ignoring his remark, she looked around the room and spotted what was required; the combined monitor and recorder. Pointing at the screen his wife said curtly, "Switch that thing on and play this tape."

The first feeling of a major disaster started to envelop Percy's mind as he shakily followed his wife's instructions. The last time he had used the player the volume had been left on high and the first sounds from the video vibrated around the office and could be clearly heard in the shop. The overwhelming sound was that of Abigail's moans of ecstasy. Percy quickly moved to reduce the volume and then his attention was drawn to the screen and he stood open-mouthed unable to comprehend what his eyes were witnessing. To his relief he knew he was not one of the participants so his wife couldn't accuse him of that crime.

When the video had finally ended he tried to speak but the words wouldn't come out. All he could do was gesticulate at the screen with a look of utter confusion on his features.

Cynthia spoke on his behalf.

"Where has that come from? At first, I thought it was a present from you to rekindle something between us."

At that suggestion he broke into a coughing fit and made gestures to be given a drink of something. Cynthia ignored his request and continued, "You have a very simple choice to make, Percy. Get rid of that tart you call a sales executive or I get back all the money I have invested in this business. Quite simple really, what's it to be?"

Matthews managed to stop his coughing for long enough to protest. "For God's sake, Cynthia, I can't just fire Abigail without good reason. She is the best sales person I have had and she would sue me for wrongful dismissal. Please, Cynthia, let's talk through this sensibly. When did this tape arrive and was there any message with it?"

"It was on the doormat when I came downstairs. This note was with it, nothing else," and she passed the crumpled note to her husband.

Percy read the note and he suddenly found a possible escape route. He stood up and said to his wife, "I think I can solve the mystery of who sent this filth. Wait here one moment, dear." Still holding the note he strode out of the office, closing the door behind him.

He called his assistant to him. "Harry, your little scheme has failed. Get your stuff and get out of my shop. You're fired."

Harry stared back at him, uncertain if he had heard correctly. When he didn't move, Matthews held up the note for him to read. Harry looked again at the message that still did not register with him, so his boss said, "I warned you after you and that damn kid came back early that if word ever got out about what you saw, it would be the end for you. Now, shift yourself or I'll call the police."

Some form of comprehension dawned on Harry but he wasn't about to go quietly. Grabbing the lapels of his boss's jacket he head-butted him on the nose.

Matthews had instinctively guessed what was about to happen and partially managed to move backwards to decrease the impact. Nevertheless the blow sent him sprawling, his nose seeping blood. But Harry was not finished. He stepped over the prone body and entered the office and confronted Cynthia Matthews as she watched the video yet again. She sat transfixed as Harry made his sudden entrance.

"I don't know what this is all about, lady, but if he thinks I told anyone about the time me and the kid caught your husband and that slut having it off, he's effin' wrong."

He turned to leave, but it dawned on Cynthia that Harry had evidence of other misdemeanours by her husband and asked the question, "Excuse me; Harry, isn't it? What happened, and when?"

Realising they were both in the dark about the mixture of events that had led to this showdown Harry explained in graphic detail of what he and Gerry had witnessed some weeks earlier.

Far from being shocked at the news Cynthia smiled and said, "I heard my husband say you were fired. I can't do anything about that but if you leave me your details I'll make sure you get at least a month's pay in lieu."

For the first time Harry noticed what Cynthia had started watching again and said quietly, "I think it's worth more than one month. How about six?"

Cynthia could see the direction of his thoughts and said firmly, "Three, and that's my final offer. Take it or leave it."

Harry thought for a moment and hastily wrote his address on a piece of paper, nodded and left the office, followed by Mrs Matthews. They found Abigail kneeling by Percy with his head on her lap as she wiped the blood from his face. On seeing Mrs Matthews she quickly pushed her boss's head away with more than a little force.

Harry retrieved his belongings and, on his way out, deliberately stepped on Percy's hand which brought a yell from the injured man.

As Harry reached the door the taxi driver pushed his way in and called, "Here Mrs Matthews, how much longer? My dispatcher is doing his nut because I'm stuck here waiting for you."

She had forgotten all about the taxi in all the excitement so she told him to leave and add an extra £10 onto the fare as his tip and order another cab for thirty minutes' time. He nodded and left. Cynthia turned her attention to Abigail.

"Your services, whatever they constituted, are no longer required here so grab your belongings and leave. The money you are owed will be sent in due course."

Abigail looked at Percy for support, but none was forthcoming. All the fight had been knocked out of him. He lay on the floor still in a daze, watching his little empire crumble all around him.

Giving Percy one final look of disdain she stood up and said glumly, "My coat is in the office along with my handbag and other things. I need to fetch them."

Cynthia nodded and allowed her to pass. On entering the office Abigail saw the last few moments of the video and understood the whole situation in an instant. It was obvious to her who the blackmailer was but she kept that to herself.

Abigail walked out of the shop without a second glance at either her boss or Mrs Matthews who locked the door behind her and then returned to the office, leaving her husband to sort himself out.

Turning the recorder off and retrieving the video Cynthia made a phone call to her son.

"Quentin, darling, I need you to come straight over to Daddy's shop in the high street. I've had to sort out an urgent problem and there is nobody left to secure the premises and close it. Be a poppet and get over here as quickly as you can, please, dear."

There was a slight moment of protest from Quentin but she won him over with the mention of the word promotion.

20

Harry kept watch on the shop from his vantage point in the pub across the road, slowly drinking himself into a deeper rage at the injustice that had befallen him.

Abigail had been the first to leave as he had finished his first pint. She didn't look too unhappy; more with a look of intending vengeance on her mind. And she wasn't heading for home either.

A younger man, whom he didn't recognise at first, arrived at the door of the shop and after he knocked a couple of times Mrs Matthews let him in. Only then did he remember the name of the person; it was their son Quentin. A second taxi arrived some twenty minutes later and the driver was told to wait in his car until he was required. After buying several more drinks and becoming increasingly abusive to other customers Harry then discovered he didn't have enough money for another drink so he had to call off his vigil and left the pub after an argument with the landlord. It must have been that kid who had sent the note to Percy's wife but what was the connection with the video he had seen? He couldn't work that one out.

The Matthews trio left the shop about an hour later, Mr and Mrs Matthews in the taxi and Quentin driving his father's car. He would return to collect his own vehicle later.

After closing the leisure centre on completing his shift, Gerry was walking home alone. Ernie and Mark were on a regular security patrol but also had the intention of checking out the potential for exploiting another business that one of the young attendees from the centre had mentioned to them.

He was so deep in thought he never heard the vehicle pull up alongside him. A woman's voice called out, "Gerry? Can I have a word, please?"

He turned to see a police patrol car had stopped by the kerbside and the passenger window was open. Recognising the wife of his former tutor, Lee Bradley, he lowered his head to be on a level with her and replied, "Oh, sorry, I was miles away, is there something wrong?"

"Nothing wrong, Gerry, Sergeant Proudfoot told me about your gran and friend in Matlock. I just wanted to pass on my condolences."

She hesitated before continuing to speak. "Get in the car, Gerry, we can talk while I drive to your place. It's on my route to the station. I'm just coming on duty."

He got into the front seat and the car pulled away from the kerb.

Gerry asked, "I thought you and Lee were moving away from the area."

"It's been delayed for a month," she said, shaking her head.

"Has Lee found another college to teach in?"

She nodded and was about to expand her comment but glanced ahead and muttered a curse under her breath. And switched on her siren and accelerated. Gerry was flung back in his seat at this sudden change in motion and he glanced ahead to view the reason. Smoke was pouring out of a building they were approaching.

The WPC put in a call for assistance and was told fire appliances were already on their way. Telling Gerry to stay where he was she jumped out of the car. However, he was already half out of the vehicle because he recognised the building that was now ablaze. It was his ex-employer's shop.

The WPC called to him while running to the side street next to the shop.

"Stay there, Gerry. I'm going to see if I can get in through the back entrance."

Reluctantly he obeyed her instruction but felt helpless. A sudden thought struck him, hoping this wasn't any of Ernie's or Mark's doing. He could hear the approach of at least two emergency vehicles speeding towards the scene. Within seconds a fire appliance and ambulance arrived from one direction while a turntable ladder arrived from another.

Gerry ran to the first appliance to tell a fireman that Karen had gone to check if she could get in through the back entrance. The officer instructed two of his colleagues to go and find her. More emergency vehicles were arriving and soon the crowd that had gathered, which included Gerry, was moved further away from the proximity of the blaze.

Two ambulance personnel were sent around the back of the building which now had flames coming out of the upper storey. A sick feeling in the pit of his stomach started to engulf Gerry, hoping Karen was still safe.

A few minutes later the ambulance crew came back into view carrying, with the aid of two firemen, a stretcher between them with a large body, covered by a blanket. From where he stood it was impossible for Gerry to distinguish who it might be. This was placed in the rear of the ambulance which sped away, sirens blaring into the night sky.

His gaze returned to the blazing building. Only a few months ago it had been a happy workplace with a friendly environment for him but those feelings had evaporated to nothing. Had it now also claimed the life of someone who had shown him sympathy and should have moved to another area to start a fresh life?

He felt his eyes moisten. Wiping his face he tried to convince himself the smoke from the fire was the cause.

Letting out a huge sigh of relief, he saw Karen being helped to walk to another ambulance and placed in the rear of the vehicle which pulled away at a more sedate pace.

The firemen now seemed to have the blaze under control so he decided it was time to go home. He had only walked about a dozen paces when he heard a call from behind.

"That's one of the two I mentioned. Arrest him."

There was no mistaking the strident tones of Percival Matthews and Gerry turned to look in the direction the voice had come from. Seconds later two strong hands had grasped his arms and pushed him against a nearby police car. He tried to struggle but his assailant was far stronger and bigger.

"Hold still, son, I want to ask you a few questions."

Gerry was slowly allowed to turn around to face the policeman who had apprehended him.

Percy Matthews strode forward and tried to grab hold of Gerry but was prevented from doing so by the officer.

"Stand back, Mr Matthews, I will deal with this if you don't mind. Now, what's your name, son?"

Once again Matthews wanted to have the first word.

"It's Gerry Reynolds. I dismissed him a few weeks ago. He and that fat slob Harry were responsible for this fire."

Holding Gerry by one arm the officer turned to Matthews.

"Mr Matthews! If you don't stop interfering I might have to arrest you as well. Now stand back and don't say another word."

Gerry spoke for the first time, "Yes, my name is Gerry Reynolds, but you said something about me being arrested. What have I done wrong?"

"I'm not arresting you just yet. I want to know the reason for you being here."

Gerry explained the reason for his presence and how he got there. The officer looked a little suspiciously at him.

"You say a police officer stopped to give you a lift and you just happened to come this way? We don't normally run a taxi service, so what's the name of this officer?"

Sensing the man was not convinced by his story Gerry sighed and gave him all the details, at the same time hoping he wasn't going to get Karen in trouble.

The officer looked carefully at Gerry then took a firmer grip of his arm.

"I don't know of a WPC called Karen Bradley. I'm inclined to think she hadn't given you a lift but that you were arrested for some other offence. So for the moment, I'm going to handcuff you and put you in my car while I make enquiries with other officers in the area."

Gerry protested and tried to struggle but he was no match for the officer.

"I'm telling the truth! She tried to get into the building but was led into an ambulance by paramedics about ten minutes later and she must be at the hospital by now. That's the truth, honest."

"Then you've got nothing to worry about, have you? So stop struggling and get in the car or I'll bring other charges."

Realising his resistance could get him in further trouble, he allowed himself to be handcuffed and bundled into the back of the patrol car. Matthews had come closer and said something to the officer who indicated to a point on the other side of the road. The shop owner moved sullenly away.

It was a further fifteen minutes before the officer returned to his car and after getting into the driver's seat he turned to Gerry.

"Nobody from my station has heard of this Karen Bradley and there are no reports of a policewoman being taken away in an ambulance so I'm taking you back to the station."

Gerry lost his temper and shouted an obscenity before yelling "Then those people you talked to must be blind, or more likely, you believe that bastard Matthews."

The officer turned in his seat and said angrily, "That's enough from you, my lad. Any more comments like that and you'll really be in hot water. Now shut it."

Slumping into his seat as the car drove away Gerry glanced out of the window on his right and caught a glimpse of a van with the emblem Acme Security on the side. He could see Ernie and Mark in deep conversation. Then they were out of view.

Ernie said with a nod in the direction of the building that had been badly damaged in the fire, "So this is what all the excitement is about. That's Gerry's old workplace. I hope he had nothing to do with it," and Mark laughed.

"Doubt it. I tried to show him how to go about it but he made a right mess of things. When I get the chance, I'll teach him how to do a proper job."

As they moved slowly along the crowded street Ernie spotted Matthews waving his arms about and having an animated discussion with a police inspector who was trying to calm the shop owner down.

"Gerry should be back at the flat by now so I'll drop you off nearby and you can give him the good news. I will come back here and try and find out some more details."

**

On his arrival at the police station Gerry was taken into an interview room, still handcuffed, and left with another officer while the one who had arrested him went to check on some details he required.

More than half an hour later he returned and signalled for his colleague to leave the room. Standing in front of Gerry he said, "If you promise to stay calm I'll take the handcuffs off and we can have a civilised chat. Any nonsense and I'll put them back on. Okay?"

Gerry merely nodded but said nothing.

"Right, I'm Constable Dave Sims and I want an off-the-record chat before taking your statement. I've made some enquiries and you were right, a WPC from another station was taken away in an ambulance as you said, she is being checked over but won't be available to speak until at least the morning. In the meantime, I want you to tell me all about your movements from early this afternoon."

"I've been at work since midday at the leisure centre until I closed up at ten o'clock. I was walking home when WPC Bradley stopped her car and offered me a lift because she wanted to talk to me about something personal."

"Like what?" was all the PC would say. Gerry was now becoming increasingly resentful at the man's attitude.

"All I'm saying on that matter is, I lost a friend a couple of weeks ago and Karen wanted to talk with me about it. What's that got to do with the fire tonight? Several people can vouch for me up until about 9.45 p.m. and that shop was well ablaze by ten thirty, so I wouldn't have had time to get there and start the fire."

"Mr Matthews thinks you were responsible for the fire. Why would he say that?"

"So that's what this is all about! When I worked for him, he was always trying to blame me for anything that went wrong until he finally sacked me. He even accused me of being involved in a break-in at the shop and it was WPC Bradley's colleague who got him to admit he was lying.

"What about checking out Harry's movements? He didn't like Matthews because he had some kind of hold on him. Then there was Abigail…"

A sharp knock on the door was followed by a second PC stepping into the room.

"Sorry to disturb you, Dave, but there's an important message for you at the front desk."

PC Sims left the room while the other constable stayed with Gerry. Time seemed to drag for him and thoughts raced through his head. What if Karen was not in a fit state to give him an alibi; could he get a message to Ernie? He would know what to do in these circumstances.

The door suddenly opened, and the PC returned, but this time he had another officer of higher rank with him. Gerry had a nasty feeling the situation was suddenly taking on a greater emphasis. He was not wrong.

"This is Inspector Gates and he is taking charge of this case."

The two constables left the room and the inspector sat down behind the table and faced Gerry. He placed a tape recorder on the desk and spoke briefly into the microphone.

"Inspector Gates at Coventry Road Police Station at 12.55 a.m. with the suspect, Mr Gerald Reynolds."

Gerry looked at him and blurted out, "Suspect? I've done nothing."

"Mr Reynolds, I want you to tell me all about your movements since nine o'clock yesterday evening and the names of any person who can confirm your whereabouts until you were arrested."

Gerry protested. "But I've already told the constable everything. I'm tired and haven't eaten anything since midday yesterday."

Inspector Gates looked back at him with a total lack of sympathy. "The sooner you give me the details, the sooner we will be finished. So tell me everything."

And to emphasise the point he tapped the recorder.

Gerry stared back at him. His hatred for those in authority was increasing by the second. However, he knew he had no choice but to repeat his story.

So he went into the smallest of detail of who could verify his movements and times he remembered. He repeated the encounter with Karen Bradley and how they arrived after the fire had been started. Suddenly he remembered something and asked a question. "As well as WPC Bradley being led away to an ambulance, someone was carried out on a stretcher. Who was that?"

Gates looked back at Gerry. This was the time to play his trump card, or so he thought.

"Finally remembered your accomplice, have you? That was Harry Brown on the stretcher. I was informed shortly before I came in here that he didn't recover and was pronounced dead on arrival at hospital."

He watched Gerry for any reaction and was not disappointed.

"My accomplice? Are you kidding me? I never trusted that fat slob any more than I did Matthews, my ex-boss. Harry physically threw me out of the shop on Matthews' orders when he fired me. He also threatened me with a good kicking if I went near there ever again."

"Can anyone confirm what you just said?"

Gerry hesitated before he answered. "Matthews will probably confirm he fired me, but there was only Harry and me outside afterwards."

Gates couldn't hide the sarcasm in his voice, "So it's your word against Mr Matthews, a respected businessman in this town."

"Not many of his former staff would agree with you on that score," Gerry retorted.

Gates changed the subject. "You seem to be on rather friendly terms with this WPC Bradley. How long have you known her?"

"I have only met her a couple of times. The first was when she and a colleague came to investigate a break-in at Matthews' shop. He lied about my tutor being off work, but Lee, the tutor, is married to WPC Bradley and she denied her husband was not in work so Matthews had to admit he was lying.

"The second time we met was at the leisure centre which she attends, and she helped me rescue someone who had got into difficulties in the swimming pool."

Gates announced grudgingly, "She is currently in hospital being checked over after inhaling smoke at the fire. I can't verify your story about how you met until she is fit to talk. In the meantime, I will have to decide whether I can release you on police bail or detain you until we interview the WPC."

"You're not going to keep me here overnight, are you? I've done nothing wrong! I had to pass the shop where I used to work, it's on my direct route home. A colleague of yours can prove I wasn't responsible for the fire, but you won't take my word for that; instead you listen to a devious sod like Matthews."

Inspector Gates glared back at Gerry and repeated his earlier comment. "Mr Matthews is a well-respected person in the business community and is a member of…"

Another knock on the door interrupted him. He gave permission to enter and the constable came in.

"Sorry to bother you, Inspector, but someone at the front desk is demanding to see you on some urgent matter."

The two officers exchanged places and Gerry leant forward and propped his head on his forearms as he rested on the table. He was tired and hungry, just wanting this farce to end.

When Gates returned it was obvious he had not received welcome news and curtly told Gerry to follow him. Getting slowly to his feet Gerry wondered what was going to happen next. He heaved a sigh of relief when he spotted Ernie waiting to greet him.

"You can leave now, Mr Reynolds, but I may need to speak to you once I have interviewed WPC Bradley."

He turned on his heels and left the two men together without saying another word.

Ernie indicated to Gerry to remain silent as they left the police station. They got into the van and Ernie started laughing. Gerry looked bemused.

"What's the bloody joke, Ernie? I've been accused of starting a fire at my old workplace. I've been stuck in that police station for about three hours, and all because Matthews spotted me walking home."

Ernie became serious and asked, "What were you doing there in the first place? I thought you took a longer route home in order not to pass the shop."

Gerry explained how the policewoman had given him a lift and what happened when they arrived at the scene of the fire and Ernie gave another short laugh and then apologised.

"Sorry, Gerry, I'll tell you what's so funny later. Anyway, Mark and I drove past the building that was on fire and knew it was your old place of work, so after dropping Mark off at the flat I returned to the scene of the fire to try and find out more details. I spoke to the landlord of the pub across the road from the fire and he told me he saw you being bundled into a different police car to the one you arrived in." He continued, "I wondered what the hell was going on, so I asked a few of the locals who were hanging around. They told me Harry had been drinking heavily all evening and cursing Matthews for sacking him and how he was going to get his own back. Added to that, he was causing so much bother in the pub the landlord slung him out and Harry disappeared for a while. Next thing, the fire started in the shop and someone said they saw a policewoman being led away by a paramedic after another person had been earlier carried away on a stretcher, who I presume was Harry."

Gerry interrupted him, "The policewoman was Karen Bradley who gave me a lift but I didn't know it was Harry on the stretcher. The inspector told me he had died from a heart attack, I think."

Ernie was silent for a while and then said thoughtfully, "I've been wondering since I heard the news what reason Matthews had for sacking Harry. He knew a lot of dirt about his boss and could have dropped Matthews in the brown stuff if push came to shove."

It was Gerry's turn to let out a small laugh which earned a quizzical look from Ernie. Gerry told him about the time he and Harry found Abigail and Matthews in the shop office and this was the explanation for his mirth.

Ernie let out a yell of triumph.

"Aha, yes. Earlier in the day, Harry had stormed into the pub and sat staring out of the window and when Abigail came out of the shop he shouted, 'Serves you right, you bitch', which caused some merriment at the bar. Mrs Matthews went to the shop to confront her husband after looking at the video I sent her, and Matthews must have blamed Harry and fired him. So the next step will be to send a message to Abigail that her secret about the drugs she pushed will be on the streets unless she moves a long way away and keeps her mouth shut." He continued reassuringly, "Don't worry about that inspector calling you back in. I told him there were several witnesses who would testify that you arrived in the police car sometime after the fire started. Gates is a mate of Matthews but he's no fool; he will leave you alone regarding this matter. But if the opportunity arises, he will try and pin something on you, so we will have to be very careful."

By now, Gerry was struggling to stay awake and he was losing interest in the conversation. All he wanted to do was go home to get some sleep and put this episode behind him.

21

Ernie decided to check on Councillor Barnes and Andrew Phillips to see if either had been approached by Abigail to establish any connection with the video sent to Mrs Matthews. It was fortunate that he had followed up his hunch. He was told Councillor Barnes was away on council business, so it only left one possibility.

"You said nobody else would know about that video as long as I cooperated with your demands!" Andrew Phillips was clearly upset about something. He had shown his visitor into the back office in order to talk privately with him.

"Calm down, Andrew. I haven't told anybody else about our little arrangement. Let me guess, you've been approached by one of the other participants from your little adventure? A female, I would guess?"

Looking a trifle embarrassed at the mention of the video being described in such a manner Phillips nodded.

"Yes, I'm sure it was the one who slapped my face. I think her name was Sally. She wants £2,000 by tomorrow lunchtime or she will go to the press. That would ruin me."

Ernie's reaction surprised him. He laughed out so loud, Phillips looked nervously at the door, half expecting someone to walk in and check if everything was okay. Then his visitor became serious once more.

"It definitely was not Sally. She died about a month ago from carbon-monoxide poisoning. But don't worry, I know who it was and will deal with her later."

The travel agent looked pensively at Ernie. "Poisoning? It was an accidental death?"

Not wanting his victim to feel any more confident Ernie replied, "Let's say it was avoidable if she had heeded advice. Now I have work to do but let me know if you hear any more from our would-be blackmailer."

**

Returning to the leisure centre he gave Mark details of what had happened to Gerry and how he had rescued him from the police station.

"Wow! That explains why he hasn't turned up this morning. Did you manage to tell him about our own little adventure last night?"

Ernie shook his head. He had forgotten all about the haul of branded perfumes they had taken as one-off payment for promising not to take further action against a reluctant business owner who wanted to be left in peace.

"Last night's episode with Gerry must serve as a lesson to us. We need to have alibis prepared when we plan a job. I've had a run-in with Gates in the past and he can be a trying bastard at the best of times. It was on his recommendation that I wasn't allowed to return to duty after my accident so I owe him."

Mark kept quiet. If Ernie wanted to get back at someone then that person better be on their guard. When Gerry turned up for work after lunch, Ernie said he had work to do in his office and he wasn't to be disturbed for anything except an emergency situation.

Making sure his office door was locked he set about sorting out Andrew Phillips' problem. Having acquired Abigail's address and phone number using techniques from his police days, Ernie dialled her number.

It was clear that the female who answered the phone had been drinking, so Ernie spoke in a very officious tone, "Am I speaking to Ms Abigail Spires? This is the police."

There was a gasp followed by a loud thud as a heavy object hit the floor. Abigail cleared her throat before speaking. "Yes, I'm Abigail Spires, what do you want with me?"

"Ah, good. Miss Spires, I understand a previous acquaintance of yours was a Miss Barbara Hutchinson who sadly died from a drugs overdose. Is that correct?"

There was another gasp and cough before her response. "I did know Babs but so did loads of other people. Why are you asking me?"

"Miss Spires, her death is being reinvestigated and we are trying to establish her movements prior to her death. A witness has come forward who claims you were with her less than twenty-four hours before she died. Do you recall this meeting? Also, were you aware Miss Hutchinson had a drugs problem and if she always went to the same supplier?"

By now Abigail was perspiring heavily and could barely hold on to the phone.

"Look, whoever you are, this all happened a long time ago and I can't remember details and I haven't been well lately. Let me have a think about it and I'll get back to you, Mister…?"

"Oh, I'm sorry, my name is Detective Inspector Gates. Have a think about what I've said and I will give you a ring early next week. One other thing, do you know a Mr Andrew Phillips and if he was an acquaintance of Miss Hutchinson, by any chance? Goodbye for now, Miss Spires."

Abigail retrieved the glass she had dropped and poured in the remainder of the vodka from the bottle. Her plans to go abroad using the money she knew Phillips would have paid her were unravelling fast. If the police had made a connection between the two of them it wouldn't be safe to have any further contact with him. That only left Percy as a source of funds.

She rose unsteadily, spilling some of the alcohol on her dress as she grabbed the phone once more. She pressed the phone's memory button and chose Percy's home number, disregarding his pleas never to do such a dangerous thing. She cursed under her breath as there was no response. It finally cut into the answering service, and the voice of Mrs Matthews purred down the line.

'I'm sorry but there is no one to take your call at present, you can leave your name and number...' and Abigail slammed the phone down before the message ended. That meant she would have to keep her rendezvous with the councillor. On the bright side, he did have access to emergency council funds and she was sure it wouldn't take much persuading on her part to make him hand over some of that money. He had done so in the past so now wouldn't be any different.

The long leather boots, matching leather mini skirt and imitation fur coat would do the trick for her. She struggled into the tight boots but failed to notice one of the heels was slightly loose.

Finishing off the remains of her drink before leaving the apartment she was annoyed to find the lift wasn't working so it had to be those damn stairs again. She cursed as the loose heel nearly made her fall but continued to the top of the stairwell and pulled open the fire door. In her impatience to leave the building she didn't appreciate the combined effect of the alcohol and cold draft in the stairwell was having on her.

On the third step the heel of her boot snapped and Abigail was thrown violently to one side with a scream that echoed all around the confined space.

Her head struck the metal handrail with a sickening thud and she tumbled to the bottom of the stairs. Her neck was broken as it hit the lower fire door at a rakish angle. Her body would not be discovered until the following morning. When news of her death did become public knowledge at least three men in the town would be able to sleep easier in their beds.

Over the next few months Ernie's mini crime wave continued to reap dividends. So much so, he had to find more outlets to disperse of his ill-gotten spoils. They still met up with the Market Man on a regular basis but he couldn't dispose of all their stock. An extra van was purchased for the task of disposal and Gerry became the main driver for these tasks while Ernie and Mark dealt with the accruement of goods.

Gerry got to know the Market Man and when he heard the young man's life story, he would often give him extra bonus payments.

"If you get the chance, son, ditch this life or you'll always be looking over your shoulder like me."

Gerry considered the advice but was caught in a dilemma. Yes, he knew he was now on the wrong side of the law and he felt uncomfortable with some of the things he was now participating in on Ernie's instructions.

On the other hand, everyone and everything on the 'right side' had been taken from him. His parents, his grandmother and especially Sally were all gone and he had nobody to turn to except Ernie and Mark. To a lesser extent, the Evans family had left the area and Lee and Karen Bradley had finally moved to another town.

He had been cheated out of his job and promising career by Matthews who was also managing to influence his friends in the police.

He was earning more money than he had done before and David Evans had not responded to his phone call about Mark moving in and sharing the rent for the flat, so he took that as a positive outcome.

Both he and Mark had a minor supervisory role over the

juveniles who attended the centre and he was proud of the fact they were influencing them to stay on the right side of the law, despite their own double life. However, as Ernie constantly emphasised, it was the adult members who attended facilities at the centre that they had to be wary of becoming suspicious.

If any did raise concerns Ernie would step in either with an alibi to allay their questions or challenge people to produce hard evidence. None did.

***

Robin Stockwell had steadily acquired enough ingredients to develop his perfume concoction to a point where it was now at the testing stage. But whose opinions would he seek and respect? He had kept himself busy for the past six months since he had started this new venture and he needed a holiday.

And there was the answer! He would visit Canada to see his granddaughter, Natalie, and her stepfather, Frank Jardine.

Frank had kept a watchful eye on Natalie since she was in her early teens when her mother died. Frank also had a healthy respect for the elderly pharmacist and his late wife and their previous visits to Canada had been warm and friendly. To complete the perfect reason to visit Natalie, she was due to have her degree awarded but that was still several months away. She would also have female friends who could express opinions on his creation.

Checking dates and times for his possible departure he found the telephone number for Andrew Phillips' Travel Agency. He and Stella had used their services in the past and the agency knew his requirements. Robin also enquired about exchanging some pounds sterling into Canadian dollars but decided to wait until nearer the travel date in case he could get a better exchange rate. With an increase in reports of damage to businesses and other vandalism being reported throughout the town he decided to keep his travel plans to himself until nearer the time.

Ernie was not too surprised upon receiving a phone call from Graham Bishop. He had guessed it would only be a matter of time before the favour was requested. His patience was duly rewarded. Bishop wanted to arrange a meeting to discuss a proposition concerning numerous valuable items that would mean a trip abroad for Ernie if he was interested.

***

Because of the knowledge he had accrued about Graham Bishop he didn't want any locals, especially his two assistants, to know about their meeting so it was agreed they should meet out of town.

"Okay, Graham, what have you got to show me that could warrant a trip abroad to dispose of these items?"

Bishop opened up the holdall he had carried into the motel room. Ernie had booked from someone who asked no questions and wasn't bothered that the booking was only for three hours. It was a regular occurrence at this time of year; short-term hire of rooms for cash.

The contents of the holdall were in cloth bags, each with a small handwritten label to describe their origin. Unknown to Bishop, Ernie had seen an identical bag a few months earlier. As each bag was emptied Ernie had to suppress his excitement at the impressive display in front of his eyes.

"Where did these come from?" he asked, even though he was certain he knew the answer. Bishop shook his head.

"I'll tell you later, if we can do a deal. Right now, give me a price and where you reckon you'll find a buyer."

"What about your usual contacts, Graham, too hot to handle or not interested?"

Bishop hesitated before answering. He was desperate to be rid of these things but he tried not to show it. Instead he made up a story to cover his tracks.

"I took them across on the ferry to Holland to a fence I used in the past, but I got a tip-off to say the police were watching his shop, so I came straight back home."

Ernie laughed out loud. "Is that so? Graham, if you tried to walk through customs carrying this little lot we would have heard the alarm bells ringing this side of the North Sea. No, sunshine, either nobody was interested, or you were offered a lousy price. Am I right?"

Bishop let out an expletive. "Damn you, Newsham, what are you offering then? This stuff is worth a mint but I can't afford to hang on to it forever."

Ernie nodded. "I'd like to know two things first. Is this everything, and where did you pick these things up? I need to know how hot they are before deciding."

Graham Bishop knew he had little choice.

"You knew Harry Brown, the geezer who died in that shop fire, a few months back. He sold me a set of skeleton keys he claimed he found at work. Well, I used them keys to do that job on the film actress in Bristol. Then I overheard that kid who works for you now talking to his bit of stuff in the library about some trinkets his grandma kept that came from South Africa. I bided my time and waited until the kid and the old lady were otherwise occupied." He pointed to the items in the cloth bags. "One bloke told me these are some kind of tribal artefacts and I could get a small fortune if I found the right dealer, but I don't have the time to go chasing round looking for some specialist dealer, so I'll take what I can and be shot of that shit."

"What about the items you stole in Bristol? From what the papers said they were worth a fair few quid. Are they part of this favour you want sorting?"

Bishop shuffled back and forth before replying. He suddenly appeared nervous.

"Most of them are in my bag. I visited a fence in London to do a deal but the bastard tried to shaft me. He had another bloke with him I'd never met before who drew a knife on me but I was too quick for the dope. I laid him out with the gun I carry for emergencies. I also put a bullet in the fence for trying to double-cross me. I only got out of there by the skin of my teeth before their mates turned up. I heard there's a price on my head for any information on my whereabouts."

Ernie nodded. "I heard there was some trouble with a small-time crook and his gang, so it was you who put paid to him. So let's have a look at what you've got in your bag. And if you're thinking of pulling a gun on me, forget it, Graham. I've left word with a few people that I was meeting you here tonight."

Ernie was bluffing but he gambled on his visitor being reluctant to want more trouble. It worked.

"I got rid of the piece back in London. It was hot anyway. I left a couple of rings behind, hoping your ex-mates might pin the whole Bristol job on them."

Ernie examined the jewellery Bishop put on the table. He remembered the press coverage of the robbery and was happy to see the most valuable items were present. He spent the next fifteen minutes examining the items with great care. He finally sat back in his chair and spoke.

"If you had come to me straight after the Bristol job we could have got at least fifty thousand for them but after you shot those two in London they've become too hot for most fences to handle. We would be lucky to get ten thousand, even if I took them abroad. And don't forget, my cut plus expenses would have to come out of the final price. As for the trinkets, I only know one specialist who might take them off our hands and he's in Australia, but I couldn't begin to guess what price he would offer."

Bishop's shoulders visibly slumped. He had hoped for twice the amount Ernie had offered him. Ever since he had stolen the items from the Reynolds' flat he had felt very uneasy, a feeling someone or something was watching every move he made:

regularly disturbed nights; having weird dreams and thinking someone was in the room with him.

Remembering those feelings, he couldn't stop himself from blurting out, "I'll do a deal with you. You give me the ten thousand up front and you take your cut and expenses from the sale of the trinkets."

Ernie sensed something had rattled the man. Was the London gang close on his case or was it something deeper? He guessed the latter, so he pressed home his own offer. "I don't know how long I would have to spend in Australia, maybe just a week or it could be longer. So I'll give you five thousand as a down payment and if the trinkets' value is enough to cover my cut and expenses you can have the second five thousand when I return. Plus we will split anything over my ten-thousand valuation of the jewellery down the middle. I can't offer any better than that."

Bishop knew he wouldn't get a better offer, but he wanted one more concession. "Okay, it's a deal. But only if I get my down payment in cash and within the next week."

Ernie shook his head slowly. "Hang fire, Graham. I need more time than that. First I have to make sure my contact is interested in these items. Then I have to arrange their safe transportation and my air fare down under along with accommodation.

"When all those details are arranged and I have a departure date for my flight, that's when you get your five thousand. Those are my terms, take it or leave it."

Bishop snarled, "Deal, damn you. But if you try and double-cross me, Newsham, I'll make sure I put an end to your security scam once and for all. I've spoken to a couple of your so-called clients and I know how you operate. Your old buddies would love to solve all these mystery break-ins and funny fires over the past year or so. Just remember that."

Ernie smiled but there was ice in his words. "And if you should try to cheat me in any way, your London contacts will learn of your whereabouts. And I'm sure Gerry Reynolds would love to know the identity of the person who, even indirectly, caused the death of his grandmother. One final point, you still have a family in Yorkshire who would be even more interested in your new address. So shall we just go ahead with our business deal and then go our separate ways without rancour?"

Ernie's last remarks shook him, but Bishop merely nodded and turned to leave but was stopped by his host.

"Before you leave here, I suggest you wipe your fingerprints off everything you've touched." For the first time Bishop noticed Ernie was still wearing his driving gloves. This amused him and he gave the faintest of smiles as he took a handkerchief from his pocket and wiped all the items that had been touched in the room. He then carefully placed all the stolen goods in his holdall and the two men left together.

The next morning Ernie called Gerry and Mark into his office. It was a rare occurrence for both to be summoned in at the same time and they both waited warily to be told the reason. Ernie didn't keep them in suspense for long. "You don't have to look so worried. I've got some interesting news that will boost our funds significantly."

Mark gave a sigh of relief, "Phew, I thought you were going to tell us somebody had cottoned onto us. What's the deal then?"

"Before I give you the details, I need some information from you, Mark. Now, tell me the truth and no details will leave this room, okay, Gerry?" and he looked at Gerry for confirmation, which he received. But Mark was more cautious.

Ernie continued. "Okay, Mark, you've mentioned your brother, Kevin, in the past and his history with the gang in Leeds. Has he ever killed anyone?"

There was a shocked silence as the question was absorbed.

Mark stared at Ernie before responding, "Is that some kind of trick question? If you think I'm going to drop my brother in it just for the sake of your curiosity, you can forget it," and he started to rise from his seat, presumably with the intention of leaving the room but Ernie motioned him to sit back down.

"It's no trick or idol curiosity, Mark. If I gave him a contract to bump someone off, would he have any qualms about doing so?"

Mark thought long and hard before answering. "If the price was right and the job was doable, I'm sure he could do it. But who's your target? If it's some innocent bystander you want to get rid of merely because you don't like that person, then no, he won't do it."

Ernie was not prepared to give any more details. Instead he said, "This person is no 'innocent bystander'. He has committed murder in the past and wants me to help him dispose of some items of value. Now, are you prepared to ask Kevin if he's interested?"

Mark looked down at his hands before mumbling, "I can only ask, but he'll want more details from you first."

Ernie smiled, "Don't worry, once I tell him the details, there's every chance, he will be interested. So, Mark, you contact your brother and ask him to call me here at the centre. Obviously, no more mention of this meeting to anyone."

Once the others had departed Ernie made two phone calls, one to the Market Man and the other to Andrew Phillips; the latter to make sure he received a favourable discount on his flight and accommodation when he travelled to Australia.

He wanted to know from the Market Man, whose real name was Richard Connelly, if he ever exported goods to the other side of the world and what measures could be taken to ensure his consignment was not searched too thoroughly for any extra items that were being smuggled into the country. Connelly agreed to send Ernie's goods in his next container which was due to leave in a month's time and would arrive a week before Ernie's flight landed.

His goods would be kept safe by Connelly's accomplice until Ernie collected the items. The charge for this service would be £1,000, payable up front, which was agreed.

***

A couple of days later Robin Stockwell phoned Ernie at the centre and asked if he could do him a favour which he was happy to undertake. Robin explained he was planning on visiting Canada in the near future and wondered if Ernie's security patrol could keep an eye on his premises while he was away. Ernie agreed and continued the conversation.

"I'm planning on taking a break at about the same time. I'm off to Australia to visit a former colleague. Actually, Robin, I might be able to get you a discount on your air ticket and foreign exchange through my business contacts. How are you coping these days? Are you still dispensing your remedies and creams?"

"Thank you for your offer, Ernie, I haven't finalised my flight details yet or given much thought about Canadian money. Thank you for reminding me, I also need to make sure my passport is valid. As for the dispensing side it's gone very flat since Stella died; one or two callers for the burns cream and herbal potions. I've formulated a new perfume I want to promote but I want the opinion of my granddaughter, Natalie, to see if it has an agreeable aroma for today's young ladies. Natalie will be a good barometer of that."

"Oh, I had forgotten all about Natalie; what's she up to these days?"

Robin was reluctant to divulge too much information about his granddaughter so he merely said, "She's doing very well and will be finishing university sometime soon. Her stepfather is very proud of her and keeps a watchful eye on things."

The conversation ended with Ernie promising to make enquiries about tickets and Canadian dollars.

Once he had received agreement from his contact in Australia that he had an interested party in the artefacts Ernie concentrated on the temporary changes he would have to sort out at the centre.

With the help and cooperation of Councillor Barnes he convinced the local authority to close the centre for a couple of weeks for refurbishment while he was away on his travels.

His next task was to get Mark and Gerry to take over the security patrols in his absence. But what seemed like a straightforward switch nearly ended in disaster.

On the conclusion of their latest meeting Ernie finished the briefing by reminding his two assistants, "Before finishing your patrol tonight, break into the Fish Bar, on Rupert Street, making it look like someone was after the night's takings. No fire or anything that dramatic. It's just a reminder to the owner that it would be wise to invest in our security offer. He wasn't that interested when I called in to see him a few weeks ago. Any problems, call me on the CB radio we installed last week."

Just after two thirty the following morning Mark parked their van a couple of streets away from their intended target. It was an area where other clients had their premises so if they were spotted they would not look out of place. However, no other single person was abroad that night.

With the aid of Gerry's keys, they gained access to the rear of the Fish Bar. As soon as they entered the building the smell of heated cooking oil filled the air and Mark became very wary. The only sound to be heard was the murmur of the extractor fans.

"There's something not right here; this place closed before midnight and those fans should have cleared the cooking smells. Just be careful, Gerry."

As they made their way to the office to carry out the task Ernie had ordered, they passed the rear of the serving area and the deep fat fryers. Gerry stopped to listen to an unfamiliar sound.

"What the heck's that bubbling noise?" he said quietly. At the same time, he put his hand on the cover of the fryer and took hold of the handle.

Seeing what his friend was about to do, Mark shouted, "Gerry! Leave it and get back!"

His warning was a split second too late. Gerry had only raised the cover a couple of inches but it was enough to allow cooler air to penetrate to the hot, bubbling fat in the fryer. With a loud whooshing sound a jet of flames shot up and engulfed Gerry's left hand. He let out a shrill scream and staggered on unsteady feet.

Mark reacted with amazing speed, pulling his friend away before he fell back towards the column of flames that was shooting into the air. With his free hand he grabbed a fire blanket next to the fryer and flung it over the flames. On finding the gas supply and temperature controls to the fryer, Mark turned them off before concentrating on helping his friend.

Gerry was in a state of shock and moaned feebly. Mark half pulled and led him out of the building. As they reached the relative safety of the yard behind the Fish Bar Gerry started to sob from the pain in his hand. While leaving the building Mark had managed to grab hold of a towel and he quickly wrapped it around his friend's burnt hand. He gave Gerry a good shake.

"Gerry! We've got to get out of here, okay? Let's get back to the van and I'll call Ernie's place on the radio. He will know what to do."

Mark managed to bundle his friend into the van. He knew it wouldn't be long before the emergency services arrived on the scene and if they were caught in the vicinity of the building they would have a lot of explaining to do, especially with the condition of Gerry's hand.

Rather than call Ernie from their current location, Mark drove for about five minutes before stopping in a side street.

Gerry's moans and groans had turned into loud curses and threats to anyone and anybody he could name.

Mark didn't bother with the niceties of CB radio speak. He switched the radio to transmit and had to shout into the handset in order to be heard over Gerry's pleading voice.

"Acme Security to base, come in, Ernie, for Christ's sake, emergency!"

There was no reply within ten seconds of his call, and he was part way through repeating his message with a few expletives when Ernie cut in, "Base to Security 1, codes only, no names. What is your problem? Over."

Mark bit his tongue before replying, "Okay, Base, have it your way! My mate has badly burnt his left hand and I need to know where to take him. No NHS facilities."

Ernie quickly grasped the situation and asked Mark for his location. Once he heard the reply he said calmly, "Base to Security 1. You're a couple of streets away from an old pharmacy. The owner will provide short-term assistance. I will meet you there in ten minutes. Over and out", and the line went dead. Ernie then picked up his phone and dialled a familiar number.

It rang more than a dozen times before a sleepy voice answered, "Hello, who is this?"

"Robin, it's Ernie Newsham. I'm sorry for disturbing you at such a late hour but I have a small emergency I need urgent help with. One of my people has badly burnt his hand. He needs to be seen at a specialist burns unit but it will take me at least half an hour to get him to Frenchay Hospital burns unit. Can you help, please?"

Robin Stockwell took a few moments to gather his senses before he replied, "I can put some of my cream onto the burn but if you say he needs a burns unit's expertise why don't you take him straight there?"

"He's in my van just around the corner from you with a

friend. I'm sorry to bother you at this time of night but it is urgent, Robin."

Ernie knew that even at his age, Robin Stockwell would not refuse to help in an emergency, and he was proved right.

"Very well, I will be downstairs within five minutes. Tell them to wait outside the door to my flat."

Ernie thanked him before putting the phone down, then he relayed the instructions to Mark.

"I will meet you at the designated place and take control. Return our vehicle to its parking point and use the office to have a rest. After assisting our colleague to obtain help, I will take him to the appropriate venue in my car."

As Robin approached his front door he heard someone knocking loudly, and he walked forward and opened the door cautiously. One person was supporting the other who was leaning heavily against him. Robin Stockwell did not want to invite two strangers into his flat so he told the taller man to wait outside for Ernie to arrive.

"What's his name, please?"

Mark hesitated for a moment and then spoke. "It's Gary."

Mark didn't want to leave his friend but knew he had little choice in the matter, so he stood back as the elderly man bore the weight of his companion and shut the door behind him.

Helping Gerry to sit down by the kitchen table he first asked what had happened. His patient was not very coherent, but he was sure he said, "Checking security of building, found someone had left deep fat fryer on and flames shot up at me, don't remember much else."

The pharmacist gently removed the towel protecting Gerry's hand which caused more cries of pain. On viewing the extent of the injury, he frowned.

"Gary, I can only put a temporary dressing on your wound, but you must get to a specialist burns unit for proper treatment or you may lose the use of your hand."

He applied his special cream to the wound and gently wrapped it in a gauze dressing. He then gave Gerry a couple of tablets and a glass of water.

"These tablets will help with the pain, but they will also make you feel a bit sleepy. Here's four more tablets but only use them if you have nothing else to take. I'm also giving you a small jar of this cream to put on as a backup help. Now remember, Gary, Ernie must take you to the nearest burns unit which is in Bristol as quickly as possible. They will be able to help you more than I can."

Gerry swallowed the tablets and spoke quietly, "Thanks, Mr Stockwell, actually my name is Gerry, not Gary. I was the person who engraved the gold lighter for your wife."

A look of comprehension crossed Robin's features.

"Ah yes. I don't think I've had a chance to thank you for that wonderful work. Well, I'm sort of glad in a roundabout way to repay you. Now let's see if your friend or Ernie are waiting for you outside."

Gerry stood up, still a little unsteady, but he managed to walk to the front door unaided and Robin opened it up and Mark was standing by, waiting for his friend.

Gerry turned to his saviour and thanked him. Robin smiled and said, "That's all right. Now remember, Gerry, straight to the hospital or that damage will be permanent."

Mark led the way as they walked slowly to meet up with Ernie. Once they were out of earshot of anyone he turned to Gerry and hissed, "Why the hell did you tell him your name, you daft sod? I told him your name was Gary. Now he's got your real name he could tell the cops and we're all in the shit."

Not willing to get into an argument with anyone Gerry said nothing and was pleased to see Ernie coming around the corner to meet them. Seeing the gaunt expression on his young assistant's features Ernie told Mark to take the van back to the centre while he took Gerry to seek further medical help. Once he had him strapped into the front passenger seat he asked, "What did Robin say about your burns, Gerry? Are they bad enough to need urgent attention?"

"Got to go to burns unit in Bristol Hospital or I'll lose my hand," was all he could manage to say.

Ernie closed the passenger door and got into the driver's seat and started the engine. He hadn't had a chance to get the full story of the accident from Mark so he was not sure if his two assistants were responsible for the fire at the Fish Bar.

By now the tablets had already started to take effect and Gerry's head slumped forward on his chest. Then he started mumbling as he dozed. His words didn't make sense at first but suddenly Ernie recognised them as being a rough transcript of his introduction to stealing from the chocolate warehouse and his meeting with the Market Man.

He couldn't afford to take the chance of this being repeated in front of strangers so he drove back to his house and managed to get his semi-conscious companion inside without any of his neighbours being awakened by Gerry's sometimes loud ramblings and cries of pain. Once he had put Gerry in the spare room and covered him with a blanket he left him to sleep away the rest of the night.

While his patient slept Ernie formulated a plan that he was sure would convince Gerry he had carried out Robin's instructions. There would be too much risk in taking him to a hospital where too many questions could be asked. Instead he decided to contact a former consultant and GP. He was no longer legally allowed to practise, following complaints from former female patients. But he owed Ernie a favour.

His skills were ideally suited to meet Gerry's current requirements, and he had his own house kitted out just like a mini clinic, with the capability to carry out minor surgical procedures.

After checking Gerry was in a deep sleep Ernie had one more task to perform before returning to his own bed. He left a phone message for Mark to collect some of Gerry's toiletries and clothes to last him at least a week and to deliver them to his house as soon as possible, and if anyone enquired about Gerry's absence, to tell them he was having a break from work for a short while.

Mark arrived with the items Ernie had requested just after nine later that morning and it was clear to Ernie that he hadn't had much sleep either. So this would be the ideal time to interrogate him about last night's events.

"Mark, I told you both it was to be made to look like a simple break-in at the Fish Bar, not a full-blown arson attack, so what happened?"

Mark gave the full details as they happened and how the deep fat fryer had been left switched on at maximum power, either accidentally or deliberately.

Ernie frowned at the last comment. Was it an accident or had the owner thought he could get away with an insurance claim for his premises being burnt down?

"I don't think it would be wise for me to contact the owner directly, but I'll put in an anonymous call to suggest it was an attempted insurance fraud. At least you made enough noise to alert the people in the flat above who managed to get out safely."

Mark asked if he could see his friend, but Ernie refused as he wanted Gerry to sleep as long as possible or until his doctor acquaintance arrived later.

"You know Gerry told that chemist bloke his real name even though I gave a false name to him earlier? If he hears about the fire and puts two and two together, he could tell the police which would mean trouble for us."

"Let me worry about Robin, I think I can convince him it was a pure accident. You had better go back to the centre for now. I will be along later once I've got Gerry into a clinic to sort his hand out."

The medic arrived just before midday and went into the spare bedroom to meet his patient.

Gerry had been awake for nearly an hour and had taken another of Robin's tablets, but it wasn't having such an immediate effect as the earlier ones he had been given.

Ernie introduced the doctor as a Mr Rogan and then left the room.

"Well, young fella, let's have a look at this hand of yours, shall we?"

Gerry drew his injured hand from under the cover and tensed himself ready for the almost unbearable pain he was about to endure when it was touched. But nothing happened.

Rogan compared the size of both Gerry's hands and shook his head.

"You can relax for now, Gerry. I'm not going to put you through any unnecessary pain just yet. I will take you to my clinic and examine your hand under a general anaesthetic and decide on your course of treatment."

Gerry looked up at Rogan with an almost pleading look in his watery eyes. "Am I going to lose my hand? I'd go crazy if that happened. Tell me, please, can you save my hand?"

Rogan put a reassuring hand on Gerry's shoulder and spoke softly, "No, Gerry, I'll make sure you don't lose your hand, but you might not have the same flexibility as you had before the accident. Now, you must keep thinking positive thoughts and that will help you to heal quicker. I will speak to Mr Newsham to arrange your transfer to my clinic. I will speak to you later, and try not to worry."

But Gerry's thoughts were far from positive. Each time he looked at the swollen hand his mind was focused on his past engraving skills he would no longer be able to accomplish.

Who was it who forecast this might happen? Then he remembered, Robin Stockwell's wife.

Had she planted the seeds of failure in his mind or had she

tried to warn him away from that path? He vaguely remembered her warning. However, his life choices were much clearer back then.

No, it wasn't Stella Stockwell's fault he found himself in this state. It was Percy bloody Matthews and the bastard who stole those items from his gran who tipped the balance. Harry had put paid to Matthews so that just left the scum who stole those things from the flat.

Concentrate on identifying that person, Gerry, a reason to get well again.

His hand started throbbing once more so he took another tablet. The pain slowly subsided but his sleep time was plagued by memories of the past.

This time three women's hazy forms were approaching him. In front was Sally carrying what looked like two dolls but then he could see they were babies. Sally turned away but the two women behind her pushed her back towards him. This time she wasn't holding anything. She held her hands in a pleading motion and tried to speak. He watched her mouth and she seemed to be saying, "All gone, all gone."

All three suddenly disappeared but not before he recognised the two other women. His grandmother and Stella Stockwell were each holding a baby.

A hand on his shoulder was gently shaking him and he awoke to find Ernie standing by the bed.

"Time to go, Gerry, we need to get to the clinic."

His companion looked up at him nervously. "Do you trust him, Ernie? Will he be able to fix my hand?"

"Since he was kicked out of the NHS he's done a lot of private work abroad and from the fees he's charged he managed to open his small clinic. I doubt there is anyone better and will do a good job on your hand."

Looking away, Gerry knew he didn't have any choice but to trust Ernie's word.

He spent the next ten days at the clinic and had numerous operations on his hand. During that time he had no visitors and felt as if he had been abandoned by everyone. However, Ernie had been busy arranging private physiotherapy sessions once he had been discharged from the clinic. Even though these sessions helped Gerry to regain some use of his hand he no longer had the dexterity of movement he had previously enjoyed.

The scar tissue only seemed to be healing at a very slow rate and the sight of his malformed fingers was sometimes too much even for him to bear so he resorted to wearing a leather boxing glove to keep it hidden from view whenever practical.

This limited his work in the centre and Ernie noticed the frustration building up in his assistant, so he took him out on his night-time patrols to show Gerry he had something to offer. However, Mark, in turn, became more resentful of this change in roles and arguments between the two became a frequent occurrence.

"You burn yourself and end up as teacher's pet while I have to stay here and fix these busted machines and any other crap that needs sorting. It's also me who has to make excuses to cover your back when the punters ask awkward questions. I need bloody help around here and if you ain't up to the job Ernie will have to find someone else to pull their weight or I'm off to pastures new and you two can get stuffed."

Ernie heard this latest argument and called them both into his office to try and resolve the problem. "First off, Mark, you're going nowhere. Try it and there might be an accident waiting just around the next corner you turn. Gerry is willing to train one of the lads who is out of work to help you in the centre. The one you know as Banjo is pretty clever with his hands and he's keen to get involved." Ernie continued, "But only with the stuff in the centre; no mention is to be made about our other activities. And you both make sure he doesn't find out what's upstairs in our storeroom. I'll tell my contact on the council that

Gerry needs to change his job role and become a trainer and you, Mark, will have more of a supervisor's role which will mean a pay rise for you both. Does that sound okay?"

Both nodded in agreement, but Mark still had a gripe he wanted resolving.

"A couple of the lads who attend the centre have said that bloke from the old chemist has been asking questions about me and Gerry. He wanted to know how and where he burnt his hand; if it was anything to do with the chip shop fire. He's getting too nosey for my liking and needs to be warned off."

Ernie frowned. "He's not the first to make that connection. One of my ex-colleagues stopped me in the street a few days ago. The answer I gave him was that you two were burning some old refuse in the backyard and Gerry had put too much petrol onto the rubbish and there was a small explosion. Stick to that story and in the meantime I'll have a word with Robin Stockwell."

Mark sneered. "He won't believe that story about burning rubbish. I tried to cover for Gerry on the night of the fire by giving Stockwell a false name but this stupid dope gave him his real name. If he goes to the cops, we're all in the brown stuff."

Gerry retaliated. "For your information, mate, I was in bloody agony that night and wasn't thinking straight."

Mark was about to respond, but Ernie put his hand up for silence.

"Okay both of you, enough! From now on you two will only use nicknames for each other, especially when you're on a job. Let me think of a couple of names that will suit your roles. In the meantime, Mark, I'm contacting your brother tonight to arrange details of the job I want him to do."

22

The next morning Ernie took his two assistants to one side, out of anyone else's hearing.

"Right, Mark, your name will be Torch and you, Gerry, will be Keys. If I need to explain I'll tell you later. Now I'm going to speak to Robin Stockwell."

He found the pharmacist sweeping up glass outside the broken window of his shop. As he got out of his car Ernie enquired, "When did this happen, Robin? Have you got someone coming to fix it for you?"

Pausing in his cleaning-up duties Stockwell replied ruefully, "I was preparing my breakfast at my usual time, about six thirty, when I heard the sound of breaking glass and I came to investigate. I'm just clearing up to make sure nobody cuts themselves on this mess. I can't afford to pay for a new window at this moment so it will have to be boarded up instead. I've got someone coming later this morning, one of Ralph Byewater's workers."

"What about the police, have you informed them?"

Robin gave him a knowing look before replying, "Oh Ernie, you should know they have better things to do with their time, but Sergeant Proudfoot said he would call in later on his way off duty."

Ernie opened the boot of his car and took out a pair of heavy-duty gardening gloves and put them on.

"Let me move those larger pieces of glass, Robin. I will finish clearing up here if you like. I need to talk to you about that incident where you helped one of my lads with his burnt hand."

Robin was silent for several moments. That was also an issue he wanted clarification on, and he believed Ernie was the person with the details. Passing the broom he had been holding to his companion, he said quietly, "If you can finish out here, I will go and make us both some coffee. I also want you to clear up something that has bothered me since that incident."

Ernie took hold of the broom and sensed that the next few minutes were not going to be as straightforward as he had hoped. Knowing Robin would not be satisfied until he had heard answers that convinced him that he was being told the truth, Ernie decided to try distraction tactics. It took him a further ten minutes to make sure no broken glass would cause any hazard to anyone walking past.

He had taken off his gloves when Robin appeared at the door to his flat and summoned Ernie to follow him inside. Indicating to a chair by the kitchen table he put down a cup of coffee in front of his guest. Ernie tried to speak but Robin held up a hand for silence.

"Thank you for helping me to clear up that glass, Ernie. I already have a busy morning ahead of me so I will come to my point straight away. How did young Gerry come to burn his hand so badly? Was it anything to do with the fire at the shop they call the Fish Bar?"

Ernie tried to look offended at such a suggestion.

"No, Robin. He and Mark had been burning some rubbish in the backyard of the centre and I think one of them must have poured some petrol over the fire and it suddenly blew up out of control. Either that or there were some old fireworks amongst the rubbish, I'm not sure…"

Robin cut him short by banging the tabletop.

"It was neither! Those burns were caused by hot fat or oil. Different types of burning liquid cause different kinds of burns and I am convinced Gerry's burns were caused by hot, burning fat. Now, Ernie, I want the truth or I will have to go to the police with this information and let them deal with it."

Ernie couldn't hide the embarrassment he felt at being caught out like this, but he wasn't about to give in to Robin's threat.

"Okay, this is what really happened. Mark and Gerry were out on their security patrol and were checking the alley behind the shops which include the Fish Bar. The extractor fans were on at the chip shop and they could smell the hot oil and knew something wasn't right. Gerry has a set of skeleton keys because they have to check some of the shops they are allowed to enter, but the Fish Bar is not one of those shops, but they decided to check it out anyway."

He explained further, "Gerry heard the bubbling sound coming from one of the fryers and started to move the cover. Mark shouted at him to stand back but it was too late, it gave the hot fat oxygen and it just flared up over his hand. Mark managed to pull him back from the flames and threw a fire blanket over the fryer which saved a lot of extra damage. Mark's shouting also alerted the family living in the flat above and they managed to get out before the fire brigade arrived. The other thing Mark discovered was that the fryer had been left on at the highest temperature. That was either accidental or deliberate, I don't know which."

Robin sat quietly for several minutes, absorbing and dissecting what he had heard. He already knew part of the facts from what Gerry had told him as he was being treated shortly after the incident, but he was still not fully satisfied with Ernie's answer.

"I understand now how the fire started but have you told the police about your suspicions?"

"No, because Gerry doesn't have a locksmith's licence to carry skeleton keys and my security business would be in trouble. You also have to understand that there have been lots of incidents that could be unfairly blamed on my lads if that got out."

Robin continued to push his point, "Gerry gave me a rough outline of what happened, so why did you lie to me, Ernie? We've always helped each other whenever possible. Why couldn't you be straight with me? If that's what really happened, I'm sure your ex-colleagues would give you a fair hearing."

Robin was not prepared for what happened next.

Ernie's face went a crimson colour, he pushed his chair backwards and stood up and shouted angrily, "Nobody will believe anything good I say about the kids who attend the centre and that especially goes for Mark and Gerry!" and he went on to tell his host how Gerry was arrested and held for several hours just because Percy Matthews accused him of starting the fire that burnt his shop down. He had a good job with David Evans but once Matthews took over the business, he made the lad's life a misery; add to that he had to cope with the sudden death of his grandmother and the tragic loss of his girlfriend, Sally.

"As for Mark, he escaped from an abusive father up north and was nearly molested by a filthy rat of a lorry driver on his journey down here. He's no saint by any means but I told him he starts with a clean slate as far as I'm concerned. I'm sorry I lied to you, Robin, but if that's what it takes to protect my lads then so be it. Nobody, it seems, is prepared to give them a second chance but me."

Before Robin could respond Ernie stormed out of the flat, got into his car and drove off at speed. Two men had unloaded large boards and other timber from the back of a lorry and had placed them against the wall of Robin's shop. Moments later Robin came out and looked around, acknowledged the men and started to approach them but noticed Jenny Potter crossing the road towards him with a worried expression on her face.

"Are you all right, Robin? I saw Mr Newsham come out of your flat and drive away at speed. I must say, he didn't look very pleased and I thought something had happened to you."

Robin shook his head. "No, Jenny, he wasn't very happy. Go inside while I talk to the men about the window."

He joined her a few minutes later and offered her a cup of tea which she declined, stating she only came over because she was concerned for his well-being after seeing Ernie drive off in a hurry.

"Don't worry about me, Jenny, Ernie and I had a small difference of opinion over a small matter and he objected to my response. Although I must say, I've never seen him lose his temper in that manner before."

"Oh, I never thought Mr Newsham had a temper, he always seems so pleasant to me. Was it anything to do with the broken window?"

Robin smiled to himself. He knew Jenny was genuinely concerned but she had a habit of sharing her news whenever the opportunity arose so he framed his answer in such a way that would not hold her interest.

"No, Jenny, it was just something of a technical nature that wouldn't make much sense to other people."

Hiding her disappointment at not having new gossip to divulge to others she gave Robin some news instead.

"My sister is going into hospital in Ipswich soon and I will be visiting her towards the end of next week. Have you booked your flight to Canada? I'm sure Natalie will be excited over your trip."

Robin scratched his head and let out a sigh. "Well, the flight is booked but an oversight on my part might force me to cancel it. I forgot to check my passport and it expired a couple of months ago. If it doesn't arrive in time I'm stuck."

"But surely you can ring up the passport people and tell them the problem? My niece was in a similar situation over a holiday last year and they sent her passport by special courier to make sure it arrived in time."

Robin let out a laugh, grabbed Jenny by the shoulders and planted a kiss on her forehead. She went bright red and looked in horror at him.

"Jenny, you're my saviour! Of course that's the answer! Stella would have checked out such details in plenty of time. Women are more organised in that way."

Pleased that she had solved his problem Jenny visibly relaxed. "What is the date of your flight and will you want your usual roast dinner after this weekend?"

He thought for a moment before shaking his head. "My flight is late on Saturday of next week. Ralph Byewater and his wife are driving me to the airport. So no dinner that weekend, thank you, Jenny. Now I must make that phone call about my passport. I'm sure we will see each other before I leave."

She took the hint and left him to his chores which included making tea for the two workers he had promised earlier. His thoughts drifted back to Ernie's reaction, especially the outburst of temper. That man had things on his mind that were troubling him, and he decided the signs were not good.

About an hour after the workmen left having completed their task, Robin Stockwell had yet another visitor. On investigating who had rung the doorbell, he found Sergeant Proudfoot admiring the handiwork of his last visitors and he said on seeing Robin, "They've done a good job here, Robin, anybody would need to use a chainsaw to get through this lot. Do you mind if I come in for a moment? I need to satisfy my curiosity over something."

Robin nodded and led the way into his flat, but the sergeant turned towards the rear of the old pharmacy.

"Sorry, Robin, but it's in here I need to check if you don't mind. I need to see that your chemicals and the like are stored safely and secure."

The pharmacist now knew why Proudfoot was keen to come and see his shop.

"I haven't forgotten about health and safety rules, Sergeant. All my materials are securely locked away in a safe place. Most of the materials I used to dispense are nearly all gone, although I've started to experiment with a new perfume I would like to develop. But those ingredients are also under lock and key."

Proudfoot turned to face him and asked, "I'm sure you are taking the necessary precautions to keep these items safe, but have you notified the local authorities about the new items you are storing? Also, are there any items here you no longer use that need to be disposed of in a safe manner?"

Stockwell knew he had lapsed in that area and attempted to defend his lack of action.

"I appreciate your need to check these things out, Sergeant, and I have yet to sort out those items I no longer use. I will make a start on that work immediately. However, I will not be able to complete that task until after I return from my trip to Canada."

Proudfoot trusted the pharmacist's word and his sincerity in carrying out the work, but he knew he had a duty to report the matter to the local authorities under the COSHH regulations.

"I appreciate you are adhering to the Control of Substances Act, but I still have to report what I have found to the relevant people. It will be then up to them to decide what to do next and how soon they act. I'm sorry, Robin. I have no choice in the matter."

Knowing the sergeant was only doing his duty didn't make Robin feel any better. It had always been his intention to safely dispose of the chemicals he no longer required, but right now was not a convenient time for him. So he resigned himself to the possible disruption in his current busy schedule and simply said, "Very well, Peter, I can only hope that council bureaucracy will continue at its present pace and allow me to prepare for my trip to Canada in peace."

The sergeant gave him a little wink. "Between you and me, Robin, the head of the environment department has just returned from sick leave and he has a mountain of cases to catch up on but I still have to file my observations."

Robin nodded in comprehension and Sergeant Proudfoot left the pharmacist to continue his preparations for his trip abroad.

***

Ernie sat in his office at the leisure centre waiting for the phone call that would, hopefully, complete his plans for getting rid of someone.

The arranged time for the phone call had passed more than fifteen minutes ago and he was on the verge of going to check if he had been given the correct time when the call was to be made. He cursed under his breath and stood up to leave the office but as he put his hand on the door handle the phone rang. He turned around and picked up the receiver and the person on the other end of the line gave the correct coded message. He replied with the agreed response.

"I understand you know the nature of this arrangement and I think if you knew the true identity things would be much clearer. Does the name…?"

Ernie gave the real name of his victim. The man on the other end of the line let out a stream of obscenities.

"Too bloody right I know him. I've a few scores to settle with that slimy toad. Am I doing this on my own or does someone else have an interest in his disposal?"

Ernie thought for a moment before replying then decided to dangle a carrot before his caller.

"One other has a similar interest and another holds our target indirectly responsible for a relative's death. I'm sure I could persuade at least one to assist you."

The caller sneered, "I don't want any bloody amateurs getting in my way so tell the second one to stay well clear. Who's the first one?"

"I thought you would have worked that one out, Kevin. It's your brother, Mark."

Kevin gave a short laugh, "Mark? Is he with you? I thought he had gone to Bristol or beyond. How come he hasn't bumped into the target if he's in your area?"

"I'll explain that once you're down here. Now, Mark told me you wanted to get out of the country after doing the job. Would Canada interest you?"

"You get me a ticket and some Canadian money and that will suit me. My passport is all up to date. If you give me about two thousand in both UK and Canadian plus the ticket, then we've got a deal."

This was more than Ernie had envisaged but as it would literally kill two birds with one stone he agreed on the price.

"Okay, it's a deal. On condition that you get down here by next Thursday and we can make final arrangements."

Kevin agreed and the call was ended.

***

Ernie had decided it would be in his interest to make peace with Robin Stockwell in order for his plan to work. First he would have to tell Mark what was going to happen, but he would not tell Gerry until the last possible moment.

Ernie had rung the doorbell to Robin's flat for a second time and as there was no response he turned to leave. As he was about to get into his car the door to the flat opened and Robin peered around to see who had disturbed him in his task of sorting out the containers of chemicals. On seeing the ex-policeman he turned to close the door, feeling that there was nothing to be gained by talking to Ernie at this moment, and started to retreat back into the flat but he was not quick enough. "Oh, Robin, have you a few minutes to spare? I want to clear up our little misunderstanding from the other day."

"Can't it wait, Ernie? I'm rather busy sorting out my stockroom before I go away."

Seizing his opportunity Ernie walked up to him and said pleasantly, "In that case, I'll give you a hand. Three people will be able to do things a lot quicker", and he tapped on the passenger window and signalled to Mark to come and join them.

Robin looked pensively at Mark. He wasn't keen on letting him come in but Ernie told Mark to go back to the car to fetch some gloves for them to use.

While he was on the errand Ernie said, "Robin, I've been thinking about our conversation the other day and I think you have a point. When we are both back from our respective trips abroad, I will accompany you to the police station and we can clear the whole matter up. Does that sound fair?"

Robin was very wary at this suggestion, but he wanted to think things over first before responding, "I'll give it some thought."

As he finished speaking Mark returned and the two visitors encroached on his personal space and he was forced to take a step backwards. Ernie gently forced his way past and said, "The storeroom is through here, isn't it, Robin?"

The pharmacist had little choice but to turn and lead the way into the room behind the main shop area. Once in the store he said very seriously, "You have to take extreme care when handling some of these chemicals, so please follow my instructions to the letter. You and I, Ernie, will move the more volatile items and you, young man, can stack those boxes in the corner to give us some space. Incidentally, I don't know your name?"

"It's Martin," Ernie said before his friend could speak. Mark took the hint and started to clear the area as requested but Stockwell put a hand on his shoulder.

"Martin, stack those boxes carefully as some still contain powders and other items that will cause burns if you get them on your skin. Incidentally, how is your friend, Gerry? Neither of you has mentioned him. I trust you took him to hospital for treatment?"

Mark's anxious glance in the direction of his boss was not missed by the pharmacist even though Ernie spoke without stopping his work.

"I took him to a private clinic where he was treated by a burns specialist. He has some movement back in his hand but it will never be back to what it was before the accident."

On hearing the mention of a private clinic Stockwell couldn't help wondering why Gerry hadn't been taken to the hospital he had mentioned as it had a formidable reputation for treating severe burn cases. It sounded like Ernie had something to hide from any inquisitive authorities. But he kept his counsel, deciding instead to follow up his concerns after his return from Canada.

However, there was one important factor he didn't notice at first as they continued working. As he moved each item Ernie asked if the container held any inflammable liquids, deliberately alerting Mark to each item highlighted.

They continued working for nearly two hours before Stockwell was satisfied he had isolated the items he wanted to keep.

Ernie casually asked Robin a question as they finished.

"What's so special about that group of containers we've put in the far corner? I notice some haven't even been opened."

Not realising he was giving Ernie the vital information he was after, Stockwell replied, "Those are the ingredients for my new venture. I've developed a new perfume and I'm taking half a dozen miniature samples in my case to Canada for Natalie to test. If she approves, I will be able to produce enough to sell as my first batch."

Ernie looked impressed and asked, "What exactly goes into making perfumes? Is it the mixture of alcohol and the different aromas, or are there any other ingredients?"

Stockwell smiled. "A small amount of petrochemicals is also included but the mixture of aromas and other items I cannot divulge and I can't give you the relative quantities, I'm afraid. Trade secrets and all that, Ernie."

"I understand, Robin. Have you received your passport yet?"

"No, it's being delivered by courier on Saturday morning. Then I will have to go and collect the air tickets and money from the travel agent. The Byewaters will come to drive me to Heathrow for my early morning flight on Sunday. It will be a bit of a rush, I'm afraid, but it can't be helped."

Ernie suddenly realised that this change of events would not fit in with his plans so he casually remarked, "Rather than you having to rush around on the morning of your flight, I could take you to the travel agent to collect your tickets and money on Friday. I don't like the idea of you walking around with all that cash on you."

Stockwell was reluctant to accept any more favours from Newsham and he tried to decline the offer.

"Thank you for offering, Ernie, but I don't want to put you to any extra trouble, I could always get a taxi back from the travel agent."

Ernie smiled and used his most persuasive tone and manner. "After all you have done for me? It will be no trouble at all, and besides, I have to go there to finalise my own details anyway. Then I can bring you back here, collect my luggage and drive down to London. It's just a pity our flights were not on the same night as we could have travelled down together."

Robin didn't have any suitable argument to the offer and reluctantly accepted.

"Very well, Ernie, thank you. I just hope Mr Phillips will let me have the tickets without showing my passport. I must admit that has worried me slightly."

"I'm sure we can convince Andrew that you will keep your word about bringing in your passport when it arrives. If you need someone to take the passport down to show him, I'll give you Gerry's number and you can ask him to run the errand."

Robin laughed and shook his head. "I'm sure that won't be necessary."

They shook hands and arranged a time on the coming Friday for Ernie to visit the travel agent. As they drove away Ernie laughed for very different reasons. He had all the information he required and he knew Mark had been listening attentively. Without realising the true nature of Ernie and Mark's visit the pharmacist had divulged enough information to sign his own death warrant. Ernie told Mark his expectations of how Stockwell would meet his end. The problem would be convincing Gerry that they had little choice in the matter.

"Your brother is arriving on Thursday afternoon and I'm putting him up in a hotel in town. If there's time I'll arrange a meeting with him for you and he can tell you who the target is. There will be no Friday-night patrol for you and Gerry, there's other business to sort out instead.

"You didn't hear me agreeing to go to the police with Stockwell after I return from my trip. I only told him as a stalling tactic as he was planning to tell them his suspicions about the Fish Bar fire before he left for Canada. If he did that then it would get the police reinvestigating some of our other activities and my contact on the police authority committee would get nervous and start panicking."

Ernie added, "No, Mark, even though he and his wife helped me in the past, Mr Stockwell will have to be silenced once and for all. Basically, it's him or us! I want you to think of a way of making a fire at his shop and flat look like a pure accident. Are you game?"

Mark was quiet for several moments before he nodded and said, "I reckon I could organise that; on my own or with Kevin?"

"Neither. Gerry has to be involved. If he is part of any incident we can incriminate him if he gets cold feet at a later date. I also want you to work on him by emphasising that if Stockwell gets a chance to talk we'll all end up inside. I'm sure you are capable of painting a lurid enough picture of what he would face."

"Okay, but when do we do this? I thought I was going to help Kevin with his job."

"Both jobs are to take place late on Friday. You will be helping Kevin by relieving Stockwell of his Canadian money and air ticket before his accidental fire starts."

Mark said nothing, merely nodding. He had always dreamed of doing a spectacular job like the one Ernie had given him. I'll show them what I can do he decided smugly.

23

It was now the Thursday before Ernie was due to fly to Australia and there was a last-minute change to plans he needed to convince Graham Bishop was unavoidable.

"Graham, I know what I said, but I was relying on my contact to send me a deposit once he had seen the goods. I'm already out of pocket myself, what with paying for sending your stuff via a secure source and my own flight and accommodation costs."

Bishop was in no mood to compromise. He was certain this bent copper was trying to con him out of the remaining £2,000 he had agreed to pay.

"I guessed you would pull a fast one, Newsham, so I took out some insurance in case you were fool enough to try. Get me my £2,000 by midnight on Friday or I'll tip off the customs people at Heathrow that you've smuggled some rare African artefacts out of the country with the help of that tight-fisted fence, Connelly."

There was only one option left for Ernie to attempt. Appeal to Bishop's sense of greed.

"Unfortunately, Graham, I'm flying out just after midnight Friday. However, I will leave £3,000 at the leisure centre for you to collect after ten o'clock that evening. If the money is not here you will still have time to stop me boarding my flight. The extra

£1,000 is a sign of my goodwill. Do you accept my compromise offer?"

The trick worked. Ernie could see, from the look in Bishop's eyes, that he was already thinking of what to spend the extra windfall on. Booze more than likely.

"Who will hand over the money if you're not here?"

"Young Gerry, you know him of course; you stole the artefacts from his gran, but he won't give you any bother. I'll tell him to let you in through the car park entrance once all the patrons have gone. I will also make it clear to him that he must count out the money in front of you. He can do that in the swimming pool area as the cleaners will still be tidying up in the cafe."

"And nobody else will be there?"

Bishop hadn't forgotten the time Gerry and that woman, Sally, had challenged him in front of his boss. Time to settle a few old scores he hoped.

Ernie noticed the gleam in Bishop's eyes, and he wasn't prepared to take any chances with Gerry's well-being, but he simply replied, "One of my security patrols may be around but I'll tell them to stay clear of the pool area. If you like, he can give you a lift home after. You don't want to be walking the streets with all that money on you. It would be a shame if you got mugged after we've taken all this trouble to finalise payment."

"I'd like to see anyone try," Bishop sneered. "Don't forget to tell your blokes, no funny business cos I can cut up rough if necessary."

After leaving Bishop, Ernie went to keep his next appointment, picked up Kevin from the train station and drove him to the hotel where his room had been booked.

"So what's the game plan regarding my dear old dad? I've brought a couple of shooters I'm giving to Mark before I disappear."

Ernie was silent for a while, pretending to concentrate on his driving. Finally, he spoke. "No guns for this job, it's got to look like an accident. A tragic case of a drunkard on his way home and falling into the river and drowning would be appropriate, I think."

"Does the old bugger go anywhere near the river? As far as I know he stays well clear of water cos he can't swim."

Ernie pulled into the hotel car park but made no attempt to get out of the car. Instead he said, "Your dad goes to the same pub every Friday night and his walk home takes him along by the river. He thinks he is collecting the balance of the money I owe him in the pool area of the leisure centre. He's only expecting to see young Gerry and a security guard. You can finish him off in the pool and dump his body in the river. Make it look like he slipped and fell in. Go and book in to your room and I'll pick you up later and show you some likely spots where someone could have an accident. But remember, Kevin, no guns."

Kevin nodded, retrieved his bag from the boot of the car and walked into the hotel.

***

Jenny Potter rang the doorbell of the Stockwell residence for the second time and was getting slightly anxious at the non-appearance of Robin and was about to return home when the door opened.

"Oh, hello, Jenny, sorry to keep you waiting, I was just doing some last-minute packing for my trip. What can I do for you?"

"I'm sorry to disturb you at such a busy time, Robin, I just wanted to let you know I'm going to visit my sister in Ipswich tomorrow, but I will not be back until after ten o'clock. I hope to see you before you leave on Saturday. Is there anything I can do to help?"

"I don't think so, Jenny, thank you for the offer. I won't be leaving until just after lunch so I'm sure we will see each other before I go."

Jenny hesitated, clearly with something else on her mind.

"Very well. I noticed Mr Newsham was with you for some time the other morning. Did you manage to talk to him about your concerns?"

Not wanting to continue the conversation on his doorstep, Robin invited his neighbour in for a few minutes. Once they were both in the flat, he said, "I still have some concerns about some of his associates but I'm sure our differences can be resolved after we've both come back from our trips abroad. Now if you will excuse me, Jenny, I still have to find one or two items to pack."

"Oh, are you sure there's nothing I can do to assist you?"

He smiled disarmingly. "Thank you for your kind offer, it's just a matter of choosing which items I will need most. However, there is one thing you could do for me when I see you before I leave. You remember I told you I was in the process of making up some perfume samples? I will leave two sample bottles of the perfume on the coffee table in the living room for you. If either of us forgets, please feel free to pick them up when you call in to check all is well in the flat. I take it you still have a spare key?"

"Yes, I do, and thank you," she said beaming broadly. It was not often she was given a present by anyone.

He gently ushered her to the door and said, "I must finish off my packing now, Jenny. So, if for any reason I don't see you before I leave for Canada, look after yourself and your cats and pass on my best wishes to your family in Ipswich."

He gave her a kiss on the forehead.

Her reaction caught Robin by surprise. She flung her arms around him, stood on tiptoe and kissed him on his left cheek.

"And please remember me to Natalie."

He nodded and let her out of the flat.

***

As instructed, Mark had begun to put doubts into Gerry's mind concerning Robin Stockwell's good intentions.

"Gerry, I'm telling you Stockwell is going to go to the police once he gets back from Canada to say he can prove you and I were responsible for that fire in the chip shop. If he does that, you, me and probably Ernie will be grilled for all the other fires and break-ins that have taken place in this town."

"But Ernie made sure we had alibis for those other jobs."

"Ernie's word will be worth nowt if that inspector – what's his name? Gates – gets involved. Ernie doesn't like him from past encounters so if you think you can stand another session with that bloke, you're kidding yourself. Think, Gerry. You won't get bail. We'll all end up on remand and that's no kindergarten, believe me. There's some tough cookies in there; some of them will make your hand an even worse mess than it is now just for fun."

"You're always making fun of my hand, Mark. I ended up like this because of both yours and Ernie's methods of trying to frighten people to pay security fees."

Mark stood up threateningly. "All you've done since you burnt your bloody hand is moan and whine. I've only poked fun about it just to get you used to how others could treat you. They'll call you a cripple or spassy, so just get used to life, you moaner."

Gerry stood up and started to walk out of the room but turned around before opening the door and said with equal venom, "Thanks a bunch, Mark! The so-called tough guy who wouldn't go near water because Daddy didn't teach him to swim. Remember who saved you, Mark? It was me."

Once he was outside the room he shivered. Mark was right, he wouldn't survive even being on remand, let alone a prison term. But what could he do about it? If Stockwell went to the police it would only be a matter of time before he cracked under questioning and gave the game away.

Robin Stockwell didn't seem like a man who would succumb to threats, bribery or blackmail, so what other options did they have? If Ernie's only alternative suggestion was the unthinkable, i.e. murder Stockwell, who would do it? Mark had let it slip that his brother, Kevin, was coming on a visit; was that the prime reason to his journey here?

His thoughts were interrupted by Ernie calling him to attend a meeting in his office in the next few minutes. He was relieved to see that there would only be the two of them in attendance.

"Gerry, I need you to do me a favour tomorrow night. I will be leaving £3,000 to be paid to Graham Bishop as part of the deal I made with him to dispose of some items on my Australia trip. Don't worry, there will be a new security guard on duty to make sure Bishop doesn't try any funny business. The guard will hold onto the money until Bishop turns up at the rear of the centre. Let him in and take him to the pool area where the money is to be handed over. If Bishop wants the money to be counted out, do it for him."

"What happens then?" Gerry asked.

"You make your excuses about going to check something in another part of the building and leave them alone in the pool area. If I tell you any more it could incriminate both of us if anything should happen. No more questions, please, Gerry."

Gerry hesitated, uncertain whether he should bring up the other subject that was concerning him.

"Mark has been making remarks about Robin Stockwell and that he plans on going to see the police after he comes back from his trip abroad. Is this true?"

Ernie looked at his young colleague for what seemed like an age to Gerry before giving his reply. "I'm afraid it's true, Gerry. And it leaves us with very little option as to how we must proceed."

Gerry sat in stunned silence, the colour draining from his face. His boss didn't have to say another word. The full realisation of what was required to be done hit him in the pit of his stomach.

Ernie noticed the change in his complexion, opened the large drawer in his desk and took out a bottle of whisky and a couple of glasses. He half-filled each glass and passed one to Gerry.

"Drink this, lad. It's not a pleasant thought but we have no choice; it's him or us."

Gerry took a swallow of his drink, coughed several times at the bitter taste and asked quietly, "Do I have to be there, Ernie? I owe him a lot."

Ernie suddenly became angry. "You owe him a lot! I owe him and his wife as much, if not more."

He regained his composure and continued, "I don't like this any more than you, but if he goes to the police it will only be a matter of time before they catch up with us. I've no intention of spending the next several years behind bars and I'm sure you don't relish the idea either. Yes, Gerry, I'm afraid you will have to assist Mark. I need a reliable person like you to make sure he doesn't leave any clues behind."

Gerry was trying desperately to find a way out for himself and he pleaded, "Ernie, I don't know if I can go through with it. What about Mark's brother? What's his part in all this?"

"Kevin is here to sort out some other business for me regarding Graham Bishop. I'm going to tell you things I didn't want you to know so are you sure you want me to carry on?"

Gerry nodded. Anything to get his mind off Robin Stockwell.

"As you know, my trip to Australia concerns items stolen by Bishop that will fetch a very good price over there. In trying to sell them off in London he shot the member of a gang and they are hot on his trail. He threatened to tell this gang about our work here unless I helped him. Nobody blackmails me and gets away with it, so Kevin is helping me sort things out.

"Another thing I found out is that it was Bishop who stole those items from your gran's flat. He apparently heard you and Sally talking in the library."

At the mention of his gran Gerry suddenly took notice and said, "Let me sort out Bishop. Kevin and Mark can deal with the other matters."

Ernie smiled, "Gerry, Bishop is much bigger and stronger than you. With the best will in the world you wouldn't manage him on your own. No, this is a family matter and Kevin and Mark have first shout on Bishop. In case you didn't know, he's their father, real name is Bryan Ramsbottom."

Gerry was speechless so Ernie continued, "Once Kevin has sorted him out, he's going to dump the body in the river to make it look like he fell in on his way home from the pub. The pool will have to be cleaned out to make sure there are no signs of someone drowning in there."

Gerry was desperate to change the subject about killing people.

"What's taking place with the refurbishment and what are Mark and I supposed to do while you're away?"

"You two can take a holiday as well. I've paid in some holiday money into your accounts but I need you to do a couple of patrols in that time, just to keep our customers happy. That shouldn't stop you going away for a break somewhere. Have you got anywhere in mind?"

Gerry was quiet for a moment, then he spoke. "I might go up to Derbyshire and visit Sally's grave. I never really got any chance to say goodbye."

His head dropped and a single tear ran down his cheek before he managed to wipe it away with his sleeve. Ernie, having noted the reaction, spoke quietly. "Take as long as you want. There won't be that much to do around here with some parts being refurbished. Just one thing, both of you make sure nobody gets into our special storeroom and that it stays locked at all times.

"I'll be seeing Robin tomorrow, so I'll make sure he's fully occupied before his trip to Canada. Mark has got special instructions that need not concern you, but you must accompany him to Stockwell's flat, understand?"

Gerry nodded, rose to his feet and left without saying another word. He was determined to get involved in some way with dealing with Bishop.

***

Later that evening and with few people around, Ernie took Kevin to a couple of locations along the riverbank that would be ideal places to dispose of Bishop's body.

"I don't want to know which location you choose to dump him, as long as it remains hidden for a while," was Ernie's only comment.

They went to collect Mark and the two brothers were left to talk family matters.

Ernie was not pleased knowing Kevin was about to pass on a pair of replica handguns that had been engineered to be capable of being lethal. Also included in the package were several rounds of ammunition to use in the guns.

Fortunately the guns would only remain hidden for twenty-four hours after the deaths of Bishop and Stockwell. At this point, Gerry would be forced to devise a plan to remove the weapons to a safer location and show them to Ernie upon his return.

The following morning Ernie took Robin Stockwell to Andrew Phillips' travel agency to collect his Canadian money and air tickets. Phillips attempted to stick to the rules about not handing over tickets until he had the passport details, but Ernie had his counter arguments ready.

"Mr Phillips, I'm sure you have known Robin as an outstanding member of this community for many years and he would never knowingly want to break any rules. But his passport may not arrive until late morning and he will be pushed for time to bring it along to you for verification."

The travel agent felt very uncomfortable in trying to stand up to the former policeman but he made one final attempt.

"I realise you will be busy, Mr Stockwell, but I have rules to follow when it comes to these very necessary procedures. I'm sorry, it's nothing personal I can assure you."

However, Ernie knew the agent's Achilles heel and played on his weakness.

"We both appreciate there are rules to stick to but you might have a sudden rush of customers tomorrow and you wouldn't want to lose a sale in those circumstances would you?"

Seeing the doubt in Phillips' eyes Ernie pressed home his alternative suggestion.

"I believe it's just a matter of filling in a form or two, so why not give Robin the paperwork now, including a spare copy in case of an error? He can fill in the details and if he has time, drop them in on his way to the airport. If he can't manage that then putting them in the post will mean you will receive the completed paperwork by Tuesday at the latest."

Both Stockwell and Phillips seemed happy with this arrangement so once Robin had signed a cheque for the tickets and money, their business was concluded, and Ernie then drove Robin back to his flat.

"Thank you for sorting out the passport problem, Ernie. I believe the courier is supposed to arrive before 9.00 a.m. tomorrow morning. I would possibly have had time to drop the forms in but as you said, there could have been a hold-up at Mr Phillips' shop. I will fill in my details on the forms right away and just have the passport number to complete in the morning and then put them in the postbox around the corner, along with the spare copy if I don't need it. I hope your trip to Australia goes well and that we can resolve the matters concerning Gerry's burnt hand when we both arrive home. I'm just a little uncomfortable about the various versions I've been told."

Ernie put a hand on his shoulder and said, "Put it out of your mind for now, Robin, events will take care of things. Just enjoy your break in Canada. One thing, can I suggest you leave those forms in a prominent place so you won't have to go hunting around for them when your passport arrives?"

"I will place them on the coffee table under the two bottles of perfume I'm leaving behind for Jenny Potter when she calls around in the morning."

They shook hands and Ernie left the pharmacist as he still had two further tasks to sort out before leaving for Heathrow and the perfect alibi.

Returning to the centre he called Gerry into his office to give him a couple of extra instructions.

First of all he was to remove the lane markers from the pool as it was overdue for a steam clean. Secondly, before handing over the money, he was to offer Bishop a glass of whisky to show there were no hard feelings between Ernie and the thief. Ernie took out a bottle of whisky from the filing cabinet along with two glasses.

Then it was time to give Mark his final orders. Ernie phoned him at the flat.

"Mark, as well as the tickets and money you need to find, there are a couple of forms that Kevin will have to complete by filling in his passport details. These forms will be on the coffee table under some perfume bottles. Robin is kindly leaving the ideal accelerant to help spread the fire."

Ernie put the phone down, still with the echo of Mark's laughter ringing in his ear. He felt a little sorry for Robin but he should not have interfered in something that was none of his business in the first place.

Once tonight's work had been completed it only left one person to be removed from the equation on his return from Australia.

***

There was no late session held in the pool area that evening so Gerry told the other staff members they could finish early. Subsequently, the cafe area was also deserted of patrons and the cleaners finished their duties ahead of schedule.

Gerry was just finishing the removal of the lane markers in the pool when he heard voices approaching from the car park entrance. Mark walked slightly ahead of a taller man who was evidently his brother, Kevin. As they came closer Gerry noticed Mark carrying a bulky package that he held close to his body.

Mark made the briefest of introductions although Kevin hardly seemed to acknowledge Gerry's presence. He gave a slight nod in his direction and then continued looking around the pool area. Gerry laid down the pole with the grappling hook on the end on top of the rubber lane markers that still had droplets of water running into the drainage channels at the edge of the pool. Mark called to him over his shoulder as he headed towards the staircase that led to Ernie's office.

"I'm taking this box upstairs and getting Kevin one of the security jackets that Ernie told him to wear. Where's the money you're supposed to be handing over?"

"On Ernie's desk," Gerry replied as he approached Kevin warily.

"Hi, Ernie told me that I'm to meet Bishop, sorry, your father, at the back door and bring him over to the table to count the money out for him. Then you take over, is that right?"

Kevin looked at him with cold eyes but said nothing for what seemed like an age. When he finally spoke, Gerry felt a chill run down his spine. "You forgot one thing, kid; then you disappear. This is a private family matter. The old man is not due for another ten minutes at least so stay well away from us if you know what's good for you."

Gerry wanted to protest but sensed he was already on dangerous ground so simply nodded his head. His only chance was to appeal to Mark, hoping he could convince his brother to allow him to stay in the vicinity. Instead he turned away and went up the staircase to speak with his colleague in the privacy of Ernie's office.

"Mark, Kevin told me that once your dad turns up, I have to leave the building. Ernie said nothing about doing that so I'm staying. If he forces me to leave then you can deal with Stockwell by yourself, it's up to you."

"If Kev says you have to scarper, I'd advise you to listen. He doesn't take too kindly to anyone who challenges him."

Mark had already pocketed the bundle of money and was about to pick up three plastic cups and a bottle of whisky, but Gerry stepped in front of his friend and blocked the exit from the office.

"Mark, listen. I'm going to make sure your dad pays for my gran's death, one way or the other. I'll stay in the background by clearing up those lane markers or doing something else. Back me up or Stockwell is your responsibility."

Mark was about to argue but was interrupted by someone banging on the car park entrance door. He pointed to the jacket on the back of a chair and hissed, "Take that to Kev, he needs it as a disguise. I'll do what I can but no promises."

Gerry grabbed the jacket and ran down the stairs and tossed it to Kevin as he was about to dash for the door, but Kevin grabbed his arm and said, "Stall him. We need to hide somewhere before he comes in. The old bastard is early for a change."

A second series of banging on the door was followed by Bishop's impatient shouts.

"Somebody let me in, or I'll break this friggin' door down. It's bloody cold out here!"

Mark placed the paper cups and bottle of alcohol onto a table and disappeared out of sight with his brother. Gerry took a deep breath and walked calmly to open the door.

"About bloody time too, kiddo. Too busy reading your comics, I suppose."

Bishop pushed past Gerry and took a couple of steps inside before stopping abruptly. He looked around suspiciously, taking in the scene before turning to Gerry.

"Newsham told me there would be a security guard here as well. Where's he hiding then?"

Gerry made a show of looking at his watch and said, "You're five minutes early, Mr Bishop, the security bloke doesn't start until ten o'clock."

As he finished speaking the sound of a toilet being flushed could be heard and he started walking towards the pool area but Bishop pulled him back by his shoulder.

"Hold it right there, sunshine. There's something not quite right here. Don't do anything sudden like, or I might be tempted to put a bullet in your backside."

"Ernie didn't tell me anything about you carrying a gun and I don't know how the security man will react."

Bishop's laugh was full of sarcasm. "Did Newsham expect me to walk in here with no insurance? Give me some credit, I've been in these situations before and nearly got caught out the last time. Now lead the way and no funny business."

Gerry walked slowly ahead, debating whether he could risk trying to warn the others about Bishop's claim to having a gun. He pushed open the swing door to the pool area and to his dismay one person was sitting with his back to the door and the other was kneeling by the lane markers, apparently trying to disconnect them into smaller, more manageable lengths. At least Gerry now knew who was kneeling and why Mark was sat at the table.

Bishop gave Gerry a none-too-gentle push in the direction of the table where Mark was sitting. He didn't seem to pay much attention to Kevin at first. Once round the front of the table he could see Mark's features and he let out a hollow laugh.

"Oh, the second of Newsham's security scam, he sure likes having kids around him. Trouble is you need real men to do work like this."

He gave a loud belch before drawing out a pistol from his coat pocket. Then he looked over at Kevin and spoke aloud. "Wait a minute! Newsham told me there would only be Cool Hand Luke here and a security guard. So who is this character playing with the rubber hoses? Get over here by the table right now or I'm liable to get very nervous and maybe shoot someone by mistake."

He gave another loud belch and rocked slightly on his heels. It was clear he had been drinking heavily. Kevin turned around and walked slowly towards him, singing softly the first few words of an old ballad.

'Oh Mine Papa'.

Bishop stared, the words not penetrating his thoughts until Kevin was about six feet away. Then the realisation dawned on him.

"Where the hell did you come from? Are you working for Newsham as well?"

Kevin continued smiling and said nothing, calmly walking behind Mark. He sat down on the chair next to his brother. Bishop looked at them both and for the first time he noted the similarity between them. He looked directly at Mark and spoke in a hoarse whisper. "You're young Mark, ain't you? I've seen you around town a few times and it kept on nagging me. Now I know why. When did you move down here?"

Mark could not hide the resentment in his voice as he spoke. "About a year ago, not that it concerns you, anyway."

303

Kevin gave him a slight nudge. "Come on, Mark, this is a family gathering, long overdue in my books. Let's have a drink to celebrate this memorable moment," and he reached for the bottle of whisky and began pouring it into the three plastic cups.

"What about stumpy over there?" Bishop asked as he kept his hand on the gun.

"He's not family," Kevin said dismissively.

Gerry clearly heard the comments but kept his thoughts on the plan he was formulating to surprise Bishop. He stood up and gathered the coils of the first lane marker, along with the hooked pole and dragged them behind Mark and Kevin to a point where they could be hung on the wall to dry. He returned to collect the next set, taking the same route as before. He did exactly the same with the next two sets of lane markers.

However, he walked behind Bishop on his next return, judging the distance between the back of Bishop's chair and the edge of the pool. The others took very little notice of his slight diversion and continued their small talk. Mark added very little to the conversation. It was mostly a two-way dialogue between Kevin and his father.

The gun was still within easy reach of Bishop's right hand but he had been lulled into a more relaxed state, possibly due to the amount of alcohol he had consumed.

As he walked behind their father with the fifth set of coils, Gerry made a motion to Kevin and Mark telling them to hold Bishop in deeper conversation. Mark didn't seem to notice but Kevin sensed something was about to happen and he sat slightly forward as he spoke.

"So how much do you reckon Newsham will get for his trip to Australia and what's your share?"

Gerry was on his return journey to collect the final set of markers and Kevin noticed that he carried the pole balanced on his left shoulder. As he passed behind their victim who had just given an estimated value of his share, Kevin sat forward and shouted, "How much did you say?"

This distraction gave Gerry enough time to swing the pole around as he swivelled on his heels and hooked the right side of the chair occupied by Bishop and pulled it away from the table. The rubber feet of the chair skated across the damp surface towards the pool edge.

Bishop let out a yell and attempted to stand up but Kevin was more alert and quicker in his reaction. Pushing the gun across the table in Mark's direction, he then gave the chair his father was still sat on a hefty kick which sent both chair and occupant into the pool. With the weight of his outdoor clothes and his lack of swimming experience Bishop disappeared under the surface of the water and didn't reappear for nearly half a minute. Kevin turned and smiled at Gerry.

"Nice one, kid, you're okay by me. Let's have that pole so that I can finish off the job I've been paid to do."

He took the pole from Gerry's grasp and turned towards the pool just as his father resurfaced, coughing and spluttering. He tried to speak but all he succeeded in doing was taking in more mouthfuls of water. Kevin knelt by the pool and held the pole out towards his father but once he had caught hold of the hook at the end he was prevented from coming in any closer to the edge of the pool and safety.

Bishop managed to shout out between gasps for breath, "What are you doing, you stupid bastard? Get me out of here. You know I can't bloody swim."

Kevin spoke in a cold, cruel tone. "Oh no, Daddyo, it's payback time for not giving me and Mark a fair chance of a good life. You were more interested in boozing and chasing skirts to care about us and our mum. Go and join the fishes where you belong!"

And with his final remark he twisted the hook from his father's grasp, pushed, and held him under the surface for the next five minutes.

This was too much for Gerry who ran for the nearest toilet to be violently sick. By the time he eventually returned to the pool, Mark and Kevin had pulled their father's body out and were searching his pockets. To Gerry, they looked like a couple of vultures feeding on their prey. The disgust was evident in his voice when he spoke.

"For God's sake, isn't it enough that we've just killed him? Do you have to squabble over his belongings so soon after?"

Kevin stopped what he was doing, walked over to Gerry and put a hand on his shoulder before speaking in a quite conciliatory tone.

"Gerry, in my business you make sure there's no evidence left behind to link you to the victim. Mark and I need to check he's got nothing in his pockets or at his digs to link us to him. While you're carrying out your next little job, I'll take his keys and give his flat the once over, okay?"

Gerry thought for a moment, nodded reluctantly and went over to the table to finish off the remains of the bottle of whisky. There would be further challenging situations to face before the night was over.

While Kevin wrapped the body in a tarpaulin Mark reversed the van through the large open door so that they could load up without being observed. Earlier that day Kevin had taken a casual stroll along the riverbank to find a suitable secluded spot to park the van.

***

Following Kevin's instructions Mark parked in the designated spot. The weather had deteriorated with heavy, blustery showers; the kind of conditions that made people think twice about venturing out on such a night.

Their plan had been to open the tarpaulin at the top of the bank and let the body slide down into the river, but it was held up by long grass at the water's edge. They couldn't leave the body in that position so both men had to scramble down to manoeuvre it into the river. But Kevin was not satisfied with leaving the body floating on the surface of the water.

He stood on the wooden jetty used by local fishermen, and with the aid of the pole and hook he dragged and then pushed the body under the wooden structure.

There were numerous discarded fishing lines, some with weights attached in the water and after much pushing and pulling he managed to wrap some over the body.

In order to make a decent job of entangling the body with the lines Kevin had to half immerse himself in the water before he was sure the body would not exit from its prison too quickly. As he pulled himself out of the water Mark hissed a warning and he just got out of the river before a silver streak flashed past the position he had just vacated. As he rolled onto the jetty he muttered, "What the hell was that thing?"

Mark shook his head in stunned silence. Kevin grabbed the pole and hook and thrust it into the water, hitting something solid with the tip of the hook. The fish swam away a lot slower than it had attacked. Kevin looked at the end of the hook and understood why. There was a residue of fish scales and a little blood on the tip of the hook.

"Whatever it was, it's not so mobile now. If there are more like that round here, I don't want to be in that water for any money!" Kevin muttered.

They found a couple of broken paving slabs nearby and slid them into the river, blocking off access to underneath the jetty.

"I need to get out of these wet clothes damn quick. I don't want to catch pneumonia so I'll get changed back at the centre and dry this lot out while you two get my tickets from the old man."

While they had been away Gerry had drained the swimming pool, ready for a steam clean later that night.

He looked on in amazement at Kevin's condition when they returned. "What happened to you? The pool would be warmer for a midnight swim compared to the river."

Kevin aimed a playful blow which Gerry easily dodged and explained briefly what had happened. Gerry nodded his head knowingly. "That was a pike. Vicious brutes, they are. There won't be much left of the body if that thing gets to it."

"I managed to clobber it with the hook and it might think twice before returning, but right now, I need to change from these clothes. Any chance of drying them out quickly?" Kevin asked, as he started to shiver.

Mark took him to the changing rooms and switched on the heaters as well as giving his brother a couple of large towels to wrap around himself to keep warm.

24

Gerry and Mark entered the pharmacy through a side door that was not overlooked by other buildings. They spent an anxious couple of minutes until Gerry found the correct key to gain entrance. Another key was required for the door leading from the pharmacy to the living quarters. Once inside, they both stood still for over a minute to check if their entry had been heard.

The ticking of a large clock standing in the corner of the hallway seemed unusually loud, but no other sound or movement could be heard in the building.

Mark shone his powerful torch along the passageway as they moved to find the lounge area where Ernie had told him the passport forms should be located. Once inside the room Gerry checked to make sure the curtains were drawn before switching on the main light.

Within seconds the forms were found under the two miniature perfume bottles on the coffee table with a note addressed to someone called Jenny. But there was no sign of any money, Canadian or otherwise, and no tickets.

Their search continued in silence but without success. The exterior pockets of a large suitcase were also gone through but only contained a small photograph album and details of an address in Canada.

Next to the case was a small cabin bag with a note attached. The note simply read: 'Liquid items to be declared'.

Inside the bag were half a dozen miniature bottles along with two larger 50ml bottles, each with handwritten labels that read:

'Munro Heather Perfume, formulated by Robin Stockwell'

A third 50ml bottle lay broken in a rubbish bag that had been placed near the door to the pharmacy storeroom, ready for disposal the next morning. The large stain on the carpet near the fireplace had almost completely dried out but the aroma of the perfume was still noticeable.

The two men continued to search for the money, knowing that it was a vital part of Kevin's travel plans. Their searching became more desperate and less careful, opening drawers and cupboards with less care or any thoughts about making too much noise.

Robin Stockwell was having a restless night. He drifted in and out of sleep. This would be his first trip abroad without Stella and while he was looking forward to meeting up with Natalie and her stepfather, Frank, the journey was causing him to have mixed emotions.

A sudden thought struck him. He had not changed his will since Stella's death and Natalie was now his only remaining relative. That would have to be rectified as soon as he returned from Canada. He sat up in bed, switched on the bedside lamp on the nearby cabinet and put on his spectacles. He reached into the top drawer to retrieve a writing pad that was kept there for such times. The pad was beneath the two bundles of money and his tickets he had placed there before getting into bed.

After writing a memo to himself about changing the will he smiled and looked upwards. Stella was still sending him these little reminders to complete tasks, even now, and he said a silent 'thank you'.

Removing his glasses, he switched off the lamp and lay down in bed, satisfied there were no more things he need worry about. He was finally ready to have a proper sleep.

However, his sleep lasted less than ten minutes. An unfamiliar sound woke him and he sat up in bed and was about to get out but on hearing a gust of wind outside, sighed and lay down once more.

Mark turned to Gerry and spoke irritably, "They're not here! We've searched every possible place downstairs, so it only leaves upstairs to look."

These were the last words Gerry wanted to hear but he knew there was little choice left open to them if they were going to succeed. Before climbing the stairs Mark spent a few minutes working out how he was going to make any fire look like an accident. He found Robin's gold cigarette lighter and slipped it into one of his pockets without Gerry noticing.

Even though Ernie had told Mark about the layout on the upper level, they made their way quietly along a corridor which had a total of four rooms along its length.

Apart from the main bedroom there were two medium-sized bedrooms and a bathroom, as well as a fourth room that had been used as an office at one time.

Now it was used as more of a display storage room. In one corner a stand with six shelves had been erected and on each shelf there were numerous bottles of varying sizes marked in a similar way to those they had found in the living room. In addition each shelf had a date and what was surely the formula of each batch. Mark read a couple of the items mentioned on the lists and gave a grim smile. Two of the ingredients mentioned different percentages of alcohol and benzene or ethanol. He indicated to Gerry to follow him out of the room and they retraced their steps along the corridor to the top of the stairs but turned away from them and made their way to the final room on that level.

Robin turned over, one eye partly open and he thought he could see a faint glow near the door to the en-suite bathroom. He blinked several times, and yes, there was something there so he reached for his glasses once more but the sound of a creaking floorboard outside the bedroom door drew his attention in that direction.

He threw back the bedcovers and was about to get out of bed when the door burst open and a bright flashlight dazzled him for a couple of vital seconds. Mark ran in first and half dived forward and swung the heavy torch, catching the old man a glancing blow on the side of the head.

Gerry found the main light switch by the bedroom door, turned it on and ran around the far side of the bed. Robin was only stunned by the blow but Mark grabbed one of the pillows and pressed it over the face of his victim. The pharmacist struggled briefly but Mark was much younger and fitter and the pressure was continued for at least another minute. When signs of resistance subsided he told Gerry to keep watch while he searched for the money and tickets.

Reluctantly Gerry took hold of the pillow but allowed Robin's head to turn to one side. Rather than having to watch the old man he followed Mark's movements around the room, failing to notice the slight rise and fall of Robin's chest, and when a hand shot up and grabbed his burnt hand in a strong grip, he let out a shout of pain and surprise. He tried to push the pillow back over Robin's face, but his one hand was no match against the strength of both of Robin's.

"Gerry! What do you think you're doing? Stop it, this is insane," Robin pleaded.

Mark stopped his searching and came back towards the bed while taking his father's gun out of his pocket.

"No, Mark! No shooting, please!" Gerry yelled.

Robin was distracted by Gerry's outburst and turned towards Mark and this gave Gerry the chance to grab the discarded torch. Without thinking he gave Robin two clubbing blows to the head and followed up by grabbing hold of the pillow, forcing it over Robin's face and applying pressure. This time there was no resistance from the pharmacist but Gerry pressed down with all his strength.

He seemed to be in a trance and was not sure how long he kept this up but a shout of triumph from Mark on finding the money and tickets broke the spell.

Gerry looked around at his surroundings and the terrible truth of what he had just done broke over him and he released and threw away the pillow.

He looked down at the face of the man who had, not long ago, come to his aid when he was in agony and feared of possibly losing his badly burnt hand. And he witnessed an even greater fear in the dead eyes that stared back at him.

He fell back in horror and landed on the floor beside the bed with a loud thump. Mark turned away from counting the money at the sudden noise and for a moment couldn't see his partner. In looking around the room his gaze briefly fell on Robin Stockwell's corpse. But the features were different to those Gerry had seen moments earlier.

Mark could only see hatred and fury that seemed to be directed solely at himself.

For a split second he thought he was going to be attacked by Stockwell but he averted his eyes and noticed Gerry's legs on the other side of the bed. He called out his name but there was no response from his friend.

Walking warily around the side of the bed he looked down at the prone figure. He gave a none-too-gentle kick at one of Gerry's feet but got no response. Then he noticed that Gerry seemed to be staring up with no real focus on anything in particular. He kicked even harder and hissed, "Gerry! Get your arse in gear. We've still got things to do."

Still there was no response. Then he remembered the glass of water on the bedside cabinet where he had found the money.

Retrieving the tumbler, Mark returned to stand over Gerry and poured the contents over his face.

The result was instantaneous. Gerry sat up with a shout and looked wildly around. Mark snarled at him, "Let's get moving, you dumb sod, there's no time for lying around. What's the bloody matter with you, Gerry?"

Gerry stood up slowly and his gaze fell on the body of Robin Stockwell, but he didn't dare look at the man's face.

"I've killed him, Mark, what am I going to do?"

Mark dropped the tumbler on the floor and grabbed Gerry by both shoulders.

"Yeah, he's dead and that's what we came here for, that and money and tickets, so let's finish the job and cover our tracks."

Gerry looked at the body once more but made no move to leave the room. Mark removed the gun from his pocket and waved it in front of his friend's face.

"I could easily make it look like you broke in alone and started the fire to cover your tracks but never made it out of the building. Time to make your choice, buddy!"

Gerry realised Mark was not joking and said in a croaky voice, "Okay, Mark, I'm coming, please put the gun away."

Mark pocketed the gun along with the money and tickets. After making sure they had not left any clues and that the scene would look like a tragic accident, both men left the bedroom and went back to the room along the corridor used as a storage facility.

Mark tipped the entire contents of one of the upper shelves onto the floor. Several of the bottles broke and the liquid briefly formed small pools on the bare wooden floor before disappearing through the gaps between the boards. He had earlier calculated that this room was directly above the main living quarters and a fire started below would quickly track its way to this area.

Moving back downstairs Mark directed Gerry to help him re-arrange items in the living room. The wicker waste bin was placed on the area where the broken bottle of perfume had spilt some of its contents. An upholstered armchair was moved next to the waste bin. The matching three-seater settee was pushed closer to the armchair and the bag containing the bottles of perfume was placed on the middle section.

Taking the two miniature bottles from the coffee table, Mark broke one open, being careful not to spill any of the liquid on his hands or clothing, and emptied the contents in a trail leading from the waste bin to the settee. He took and broke the second miniature and carried it out in the direction of the hallway, again leaving a trail of perfume on the carpet.

Making a hole in the base of the rubbish bag he pushed the two broken bottles inside.

Earlier, when he had picked up the gold cigarette lighter, Mark had noticed a refill liquid gas canister for the lighter and a packet of small cigars. The waste bin had several pieces of paper inside so he poured some of the liquid gas over the paper and returned the canister to its original position. Gerry was told to slightly dampen a couple of other pieces of paper in the kitchen sink and bring them back. He looked puzzled at the instruction but did his bidding.

While his companion carried out the task Mark lit one of the cigars and inhaled the smoke a couple of times to make sure the cigar would not go out. Gerry came back with the damp paper and placed it in the bottom of the waste bin over the other contents. Mark took the note that had been left for Jenny and placed it over the other papers. Then he turned to Gerry.

"Get back to the door we entered through and have it unlocked so that we can scarper from here once I start this fire but make sure you lock the door when we leave. And no running, just walk quickly. Got it?"

Gerry nodded and left, glad to be away from this place of death.

Neither had noticed the faint outline of a female person watching them from the bottom of the stairs. As Mark placed the still burning cigar carefully on the top sheet of paper the figure disappeared from that spot but reappeared at the bedroom door, to be joined by a male figure.

Mark watched carefully as the cigar started to burn a hole in the paper, knowing that the damp material would slow its progress sufficiently to give him time to escape from the ensuing inferno. Satisfied, he turned around, switched off the light and headed for the side door. Gerry was waiting anxiously for him to appear, the key already placed in the lock on the exterior of the door.

Mark was two paces from reaching him as they both heard the dull roar of the waste bin fully igniting. Mark pushed his colleague outside as a second sound reached their ears; this time it was the armchair catching fire.

"Lock up and let's get the hell out of here. It's going up faster than I expected!"

They reached the main street in ten seconds and could already smell the first shafts of escaping smoke. Within five minutes they had arrived at the leisure centre and only then did they hear the first emergency vehicle's siren in the distance.

Kevin was waiting for them in Ernie's office, fully dressed in his now dry clothes and helping himself to another bottle of whisky from the filing cabinet. He also had more money stacked in small piles in front of him and looked pleased with life.

"Did you get the tickets and cash?"

Mark nodded. "Where did that lot come from?" he asked.

"I found a spare tracksuit in the changing room, so I borrowed it and went round to the old man's flat and this is what I found. It's pretty handy when you know people's habits and their hiding places."

Mark removed the tickets and money from his pockets and asked, "What's my share of his money then?"

"You both get £1,000 each but don't let Ernie know."

Mark protested, "Why should Gerry get any of it? He was our dad, not his!"

Before Kevin could respond Gerry turned to Mark and stared at him. "I don't want any of your blood money. Keep it all to yourselves! I've had enough of killing and I certainly don't want paying for any part of it. I really think you would have shot me back in Stockwell's flat if I hadn't moved."

Kevin's reaction surprised them both. "Mark, you actually took the old man's gun on that job? How stupid can you get?"

There was defiance in Mark's response, but not for long!

"What difference does it make what gun I took? The ones you gave me are here in this office."

Kevin roared back at him and gave the desk a heavy thump with his fist to emphasise his point.

"You idiot, Mark! The guns I left with you are replicas that have been engineered to work with real bullets. They can't be traced to any crime.

"The old man's gun could have come from anywhere with a load of history behind it. He wouldn't have thought of that or really cared knowing him. You've got more brains than that so bloody well use them."

Mark looked down at the floor. He loathed being spoken to in that manner, especially in front of someone else. Kevin continued, "I don't know what went on between you two to warrant shooting Gerry, that's up to both of you to sort out. Just give me Dad's gun right now!"

Mark hesitated for a second, but it was enough defiance for Kevin to spring to his feet and demand "Give!"

Mark knew better than to argue with his big brother. He took the gun out of his pocket, put it on the desk and stomped sullenly out of the office, slamming the door as he left. Both men watched him leave. Kevin shook his head and turned to Gerry.

"I need to leave within the next hour. Ernie arranged for me to meet up with someone called the Market Man who's giving me a lift to Heathrow. Mark can give me a lift in the van and I'll throw the gun in the river near where we dumped the body."

Gerry suddenly remembered he had something to pass on to Kevin. He took some papers from an inside pocket of his jacket and put them on the desk. "These are the papers Ernie said you needed to fill in with your passport details."

Kevin nodded and smiling, he picked up a bundle of money and thrust it into Gerry's hand.

"Willingly or not, you helped me tonight so take this. I don't care if you put it in some charity box or something else but take it!"

He knew it would be unwise to argue with him so Gerry thrust the money into his pocket and nodded a silent thank you. He knew what he would use the money for when he had the chance. He turned towards the door but Kevin called him back.

"It's none of my business, Gerry, but it's my guess someone like Ernie suckered you into this business. Take my advice, don't put all your trust in a bent copper, they're sly bastards and they know both dark sides of the law. And watch your back."

Mark was sitting on a table near the pool and turned accusingly to Gerry.

"You had to open your big mouth about the gun, didn't you? That was the only memento I had of my dad, now Kevin's got it," and he stood up and tried to barge past Gerry, but his companion stood his ground.

Gerry replied, "I think, and so does Kevin, that I've done you a favour by telling him. And Mark, I'll never go on a job with you if you're carrying a gun, but I bet Ernie won't let you anyway."

He stood aside to let Mark pass then went to change into his working clothes to start steam cleaning the now empty pool, hoping that it would take his mind off the night's events, though he doubted that would ever happen.

He was fully occupied in this task when Mark and Kevin left nearly an hour later to meet up with the Market Man. Mark was carrying the box containing the guns.

Neither would have seen the tears streaming down Gerry's face or heard his raking sobs above the commotion caused by the steam cleaner. He was glad to be alone and tried to concentrate on the job in hand.

Sometime later he only just heard the loud banging on the rear door and tried to ignore it. Whoever it was would soon give up. But the persistent sound continued, and Gerry climbed out of the pool and walked to the door and called out, "Who is it? The centre's closed, so go home and sleep it off."

He turned around and started to walk back to finish the steam cleaning, when a voice called out, "This is the police, open up right now."

Gerry's heart missed a beat for he recognised the voice of Inspector Gates. Had they been seen leaving the pharmacy or left an obvious clue behind? He knew if he ran he would not get very far.

"Hang on, while I fetch the keys," he called back, stalling for time to think of an alibi. He managed to calm down and hoped his story would be plausible. When he opened the door the smell of smoke was strong in the air as Gates pushed his way into the building.

"What the hell are you doing here at this time of night?"

Gerry told him the truth. "Steam cleaning the pool after some late swimmer left a deposit in the pool."

"Couldn't it wait until the morning?" was the suspicious response.

"No, I have to do it now. There won't be time before the schools swimming gala starts later on this morning. I'm late finishing because the bloody steam cleaner packed in and I had to repair it. Is there a fire somewhere?"

"You must be deaf if you didn't hear all the commotion outside."

"I couldn't hear or smell anything because I've been using the steamer down in the pool area."

Gates looked as if he wanted to press Gerry further, but his police radio blurted into life and he walked away without saying a word. Gerry closed the door and started shaking so much he had to lean against the wall until it eventually subsided and he had calmed down. He sank down on his haunches and stayed in that position for more than five minutes before returning to complete the cleaning of the pool.

***

Kevin told Mark to stop the van near the spot where they had earlier deposited their father's body. A red glow was still visible in the night sky, firm evidence that the fire at the pharmacy was still burning nearly two hours after it had begun.

After checking the coast was clear Kevin went down the slope to the jetty and threw his father's gun into the middle of the river. After taking a last glance at the final resting place of his parent he strode back up the slope to the van. As he got back in, he commented, "You made a good job of that fire, there shouldn't be any evidence left by now."

Mark said nothing, it was beginning to sink in that this might well be the last time he saw his big brother. Kevin was aware of his manner and he too was feeling a little melancholy but neither spoke, not even when Kevin walked over to meet Connelly to continue his journey.

Kevin was in deep discussion with the driver when they left the meeting place and he never saw Mark wipe away a tear from his cheek.

By the time Mark came back into town the first signs of the coming dawn were starting to appear and there was still a strong smell of smoke hanging around. He had taken a slightly different route back to the leisure centre in order to pass the scene of his night's dastardly work.

There were still four fire appliances at the scene. The outer shell of the building was still intact but the roof and upper floors had collapsed and the former pharmacy was now just a mass of smoking rubble. Driving away he knew he could not have done a better job and a macabre sense of pride and satisfaction dispersed the earlier feelings of sadness. On the way back from taking Kevin to meet up with Connelly he dropped off the guns at the flat. He was about to get out of the vehicle, but spotted a piece of paper on the floor in front of where Kevin had been sitting. Opening the folded paper he read the following words:

'Don't get too down in the dumps Mark, if I don't like Canada I might consider coming back to show Ernie how to run a proper security scam. Cheers, kiddo.'

Mark smiled and pushed the note into his jacket pocket. He returned to the pool area to find Gerry had finished the cleaning operation and was in the process of refilling the pool for the last time before the centre closed for the refurbishment. He decided it was time he pulled rank on Gerry.

"Seeing as I've been here longer than you, that makes me the more senior member of staff, so I'm taking the weekend off and you can secure the place tonight after everyone has left."

Gerry saw through this ploy immediately so he countered with the following remark, "Fair enough, but as the senior member of staff left here, you must be the one to deal with the workers when they come in next week to start the refurbishment. And as I'll be here today in charge on my own, I'm going home now to grab a few hours' rest." And Gerry left before Mark could argue.

On his way home he walked past the mound of rubble that was once a venue many people had called in to seek advice, help or both, including his grandmother. As soon as he reached the end of the street to pass the pharmacy he knew it was a big mistake taking this route. He was so transfixed by the destruction he nearly walked into Sergeant Proudfoot who was giving instructions to a female constable. Gerry couldn't help but hear what the sergeant was saying because he had to shout over the clamour that was going on around.

"She can't be at home or she would have been out here already so when you see Miss Potter let me know straight away. This news needs to be broken to her gently as she was almost like family to Mr Stockwell."

Gerry didn't want to hear any more of what the sergeant was saying so he retreated from the scene without being noticed by the police officers. He had not wanted to be reminded about such matters. His guilty feeling was almost more than he could bear.

As he left the scene another figure approached Proudfoot. A courier had turned up with a special delivery of a passport and insisted on confirmation that he could not complete the task. Proudfoot instructed his colleague to sign his paperwork and told the courier to leave the area immediately as he had more important work to follow up at present.

Having been on duty since before midnight he needed a few minutes alone to digest what had happened. He went to his patrol car in the hope of getting a few minutes to gather his thoughts.

Rubbing his eyes he was just starting to relax into his seat when a tap on the driver's window brought the sergeant back to the current situation. He reluctantly wound down the window to see what his colleague wanted. She told him that the fire personnel had made a significant discovery. Proudfoot sighed and climbed out of his vehicle to approach the wreckage of the building once more.

The senior fire officer told Proudfoot that his team had discovered a body amongst the rubble and he required the sergeant to witness the removal of the corpse. He nodded but glanced over his right shoulder as he heard a vehicle approach.

Recognising the driver he asked the fire officer if his team could wait a few minutes as he didn't want the new arrivals to witness the removal.

Proudfoot approached the limousine as the driver wound down his window and surveyed the scene before him. He turned to the passenger sitting next to him and told her to stay in the car as he opened his own door to get out. Proudfoot put a hand on the arm of the driver and spoke in a quiet tone so that nobody else would hear.

"Ralph, it would be better if you took your wife away from here, the fire people are about to complete a grim task."

Ralph Byewater glanced at the ruins and then back at the police officer he had known for many years and spoke only one word. "Robin?"

Proudfoot nodded grimly.

"Has anyone been to tell Jenny Potter?" Byewater asked, unable to disguise the tremor in his voice.

Proudfoot shook his head, "She's not at home. My wife bumped into her a couple of days ago and Ms Potter said she was going to visit her sister in Ipswich."

Byewater gave a small sigh of relief. "I don't think it would be wise to let her come back here with all this activity going on. I imagine the investigation into the cause will take some time to sort out. We would be happy to put her up while things get sorted."

Proudfoot nodded. "That would be very kind of you, but she will insist on her cats coming too."

"Oh yes, the cats, but I'm sure we will manage. I'd better go and break the news to my wife. Thank you, Peter."

The sergeant smiled his thanks and went to consult with the senior fire officer after watching the limousine pull slowly away.

"It should be okay to remove the body now. Will all this have to be pulled down?"

SFO Collins gave the thumbs-up to his men before replying, "As you can see, Sergeant, the whole roof has collapsed but the outer shell of the building appears to be quite stable for the present anyway. But I'll leave that decision to the local authorities."

"Any idea what caused this?"

Collins shook his head. "Too early to speculate. That will be the task of our investigation team who will be here later. One thing I will say though, once the fire started it spread damned quickly. Whatever was stored in there made sure of that."

Proudfoot hesitated before telling Collins of his visit a few days earlier and the report he had made to the council regarding the contents of Robin Stockwell's storeroom.

Collins sighed. "Well, you did the right thing in one respect, it is the council's responsibility, but maybe a quiet phone call to one of my station officers might have got things moving a lot quicker."

"I had thought about taking the second course you suggested but I have an inspector who insists on everyone going through the proper channels, but that didn't help poor Robin."

Collins replied sympathetically, "Well, what's done is done. Perhaps the council should have been more on the ball and checked things out once the pharmacist had retired."

The body was removed and placed in an ambulance to be taken to the mortuary pending a post-mortem and subsequent inquest.

It was now late afternoon. Sergeant Proudfoot had gone off duty. A lonely figure stood on the corner transfixed by the scene facing her. A single fire engine stood in front of what had been a solid familiar building when Jenny Potter had left to visit her sister a couple of days earlier.

A few wisps of smoke rose into the clear afternoon sky as the fire personnel moved around over the mound of rubble, making sure there were no hot spots left to reignite. One of Jenny's neighbours came over to try and speak to her but she didn't seem to notice their presence. It was only when a young policewoman stood in front of Jenny that the spell seemed to break.

"Miss Potter? Sergeant Proudfoot asked me to look out for you. Can we go inside your house where we can talk in private please?" and she gently, but firmly, turned the older woman around to face her own home. The WPC had been given details of who to contact if Ms Potter arrived on the scene. Once inside the house, Jenny had several questions on her mind but the first one caught the policewoman a little by surprise.

"I hope someone has informed Mr Stockwell about this. He left for a trip to Canada this morning."

WPC Rudge tried to ignore the question and said softly, "Miss Potter, Sergeant Proudfoot thinks it would be best if you stay with someone for a few days until things return to some sort of normality here. If I can use your phone, I will contact someone to collect you."

"Collect me!? Whatever are you talking about, young lady? I am quite capable of looking after myself, thank you. Now, you have not answered my question I asked earlier. Has Mr Stockwell been informed or not?"

The look on the policewoman's face suddenly told Jenny the devastating news and she took a pace backwards and collapsed into the armchair, bursting into floods of tears. It took several minutes for these to abate and she mumbled the same phrase several times before her companion could understand what she was saying.

"Your cats? I'm sorry, Miss Potter, what have they got to do with this matter?"

Jenny wiped her eyes before replying, "My cats are with a neighbour at number 36. Could you collect them for me and then make me a cup of tea in the kitchen, through there, please?" She pointed in the direction of the kitchen.

"Okay, I'll do what you ask but I need to make a phone call first. I will be back in a moment."

She dialled the number her superior had given her, but it was engaged so she went to the kitchen to make them both a cup of tea. On returning to the lounge she found Jenny standing by the window, staring once again at the scene across the road. Taking the elderly woman by one arm she managed to return her to her seat.

"Excuse me, Miss Potter, I didn't manage to speak to anyone last time, so I need to try the phone again."

"Who are you calling?"

Rudge hesitated but felt she had no option but to tell the truth. "Sergeant Proudfoot asked me to contact Mr and Mrs Byewater to ask them to collect you and take you back to stay with them. He didn't feel you would want to spend this time on your own."

Jenny Potter sat up in her chair, suddenly quite indignant.

"I thank you and Sergeant Proudfoot for your concern regarding my welfare, but this is my home and I shall remain here. So once you have finished your tea, would you please go to number 36 and collect my cats? They are all the company I require at present."

Not wanting to upset her host by trying to force the issue the WPC proceeded to carry out her request. The sergeant would have to deal with Ms Potter in his own way, if he dared.

Once she was alone with her two cats Jenny sat back in her chair and sobbed until she could cry no more. She fell asleep, exhausted, with her feline companions meowing in unison to their mistress's distress.

The coldness of the room awoke her in the early hours of the morning and she climbed the stairs to her bedroom, removing her shoes before getting into bed fully clothed. This had never ever happened before in her life but it was of little concern at this moment.

The late morning sunshine was streaming into her room when she finally awoke. Not even the activity of workmen, erecting scaffolding to facilitate a large screen to hide the area around the devastated building, had penetrated her sleep. Nor had she been disturbed by the repeated ringing of the phone next to her bed.

Both cats were lying next to her and it took several moments for Jenny to recall the reason she was in bed still fully clothed. Dabbing her eyes with her lace handkerchief, she arose from the bed and walked to the window to survey the scene outside.

Despite it being late Sunday morning there was lots of activity in the area. A fire engine and a large police forensic van were parked next to the devastated building and there were several people in white overalls milling about.

Tears started to run down her face as she turned away from the window. Would she ever be able to look out of her house again without feeling this desperate loss? The message light was flashing on her phone but it was ignored. There was nobody she wanted to talk to at this time who could help ease the terrible pain she was feeling.

25

After overseeing the swimming gala and closing the leisure centre on the Saturday evening, Gerry had returned to the flat expecting Mark to be lounging around as usual. But there was no sign of him. All he found was a note on the dining table which read: 'Passports arrived so have managed to book a late holiday with Club 18-30 in Majorca, will be back in about 10 days mind the fort. Mark.'

Crumpling up the note and throwing it in the kitchen waste bin he shouted, "Bloody typical of you, Mark, look after number one and sod your commitments."

He found his passport and put it into a drawer in his bedside cabinet, not knowing if he would ever use it.

Because of his colleague's selfishness this meant he would have to postpone plans to visit Sally's grave until Mark returned. He would now also be responsible for letting the refurbishment team into the centre on Monday morning and be available to answer any queries they may have about the work to be carried out. As for the security patrols Ernie had mentioned, they would have to wait until Mark came back. This didn't bother him too much as he had felt uneasy about going on those patrols ever since his hand had been burnt so they were bottom of his priority list.

Even though he had only eaten one light snack in the centre cafe in the last thirty-six hours Gerry had very little appetite and decided to have an early night. His sleep was disturbed by sounds that seemed to emanate from different parts of the flat and had him repeatedly getting out of bed to investigate. On the fourth occurrence the noises seemed to be coming from Mark's bedroom and on entering the room he made a discovery that shook him.

He found the light switch as he stood in the doorway and took a further step inside. As he did so he could have sworn someone or something brushed past but without any sound.

Looking around the room there seemed to be nothing out of place until he noticed one of the drawers on the bedside unit was half open. That drawer was definitely closed when he had come to check if Mark was in his room earlier in the evening. He bent down to look into the drawer and discovered a large wooden box that took up most of the space.

Gerry knew he shouldn't be going through another person's possessions but his inquisitiveness got the better of him. It was a very tight fit and it took him several minutes to prise it out of the drawer. He was surprised at the weight of the box and almost dropped it until he managed to get a firmer grip.

Placing the box on the bed he noticed the name etched onto the lid, Kevin Yarrow. It could only belong to Mark's brother, but what was inside? There was a small lock set into the front of the box but a further search of the drawer did not reveal any key. He retrieved his set of skeleton keys from his own room and set about finding a matching key for the lock.

There were only four possible keys that could fit and to Gerry's relief, the third key did the trick. But his euphoria was short-lived when the contents of the box were revealed to him. There were two oily rags inside, and within each rag was a revolver. Also in the box were several clips of ammunition for the guns.

He sat on the bed staring at the box and its contents. Was Mark just looking after the guns until his brother returned?

No, he remembered being told that Kevin was escaping to Canada to start a new life. That meant that Mark was the new owner of the firearms. Recalling the incident in the Stockwell bedroom sent a shiver down Gerry's spine and proved that Mark was familiar with handling such weapons.

But Ernie would not allow such folly to take place. Or would he?

Having already been a near victim of Mark's volatile temperament, Gerry was not prepared to let the guns remain in the flat a moment longer than necessary. So they had either to be disposed of or moved to a safer place. But where, was the question.

The obvious answer would be the leisure centre and they had to be moved while both Mark and Ernie were away.

But he had to do more than just move the guns. Once Mark returned from his holiday he was almost certain to check that his possessions were still intact. A delaying tactic would be necessary to prevent him from discovering his loss.

It was getting late and Gerry decided to leave the task of hiding the guns and ammunition until the morning. He returned everything to the box and took it into his own bedroom. At least he knew they would be safer with him.

It wasn't often that Gerry had bad dreams but that night his sleep was punctuated by several.

The first dream involved Sally. He was standing in a large room he didn't recognise. Someone called him from behind and he turned around to find Sally standing in the doorway. She beckoned him to follow and then disappeared. Outside the room there was only one way he could go, up a set of stairs with Sally at the top urging him to follow her.

Once again she disappeared and he called out her name but there was no sign of his one-time lover. He wandered into another room which had a window open. Walking over to see if there was any sign of his former love, he stood by the open window and heard the sound of footsteps rushing towards him. He spun round but a figure of an unknown person pushed Gerry backwards towards the open window.

He felt himself falling and woke up in his bed, covered in sweat and panting for breath.

He slowly regained his composure and was mystified as to why Sally would lead him into a trap. He lay back in the bed and was soon asleep again. But the dream was repeated several times, with other people from his past leading him into the same situation and ending in identical fashion to his first dream.

The final dream had a slightly different ending. Standing by the open window once more, he turned around to see that the room was on fire. Looking out of the window he noticed three men dressed as firemen holding out a blanket for him to jump into, and recognised the men as Ernie, Mark and Kevin.

But as he jumped they withdrew the blanket and laughed out loud as he fell past them into a dark hole.

When he woke up this time he found himself shouting at the top of his voice, "Why, why, what have I done wrong?"

Not only was he bathed in sweat, the bedclothes were also damp and in complete disarray. Even though it was still in the early hours of Sunday morning he decided his time would be better spent in sorting out the problem of finding a safe hiding place for the guns.

After eating a quick snack for breakfast he went out into the backyard of the flat to try and find an object that was of a similar weight to the guns and would fit into the box. He spent the next half an hour going back and forth until he found something that he was satisfied would be a close match.

A slightly chipped house brick wrapped in one of his old T-shirts to prevent the brick sliding around was the best solution. Merely locking the box up again would not prevent Mark from discovering the switch, so he had to find a way of delaying him. And he hoped the answer was in Ernie's office.

As the centre was closed for the duration of the refurbishment work he could hide the guns in their upstairs storeroom where no outsiders would have access. However, he knew Mark also had a key to that room, along with Ernie, so to keep Mark at bay until he had explained things to Ernie, the lock would have to be changed.

Gerry knew the scariest part for him would be carrying the guns through the streets back to the centre. He could not risk walking his normal route as it passed close to the burnt-out pharmacy and there would still be a police presence in the area.

Ernie had once told him to look as if he didn't have a care in the world when he was carrying out a task that could make him appear nervous. That way, you were less likely to attract attention to yourself.

Even with this thought in his head Gerry felt that every person he passed was observing him with suspicion while walking to the centre carrying the guns and ammunition in a backpack. But nobody he passed paid him any attention.

Everyone seemed to be headed for, or away, from the carnage in the nearby street.

Once he was inside the sanctuary of the centre he broke out into a cold sweat and leaned against a wall to regain his composure. Gerry took the stairs to the storeroom two at a time. The sooner he hid the contents of his backpack the better.

While unlocking the door he cursed himself for forgetting to bring along his tools to change the lock. Once inside the room he took out the contents of his bag and hid them in the furthest corner from the door amongst some builders' equipment. After closing and locking the door he went to the centre's maintenance store to search for a replacement lock but couldn't find one that would fit.

Checking the time, he decided to go to a hardware store across town, but he had a wasted journey as they didn't have the correct size of lock he required. However, he could order one that would arrive within a couple of days.

Disappointed but not disheartened, he still had time to change the lock before either Mark or Ernie returned from their respective trips. Gerry trudged back to the centre to find the other item he required to delay Mark from opening his brother's box. Thankfully, he found the item in a drawer of Ernie's desk in his smaller office next to the reception area. At least he could put one part of his delaying tactics into operation. Returning to the flat, he was happy in the knowledge he could keep Mark away from the weapons for the time being at least.

Still feeling hungry he prepared himself the first proper meal he had eaten in nearly two days and then collected the tools he would require to deny Mark access to the interior of the box.

Placing the box on the kitchen table he used his own keys to unlock it once more.

First, he placed the brick wrapped in his old T-shirt inside the box. He then took the tube of super glue borrowed from Ernie's desk and carefully put a couple of drops into the lock recesses and applied liberal amounts of glue to the edges of the lid for good measure.

The box was locked and he waited a few minutes before trying to unlock it again. As he had guessed, the lock would not budge and the box remained firmly sealed.

The box was returned to the bedside drawer where he had found it the previous evening and made sure the drawer was left in the exact condition as when he had found it. Now he would have to wait for Mark's return and hope that he could distract him until Ernie returned.

***

The refurbishment team arrived on the Monday morning and Gerry showed their supervisor, Adam, around the centre and handed him a set of keys so they could let themselves in each day.

"On my list of work, I have: clean and re-tile the swimming pool area; update equipment in the cafe kitchen and re-lay a new floor in the gymnasium, along with various painting and decorating tasks in the reception area. Is there anything to add to the list?"

"The two office areas need no work done as well as the upstairs storeroom. We've already given those rooms a coat of paint. But Mr Newsham asked if you could check the safety of the outside staircase that leads to the exterior balcony."

Gerry also told him which parts of the centre Ernie wanted to be kept off limits.

Adam nodded but added, "That's fine. Oh, by the way, just to let you know, a Councillor Barnes has taken an interest in this project and he may pay a surprise visit during the work. Not sure why he's so interested; it's nothing to do with his department."

Gerry understood immediately but said nothing to the supervisor. Ernie had left instructions of what to say to the councillor if he started to get too inquisitive. As well as having to change the door lock to the storeroom, Gerry would have to dismantle some of the exercise equipment in order for part of the refurbishment work to be carried out. This would give him the legitimate excuse to be on hand should Barnes turn up at the centre.

Late on the Friday afternoon of the first week of the refurbishment work Gerry was moving the last piece of exercise equipment to allow the workmen full access to replace the flooring.

"I believe you are Mr Newsham's assistant. I need the keys to his office, please."

Gerry looked up from his work to face the person who had addressed him. A man in his late forties with a chubby face and receding hairline stood before him. He wore a very expensive suit and had an air of impatience about him.

Even though Gerry recognised this man from a grainy video he asked innocently, "I'm sorry, this centre is closed for refurbishment. Who are you and why do you want to go into Mr Newsham's office?"

"I am Councillor Barnes and I want to go to Mr Newsham's office immediately so give me the keys."

"I'm sorry, Mr Barnes, I have strict instructions from Mr Newsham not to allow anyone into his office while he is away. If you tell me what it is you hope to find there I will look for you."

"I am quite capable of looking for myself, thank you. Just give me the keys and get out of my way," Barnes snapped back.

But Gerry stood his ground and said quietly so that nobody else would hear, "Councillor Barnes, Mr Newsham doesn't keep personal possessions like videos for example, in his office. They are locked away in his home and his house has a very good alarm system protecting it."

Barnes' face went from bright crimson to a sickly grey as he realised that others might know of his past secret. For a moment Gerry wasn't sure if the man was about to assault him, but instead, he gave a short choking cough and stormed out of the building. Moments later, Adam the supervisor, approached Gerry. "The councillor didn't look too happy, did you upset him? Anyway, me and my team are leaving now. We've just finished re-tiling the pool area and there's no point starting on the next bit of work until we come back on Monday. By the way, I've looked at the exterior staircase and Ernie is right, it's not safe so I will get it pulled down when we get back on Monday. In the meantime I've hung a sign at the bottom of the stairs to say the structure is unsafe and should not be used."

Gerry nodded his thanks and watched as Adam and his team left the building. He had collected the new lock for the storeroom door that morning and decided to replace the old lock before going home.

He had finished the task and was about to leave the building when he heard a crashing sound followed by someone's loud scream. The noise had come from outside. After hastily locking up he went to investigate. Cautiously walking around the side of the building he turned the corner and found the source of the commotion.

The first nine steps of the staircase to the outside balcony were still intact but the next two steps lay in broken pieces on the floor underneath. Hanging on to the stair above as if his life was in mortal danger was Councillor Barnes.

One of his trouser legs was torn and blood was oozing from several cuts and grazes on his leg. Gerry walked over and stood to one side of the staircase and looked up at the forlorn figure.

"What do you think you're doing, Mr Barnes? Didn't you see the sign saying the stairs aren't safe?"

Barnes turned his head to look at Gerry but ignored his question. Instead he shouted back, "Don't just stand there, get me a ladder or something before I fall and break a leg. I can't hold on for much longer."

"Mr Barnes, your feet are no more than three feet off the ground. I'll remove the broken pieces of wood so that you will have a safe place to land and I can catch hold of you to make sure you don't hurt yourself."

He moaned, "I need something soft to land on, I might break an ankle!" but as he spoke, his grip on the wooden plank started to slip.

Gerry saw what was about to happen and stepped forward to break his fall. He was tall enough to just about put his arms around the waist of Barnes and lowered him to the ground as the man's grip finally failed.

Rather than show any gratitude for the help he had been given Barnes pushed himself away from the younger man and turned to accuse him. "I'm going to claim compensation for the injuries to my leg and the damage to my suit from you and Newsham."

Gerry smiled mockingly, "And what about the sign that the supervisor put on the stairs to say they were unsafe and not to be used?"

"There was no such sign or notice that I could see," was the reply from Barnes. Without another word he hobbled away and headed for his car which was parked nearby, but Gerry spotted something lying on the floor near the broken steps.

He picked up the paper and read it out loudly for Barnes to clearly hear him:

"'DANGER: These stairs are not safe. Do not use them under any circumstances.'"

The right hand of the councillor automatically went to the rear pocket of his trousers as he half turned to face Gerry. The guilty look was written all over his face and he cursed loudly and continued the unsteady walk towards his car.

He waited until Barnes had left the car park and went back inside to secure the building for the weekend after completing an extra task of copying the notice left by Adam.

He attached the notice to the bottom of the staircase and went home.

When he returned to the centre on the following Wednesday the lower section of the stairs had been removed thus denying any further access to the exterior balcony.

He had been monitoring any phone calls to the office during Ernie's absence and was surprised to hear a message from the man himself. It simply said that he had completed his business a lot quicker than expected and he would be arriving back home on the following weekend. It would be interesting to see who returned first, Ernie or Mark.

A phone call to the flat late on the Sunday evening gave Gerry the answer.

Ernie's tired voice aroused Gerry from his dozing.

"Gerry. I landed at Heathrow this morning and drove straight home. It was a very successful trip but I'll tell you and Mark all about it tomorrow morning at the centre. Make it about ten o'clock. Did everything get sorted by you two?"

Gerry had tried to put the events of that particular weekend behind him but Ernie's comment brought them back into focus. He answered quietly, "As well as could be expected but enquiries are still being made about the fire. Mark is not back from his holiday break yet. I've been holding the fort on my own since you left."

"Where has he gone to? Look, don't bother telling me now, you and I can talk things over in the morning." The line went dead.

Gerry was relieved that he would be able to inform Ernie about all the events that had taken place in his absence without Mark being present.

Arriving at the centre some thirty minutes before he was due to meet Ernie he was surprised to find his boss already on site and talking to Adam as they observed two workmen completing the demolition of the external staircase.

Gerry related the visit by Councillor Barnes on the previous Friday evening and how he had to be rescued after attempting to climb up the stairs. Adam asked why would someone try to climb such an unsafe construction but Gerry shrugged his shoulders without answering.

All three men went inside and after Adam had given Ernie a progress report on the refurbishment, he went to join the rest of his team. Ernie indicated to his assistant to follow him to his office but not to speak until they were inside and out of earshot of anyone else.

"So why was Barnes fool enough to climb those stairs? I saw your signal to Adam to drop the subject."

Gerry gave a little smile; this guy didn't miss much.

"Councillor Barnes paid us a visit on Friday and wanted the keys to this office, but I didn't let him in. I was just closing up when there was a crashing sound and a yell outside. I went to look and found him hanging on for dear life with blood dripping from scratches on his legs and his suit trousers torn to shreds."

"Okay, leave that with me. I think the councillor needs a reminder that he's not in a position to bargain. Now tell me about Bishop and the pharmacy fire."

Gerry wanted to delay talking and thinking about Stockwell's death so he gave details of Bishop's demise. He

left out the news that Bishop had pulled a gun on them until the end so that he could justify his actions regarding Kevin's present to his brother. Upon the mention of Mark threatening him with the same gun when they were in Stockwell's bedroom Ernie's face went crimson and he thumped his desk. "Has he still got his father's gun?"

Gerry shook his head and explained Kevin's reaction when he found out about the weapon and its subsequent disposal. Ernie heaved a sigh of relief until he was told of the discovery he had made in Mark's room at the flat. Once again, Ernie's desk felt the force of his anger. "Are those guns still in the flat? If so, we will have to move them before Mark returns."

Again, Gerry shook his head. "No, they're in the storeroom upstairs amongst the builders' material but I've changed the lock on the door. Mark will need to have access to that room or he will get suspicious once he discovers the switch I made."

On hearing the last comment Ernie gave a faint smile. "Switch? Tell me more?"

He was given the details. By the time he finished telling the story Ernie was rocking with laughter. "Well done, Gerry! You could always suggest that Kevin had made the swap before leaving just to delay things. Right, get him a spare key cut for the storeroom after I've moved the guns to a safer place. I'll let

Mark give me his version of the fire, unless you want to mention anything else now?"

Gerry stared down at his hands and was silent for a moment. Ernie guessed he wasn't sure how to communicate his real feelings so he waited patiently for the young man to speak in his own time. Finally, Gerry cleared his throat and said, "Until I joined you, I'd never broken the law or been in any kind of trouble. In the past two weeks I've been involved in a couple of murders and before that, taken part in a number of burglaries. But from now on, I'm having nothing to do with any of your schemes that involve anyone else getting hurt, and if you or Mark try to trick me into doing so, you'll never see me again."

He stood up and headed for the door, but Ernie called him back. "Gerry, stop right there."

He hesitated and looked over his shoulder and in that time Ernie had reached him and blocked his exit from the room. He took Gerry's arm in a vice-like grip and marched him back to his chair and ordered him to sit down.

Ernie sat back at his desk but when he spoke there was no denying the menace in his voice.

"Like it or not, Gerry, you're in this little club as deep as me and Mark and nobody is just going to walk away from it. Okay, as I told you before, Stockwell was about to make life very difficult for us so we had no choice but to silence him. As for Bishop you knew he stole those items from your gran's flat and you swore vengeance, remember?"

Gerry stared straight ahead, saying nothing, so Ernie continued, "When you and me or you and Mark go out on a job I can't give a cast-iron guarantee that some daft sod won't try to stick his nose into our business or some copper won't happen to amble by and catch us in the act of enforcing our security business. You think I, or Mark are going to just stand there with our hands up? No chance! And neither will you unless you want to spend the rest of your life inside. I don't get any satisfaction from hurting someone just for the sheer hell of it. Maybe Mark does but not me or you. But any witnesses who could identify us have to be stopped from doing so. Gerry, I try to plan our jobs so that there is the minimum of risk of us getting caught, but sometimes things don't work out that way."

Numerous thoughts and feelings ran through Gerry's head as Ernie spoke; hostility, fear, defiance, but most of all loathing. Not just at some of the truths he had been forced to accept but loathing at his own weakness and the limited choices he would be left with to pursue.

"Listen, Gerry, I want you to take a few days away from here. Forget the last couple of incidents. You've been a damned good worker in the centre and you deserve a break. I seem to remember you mentioning you wanted to visit Sally's grave in Matlock. It would also be better if you weren't around when Mark comes back so that I can smooth things out over the gun issue."

Gerry looked up at the mention of Sally's name. "I don't know anyone in Matlock who could direct me to where she is buried so what's the point?"

Ernie took out a pad from the desk drawer and wrote something down and passed it to him. "That's the contact details of a B & B in the town. Give it a ring. They may know some details or gossip about recent events."

Gerry wanted to ask how long Ernie had held these details from him but right now he didn't trust his boss to tell him the truth. He took the piece of paper and started to rise from his chair, but Ernie held up a hand.

"Hang on, Gerry, there's a couple of things I need to say. First, I'll give you a lift back to your flat and you can give me the box that held the guns. We'll go in the security van, because knowing Mark he will have left the petrol tank low as usual. But remember, Gerry, if you try to do a runner while you're away, I'll find you and sort things out once and for all. This is a final warning. The only way you or Mark will be able to leave our group is feet first. Do I make myself clear?"

There was no mistaking the threat in Ernie's last comment. Both men stood up and left the room together and walked in silence to the vehicle. Ernie unlocked the door and was about to climb in when he noticed a scrap of paper in the footwell of the van.

He had repeatedly told Mark about throwing sweet wrappers and other rubbish around on the floor inside the van. Picking up the piece of paper but before stuffing it into his coat pocket to dispose of later he read the writing scrawled on it. Instead of discarding the note he folded it carefully and put it into his pocket.

When they arrived at the flat Ernie asked Gerry how he discovered the box in Mark's room. Feeling a little foolish at the explanation he offered, it was obvious that Ernie wasn't convinced by the story.

"He won't buy that one, Gerry, let me think for a moment."

He looked around for a few minutes before he decided.

"Okay, you arrived home on the evening he left to go on his holiday. There was a noise in this room and at first you thought it was Mark and you called out to let him know you were back. Then there was a second, much louder sound and a curse that you knew it wasn't Mark. Banging on his door didn't bring any response so you opened it just in time to see a young kid climb out of the window. He was too quick for you and because it was dark outside you didn't get a good look at him. That's when you saw the half-open drawer and you showed me the box when I came back this morning."

"What about the guns being removed from the box?"

Ernie's answer was immediate, "Simple, you swapped the brick for the guns because you didn't want them to fall into the wrong hands, especially any of the kids who attend the centre."

Gerry was not completely convinced by Ernie's version of events, but he couldn't think of anything better, so he gave a resigned nod.

"Okay, that's sorted so now you pack a bag for your trip to Matlock and leave either later this afternoon, or at the very latest, first thing tomorrow morning. I don't want Mark coming back and finding you here. I need time to decide what to do with those guns."

Gerry started packing as soon as Ernie had left, but a sudden fear hit him harder than he would have expected. He had never met any of Sally's family before. Would they hold him responsible in any way for her death? And would he find out the true reason why she left so suddenly?

26

It was just after ten o'clock at night when the coach pulled into the bus station in Matlock. There was no one around for Gerry to ask directions to the B & B address that Ernie had given him. Having booked for three days, he allowed himself that amount of time to find out the truth about Sally's death.

No staff were visible within the bus station, so he had little choice but to walk around the town in the hope of finding someone to ask directions.

At first it seemed as if the whole place had decided to have an early night. Not a solitary person passed him as he trudged the lonely streets.

He was about to enter the first pub he came across when a car pulled up just behind him. A voice called out, "Excuse me, sir, can I have a word with you before you go in there?"

He turned to see two policemen get out of their patrol car and walk briskly towards him. He waited for them to reach his side before asking, "Thanks, you'll save me the bother of going in here. Can you tell me, am I heading in the right direction for Vicarage Road?"

The older policeman spoke first. "What business do you have in Vicarage Road if you don't mind me asking, Mr... ?"

Gerry was tired after his journey, but experience had told him not to be flippant with his answer, as Mark had once been when they were walking home from work one night. His caustic remark nearly had them arrested.

"I'm Gerry Reynolds and I've booked into a bed and breakfast establishment there for a couple of nights."

The younger officer chipped in, "What number in Vicarage Road and do you have a contact name that we can check it out against?"

Gerry sighed and took out a piece of paper he had written the details on and passed it to the officer who took it off him and immediately returned to the patrol car. His colleague looked carefully at Gerry and asked casually, "Is this your first time in Matlock, Mr Reynolds?"

Not wanting to drag the conversation on for any longer than necessary he gave details of the last time he had been in the town and why he was returning. On hearing the reason for Gerry's visit the officer relaxed.

"Yes, I knew I'd seen you before. I recall that incident. You might not recognise me, but I was the officer who stopped you walking down the street after you got out of the taxi. Remember?"

Gerry didn't recognise the officer, but he was prepared to accept the man's recall of the day. He just wanted to get into his digs and catch up on his lack of sleep. The other policeman came back from the car and said something to his colleague and they both turned around and walked briskly back to their patrol car. As he got into the driver's seat the older officer called out, "Vicarage Road is back in the direction you were walking from. Go back to the last junction, turn right and it's the second street on your left. The B & B is on that corner."

Without any further explanation for his brief apprehension the car sped away, siren blaring and blue lights flashing.

As they departed Gerry realised that the younger officer had kept the details of where he was staying. Fortunately, he had memorised the address and name of the owner and managed to gain access to his room without further delay.

He slept soundly that night and was the last person to enter the breakfast room. The four other guests soon dispersed which gave him the opportunity to try and gain some local knowledge from the proprietor.

When she approached his table to ask if he had finished his breakfast, Gerry seized the opportunity to enquire, "Excuse me asking, but do you remember an incident here in Matlock several months ago where a young woman died from carbon-monoxide poisoning?"

The blonde woman's demeanour changed abruptly. Before Gerry had posed his question, she had been the ideal hostess but now she looked at him warily.

"Are you a reporter? I'm sick and tired of your kind snooping around trying to dig up some dirt on our Sally!" she said with a hint of loathing in her voice.

Taken aback by the sudden change in the woman's manner Gerry managed to stammer out a denial.

"No, no. I remember seeing something in the papers, that's all. From what you just said, were you related to Sal in any way?"

"Every reporter in town and beyond knows I was her second cousin. You called her Sal – she was quite particular about who she let use that name."

Before he could stop himself, Gerry's eyes filled with tears and he hastily wiped them away, but his actions were noted by the woman and she sat down on the chair across the table from him. She also had some difficulty in hiding her emotions but managed to control them better than her guest.

Neither spoke, both trying to come to terms with the situation that had aroused such emotions within them. The woman broke the silence by standing up and announcing, "I think we need to talk about Sally at some time but not now. I've got chores to complete to keep this place running. If you have had any involvement with her in the past, then we'll talk later when I've finished. But I warn you, Mr Reynolds, if you've just come here as a reporter or some kind of thrill seeker, I'll tell my husband when he gets home tonight and he'll sort you out, good and proper."

Before Gerry had a chance to respond she walked out of the dining room, dabbing her eyes as she entered the kitchen.

Either he had stumbled into an atmosphere that would give him some answers or one that would seek to blame him for their grief and seek revenge. However, he never thought for a moment that a third option could exist.

Not wanting to miss the opportunity to speak to the woman he stayed in his room until the early afternoon. His patience was rewarded when a soft tap on the door had him dashing to answer the summons.

She stood in the hallway outside his door, dressed in what Gerry could only think of as a party dress. Having showered and put on make-up he immediately noticed the family resemblance to his Sally and he couldn't speak as he beheld the person facing him. For a split second he was convinced it really was Sally standing there.

When he found his voice, the comment he made would haunt him for several months. "If I didn't know better you could be Sally's twin."

Realising his remark could have upset her he tried to stammer an apology, but she gave a little laugh and said, "I'm sorry if I've startled you by appearing this way but yes, Sally and I were often mistaken for sisters when we went out on the odd occasion. If it upsets you I'll go and change into my working clothes."

"No, it's okay. Sally never spoke about any relatives. One thing I've never found out is why she suddenly moved here. One minute she was around, the next, she had left."

The woman's expression changed, and her voice lost its warmth and became serious once again. "Is it okay if I call you

Gerry? My name is Valerie by the way. Let's go into my private lounge where we can talk without being disturbed."

Gerry nodded and followed her downstairs, steeling himself for what he hoped would be the answers to his questions.

Valerie sat down on a spacious settee and motioned for Gerry to sit next to her, but a nagging doubt warned him to be careful and he chose an armchair opposite the woman.

A flicker of annoyance crossed her features but was gone in an instance. Instead she changed her seating position to a more provocative one. She smiled and said quietly, "When did you last see Sally?"

Gerry was surprised at how long it had been since he and Sally had spent time together. Looking at his hands which were shaking slightly, he said, "It must be at least eight months since I saw her. But we spoke on the phone a couple of times. That would be about six months ago."

"Did Sally mention anything in particular during that conversation, about herself, I mean?"

He was reluctant to divulge too many details, so he simply said, "I asked her to come back to Clapfield but Sally said it wasn't possible at the time, so she invited me to come and stay with her."

"Nothing else?"

Gerry hesitated before replying, "Only that there was some news she wanted to share with me. I don't suppose you know what that news was, do you?"

Before replying Valerie stood up and went to a cabinet in the corner of the room and poured two drinks. She handed one to Gerry and sat down before speaking. "When Sally died, she was nearly four months pregnant."

She watched carefully for his reaction, which didn't take long to happen. He emptied the contents of the glass in one swallow and started coughing. She sat back and watched until he had finished and had recovered some of his composure. Then she continued, "She was expecting twins. She also told me that the father was going to visit her just before she died but the bastard never showed his face."

Gerry was speechless, so she continued, feigning anger, "She mentioned you a couple of times, but you only turn up months after she died. I don't call that being much of a friend, do you?"

He smarted at the obvious jibe but replied with more than a little anger in his voice.

"Valerie, if you want to know, I came to Matlock on the same day her body was found. I arrived on her doorstep just before the doctor who attended came out to confirm her death to the police."

The memory brought tears to his eyes, but he continued, "The doctor saw I was in a state of shock and took me to the ambulance to help calm me down. Then the police took me away so that I could contact someone to come and collect me. I was given assurances that someone would keep me informed about funeral arrangements but nobody did. There was noone else I knew in Matlock so I kept ringing the police but they told me nothing. Then I had an accident and had to have several skin grafts with limited success."

As he finished his last statement, he took the leather glove off his left hand. The revulsion at the sight of his disfigurement was clear to Gerry so he quickly covered the injury.

Valerie was in a mild state of shock and couldn't clear her mind of the gruesome image she had seen. The planned seduction of Gerry she had hatched up with her husband was now the furthest thing from her mind. They would have to think of some other way to exhort money out of him.

Unwittingly Gerry provided her with an alternative method.

"I'm sorry for showing my hand to you like that, it's not a pretty sight, but I had to explain why I haven't come sooner. Valerie, I came here to visit Sally's grave and pay my respects privately, but I still can't understand why she didn't tell me she was pregnant a lot sooner. Things could have turned out a lot better for us both."

The woman replied, "I think she wanted to get away from familiar surroundings to decide the best course of action to take. Continue with the pregnancy, or have an abortion, and whether the father would support her in whatever decision she came to."

Something about Valerie's smile troubled Gerry. Was she being honest or goading him into a reaction he would regret later? Instead he gave the only answer he knew was true.

"If Sally had confided in me, I would have come here much sooner and fully supported her in the decision she clearly made to go ahead with the pregnancy. Once my grandmother died I had no reason to stay where I was and I'm sure I could have found a job here to support all of us financially. I also have some savings that I could have used if necessary."

A noise made Valerie jump to her feet and go into the other room, closing the door behind her. She glared at the man leaning against the kitchen worktop.

"Stan, I told you to keep the noise down, you'll soon know if I need a hand."

Stan gave a crooked smile and whispered, "You must be losing your touch if you haven't managed to seduce him by now, or is he queer?"

"I'll explain later but I'm not going down that line. I'll try a different tack so keep the noise down."

"I heard what he said about savings so make sure you get a decent amount out of him or I'll take over," Stan snarled.

She ignored his last comment, turned on her heels and went back to join Gerry in the lounge. "Sorry about that, I've got a repair man sorting out the dishwasher and I thought he'd knocked something over. He can be a bit clumsy at times. Now where had we got to? Oh yes, you said you could have supported Sally. Did you have anything to add?"

Gerry nodded, "Yes, one of my main purposes for coming here was to visit her grave. Can you tell me where she is buried?"

Valerie's smile disappeared, to be replaced by her crestfallen look. She wiped an imaginary tear away and said quietly, "There is no grave, Gerry, Sally and the twins were cremated together. We enquired about the cost of putting a small plaque on top of burying her ashes but I don't have that kind of money to do so."

Without thinking Gerry asked what the price was being quoted.

"Around £2,000 just for the plaque. Any inscription would add to the cost."

Valerie's haste in replying should have warned Gerry but the tone of the conversation had dulled his capacity to think clearly. His grandmother had also been cremated but a couple of insurance policies had covered the vast majority cost of her funeral and he had thrown away the receipt from the undertaker without giving it any thought.

But he was smitten by the desire to make amends for not being around to help Sally in her time of need. And the money Kevin had made him take could go towards the cost this would entail.

He had brought it with him to Matlock in the forlorn hope of using the tainted money to do some good.

"I've got about £1,500 with me if that can help progress things, and I could send you the balance when you have the final price."

Valerie sat dumbfounded. Was it that easy to con this fool out of his money? What could the limit of his gullibility amount to?

Gerry gave her the answer.

"Is there something wrong with my offer, Valerie? I know now that I should have made more of an effort to visit Sally and I will regret not doing so for the rest of my life. I just want to try and do the right thing for her memory. There is one other thing I need to say. When you have the date for the burial of the urn I will need to come back here for the ceremony because there is something I want to put in the urn to be buried along with the ashes."

She had recovered her composure by now and said softly, "Of course you must come to the ceremony, Gerry. What is it you want to place in the urn?"

He felt a little embarrassed at what he was about to say but he knew it would be the kind of gesture Stella Stockwell would understand.

"I did some work as an engraver for an elderly client and because she was so pleased with the task I carried out she gave me a brooch and told me I was to give it to my first real love. I never had chance to give it to Sally…" As he finished, he was overcome with grief at the thoughts and memories it rekindled and he burst into tears.

Valerie sprang to her feet and crossed the short space between them and flung her arms around his neck, drawing his face onto her bare shoulder.

"Oh, Gerry, that's a beautiful gesture, don't cry. Sally would understand."

At the mention of her name the sobs became louder and Valerie clung on even tighter. She glanced to her right as she heard the kitchen door open and her partner stood perplexed at the sight before him.

She silently mouthed the words 'Get out, you idiot' and gave him a look that warned the man not to interfere, to which he gave a little smile of acknowledgement and stepped back into the kitchen. Gerry had not noticed the intrusion but gently leant back and pulled away from Valerie's embrace.

Taking a handkerchief from his pocket he wiped his face and spoke in a subdued voice, "I'm sorry about that. I thought I had more control of my emotions."

"I should be the one to be apologising, not you, for questioning your love for Sally. Do you mind if I see the brooch and who was that lady you mentioned? Shirley something; a close friend of yours?"

"Her name was Stella Stockwell. I engraved a gold cigarette lighter she was giving her husband on their golden wedding anniversary. She gave me the brooch as a thank you because it reminded her of someone. I think Sally met her a couple of times. I'll go and fetch it now and bring the money for the deposit on the plaque."

Valerie nodded and as soon as he had left the room, she dashed into the kitchen to speak to her partner. He leered and said, "Change your mind, did you? Anyway, that was a quick one by your standards."

She glared back at him. "Nothing like that at all if you must know, Stan. He broke down when he started talking about the girl. So far, I've got £1,500 out of him and there could be more but let's wait and see. He'll be back down with the money and some kind of brooch. Anyway, we'll have to act quickly."

She turned her head when she heard Gerry coming back down the stairs. Putting a finger to her lips she pointed at Stan to motion for silence and returned to her seat on the large settee.

To her surprise, Gerry sat next to her and handed over an envelope. She took it and then planted a kiss full on his lips.

The thought of his crippled hand rubbing over her body made her pull away from the kiss just as quickly. Gerry blushed slightly and suddenly said, "I hope you don't mind me asking one small favour? Would it be possible to include my name on the plaque? I'm not sure how it could be phrased. And as long as the rest of the family don't object."

She looked puzzled for a moment but recovered herself in time. "There is no other family member still alive, apart from me that is. But once you've sent the balance of the money, you can let me know the message you want put on the stone. I'm afraid we will have to finish this meeting soon as I have to prepare the dining room for breakfast for you and the rest of the guests. Will you be okay for now? It's been quite emotional for both of us."

"Yes, I'll be fine. As there's nothing else for me to do here right now I will book a coach back home tomorrow and wait for you to give me the final figure so that I can send you the balance. I will pay my bill before I leave, if you can have it ready for me, please."

"Will that be cash or by card? I could give you a small discount for cash if you prefer," she said with her disarming smile at its fullest.

"Okay, I'll pay cash if you tell me where the nearest ATM is situated."

She nodded and gave him directions. As soon as Gerry left the room, she returned to the kitchen to confer with Stan. "Take this brooch to a pawnbroker who won't ask too many questions. It might not fetch much but it's got gold lettering on the back. Make up some story about someone who couldn't pay their bill or something like that. I've got that mug's cash and I'll have a bit more tomorrow when he pays his bill."

"What if he enquires about the ashes at the undertakers?"

She looked at Stan with disdain. "What do you take me for? Dumbo? There are several undertakers in the area and I didn't even have to give him a name of one. Besides the ashes were scattered in the Garden of Remembrance next to the crematorium. No way was I going to fork out any money for her bloody ashes. She never did me no favours!"

Stan laughed. "What about Sally's mum?"

"She's been in the nursing home for the past couple of years and doesn't know what day it is anyway. She probably can't remember having a daughter. That side of the family disowned me after I did time inside, so sod them. That bloke Gerry would describe me as a blonde, but we know different."

And as she finished speaking, she removed the blonde wig to expose a close-cropped brunette mop of hair. She continued,

"I'll hang onto the money for now while you sort the brooch out. I'll meet you back at the flat once Mrs Simmons comes back on Saturday and pays me for looking after this place. I told her I wasn't staying on after she returned so we can go on holiday on our proceeds."

Stan moved forward and put his hands around her waist.

"You know something, Diane, I'm not sure which I prefer, you with the wig on or off," and he leaned forward to give her a kiss, but she slipped out of his embrace.

"Uh no, not now! Plenty of time later once this caper is over."

She left him standing in the kitchen on his own.

There were several things to sort out the next day once Gerry had booked out. Diane conveniently forgot to give him the promised discount for paying in cash and had guessed he would be too embarrassed to remind her of the offer. The same trick had been used with some other guests who had paid in cash, thus adding to the ever increasing sum of money she had accrued while running the B & B.

The owner, Valerie Simmons, had left Diane in temporary charge while she went on a month's cruise around the Caribbean, not realising her deputy was embezzling funds from her business by not entering the names of all guests who had stayed at the guest house.

But Gerry's arrival had been an unexpected bonus. Diane had cleared out Sally's belongings from her house and had found a couple of references to him, including his telephone number. When he had made his booking to stay at the B & B, having quickly formulated a couple of different schemes to trick him into handing over some cash, it turned out to be much easier than she could have dared hope.

There had to be no evidence of Gerry and the seven other guests who had stayed and paid in cash but had not been entered into the official register. Diane had made a profit of nearly £2,700 from this scam in the three weeks she had been in charge. All other current guests would have left by midday on that Friday.

She had even gone to the trouble of replenishing the food and other items consumed by the unregistered guests so as not to arouse the suspicion of the owner.

Just before retiring for the night Diane received a phone call from her partner.

"Nobody will touch that brooch; there's some inscription on the back that's putting off my contacts and the best offer I was given was £20 so what do you want me to do, sell or hang on to it?"

She was convinced the brooch was worth far more. "I've made a nice little profit here so hang on to it, I'll bet we will get more if we flog it abroad. I can't stay chatting; I need to have an early night so that I can be long gone before Ma Simmons turns up."

She was alone in the house that night and was not prepared for the images that haunted her dreams.

The first dream involved the brooch, showing Gerry giving it to Sally who was then replaced by an elderly lady Diane did not recognise.

She was then led down a dark corridor that opened out into a large meadow which was full of flowers and several people dressed in striped clothes. The other thing Diane noticed about these people was everyone, including the children, had shaved heads.

Instinctively she placed one of her hands on her own head and discovered that it had been shaved in the same way. The next moment the woman had led Diane to the front of a queue that was filing towards a large building with two large chimneys billowing out dark, rancid smoke into the air. Diane tried to run but the other people behind blocked her escape and started laughing as they pushed her towards the open doorway.

She awoke bathed in sweat and shaking uncontrollably, only then comprehending the significance of the other people's appearance. As in the dream Diane put her hand onto the top of her head and was relieved to discover the familiar cropped mop of hair was still intact.

Getting out of bed, Diane put on her dressing gown and went downstairs to raid the drinks cabinet Mrs Simmons kept for special occasions. Her hands were still shaking slightly as she poured the second drink in an attempt to wipe the images of the dream from her mind. Tiredness took over and she reluctantly went back to bed, sleeping for about two more hours before being haunted by the arrival of another dream. This time she was with Stan in an open-top sports car and they were driving down a country road laughing and joking at their good fortune. Diane glanced to her left and saw the same building with two chimneys billowing out smoke. She screamed at Stan who was distracted and had to swerve violently to avoid a giant dumper truck that was heading straight for them.

The building had disappeared but in its place was a yawning chasm and the car was pushed over the edge. Once again Diane awoke shaking and sobbing.

When she eventually managed to calm her nerves, she remembered Stan didn't own a sports car and sleep enveloped her once again with no further such dreams.

∗

Gerry arrived home in the late evening and was glad to discover Mark was not around but there was a message on the answer phone from Ernie.

"Gerry, not sure when you're coming back tonight but Mark and I are going out on patrol. He's not very happy about the guns but I told him there had been an attempted break-in at your flat and you moved the guns for safe keeping, so stick to that story when you meet up."

He had to listen to the message a second time before deleting it from the memory of the phone.

He heard Mark enter the flat about three o'clock in the morning and braced himself for a visit to his room. Sure enough, there was a loud rap on his door and Mark pushed against the door but Gerry had locked himself in the room. The shout from outside told him Mark was not in the best of moods.

"Open up, Gerry, or I'll kick this bloody door in. You and me need to talk and I ain't waiting till morning."

"Okay, keep your hair on. Just give me a minute to wake up properly. I've been on a coach for the best part of yesterday."

There was a muffled threat from the other side of the door but no further comments. Gerry put on a pair of jeans and T-shirt before unlocking his door and meeting Mark in the lounge. Mark rose from the chair and stared menacingly at him.

"Why the hell did you give those guns to Ernie? Kevin gave them to me for my use. You had no right giving them to that ex-copper."

"Did Ernie tell you about the break-in? You must have left your window open when you buggered off on your holiday. Someone had got into your room and the window was open when I checked it after hearing noises."

Mark was spoiling for a fight and snarled, "I'm damn sure I didn't leave any window open. This is the story you and Ernie have concocted just to hide the guns from me. You've no bloody right! Kevin gave them to me so hand them over, Gerry, or so help me I'll beat the hell out of you if you don't!"

Gerry managed to hide the fear he felt and spoke calmly. "Mark, I heard noises in your room and when I went to investigate, the drawer of your bedside cabinet was fully open and I could see the box in there. A few minutes more and that person would have got hold of the guns. It was lucky the box was jammed tight in the drawer.

"Just think, Mark, if the police had found out about the guns they would have been crawling over here and the centre and discovered the stolen stuff there. That would have meant curtains for us and Ernie. And even Kevin if they caught up with him. At least this way the guns are safer where they are and we're still free to carry on."

Mark calmed down slightly as he followed Gerry's reasoning but still felt aggrieved.

"Maybe so, but I still need to have a bit of practice now and then."

"Remember what Ernie said about using guns? That would make the police even more determined to catch us. And Ernie's contact on the police authority would get cold feet, from what I've seen of him."

Mark looked puzzled. "How come you know who he is and how did you meet?"

This gave Gerry the opportunity to turn the conversation to a different subject and he relayed the story of Councillor Barnes and his attempts to search Ernie's office for the incriminating video tape. When he finished with the part about the councillor falling through the outside staircase and ripping his expensive clothing Mark was laughing.

Mark stood up to leave the room but not before saying, "I'll explain more in the morning but Ernie reckons it would be a good idea to make the nightly patrols more noticeable but at the same time, you and me go out on foot to do a few jobs on our own."

The relief was clear to see on Gerry's features. It looked as if Mark had accepted his explanation.

But nothing could be further from the truth. As soon as he had left the room and closed the door, Mark muttered to himself, "Oh no, kiddo, you and me have unfinished business over those guns but I can wait."

It was a couple of days later before Ernie summoned them into his office to explain his new working methods.

"We're going to rotate duties in this way from next week. I will go out on patrol on my own while you two break into businesses that refuse to play ball. Just make it obvious that you've been in and taken stuff or caused some damage. The Market Man has gone away on a trip to South America and I've got the use of his new van for a few weeks. It's almost identical to ours so we'll swap the logo and number plates. I'll drive that vehicle and you will have use of ours, but only if you need it to transport goods back here. If you're going just to cause damage it would be best if you are on foot for a quick getaway. We will stick to the same number of patrols per week so as not to arouse suspicion. Any questions?"

"You mean we will be doing all the break-ins while you swan around in the van each night?" Mark asked sarcastically.

"No, Mark, we will rotate the duties when I say so. You might be doing the patrol while Gerry and I do the other stuff, or you and Gerry swap the patrol duties and I go to persuade any reluctant clients the error of their ways."

Gerry chipped in with a query. "There's usually two of us on security patrol. If we are being watched, won't that look odd?"

Ernie's answer surprised them both. "There's a couple of the older kids that are regulars at the centre want some pocket money so I'm letting them join me on patrol on odd days."

Gerry was not happy. "Ernie, you distinctly said we weren't to involve any of the kids in our business, so why the change of heart?"

Ernie shook his head. "They're not getting involved in our business in any way. They will only go out on patrol with me and that's all it will be; a genuine patrol. And don't give them any reason to be suspicious, especially you, Mark."

"But why?" Gerry persisted.

Ernie replied, "I've heard mutterings amongst some of those attending the centre linking us with the break-ins. By taking a couple of them out on patrol I want to show them it's all above board; a security patrol, nothing more, nothing less."

The other two said nothing so Ernie continued, "Tonight, Mark, it's you and me again on patrol. Gerry, you can come out with me on Tuesday."

Before he could say anything else his phone rang. The receptionist told Ernie someone wanted to speak to him. When he was told the name, Ernie cursed quietly but said he would meet him in his office downstairs in a couple of minutes. He put the phone down and addressed Mark and Gerry.

"I've got an unexpected visitor downstairs, so I want you two to keep your heads down until he's gone."

"Who is it?" Mark asked.

Ernie hesitated before saying one word, "Proudfoot", and left the room.

Mark scowled at Gerry. "It's at times like this when I wish I knew where those guns are hidden. If the cops have sussed us out then I want to go down fighting."

Gerry looked at him with incredulity. "Are you crazy? We don't know what the copper is here for. It could be something totally innocent, and you want to start a war with your bloody guns. Let Ernie handle it, it's his ex-mate he's meeting, for God's sake."

Mark turned to face his companion with a look of pure malice on his face. "You think Ernie is your bloody mate and tells you the truth all the time, yeah? Well, I know him better than you, Gerry baby, and I bet you anything one of his dark secrets from the past involves you in some way."

Gerry laughed. "You're crazy, Mark. Until I got involved in this security caper of his I'd only met him as a customer in Mr Evans' shop."

"I still think he's more tolerant of your mistakes than anyone else. To me, that smells of favouritism for some reason or other."

Gerry sensed he was being wound up by his colleague, so he said nothing.

Ernie met Peter Proudfoot in the foyer and invited him to enter his downstairs office.

Once both men had sat down facing each other over the large desk Ernie opened the conversation. "So, Peter, to what do I owe this visit? I thought you were a busy man these days."

Rather than come to the point immediately the sergeant said quietly, "Yes, enough to keep me busy. How was your trip to Australia?"

Ernie knew his ex-colleague well enough to know he would only come to the reason for his visit when he was good and ready. But he wasn't going to let him dictate the pace. He had a good idea why this meeting was taking place.

"Peter, we are both busy people and I don't have time for idle chit-chat right now, so can I assume this visit is to do with Robin's tragic death?"

Proudfoot gave a small cough before responding. "Very well. I know you travelled to Australia on the day before the fire and would not have had any direct involvement in the blaze."

Ernie put his hand up and spoke in clipped tones, "Stop right there, Peter! I had neither direct, nor indirect involvement, or even prior knowledge of the fire. Damn it, Robin and Stella brought me back to full health and I counted them amongst my closest friends."

It was Proudfoot's turn to hold up his hands in submission. "I'm sorry, Ernie, that didn't come out as I intended it to. I apologise. With this investigation and all the other break-ins continuing I've been on double shifts for the past week."

For the first time he noticed the look of exhaustion in his ex-colleagues features and the slump of his shoulders made him look ten years older. The sergeant continued, "I've spoken to young Gerry and he told me what he and the other lad, who works for you, were doing. But there's one character we are anxious to have a word with. Have you seen anything of, or heard rumours about Graham Bishop since you came back?"

Ernie had not been prepared for this turn of events, so he asked cautiously, "What makes you suspect Bishop?"

"Something Gerry let slip when I had a brief chat with him. He remembers Bishop threatening to burn David Evans' shop down some time back, unless he paid protection money. No sign has been seen of friend Bishop since the Stockwell fire."

Ernie was genuinely surprised at the first part of Proudfoot's comment. But he decided to take a gamble.

"That's the first time I've heard about such threats, but I've just remembered something totally unconnected.

"It's not the first time he's disappeared on an extended leave of absence. I heard rumours that he had tried to pull a fast one over some items he was trying to flog to a London mob. They were not at all happy with Mr Bishop and wanted to even things up."

Proudfoot perked up at this news. "We checked out his whereabouts leading up to the fire and he was definitely at his favourite watering hole that evening but left early to keep an appointment with someone."

The subject was getting too close to home for Ernie's liking, so he tried to change tack.

"What about my old mate, Inspector Gates? Hasn't he come up with an answer?"

For a moment Proudfoot looked surprised at Ernie's comment.

"Oh, you haven't heard the latest? Gates has been promoted to chief inspector and gone up north to run their regional crime squad. I've got a new boss now, an Inspector Stevens."

For a second Ernie's spirits lightened. With Gates out of the way would there be a chance of getting his job back in the force? Then reality took over. Gates had finished any chance of him returning with his damning report that even a top lawyer couldn't fight.

Proudfoot interrupted his thoughts. "Well, there's not much else to say. I'm off to catch up on some much needed shut-eye. If you do hear any news of Bishop, be sure to let me know."

"You can depend on it, Peter," Ernie replied, still feeling some rancour at Gates' involvement in his dismissal from the force.

After showing the sergeant out Ernie returned to his upper office to share the news with Mark and Gerry.

"You two might have got lucky. The police have Graham Bishop down as their number one suspect for the Stockwell fire."

"How come?" Mark asked.

"Thanks to Gerry here who told Sergeant Proudfoot that your father once threatened to burn down the shop he worked in. Do you remember saying that?" he said, turning to face his assistant.

Gerry merely nodded but remained silent. The memory conjured up another reminder of Sally. His eyes glazed over, and he left the room. It was time to make a phone call.

"Vicarage Road B & B, can I help you?"

Gerry was a bit surprised at the voice of the woman who answered the call. It definitely was not the woman he knew as Valerie. This person sounded a lot older.

"Hello? Vicarage Road B & B, can I help you?" the woman repeated with a slight hint of irritation in her voice.

Gerry replied to this less than homely greeting, "Could I speak to Valerie, please?"

It was the woman's turn to hesitate but when she finally answered the temperature in her voice had dropped several degrees.

"Excuse me! This is Mrs Valerie Simmons speaking! Now would you mind telling me your name and purpose of your call or I shall put the phone down?"

Gerry had a sudden thought and replied, "Mrs Simmons, my name is Gerry Reynolds and I stayed at your B & B last week and the lady in charge told me her name was Valerie; your daughter, perhaps?"

The frosty reply came back, "Mr Reynolds, I do not have a daughter. You say you stayed here last week. Wait one moment while I check the guest register."

The only sound to break the silence for the next few minutes was the intermittent turning of pages and rustling of paper. When she returned to the phone the irritation in her voice had barely diminished.

"Mr Reynolds, I have no record of anyone with that name staying here, and I have gone back to the time before I went on holiday. Are you sure it was here at my establishment that you stayed?"

"I'm certain I stayed at your place. I can describe the room and view in detail if you want me to do so and a rough description of the four other guests who were also present."

Valerie Simmons gave a deep sigh and spoke in a clipped tone, "Mr Reynolds, or whatever your name is, apart from one other guest who only stayed here for the first two days of the week you mentioned, nobody else booked in. So whatever your motive is for calling me, you have wasted enough of my time. Goodbye."

Gerry shouted down the phone at her in desperation, "Wait! Mrs Simmons, do you remember the pregnant woman who died from carbon-monoxide poisoning in Matlock a few months ago?"

"Yes, I remember the incident. Why do you ask?"

"The lady who was in charge of your B & B called herself Valerie and claimed she was the second cousin of the woman, Sally Edwards, who died."

Mrs Simmons' voice mellowed, "Yes, that is true. However the lady I left in charge was called Diane. What has this got to do with you?"

Alarm bells were starting to ring in his head, but Gerry felt he had no choice but to respond and was reluctant to go into great detail. He hoped she would not press him on the matter.

"Sally was my girlfriend and I went there to visit her grave."

There was an audible gasp on the phone followed by a long silence before Valerie Simmons spoke again in a more sympathetic voice, "Oh, I'm so sorry, Mr Reynolds. But weren't you notified that her ashes were scattered in the Garden of Remembrance?"

It took a full minute for her comment to sink in and even then, Gerry had difficulty in comprehending fully what it meant. Once he grasped the situation all he could repeat to himself was the phrase, "I've been conned! That sly, devious bitch has conned me!"

Valerie Simmons was unsure as to who Gerry was referring to and asked him to repeat what he had said more slowly.

Having had a moment to gather his thoughts he said instead, "Mrs Simmons, I believe Diane, if that's her real name, has swindled me out of some money and she has probably done the same to you."

"I'm not sure I follow your train of thought, Mr Reynolds, please explain."

Gerry did so.

"If my name and the other people I saw in the breakfast room that morning are not in your guest register and we all paid cash then I'm guessing Diane will have pocketed the money for that week. How long had she been left in charge?"

"Just over three weeks," the landlady said quietly. "If that's what she has done it could amount to near £3,000. Oh my God, I'm calling the police immediately."

It was Gerry's turn to show some sympathy, however he didn't want his name mentioned in any enquiry.

"I'm sorry, Mrs Simmons, I've lost considerably less than you. But I don't want my name mentioned in any of this. I will deal with it in my own way. But would you please keep me informed of any developments."

"But how do I explain to the police how I came to discover this fraud?"

"Give any name you like but don't use mine. After all, you don't have any further details about me, do you?"

She agreed and added, "There are a few other checks I can make first before calling the police. For instance, I have a contract with a laundry company and I can check how much linen they have collected while I've been away. If it doesn't tally with the number of bookings shown then that will confirm your allegations. I will keep you informed of developments, Mr Reynolds."

Only after he put the phone down did the sense of nausea hit him. He thought he had done something to keep Sally's memory alive. Instead he had been taken advantage of by a con artist.

Nobody could be trusted any more, so, from now on whatever he could get hold of was his and nobody better try and stop him. He had tried to stay on the right side of the law but coppers like Gates wouldn't believe him.

He vowed that he would stop short of using violence for violence sake unless it meant there was the risk of losing his freedom. An acceptance had slowly built up within him that he grudgingly had to admit to an increasing buzz of excitement when he was out on a job with either Ernie or Mark, a feeling he had never experienced in his earlier life. It was getting easier to understand the logic of the way his colleagues looked on their lives as they did.

27

Ernie couldn't help noticing the change in Gerry's attitude over the recent past, so he decided to challenge his assistant.

"You've been quieter than usual for the past few days. Do you want to talk about whatever's on your mind?"

"No thanks, I'll sort it out for myself. I just need time to come to terms with a few things, that's all."

Ernie shook his head. "No, Gerry, this is to do with Sally and your trip to her grave, isn't it?"

He was surprised at Gerry's reaction.

"Just drop it, will you! I'll deal with it in my own way so back off!"

If Mark had spoken to him like that Ernie would have taught him a lesson of who was boss. But it was out of character for Gerry to act in that way. He was convinced he was right that it involved Sally, but he let the matter drop.

Gerry had heard nothing from Valerie Simmons regarding Diane and her husband so after his confrontation with Ernie he decided to give her a call.

"Vicarage Road B & B, can I help you?"

Another unfamiliar voice greeted Gerry. He sighed. *Please don't put me through that same identification routine again* he pleaded to himself.

"Is Mrs Valerie Simmons available, please? My name is Gerry Reynolds."

There was a short silence before he heard the more familiar voice of the proprietor who sounded rather subdued. "Hello, Mr Reynolds, I take it you've heard the terrible news?"

"I'm sorry, Mrs Simmons, I don't understand. What news are you referring to?"

Gerry could have sworn he heard something that sounded like a sob before she replied, "It's poor Diane. She, and her husband Stan, were both killed in a car crash last weekend. Diane may have had her faults but not even she deserved such a death. I'm sorry, Mr Reynolds. It's too upsetting for me to say any more."

Before she had time to put the phone down, Gerry asked, "It may be upsetting for you, but could you give me a couple of details, please? What was Diane's surname and where exactly did the accident happen? If I have those details, I can look up the story myself."

Valerie cleared her throat before speaking. "Her married name was Adams, but she stopped using that when they released her from prison and the accident happened somewhere in Kent. Now I'm afraid that's all I can tell you. If you want to know more, you will have to ask the police. I'm sorry I can't help you any further. Goodbye, Mr Reynolds."

Before Gerry could ask another question, the line went dead. There would be no point in phoning her back. There was a finality to her last remark. Gerry couldn't go to the police so he waited a couple of days then approached Ernie. He knew an apology for his outburst earlier that week would be the least his boss would demand of him. Once that was out of the way Ernie made him divulge the full reason.

"What's your interest in this Adams woman?" he asked and wouldn't agree to make any enquiries until Gerry told him the full story.

Gerry finished by saying, "As well as the story of the accident, I want to know why she was sent to prison."

It took Ernie's contacts nearly a week to come back with the answers but before divulging the information he wanted an answer from Gerry.

"How much did she squeeze you for?"

He looked totally embarrassed when he admitted, "Over £1,500 in cash, plus the brooch Mrs Stockwell gave me that was meant for Sal."

Ernie's smile had no warmth in it. "You got off lightly there, Gerry. Adams and her boyfriend stole the life savings of an old lady after knocking six bells out of the old dear. Fortunately, she survived the beating but ended up in a nursing home because she was no longer capable of looking after herself. As for the accident, hubby Stan bought an open-top sports car with your money and no doubt other illegal proceeds and it's believed they were heading for Dover to skip abroad. According to witnesses he suddenly seemed to lose control of the car and they were both thrown out into a field. Unfortunately, right into the path of a large combine harvester! Stan hit the body work of the machine and broke his neck. Your friend Diane was not quite so lucky."

"How so?" Gerry was puzzled for one moment, until Ernie explained.

"As I said, Stan was lucky, but Diane was thrown into the machinery itself! By the time the driver managed to stop his machine, there wasn't much left of her ladyship."

Gerry grimaced and looked away, but Ernie had one other piece of information.

"In the glovebox of the car they found your brooch. If you can make a positive identification of the item there's a good chance you could claim it back."

Gerry said nothing. He was stuck in a dilemma. It was meant to be and should have gone to Sally. It had been his intention to give it to her while she was alive but that opportunity was cruelly taken from him. The only other alternative was to have the brooch buried with her ashes and those of the twins but Diane's cruel deception denied him even that solace.

He stood up abruptly and spoke to Ernie as he headed for the door. "No! I don't want it back, too many negative memories. Besides, I can't meet Mrs Stockwell's conditions of giving it to 'my first love'. Let someone else try."

When he was on his own in the room Ernie took a box out of his pocket and looked at the brooch inside. If Gerry didn't want it then he would keep it until he could find a suitable person of his own.

Ernie also left the room and failed to notice the outline of an old woman who hung her head and wept ghostly tears.

Ernie and Mark were in deep conversation when Gerry arrived for work the next morning. It was unusual for Mark to get to the centre before his flatmate, unless there was a special reason. As he joined the other two Ernie told Mark, "It's only fair we tell Gerry what we've been discussing, Mark. We'll talk about it over lunch. In the meantime get together those details I requested."

Mark nodded and walked away towards the pool area with a wide grin lighting up his features. Gerry tried to speak but Ernie interrupted him. "Not now, Gerry, it will be explained to you later but do me one big favour. Put in a couple of objections to what we're planning but back down when I insist on one point."

Gerry was even more confused at Ernie's last comment but he had no chance to ask for at least a hint of what was going on so he went to join Mark in preparing the pool for the morning session, hoping his colleague would shed some light on the mystery. No such luck. Mark was on cloud nine, completely encased in a world of his own.

The upstairs office was being redecorated so they met in the second office downstairs. Ernie began the conversation, "Okay, Gerry, this is what will be happening in the near future. Kevin wants to return to this country but he's strapped for cash and he's asked Mark for help."

"Does that mean he'll be joining us here?" was Gerry's first thought.

Mark spoke before he could be stopped and ignored Ernie's look of annoyance. "Why not? He could teach us all how to get even better results."

"Yeah, by using guns, I'll bet!" Gerry muttered.

"There will be no guns around here while I'm in charge," Ernie snapped and he continued, thus preventing the other two from getting into another argument.

"We do owe Kevin a big favour. After all, we couldn't have got rid of Graham Bishop on our own. And remember, Bishop is being blamed for Mark's handiwork. Gerry, if you are in agreement, I will draw the money from the account I set up to hide our earnings from the scams. I think £10,000 will be enough to cover his air fare and set himself up when he gets back over here. Mark did you get the details of where to send the money?"

Mark nodded. "It's a Western Union office in Toronto but none of his old mates will fund him although they have the details as well."

A look of concern showed on Ernie's face. "Damn, can you get in touch with his mates in Leeds? I forgot to mention before, Gates has been promoted and joined the regional crime squad in that area and Kevin's mates better be on their toes."

Mark nodded again and said he would contact someone once he got home.

"Better still, use the phone in here once we've finished lunch."

Ernie and Gerry left Mark alone to make his call and once they were out of earshot of anyone else Ernie asked quietly,

"Gerry, you don't think I would let Mark get his own way with the guns issue, do you?"

Before Gerry could respond they were joined by Mark who didn't look very pleased.

"Problem, Mark? Did you make contact?" Ernie asked.

"Yeah, I got through and was told they already knew about Gates. He's picked up one of their couriers and was still questioning the kid. They wouldn't let him see a lawyer."

Gerry spoke sympathetically, "Unless he's got the skin of a rhinoceros, Gates will break him."

Mark gave Gerry a disdainful stare. "That kid is no southern softie like someone I know."

Ernie could see what was about to happen and only just managed to get between the pair before they came to blows.

"That's enough, Mark! What we have to decide is whether we send Kevin the money or wait a while longer for things to cool down."

"Kev is broke. He needs that money right now. If he doesn't have it by tomorrow he's liable to do a stick-up."

Ernie was thoughtful, weighing up the situation. Finally he made his decision.

"We can't risk that. I'll send the money this evening. You two will have to do the patrol tonight. And I don't want any problems from either of you. Understood?"

Both nodded and Ernie continued, "Okay, Mark, I need a password that Kevin will know. I don't suppose he's got a favourite, has he?"

Mark stayed silent for several moments before picking up a pen and writing something on a nearby pad and passing the sheet to Ernie.

"I don't want anyone else to know, okay?" and walked out of the room, slamming the door behind him.

Ernie looked at the writing and he only just about managed to stifle the laughter welling up inside his chest.

Later that evening, after Mark and Gerry had gone out on patrol, Ernie went home to make a long-distance phone call.

Before doing so, he took the folded slip of paper out of his pocket, the same piece of paper he had found on the floor of the van upon his return from the trip to Australia. He smiled as he said quietly to himself, "I'm afraid you won't get the opportunity to show me how. Sorry, Kevin."

The female voice on the other end of the line was courteous but efficient, and Ernie warmed to the strong Canadian accent.

"RCMP Headquarters, Toronto, how may I help you today?"

Ernie cleared his throat before speaking. "Ah, good evening. My name is Chief Inspector Gates of West Yorkshire Regional Crime Squad. May I speak to your armed robbery response unit, please? I have information about an incident that has been planned in your area."

"Hold one moment, please, sir, and I will transfer you to one of my colleagues."

There was a thirty-second delay before another person took over the call.

"Inspector Frank Jardine speaking, I understand you have information about a possible felony that is about to take place. Is that correct, sir?"

"That is correct. We understand it is planned to take place at the Western Union office in the proximity of the main bus and coach station."

After a short pause Jardine responded, "Chief Inspector, do you have a description of the people planning this robbery?"

Ernie pretended to rustle papers before answering, "Only one person as far as we know. The last name he used in this country was either Kevin Yarrow or Kevin Ramsbottom. I must emphasise, Inspector, he is under suspicion for the murder of a Graham Bishop before he left the UK some five months ago. He is known to be a member of a local gang and frequently uses firearms in his robberies. As far as we know he is planning to carry out this felony at around eighteen hundred hours, Toronto time."

Jardine suddenly sounded annoyed. "Then, Chief Inspector, why weren't we informed a lot sooner that this person was in our country?"

Ernie hesitated. The conversation was getting too complicated to continue so he started to reply and then remained silent. "It was only brought to our attention a few days ago by..." and then stayed silent, waiting for Jardine to respond.

"Hello, Chief Inspector, I didn't catch the last part of what you said. Could you repeat it, please?"

Ernie did not respond until Jardine repeated his request then simply said, "Hello, Inspector Jardine, can you hear me?"

Jardine responded, this time the irritation clear in his voice. "Mr Gates, I still can't hear you. Are you still there?"

Ernie waited another ten seconds before holding the phone at arm's length and calling to an imaginary person. "Davies! This bloody phone has gone on the blink again, get it sorted," and quietly replaced the receiver.

Jardine heard the click as the line went dead and sat for a moment, pondering whether to take any action. But a call about a possible firearms offence could not be ignored. He picked up the phone again and told the operator, "Chloe, dispatch two units to the Western Union on Prince Street. I'm on my way there now. Oh, and get a message to Natalie. Tell her I can't keep that dinner appointment tonight. I'll contact her later."

He quickly retrieved the body armour from his locker and went to change before leaving the office.

Meanwhile Ernie went to his bed, happy in the knowledge that another challenge to his authority would not arise. Would there be others? Well, he was ready if they showed their hand.

To complete the betrayal of Kevin he had already withdrawn the £10,000 from the funds as agreed and banked it in a new account of his own.

There was one other possible loophole to check and close if necessary, but he had to wait for developments to unfold. It was several weeks later when he received a phone call from an agitated Andrew Phillips asking to see him urgently. Ernie obliged and called on the travel agent the next day. On his arrival he was ushered into the back office after Phillips instructed his assistant not to disturb him for any reason. He didn't wait for any formalities to be carried out.

"Ernie, a trade magazine arrived yesterday with a request to any travel agents in this country to check if they have handled a certain ticket for a flight to Canada. It's the ticket I issued to Robin Stockwell."

Ernie appeared to be deep in thought for several moments.

"Perhaps someone broke in and started the fire in Robin's flat, found the ticket and either sold it to another person or used it themselves. What's the problem?"

"But Ernie, the coroner's verdict was accidental death. They think Robin left something burning in his lounge and that started the fire. If the ticket was stolen as you suggested, then it was no accident."

Once again Ernie spent more time in thinking through his answer. He had to convince the travel agent to remain silent.

"It could be possible your theory is correct, Andrew. However, if this evidence of the ticket being used was not submitted at the inquest, the coroner was justified in coming to his verdict of an accident. Don't mention this to anyone else until I've had a chance to look deeper into this matter. Remember, Andrew, if someone did start the fire and that person or persons, are still in the area you could be in great danger if they found out you had this evidence. As I said, I can make more discreet enquiries than you and as soon as I know something I'll tell you."

"But what if someone does find out I have this evidence and comes after me? Shouldn't I go to the police?"

Ernie glared at him. "On no account should you tell the police. Not only would it make them look foolish, it could still reach the perpetrator's ears and I might not be able to help you. So Mum's the word, Andrew."

Ernie stood up to leave, noting his host's hands were shaking and his face bathed in sweat. There would be no trouble from Andrew Phillips for now, he surmised.

***

After waiting in vain for contact from his brother, Mark checked with Ernie to make sure the money had been paid. He was shown notice of the withdrawal of the agreed amount but never saw details of where it was paid.

"As you can see, Mark, he's received the money so maybe he's fooled us and gone somewhere else. I don't know. He's your brother. Can't you check with his friends up north?"

Mark did just that and received the grim news of his brother's death at the hands of the RCMP. He tried to blame everyone else and, at first, Ernie gave him a wide berth to get over his initial grief. But when he started antagonising Gerry he gently, but firmly, reminded him that it was he who insisted on going ahead with the transfer of the money while CI Gates was still questioning one of Kevin's former associates in his home town.

Mark then decided he would go back home to find and kill Gates.

As a last desperate measure Ernie took Mark back to his house and got him so drunk he passed out and didn't come round for nearly forty-eight hours. Ernie heard raking sobs coming from the room where he had left his distraught colleague. Only when there was no further sound coming did he check to see that Mark had fallen into another sleep.

It was a further twelve hours before he stumbled back into some sort of contact with the outside world.

Ernie took him to a nearby cafe in Hereford Road for something to eat. Mark sat silently and sullenly while waiting for the light snack to arrive. There was no attempt at conversation between the two as they sat in the corner by a window. Ernie paid careful attention to Mark as he observed people walking past outside.

There was very little reaction until a police car slowly cruised by and stopped a few doors away down the street. Mark never took his eyes off the car as the two occupants got out and went into a recently opened electrical store. Ernie gave him a kick under the table, just hard enough to draw his attention away from the two constables. He pointed at the food on his plate and then indicated that they would be leaving soon.

While Mark finished his meal Ernie casually glanced around at a few of the other patrons of the cafe and noticed that a couple of them had been observing Mark in particular. When they realised Ernie was looking in their direction they quickly averted their gaze.

Mark pushed his plate away and both men stood up. Ernie took the dishes back to the counter and earned a nod of thanks from the patron. Recognising Ernie, the woman spoke.

"Thanks, Mr Newsham. Did you hear about the break-in at that new shop the other night?"

Ernie shook his head. "No, I've been looking after my young colleague for the past couple of days. He's just had some sad news and needed to sort himself out. Much taken, was there?"

"A few electrical items I believe, and a fire was started in an outside storeroom. The man who used to run the shop, Tony, was well liked in the area but sacked about a month ago and a pompous man named Matthews took charge. He won't get much sympathy from any locals with the attitude he had."

Ernie shook his head and simply said, "Some people never learn, do they? Thanks for the meal. Bye."

As they left the cafe Ernie indicated to Mark to stay silent until nobody else was nearby. They walked in silence with Mark constantly looking around and if a police car passed by, he would follow its progress until it disappeared from view.

By the time they arrived back at Ernie's house the angry look Mark received from his boss spoke volumes. Once indoors Ernie made his feelings known.

"What was one of the early points I made to you about trying to appear invisible and not drawing attention to yourself? You might as well have been carrying a large sign with the words 'I hate the police' in bright colours and shouting out the message from a megaphone and you couldn't have drawn any more attention to yourself."

Mark stood stock still, trying to emit a defiant air but failing miserably. Ernie continued, "You drew attention to yourself in the cafe. Patrons were watching you staring at the two police officers. And do you think those officers didn't see you watching them, or the ones in the police car that passed us on the street? That's part of their basic training, Mark. It's called observation! If you carry on like that you'll be picked up and taken in for questioning."

He mellowed his tone slightly. "I'm sure you heard the cafe owner talking about the break-in those officers were investigating. Well, that was Gerry and me at work and tonight you two are going to complete the job."

Mark looked Ernie straight in the face and asked, "Why?"

"That shop belongs to Percy Matthews who used to be Gerry's boss and he worked there a few times before joining us. Gerry got on well with the manager but Matthews sacked him for no real reason and he's upset a few other locals as well with his style of dealing. A decent fire should show Matthews he's not wanted in this town and also be a timely reminder to other traders who think they don't need protection."

"What's wrong with you and me doing the job instead?"

"The Market Man finally comes home today and we've arranged a meeting for tomorrow morning, so it's you and Gerry, I'm afraid."

Mark gave a resigned nod and seemed to accept his boss's instructions, but he would be the one who was going to decide on how they would tackle the night's work. Ernie had not said anything about confining the fire to just the one building.

Ernie dropped Mark off at the flat and then continued to the centre to relieve Gerry of his duties and to enable him to have a rest before their night's work.

On arriving back at the shared flat, Gerry had a surprise for his partner in crime. He knocked on Mark's door. When there was no response, he placed a carrier bag on the end of the bed as Mark slept, and quietly left the room.

Mark did not have the courtesy to knock before entering Gerry's room a few hours later and nudged his companion until he woke up.

"Where did these come from, Gerry?" he said, holding up a new pair of trainers.

Gerry sighed, rubbed the sleep from his eyes and said drowsily, "Matthews' shop on Hereford Road that me and Ernie turned over the other night. They were the only ones in your size."

"But there's no buckle on the left shoe. I notice your pair has one on each heel."

Gerry was now fully awake thanks to this interruption.

"As I said, the only pair in your size. Serves you right for having big feet."

Mark was about to throw the footwear at his friend but had a sudden thought. He couldn't remember the last time anyone, including Kevin, had given him a present, apart from the guns. Instead he turned round and as he left the room he said quietly, "Thanks, mate."

In the darkness and thankful silence Gerry lay on his bed thinking about how his life had changed over the last few months. He had gone from being a hard-working, honest man to a thief and murderer.

As he tried to put this last thought out of his mind he started to doze off when the image of an elderly woman appeared and he heard the words:

"If you continue using these hands with their natural skills you will become very successful. Take care of them, my dear. But a word of caution. Do not let others distract you from this path you have chosen, or the success you deserve will elude you."

These words took his mind back to the meeting with Stella Stockwell in his old but safe workplace in David Evans' shop.

A few tears ran down his cheeks and he quietly cried himself to sleep, knowing it had all been taken away from him.

South Dublin Libraries

www.southdublinlibraries.ie

28

For the next several months Ernie Newsham, Gerry and Mark continued their mini crime wave, evading all attempts by the police to apprehend them.

There were both arrivals and departures at Clapfield Police Authority. One notable arrival was PC Vic Holland, although the first six months did not leave a lasting impression on his superiors.

Inspector Stevens opened the personal file on his desk and started reading the career details of PC Victor Holland.

Sergeant Proudfoot sat across the desk from him, waiting for his superior to complete his detailed examination in order to come to a decision. Finally, Stevens sat back in his chair.

"Up until the tragic death of his wife, Holland had an exemplary record, having satisfied the promotion board that he was ready to take on the position of sergeant. Then he blots his copybook with that damned assault on the lorry driver. Mind you, who in all honesty could say they wouldn't have reacted in similar circumstances? Yet since he was transferred to this station he's just seemed to want to hide in the background."

Proudfoot added his own observation, "And he didn't exactly enhance his standing with the performance on recovering that body from the river. But to be fair, something had made a right mess of Bishop's corpse."

Stevens nodded and added, "Hmm, perhaps we should have put him on indefinite sick leave then, but we were well below on our numbers. No, Sergeant, as you have mentioned a number of times before, he looks in poor shape and the medical route is the only real option open to us. Give me five minutes and then send him in."

Proudfoot stood up and left the room. He was back within two minutes.

"I'm sorry, sir. Holland went off duty over five minutes ago."

Stevens swore under his breath and said, "When is he back on duty?"

The sergeant looked at his staff duty roster before replying, "He's on nights until next Monday. Do you want me to leave a message for him, sir?"

Stevens let out a sigh. "Yes, do that, Sergeant, but I still need to talk to him about it anyway. Arrange that, please. In the meantime, I will contact the Medical Examination Board to arrange a suitable date and time."

***

Meanwhile, unaware of this pending appointment Vic Holland continued his search for the new chip shop he had been told about, not knowing that shadows from the past were about to change the course of his life.